What the critics are saying...

Blue Ribbon Rating: 5"This book is a perfect holiday read to settle down with." ~ *Angel, Romance Junkies*

"*Holiday Heat* is a fabulous collection of sizzling Christmas stories which you shouldn't dare miss!" ~ *Julie, eCataRomance Reviews*

"*Holiday Heat* is a collection of stories from three talented authors that is guaranteed to put a smile on your face." ~ *Angela, Romance Reviews Today*

4 Angels "*Holiday Heat* is a heartwarming story of three sisters finding love at Christmas..." ~ *Tewanda, Fallen Angel Reviews*

Holiday Heat

Lynn LaFleur
Jan Springer
Katherine Kingston

ELLORA'S CAVE
ROMANTICA PUBLISHING

An Ellora's Cave Romantica Publication

www.ellorascave.com

Holiday Heat

ISBN # 1419952471
ALL RIGHTS RESERVED.
A Wish Granted Copyright © 2004 Lynn LaFleur
Jade Copyright © 2004 Jan Springer
The Last Candle Copyright © 2004 Katherine Kingston
Edited by: Raelene Gorlinsky, Mary Moran and Briana St. James
Cover art by: Syneca

Electronic book Publication: December, 2004
Trade paperback Publication: August, 2005

Excerpt from *Happy Birthday Baby*
Copyright © Lynn LaFleur, 2003
Excerpt from *A Hero Betrayed* Copyright © Jan Springer, 2004

Warning:

The following material contains graphic sexual content meant for mature readers. *Holiday Heat* has been rated *E-rotic* by a minimum of three independent reviewers.

Ellora's Cave Publishing offers three levels of Romantica™ reading entertainment: S (S-ensuous), E (E-rotic), and X (X-treme).

S-*ensuous* love scenes are explicit and leave nothing to the imagination.

E-*rotic* love scenes are explicit, leave nothing to the imagination, and are high in volume per the overall word count. In addition, some E-rated titles might contain fantasy material that some readers find objectionable, such as bondage, submission, same sex encounters, forced seductions, etc. E-rated titles are the most graphic titles we carry; it is common, for instance, for an author to use words such as "fucking", "cock", "pussy", etc., within their work of literature.

X-*treme* titles differ from E-rated titles only in plot premise and storyline execution. Unlike E-rated titles, stories designated with the letter X tend to contain controversial subject matter not for the faint of heart.

Contents

Prologue
~9~

A Wish Granted
Lynn LaFleur
~17~

Jade
Jan Springer
~113~

The Last Candle
Katherine Kingston
~265~

Prologue

Fragile glass figurines rested in a cushioned box—stars, Santas, trees, toys, even a miniature Noah's Ark with a host of small animals to surround it. Shiny colored balls of red, green, blue and gold snuggled in individual containers, with lacy, white crocheted snowflakes floating among them. Three strings of Christmas lights had a few blinking bulbs interspersed among the steady ones. The angel tree-topper's plaster body wore a blue satin robe below its light-brown floss hair and glowing, golden halo. Most precious of all, though, was the one single bubbling candle light, wrapped in layers of plastic to protect it.

Three other boxes of decorations were scattered around Lindsey Hart's living room, but those contained things she'd bought herself over the last few years. Some nice pieces nestled in them, in truth—consolation prizes she awarded herself at the after-holiday sales for surviving another lonely Christmas while helping others find their dreams. None of them meant much to her compared to these.

These were Gram's last, most precious gift to her.

"There's magic in them, Lindsey," Gram had insisted, four years ago, as she lay dying. "And you have it in you to unlock the power. The candles especially. Wait for them to show you their message, then act. Act boldly, no matter how absurd it appears. Someone's life will be changed, and they'll thank you for it."

"I don't understand, Gram." Lindsey barely restrained a sob on the words.

A thin hand lay gently over hers. "You don't need to understand now," Gram assured her. "Just remember when the time comes."

"There will always be magic in those ornaments, Gram. Because they were yours. I'll never...forget." Tears streamed hot and heavy down her cheeks.

Gram managed a smile that turned her thin, weary face radiant. "No. They have more magic than that. You'll see. Trust me." She sighed and had to wait a moment to gather her breath again. "There is magic, and in the end, you'll benefit as well, but it carries great responsibility. Take care of your sisters, Lindsey."

Only later would Lindsey understand that the last sentence wasn't a *non sequitur*.

She'd wanted to ask Gram to explain more, to tell her what kind of power the candles held, how she should use it, but the old lady was too tired. Unfortunately, she never got another chance. Gram died later that night, unexpectedly but peacefully, as she slept.

Lindsey had to tell her sisters, Crista and Jade, that Gram had passed away before either of them could get there to say goodbye. When they did arrive, the sisters huddled together for a long time over the next few days, holding onto each other as the tears flowed. Their parents had died some years before and Gram was all they'd had. With her death, they had only each other. And though they lived far apart, they kept in touch by phone and through annual get-togethers.

They met with Gram's attorney, a friend of Lindsey's from law school days, and learned that in addition to inheriting equal shares of Gram's modest estate, they'd each received specific bequests of some of her most treasured possessions. For Lindsey it had been the box of Christmas ornaments and Gram's prized crystal flower vases.

She didn't believe the ornaments could possibly have the magical power Gram had attributed to them, but she treasured them, nonetheless.

That first Christmas after Gram's passing, there were four candle lights ready to insert into the string of lights. Each glowed and bubbled merrily during the holiday season, reminding her of the way Gram's spirit had lit up her life.

On Christmas Eve, Lindsey got her first taste of the magic Gram had promised. A red-and-orange bubble light suddenly flared brightly, almost like a small explosion, except no noise accompanied it and the glow held steady for a long time. Drawn by the sudden brightening, Lindsey moved over to the tree to stare at it.

In the golden yellow halo around the flaring bubble light, she saw…movement. Small figures. A tall, thin woman of late middle age, with dyed flame-red hair and…a dog? The red-haired woman had to be Joanna, a neighbor of Gram's for the last twenty years. She'd been a close friend of Gram's for most of those, too, even though Joanna had been almost twenty years younger. Both women had been widows for a long time, with a shared interest in scouring flea markets. They usually returned with dubious collections of odds and ends.

But Joanna didn't have a dog. In fact Lindsey couldn't imagine fastidious, neat-freak Joanna with a pet of any kind, a creature that would shed on her furniture and track mud on the carpets.

In the vision, though, Joanna clutched the leash of a brown, black and tan creature that looked like a cross between a basset and a beagle. She laughed as the dog trotted along the park walkway, nosing at leaves, and suddenly strained to chase after a chipmunk.

The vision faded, went misty and reformed. She saw the dog again, but not in the park this time. In fact, it was in a box of some kind, a concrete box with bars…a cell at the pound. Instead of capering in the fresh air, the animal curled in a ball, eyes half-open in a droopy stare, only rising to attention and yipping each time someone came near, then settling down with a sad little whine and shake of the tail when the person left again.

Then it was gone. Dog, Joanna and the golden flare all disappeared. The bubble light blinked a few times and went out.

Lindsey tried to reseat it in the socket, and tapped it a couple of times, but it appeared the bulb had blown. She mourned it, since it had been one of the flea market treasures that Gram had somehow imbued with her own magic.

Wait for them to show you their message, Gram had said, *and then act boldly on what you see.*

What was she supposed to do—? Oh, no, please!

That wasn't acting boldly, it was acting foolishly. And arrogantly. What gave her the right to decide Joanna needed a dog in her life? And not just any dog—a pound-puppy mutt with big, sad eyes.

No way. She wasn't going to present Joanna with an unknown and unwanted dog, just because her own imagination had cooked up a weird vision showing them happy together. Not in this lifetime.

Act boldly… Someone's life will be changed.

Well, yes, but Gram hadn't promised their life would be changed for the *better*. A dog was a big commitment, and possibly a burden, for a woman living alone.

Act boldly.

Hell.

Lindsey got her coat and headed out for the pound, leaving quickly before she had time to think too much about it and convince herself it was an entirely foolish notion. She immediately retraced her steps when she got out her door and realized she had no idea where the pound was. She looked it up in the phone book. If the dog was there, she might start believing there was some kind of truth in the vision.

The dog was there. It sat up and stared at her when she approached its cage, tail pounding the ground in hopeful rhythm.

Lindsey had nothing against dogs—as long as they didn't jump on her, shred her pantyhose, goober her face or leave muddy paw prints on her clothes.

This one was smarter than he looked. When the attendant opened the door to the cage, he marched out, sniffed at her feet and wagged his tail, but he didn't attempt to jump up or kiss her. Lindsey paid fifty dollars for shots and worming medication, then loaded the dog into the back of her car.

An hour at the pet store and an additional ninety bucks later, Lindsey drove to Joanna's home. She parked at the curb and sat there for the next ten minutes trying to work up her nerve to take the dog in. She glanced back in time to see him slobber on the bright red bow she'd bought him, along with a food dish, retractable leash, crate, and fifty pounds of premium dog food.

Joanna would probably give her an earful and tell her to take the mutt right back to the pound.

Lindsey stared at the front door of Joanna's home until something cool and damp licked across the back of her neck. "All right, all right, you're eager to get to your new home," she said to the dog, reaching back to push him away. "Let's go."

Joanna answered the door after the second knock and greeted Lindsey with her usual warmth. It quickly changed to puzzlement when she noticed her companion.

"You've got a dog?" Joanna went down on one knee to pet the mutt and let him kiss her hands. "He's adorable. When did you get him?"

"Um…actually, I don't have a dog. He's yours. Merry Christmas."

Joanna's head jerked upward and her eyes widened. "Lindsey!" Joanna's expression changed and sudden tears glittered. "How did you know? It's been so lonely since your Gram died, and I've been thinking about getting a dog, but I hadn't told anyone yet."

Lindsey felt as though she'd been punched in the gut. "I suppose…in a way…this is a gift from Gram."

"Oh?"

In the face of Joanna's skepticism, Lindsey didn't want to explain, but she owed it to both Joanna and Gram. When she finished the story, Joanna looked flummoxed but not nearly as disbelieving as Lindsey expected.

"It would be like Nora to find a way to watch over us even after she's gone from this world," Joanna finally said.

Lindsey helped Joanna set up the food dish and crate, then departed, leaving dog and mistress cuddling up together on the sofa.

Three weeks later, Joanna met a man while walking the dog, now named Noah, in the park. Sam was walking his retriever, and the leashes somehow got tangled as the two dogs nosed each other.

Six months later Joanna and Sam married. Both dogs went with them on the honeymoon.

The next Christmas, Lindsey set up the tree the day after Thanksgiving. She waited, not too patiently, for another candle flare, wondering what this one would bring.

A Wish Granted

Lynn LaFleur

Prologue

Lindsey stared into the candlelight and wished she wasn't seeing this. The dog last year had been bad enough, but this…

Mrs. Claus's Grant A Wish Foundation? She'd never heard of it before. But there was a sign there with an 800 number clear and easy to read. Crista stood to one side, though it didn't appear she was anywhere near the sign. She still looked so heartbreakingly sad, the way she'd looked at Joe's funeral.

Lindsey and Jade had felt so helpless then. Still did, in fact. There was so little they could do to help Crista. Only time could heal the wound left by her husband's death.

Did this vision mean that now there was something Lindsey could do?

Wait for them to show you their message, Gram had said, *and then act boldly on what you see.*

The dog had worked out well last year. Joanna and Sam were so happy. And so was Noah, settled into a home where he was loved and cared for.

Lindsey pulled her attention back to the vision. Way in the background was a snowy landscape, with a single cabin standing out in the blizzardish conditions. A light glowed warmly in the windows. A light for Crista?

What was she supposed to do, though? Call the 800 number? And ask Santa Claus for help?

Crista would probably wring her neck if she knew about it.

Chapter One

Crista Farrell folded her arms across the steering wheel and stared at the stormy water of Hood Canal. The line of snow-covered hills in the distance was the only thing that separated the gray water from the cloudy sky.

The colorless scenery fit her mood perfectly.

Crista leaned back in the seat and closed her eyes. She hated self-pity, and it had consumed her for the last eight months. She didn't know what to do to make it disappear from her life. Her sisters, Lindsey and Jade, had tried to cheer her up, and so had her friends. Nothing had worked to bring any happiness back into her life.

Despite trying to hold them back, tears filled her eyes. She was so tired of hurting. She tried to tell herself that there were so many people in the world a lot worse off than she. That knowledge didn't help her feel any better.

Tears trickled from her eyes and ran down her cheeks. Crista angrily swiped at them. *Stop it! Joe is gone. No amount of tears will bring him back, no matter how much you want him back.*

Her tears slowed, although they still clouded her vision. This had been a mistake. She'd driven here on impulse because she and Joe would've been married two years today. They had stood on the shore one year ago, only a few yards in front of where her car was now parked, and planned their future. They'd talked about the phenomenal success of her hair salon and the steady growth of his investment firm. They'd talked about shopping for a larger house, and when they would start a family.

Crista laid her hand on her flat abdomen. They'd decided to wait another year or two to start a family. She desperately wished they hadn't waited. If she had Joe's child growing inside her, a part of him would still be alive.

Would *always* be alive.

She wasn't supposed to be a widow at twenty-six. She and Joe were supposed to have a long life together. That life had been snatched away from her because some *idiot* had run a stop sign and plowed into Joe's car. He had died instantly and hadn't suffered. That knowledge gave her comfort.

It was the only comfort she'd had in eight months.

Light, fluffy flakes of snow began to fall. How appropriate for the first day of winter. Wrapping her coat tighter across her chest, Crista studied the flakes as they slowly accumulated on the windshield and hood of her car. Although she rarely watched the news because she'd grown tired of seeing nothing but bad things, she faithfully watched the weather every evening. She didn't remember any mention of snow in the weather forecast. While snow was always a possibility, December along Puget Sound usually meant rain.

When the snow completely obscured her vision through the windshield, Crista decided to leave. She turned the key in her Nissan's ignition. Nothing happened. She heard no sound, not even the grinding of a motor struggling to turn over. Frowning, Crista tried again. Still nothing. How odd. She never had trouble starting her car. Although four years old, it still ran perfectly.

One more time produced the same result. Crista rested her head on the steering wheel and sighed deeply. *Great. Car trouble on top of self-pity. This is turning out to be a shitty day.*

A shiver ran through her, an indication of how cold it had turned. She had to get out of here. Since her car wouldn't start, she had no option but to call Joe's brother, Gene, for help.

Crista reached for her purse and removed her wireless phone. The indicator showed no signal available, but she tried making a call anyway.

Nothing.

Okay, now what? I can't just sit here and wait for someone to come by and rescue me. There hasn't been one vehicle drive by here in the last hour.

Walking appeared to be her only choice.

Crista buttoned her coat and pulled the collar up in back to cover her neck. She dropped her wireless phone and keys into her purse, took a deep breath, and left the car.

The snow seemed to be falling harder now. Stuffing her hands in the pockets of her coat, Crista trudged up the incline to the road. Visibility became more difficult because of the falling snow and approaching dusk. Sunset would occur in less than an hour. She had to find help somewhere. Traffic could be heavy along Highway 101 in the summer, but very sparse in the winter, especially during a snowstorm. She knew there were houses along this road, as well as vacation cabins, although she doubted if anyone would be at their vacation cabin now, only four days before Christmas. People were gathering with their families, spending time with their loved ones at this most special time of the year.

Tears tightened Crista's throat. Jade had invited her to come to Florida, and Lindsey had also extended the invitation to visit her over Christmas. Crista had turned down both of them. She had to be *here* on her anniversary, in Washington, where she and Joe had spent their short life together.

Now, with the snow falling even harder and the sky turning darker, Crista wondered if she should've accepted one of their invitations.

She reached the highway and stopped. *Left or right? Think, Crista. Did you see any houses or cabins?*

No, she hadn't. That meant she should turn right, instead of the way she'd come.

Ten minutes of brisk walking made Crista thankful she used a treadmill regularly. Ten minutes more and she decided not even a treadmill could prepare her for walking in the biting cold. Her lungs burned. Her throat felt raw. Small pellets of ice now mixed with the snow and stung her cheeks. It didn't take a medical degree for her to know she had to find help, and quickly.

The approaching vehicle didn't register until a flash of headlights illuminated the highway before her. Crista turned and shielded her eyes from those lights. The vehicle slowed to a stop beside her.

A tow truck! Perfect.

She ran around the front of the truck to the driver's side. "Oh, I'm so glad to see you! My car…"

Crista stopped when the driver rested his arm on the frame and leaned out the window. He looked just like Santa Claus. He wore a Seattle Mariners baseball cap and a plaid flannel shirt instead of the normal red velvet. Otherwise, with his snowy white hair and full beard he could be Santa's twin brother.

He smiled. "Hi, little lady. Need some help?"

"Yes, please."

"Climb into the truck. No reason for you to stand out there in the snow."

"Thank you." She jogged back to the passenger side and climbed up on the bench seat. The warmth inside the truck made her shiver. She stuck her feet as close to the heater vent as she could get them. "My car broke down a mile or so back."

"The little Nissan parked by the water? I saw it when I drove by."

"Yes, that's it. Can you give me a jump, or tow me to a service station?"

He stroked his beard. "Well, that's a problem. This truck isn't exactly the newest model. My winch jammed on my last tow."

"What about jumper cables? Maybe it's just the battery."

"I lent my jumper cables to a friend last night. Do you have any?"

Crista could almost hear Joe yelling at her to keep her trunk supplied — especially with jumper cables — in case of an emergency. "No." She bit her bottom lip. "Can you call for another truck?"

"Well, that's another problem. There's no signal here for my cell phone, and my scanner's busted."

Some help you *are,* Crista thought. Immediately, she regretted her ungrateful thought. Surely, somehow, he could help her.

"I'm sorry I'm not more help," he said, "but I'll be glad to take you wherever you need to go. Maybe there's someone up the road a piece with a phone."

"I don't think there's anyone up here this time of year."

"It won't take long to find out. You need a few minutes in this warm truck anyway."

"The heat does feel good. Thank you."

He winked at her, then put the truck into gear.

Crista settled back in the surprisingly comfortable seat. She looked around the interior of the truck. She'd never been inside a tow truck so didn't know how they should look, but she'd describe this one as…comfy. Soft Christmas music came through the speakers. A cup sitting in a holder on the dash held what looked like hot chocolate. A plastic bag of homemade cookies sat on the seat next to the driver. All the comforts of home on wheels.

"What's your name, little lady?"

"Crista Farrell. And yours?"

"Folks call me S.C."

S.C. Short for Santa Claus, maybe?

Shaking her head, Crista chuckled to herself. If Lindsey were here, she'd believe this man was Santa. Lindsey believed in the magic of Christmas. She swore the ornaments that she'd inherited from Gram were magic.

Crista stopped believing in magic when her husband was taken away from her.

The truck jerked and spit. Crista instinctively grabbed the edge of the seat. "What's wrong?"

"I don't know. She's been acting up lately."

The truck jerked and spit again before the motor died. S.C. tried to start it once more. His effort produced nothing but a grinding sound.

"Well, this is embarrassing," S.C. said. "The tow truck driver needs a tow."

Crista didn't find his joke amusing. "Isn't there anything you can do?"

"I'll take a look under the hood, but it sounded pretty bad." He reached for his door handle, then stopped. "Looks like there's someone on this road after all."

Following the direction of his gaze, Crista squinted through the falling snow to see lights from a cabin.

"I'll walk up there and see if we can get some help," S.C. said.

"No, *I'll* go. You see if you can get your truck started."

S.C. hesitated, his hand still on the door handle. "I don't like the idea of a pretty young thing like you walking up to that cabin alone, and in the snow."

"I've already walked in the snow tonight. Walking a bit more won't hurt me. And I promise you, I can take care of myself. I have a black belt in Aikido. And if that isn't good enough…" Opening her purse, she withdrew a .22 caliber Jennings automatic and held it up for S.C. to see. "…I have this."

S.C.'s eyes widened. "I'm convinced."

Leaving the warmth of the tow truck wouldn't be easy. Crista climbed down from the truck and took off toward the cabin. She estimated she had to walk about 100 yards before she turned up the narrow driveway to the cabin. The heavy falling snow made it difficult to see, and even more difficult to walk.

The paved road became more slippery by the minute, and Crista had to step carefully to keep from falling. What should have taken her only ten minutes to travel took three times as long.

The driveway climbed uphill at a steep angle, making the walk even harder. By the time she made it to the front door of the cabin and underneath the small overhang, Crista was struggling for breath. She shivered from the cold and her wet clothes. Her hand trembled as she tugged off her glove so she could knock. She gasped when her knuckles touched the wood. Knowing no one could hear that pathetic attempt at knocking with her numb fingers, she beat on the door with the side of her fist.

Crista was about to beat for the third time when the door opened, leaving her hand in midair. She stared in shock. The man who stood before her could easily pass for Robert Redford when he played the Sundance Kid.

"May I help…" He stopped and his gaze passed over her body. "My God, you're soaked! Get in here."

He took her hand and dragged her inside the cabin, shutting the door behind them. "What are you doing outside in the snow?"

"My car broke down, and the tow truck driver who picked me up can't get his truck started. May I use your phone to call for help?"

"Of course. It's over here by the couch."

Crista had only a moment to glance around the small cabin as she followed him the short distance to the end table. It was one large room, the only door leading into the bathroom. A counter separated the living room from the kitchen. The furniture was leather, the décor masculine. He obviously lived here alone.

He pointed to a plain black push-button telephone. "Help yourself."

"Thank you." Picking up the receiver, Crista began to push the buttons of Gene's phone number. She'd punched in four digits before she realized she heard nothing.

She held out the receiver toward him. "There's no dial tone."

"What?" He took the receiver from her, listened, then pressed the button on the cradle several times. "I guess the storm took it out. That's never happened."

"Do you have a cell phone?"

"Yes, but there's no signal up here."

"I didn't have one on my cell either, but I thought since your place is on a hill…" Crista stopped and sighed. No phone. This day just got better and better.

"I can take you somewhere so you can use a phone."

Crista looked at him. He had dark blond hair that swept over his forehead, touched his ears and covered his collar in back. His eyes were a deep blue and surrounded by long lashes. A dark blond mustache touched his upper lip. A straight nose, strong chin, and high cheekbones completed the picture. He was definitely one of the most handsome men she'd ever seen.

Being handsome didn't mean he wouldn't also be dangerous.

Crista knew she had no choice but to go with him. They could pick up S.C. on the way. Despite her self-defense training and the pistol in her purse, she'd feel better if the older man rode with them. "I'd really appreciate it."

"No problem. I'll grab my keys and jacket." His gaze swept over her again. "Would you like a jacket? I have an extra one. It'll be big on you, but at least it'll be dry."

Crista smiled. "No, thank you, I'm fine."

He returned her smile, which made him even more handsome. A tiny fluttering in her stomach surprised Crista. She couldn't *possibly* feel anything for this stranger. Her heart still belonged to Joe.

He opened the front door and stood to the side to let her exit first. "Can we pick up the driver too?"

"Sure. Where is he?"

She motioned toward the spot where S.C.'s truck had died. "He's over…" She stopped. S.C.'s truck was gone.

"He's over where?"

"He was right there." Crista looked up and down the road, but saw no sign of S.C.'s truck. "He's gone."

"It's almost completely dark. Maybe you just can't see the truck."

"He left the headlights on and he had the hood up when I left him. He stuck one of those hanging lights under it. We'd be able to see it from here."

"He must have gotten his truck started."

"I guess." *Surely he wouldn't have just* left *me here with a complete stranger.*

"He's probably gone to get your car."

"He couldn't have. He said his winch didn't work."

He jiggled his keys in his hand. "Do you want me to drive you there?"

Crista looked at the landscape. Several inches of snow and ice covered the ground and driveway, with still more falling. Getting down the steep driveway wouldn't be easy. "Can you? The driveway looks icy."

"My SUV has four-wheel drive, and I'm a good driver." He smiled. "I'll get you there, I promise."

Chapter Two

Jeffrey Bower held the passenger door of his SUV open so the young woman could climb in. She gave him a gentle smile.

Jeff would swear his heart skipped a couple of beats. *She's so lovely*. He couldn't help staring into those incredible icy blue eyes a moment, admiring the dark brown hair that brushed her shoulders, before he closed the door. He'd come to his cabin to be alone, to try and decide if he'd done the right thing ending a two-year relationship. Dealing with a stranded woman hadn't been in his plans, but he couldn't possibly turn her away when she needed help.

Knowing she had to be cold in her damp clothing, Jeff hurried around to the driver's side and climbed inside. He turned the key in the ignition. Nothing happened. He tried again, but the engine still didn't turn over. That didn't make sense. He'd never had any trouble starting his vehicle.

He heard her sigh. "Don't tell me it won't start."

"Okay, I won't tell you."

"But it won't start."

"You told me not to tell you."

She sighed again and pushed her hair back from her forehead. "I don't believe this. How could three different vehicles have trouble starting?"

"I'll take a look under the hood, but I'm not a great mechanic."

She turned her head away from him. Jeff leaned forward, trying to see her face. He couldn't see her clearly in the dim light, but he thought he saw the sheen of tears in her eyes.

"Hey, it's okay," he said softly. "I'll figure out something. I'm not a complete idiot when it comes to cars." He hesitated a moment, then reached over and touched her shoulder. "Why don't you go back in the cabin where it's warm? I'll see what I can do."

She looked back at him, blinking away the tears. "Okay," she whispered. "Thank you."

The sad look in her eyes tugged at his heart. A wave of protectiveness surged through him. He didn't even know this woman, so that surprised him. He shouldn't be feeling *anything*, other than a desire to help her.

She climbed down from the SUV and returned to the cabin. Once the front door closed, Jeff opened his door and went to the back of the vehicle to get his tool box.

* * * * *

Crista stood before the fireplace, staring into the flames. She'd removed her wet coat and draped it over one of the kitchen chairs that she'd moved closer to the fire. Her wet boots sat on the hearth. Her clothes would be dry soon and she'd be ready to leave. She just needed a way to get home.

Home, to her empty house.

She'd always loved the small house in Tumwater that she and Joe bought before their wedding. The natural cedar siding let it blend in perfectly with the tall cedar and fir trees on their three acres. She'd insisted that whatever house they bought have a fireplace in the living room. Joe had topped that. In addition to the living room fireplace that already existed, he'd had one built in the master bedroom while they were in Hawaii on their honeymoon.

Now, the cozy house she loved seemed so lonely.

Tipping her head back, Crista closed her eyes and sighed. Eight months. She'd hurt for eight months. She didn't know how *not* to hurt. Yet she wanted more. She wanted to share her life with a man who loved her. She wanted children.

She wanted to live again.

I miss you, Joe, but you're gone and I'm alive. I don't want to be alone. If something had happened to me, I'd want you to find someone else. I have to believe you'd want the same for me.

She didn't know how to go on without her husband, but she had to find the strength to do it. Coming to the canal where she and Joe had spent their first anniversary had been to say her final goodbye to her husband. She'd always love Joe, but she'd mourned long enough.

Her new life started now.

The front door opened. He came in, along with a gust of cold air and snow. One look at his face told Crista that he hadn't been successful in starting his vehicle. "No luck?"

He shook his head. "No." He slipped off his jacket and hung it on a hook next to the door. "I can't find any reason why it won't start. I guess the battery's dead."

"I don't suppose you saw any sign of S.C.?"

"S.C.?"

"The tow truck driver."

"I didn't see anyone, or any vehicles. The road is completely deserted."

"I thought maybe he might come back with help." Crista slipped her hands into the back pockets of her jeans. "The initials fit him. He looks just like Santa Claus."

Chuckling, he stepped closer and held his hands up to the fire. "Maybe he's getting an early start on his deliveries."

"I hope his sleigh works better than his tow truck."

"Yeah."

Crista looked at him from the corner of her eye. He didn't say it, but she knew without him having to say anything—she had to spend the night here, and possibly longer than that. If he couldn't get his SUV started and the phone remained out of order, they had no way to get out of here.

"So, what's next?" Crista asked.

That got him to look at her. Crista inhaled sharply. The firelight illuminated half his face while the other half remained in shadow. She hadn't seen such a handsome man in a long time. Joe had been good looking, but not send-your-hormones-into-a-frenzy handsome like this man.

His body fit his good looks. Tall, broad shoulders, strong arms and thighs, flat stomach. He had the kind of body that women fantasized about having next to them in bed...or on top of them in bed.

A quick glance at his crotch proved he didn't lack anything there either.

A tickle of awareness surprised her. Although Crista hadn't wanted to be with a man since Joe died, she still had feelings. There had been many mornings when she'd awakened hot and aroused, when she'd longed to feel a man's strong arms around her. She and Joe had enjoyed a very healthy sex life. She missed that closeness, that feeling of fullness when Joe had slid his cock inside her.

A plastic dildo was a poor substitute for the real thing.

"I guess you realize you're stuck here with me."

His words brought her back to the present. Crista nodded. "Yes, I realize that."

"I won't hurt you. I hope you believe that."

"I do. I...trust you."

He smiled. "I'm glad." Turning to face her, he held out his hand. "Since we're stranded here together, we should introduce ourselves. I'm Jeff Bower."

She accepted his hand. "Crista Farrell."

"Crista. That's an unusual name. And very pretty."

His gaze traveled over her face in obvious masculine interest. Awareness tickled her again.

Uncomfortable with her feelings, Crista withdrew her hand from his and slipped it back in her pocket. Feeling desire for a man she didn't even know shouldn't happen.

Jeff cleared his throat. "Would you like some coffee or hot tea?"

"Hot tea would be wonderful."

"Sweetened or not?"

"Two teaspoons of sugar."

"One mug of hot tea coming up."

He crossed the room and entered the small kitchen area. Crista watched him for a moment as he moved around, preparing the tea, then shifted her attention to the cabin. Wood beams crossed the high ceiling. The wall to her right contained a floor-to-ceiling bookshelf, filled with books. A leather couch sat before the fireplace, flanked by two end tables holding small lamps. Two matching recliners completed the arrangement. The sleeping area to her left contained a queen-sized bed, dresser, cedar chest, and a nightstand on either side of the bed. She could see a claw-foot tub through the open bathroom door. All the furnishings appeared old, perhaps even antique. While not very large, the cabin looked homey and comfortable.

Crista wandered over to the bookcase. Standing with her hands behind her back, she perused the titles and authors. He had a wide variety, including medical thrillers, science fiction, horror, and comedy. She saw books by current fiction authors Koontz, Clancy, Crichton, Patterson, King, Heinlein, and McCaffery, mixed in with classics by Christie, Poe, Wells, Hemingway, and Dickens. Nonfiction books and autobiographies were scattered among the works of fiction. She wondered if he'd actually read all of these, or if most of them were for "show".

Jeff stood ten feet away from Crista. He studied her as she looked at his selection of books. The dim light from the one burning lamp and the fire turned her skin golden and gave her hair red highlights. His gaze wandered down her voluptuous body. Full breasts filled out her maroon sweater. Tight jeans hugged rounded buttocks, then tapered down her long legs. He guessed her height to be five feet five or six, a perfect complement to his six feet one frame.

Stranded with a beautiful woman. Jeff could think of worse things to happen. And if he hadn't been raised a gentleman, he could easily take advantage of the situation. He loved sex, especially with women built like Crista. He'd always thought a full-figured woman much more sexy than one model thin.

Being stranded together didn't mean she'd automatically fall into bed with him. They'd known each other less than an hour. Besides, she seemed…sad, and alone.

Jeff stepped closer and held out one mug. "Here's your tea."

She turned to him and accepted the mug with her right hand. "Thank you."

Jeff watched her as she sipped her tea. Those huge eyes surrounded by thick lashes, a cute turned-up nose, full lips, an oval face…they all combined to make her stunning.

Crista cupped her left hand around her mug. That's when he noticed her wedding band.

He crashed back to earth with a thud.

"I'm sorry you aren't able to call your husband. Does he know where you are?"

Gripping her mug tighter, she shook her head. "My husband… He was killed in a car accident eight months ago."

A widow, so young? She couldn't be any older than her mid-twenties. Jeff didn't know what to say. "I'm sorry" seemed so inadequate.

Before he could say anything, she raised one hand. "I didn't mean to dump that on you."

"You didn't dump anything on me, Crista," he said softly.

Talking about her late husband obviously upset her. Jeff decided changing the subject would be a good idea. "Are you hungry? I made a beef stew earlier. I'm no master chef, but I do make a mean stew."

She remained silent for a moment, then gave him that gentle smile again. "Actually, food sounds pretty good."

"To me too. Enjoy your tea while I warm up the stew and make some biscuits."

"You make biscuits too?"

"Yeah." Jeff grinned. "As long as they come from a can."

Crista released a tinkling, feminine laugh. The sound touched his heart. He always enjoyed hearing a woman's laughter.

Jeff gestured toward the couch. "Make yourself comfortable. I'll have everything ready in a few minutes."

Chapter Three

The stew was thick, loaded with vegetables, and delicious. Crista didn't realize the extent of her hunger until she started eating. Her appetite had been non-existent since Joe died. She'd lost twenty-five pounds in eight months. Since she'd always been full-figured, she'd been happy to say goodbye to that weight, and would love to get rid of another fifteen. Unfortunately, very little of that weight had disappeared from her breasts. Joe had loved her large breasts. Crista would gladly give up a couple of cup sizes for more comfort.

"Jeff, this is wonderful."

"Thanks. I like to cook, but don't get the chance to very often. Lots of late nights at work usually mean I pick up something on the way home. I'm on a first-name basis with the owners of every pizza place and Chinese restaurant between my office and my house."

"I know what you mean. I like to cook too, but cooking for one isn't worth the hassle."

He looked at her, his expression serious. Crista braced herself for the questions about Joe. She knew people meant well, but she didn't want to talk about how her husband died, or her life without him.

Instead, Jeff asked, "Where do you work?"

Relieved at his change of subject, Crista took another half a biscuit from the plate in the center of the table. "I own a hair salon in Olympia. I have three stylists who work full-time, and two who work three days a week."

"Sounds like a successful place."

"I work long hours, but I make a good living. And I enjoy it. I have a lot of wonderful clients. My stylists have their own rooms and pay me rent. I take care of the utilities, laundry, supplies, things like that. It works out well for all of us." Crista popped the last bite of biscuit in her mouth. "So, what do you do for a living?"

"Would you like more stew? There's plenty."

Crista tilted her head. "You didn't answer my question."

"Talking about work is boring. I'd rather eat."

"Wait a minute. You asked me about my job. Why won't you tell me about yours? Do you do something…" She looked from side to side, playfully checking for anyone who might overhear their conversation, then leaned forward and lowered her voice. "…illegal?"

Jeff laughed. "Hardly." He rose and turned toward the stove for more stew. "I crunch numbers at a paper company."

"Ah, you're an accountant."

"Of sorts." He gestured toward her empty bowl. "Want more?"

Crista shook her head. "I'm fine."

Jeff returned to the table and dug into his second bowl of stew. Crista pushed aside her empty bowl, rested her folded arms on the table, and watched him. She hadn't been this close to a man in a long time. Male customers playfully teased her, male friends phoned often to make sure she had everything she needed. This was different. She and Jeff were totally alone, cut off from the rest of the world. No phone, no transportation, and the heavily falling snow meant they might be alone for several days.

A gust of wind rattled the kitchen door. The unexpected noise startled her.

"Don't be afraid of the storm," Jeff said. "You're safe."

"I'm not usually afraid of storms. I like the clouds and rain here."

"Here? Does that mean you aren't a native Washingtonian?"

Crista shook her head. "I'm a native New Yorker. I grew up in a small town called Winterland."

"Sounds…Christmasy."

She grinned along with him. "Very. Lots of snow in the winter, friendly people, my sisters and grandmother. I had a great childhood."

"How did you wind up all the way across the country in Washington?"

"Joe, my husband. Three years ago, he and two friends went to New York City for a series of seminars. They did the tourist thing in the city after three days of lectures and classes, then decided to get in some skiing. We literally ran into each other at a restaurant in Winterland where he and his friends stopped for lunch. He offered to take me out to dinner as an apology for almost knocking me to the ground. I accepted."

Crista smiled. She remembered the horrified look on Joe's face when she'd almost fallen. He'd been mortified that he could've seriously hurt a woman. "We hit it off right away. He spent more time with me than his friends the next two days. When he invited me to visit him in Olympia, I accepted. I went there a month later and stayed."

"Sounds like something from a fairy tale."

"My relationship with Joe was like a fairy tale."

"And cut short much too quickly."

"Yes," she whispered.

Tears pricked her eyes. Crista blinked them away. She refused to shed any tears in front of Jeff. Instead, she changed the subject.

"So, where's dessert?"

"I just happen to have dessert. My parents' housekeeper always stocks me up with way more than I can eat when I come here." Jeff rose, collected a rectangular plastic container from the cabinet, and returned to his chair. "Ta da!" he said as he removed the lid.

Crista bit back a grin and peered into the container. "Ooh, brownies! With nuts?"

"Of course. Help yourself while I start some coffee."

"None for me. I drink decaf."

"So do I."

Joe had refused to drink decaf. He claimed there was no reason to drink coffee if it didn't give you a jolt.

Crista took a brownie, tore it in two, and took a bite. The taste of chocolate and walnuts exploded on her tongue. She chewed slowly, savoring the moist treat. Joe hadn't been a chocolate fan, but had loved the peanut butter bars she'd bake for him.

She wondered how long it would take before she didn't compare Joe's likes and dislikes to everyone else's. Thoughts of him still filled her mind every day, although not as often. Where she used to think of him every few minutes, now she thought of him every few hours.

Maybe I really am starting to heal.

"Do you take milk or sugar in your coffee?"

Jeff's question made Crista look up at him. She'd never put a lot of emphasis on a person's appearance. How a person treated their fellow man was more important to her than hair or eye color. Looking at Jeff, with his longish blond hair and sexy blue eyes, made her breath catch and her heart beat funny.

"Crista? Milk or sugar?"

"Uh, yes, please. Milk. I like milk in my coffee."

The amusement in his eyes made heat climb in her cheeks. *You're being a twit, Crista! Good grief, he isn't the only handsome man you've been around in your life.*

True, but Crista hadn't been around *any* man since she'd starting dating Joe. He'd been her whole life since their first date. Imagining herself being intimate with any other man... She simply couldn't do it. She couldn't give her body to another man.

Crista hadn't been a virgin the first time she and Joe made love, but her total experience with sex had consisted of a couple of times that were best forgotten. Joe had been...perfect. Their lovemaking had been slow and tender or fast and hard, depending on her mood. He'd loved foreplay, especially caressing her breasts. Seeing her body always pleased him. Touching it pleased him even more.

He'd known her so intimately, had known exactly how to give her the most pleasure. Right from the start of their relationship, he'd been an incredible lover.

He'd done things with his tongue that were probably illegal in some countries.

She missed sex. She missed it a lot.

"How are the brownies?" Jeff asked. He set their mugs of coffee on the table and returned to his chair.

"Wonderful."

"Ida's a great cook. She's worked for my parents as long as I can remember." Jeff took a brownie and ate half of it in one bite. "When I told her I was coming here for a few days, she loaded me up with casseroles and pre-cooked meals and desserts. There's no chance of us running out of food." He chuckled. "She still treats me like I'm ten."

If he grew up with a full-time housekeeper in his home, he must come from money. Not bad for an accountant at a paper company. "She sounds wonderful." Crista finished her brownie and washed it down with coffee. "So, why are you here alone so close to Christmas?"

Jeff stopped in the act of reaching for another brownie and looked at her sharply.

"Did I ask the wrong thing?"

"No. I just...wasn't expecting that question."

"You don't have to tell me, Jeff."

"You've been very open with me. I should be just as open with you. After all, we have a lot of time to kill, right?"

"That we do."

Picking up his coffee mug, Jeff leaned back in his chair. He slowly sipped the hot brew before speaking. "I was involved with someone for almost two years. We'd known each other practically our whole lives. I never officially proposed to her, but our families and friends assumed we'd get married someday." He set his mug back on the table. "I finally realized I didn't want to marry her, that I didn't love her the way a man should love a woman he plans to spend the rest of his life with. I broke up with her last week."

"How did she take it?"

"Not well. She ranted and raved and cried and called me some very nasty names. I'd never suspected Becky knew that kind of language." Leaning forward again, he rested his arms on the table. "But not once during her outburst did she say she loved me."

Crista remained silent, letting him speak at his own pace.

"I mentioned that little fact to Becky, and she had no response. I think she thought of our relationship just like I did— it was comfortable. We were there for each other in good times and bad, had great sex…" His eyes widened. "Oops. I probably shouldn't have said that part. I don't usually talk about sex with a woman I barely know."

Crista couldn't help chuckling at his discomfort. "It's okay."

Jeff cleared his throat. "So, what shall we do to pass the time?"

"Watch television?"

"Nope. No TV, no radio. I have a CD player and a lot of books. This is my place to get away from the world, and I don't want anything outside my front door to intrude on my space."

"I rarely watch TV anyway." Pulling her mug closer, she cupped it in both hands. "I'm enjoying talking to you."

Jeff smiled. "Me too." He snapped his fingers. "I have a deck of cards. How are you at gin rummy?"

"Excellent."

"Ah, I sense a challenge in your tone."

Crista smiled. She liked playing with him. "I always beat my sisters."

"Well, I happen to be an excellent player too. You game?"

"I'm game."

* * * * *

Crista totaled the amount one more time. Jeff braced himself for the outcome.

Grinning wickedly, she laid down her pen. "You owe me $98.36."

He winced. "Damn. Will you take a check?"

"Of course, with proper ID."

Chuckling, Jeff shook his head. "You weren't kidding when you said you're an excellent gin rummy player. I never should have agreed to your double or nothing bets."

"I've bought a lot of shoes with the money I've won from my sisters."

"I'll bet."

He leaned back in his chair and watched her shuffle the deck. They'd played cards for three hours and she'd talked most of the time, which was what he wanted. He'd learned more about her life in Winterland. She'd told him about her two sisters, and being raised by her grandmother after her parents were killed in a skiing accident. She'd talked about her salon and how much she enjoyed her job.

She'd told him today would've been her second wedding anniversary.

Jeff couldn't imagine losing a mate to death, especially so young. He and Becky had been together a couple of years, but the deep, forever love simply hadn't existed between them.

He wouldn't settle for anything else.

At thirty, thoughts of marriage and a family entered his mind almost daily. He wanted to share his life with a woman, a woman who loved him as deeply as he loved her. He wanted to tuck his kids into bed at night, help them with their homework, coach a Little League team.

He wanted to end each evening making love with his wife.

Thinking about making love drew Jeff's attention back to Crista. He watched her hands as she shuffled the deck. Slim, graceful fingers. Medium-length fingernails painted a shiny maroon, almost the same shade as her sweater. Hands that could give a man an incredible amount of pleasure.

His gaze traveled up her arm. Long, ivory neck. Silky hair that brushed her shoulders. Full lips, made for kissing…or sliding over a man's cock.

Stroking his mustache, Jeff studied her large breasts. They would easily fill his hands, perhaps even overflow them. They would be as ivory as her neck with pale pink nipples. Or perhaps rose-colored ones.

His mouth actually watered with the desire to taste them.

It took Jeff a moment to notice she'd stopped shuffling the cards. Slowly, he raised his gaze back to her face. An unusual heat climbed into his cheeks. She'd caught him ogling her breasts.

"They're real, I promise," she said dryly.

"I didn't mean…" Jeff cleared his throat, not sure what to say.

"Don't be embarrassed. I've caught a lot of men looking at my breasts. Besides, women look at men just as much as men look at women."

"You think so?"

"I *know* so. When you got up to make coffee, I…"

She stopped. An adorable blush bloomed in her cheeks. Jeff struggled not to smile. "You what?"

"Nothing."

Jeff leaned forward and rested his arms on the table. He couldn't resist teasing her. "When I got up to make coffee, you looked at my ass. Or maybe my crotch. Is that what you were going to say?"

He saw her throat work as she swallowed. Then she laid down the cards and leaned forward too, her chin high. "Yes, I looked at your ass. If you don't want women to look at it, you shouldn't wear such tight jeans."

"I didn't expect to have a woman in my cabin looking at my ass, so I didn't think about the tightness of my jeans. I wear what's comfortable."

"Comfortable looks very good on you."

Their faces were close, no more than eighteen inches apart. If Jeff moved a few more inches, he wondered if she would meet him halfway until their lips touched.

Awareness filled her eyes...the awareness of a woman for a man. Her gaze moved from his eyes to his lips and back again.

Jeff moved closer. So did Crista. A mere six inches away, she stopped and abruptly pulled back.

"I, uh, I think I've taken enough of your money for tonight."

It took much longer for Jeff to lean back in his chair. He still wanted to taste her lips, her tongue. He wanted to pull her from that chair and wrap his arms around her, feel those luscious breasts against his chest. He wanted...

Picking up their coffee mugs, Jeff carried them to the sink. He'd never felt such a strong attraction for a woman so quickly. It had to be their situation. Crista was a very lovely woman, and they were stranded together. Not able to move more than a few yards away from her in the small cabin was playing havoc with his hormones.

"It's getting late," Crista said. "Where can I sleep?"

Jeff turned to face her. Leaning against the counter, he crossed his arms over his chest. "In my bed."

Chapter Four

Her eyes widened. Jeff bit his tongue to keep from laughing. He knew he shouldn't tease her so unmercifully, but couldn't resist. The pink coloring her cheeks made her even lovelier.

"Your bed?" she squeaked.

"Yeah. It's *very* comfortable." He paused when she fidgeted in her chair. "I'll sleep on the couch."

Her shoulders slumped. He didn't know whether to be amused or annoyed at her obvious relief. "That's very nice of you, but I'll take the couch."

"I don't mind—"

"Jeff, you're a lot taller than me, and a lot more…husky. I'll take the couch."

Husky. He wondered if that meant she approved of his body. "Whatever you want." He pushed away from the counter and headed for the sleeping area. "I'll get you a quilt and pillow."

Kneeling before the cedar chest, Jeff sorted through the extra bedding until he located a sheet and quilt. He had no extra pillow in the chest, so took one from the bed. When he turned around, Crista stood between him and the bathroom.

"Will this be enough for you? I only have one extra quilt."

"I'm right by the fire. One will be fine." She slipped her hands in the back pockets of her jeans. "Do you have anything I can sleep in?"

Jeff hadn't thought of that. Of course she wouldn't want to sleep in her clothes. "I have some sweats. Will they be okay?"

Crista nodded. "I don't suppose you have a washing machine and dryer here."

"Nope, 'fraid not. You can rinse out whatever you need to and hang it over the shower rod."

His idea must not have appealed to her. She looked down at the floor for a moment before she released a heavy breath and raised her gaze back to his face. "I know we're both adults, and I know you've seen women's underwear, but the thought of my bra and panties just…hanging around makes me uncomfortable."

"So don't rinse them out."

She wrinkled her nose.

Jeff chuckled at her expression. "I have plenty of sweats. Ida makes sure I have extra clothes as well as lots of food. You can put your clothes in a bag and wear mine."

"With no underwear?"

The idea of being around him without wearing her bra and panties obviously made her uneasy. To try and ease her mind, Jeff teased her again. "I'll make you a deal. I won't wear any shorts. How's that?"

She chuckled. "You'd do that for me?"

"Absolutely, without hesitation."

"Such a gentleman."

"My mom would be happy to hear you say that." Jeff laid the bedding on top of the cedar chest and turned toward the dresser. "Do you have a favorite color? I think Ida packed a pair in every color there is."

"I'm not picky."

Opening the second drawer, Jeff grabbed the pair of sweats on top. "How about these? I don't know why Ida bought purple sweats for me. I never wear purple."

"Those aren't purple, they're plum."

Jeff frowned. "Crista, guys understand eight basic colors. Plum is a fruit, not a color."

Crista giggled and took the sweats. "Thank you."

"The bathroom is all yours while I make up the couch."

The gentle swing of her hips drew his gaze. He watched her until she shut the bathroom door. Her ass filled out those jeans so nicely…

Get your mind off sex, Bower.

Easier said than done when a beautiful woman occupied the bathroom only a few yards away from him, a woman who happened to be taking off her clothes right now. He hadn't heard the lock click. He could walk over there, open the door, touch her…

Jeff quickly gathered up the bedding and crossed to the couch. He had no right to think of Crista in a sexual manner, simply because they'd shared a few hours together. She'd called him a gentleman. He'd better start acting like one.

She came out of the bathroom a few moments later. The sweats were too large, and she'd washed the rest of the makeup off her face. She still looked incredibly lovely.

Jeff struggled to keep his gaze on her face and not let it drop to her unbound breasts.

"Thank you for making up the couch."

"No problem."

He didn't want to say goodnight. He wanted to sit with her by the fire, listen to her talk more about her sisters, her childhood. Instead, he smiled and said, "See you in the morning."

* * * * *

The sound seeped into his consciousness. Jeff frowned and moved his head on the pillow, trying to block out the sound and go back to sleep.

When he heard it again, Jeff raised his head. It sounded like a moan from someone in pain.

The only light in the room came from the fire. It illuminated Crista's thrashing form on the couch. Jeff threw back the covers, hurried across the floor and dropped to his knees next to her. He touched her shoulder lightly.

"Crista. Crista, it's Jeff. Wake up."

When Crista continued to toss and turn, he slipped his arms underneath her and pushed her into a sitting position. "Crista," he said, his voice stronger.

She shuddered and lifted her lids. Her eyes appeared glazed and unfocused. He waited for her to recognize her surroundings.

"Jeff." Her voice sounded hoarse until she cleared her throat. "What happened?"

"You tell me."

Slowly, she swung her legs off the couch and straightened. Jeff sat beside her, resting his arm along the back of the couch behind her.

"Did you have a bad dream?" he asked softly.

Crista frowned and pushed her hair back from her face. "I'm not sure. I…" She stopped. Jeff could tell by the sudden change in her expression—from puzzlement to realization—that she remembered what happened. "I was dreaming about Joe, about when he died." She crossed her arms over her stomach. "I haven't dreamed about the accident in a long time."

Not sure what to say to ease her pain, Jeff remained silent.

"I had a nightmare every night for weeks after Joe died, at least on the nights when I could sleep at all. They tapered off to a few a week, then a few a month, until they stopped." Tilting back her head, she squeezed her eyes shut. "What made it come back tonight?"

"It's your anniversary."

Such a simple explanation, but one she obviously hadn't considered. Crista looked at him. Tears shimmered in her eyes. "Yes, it is," she whispered.

A lone tear slipped down her cheek. Jeff cradled her jaw and wiped the tear away with his thumb. "I'm so sorry you're hurting."

He wanted to hold her, comfort her. The need to protect her almost overpowered him.

Crista leaned forward and chafed her arms. "I'm so cold."

Jeff didn't think twice about it. He had to help her in whatever way possible. Scooping her up in his arms, he headed for the bed.

Crista released a squeak and grabbed his shoulders. "What are you doing?"

"Taking you to bed."

"Now wait just a minute—"

"Crista, you're shivering. I don't have any other quilts." He placed her in the spot where he'd slept and pulled the covers over her. "There's nothing warmer than another body." Rounding the foot of the bed, he climbed in beside her and pulled the covers over himself. He tugged her into the curve of his body, her back to his chest. "Get some sleep."

She remained stiff, which didn't surprise him. He lay perfectly still, his arm over her waist, and waited for her to relax. It took several moments, but he finally felt the tenseness leave her body. She shifted to what he assumed would be a more comfortable position for her and released a deep breath.

Jeff smiled and closed his eyes.

* * * * *

Crista didn't want to awaken. She felt too comfortable to move. A delicious heat warmed her back, buttocks, and thighs. Crista snuggled closer to it and sighed contentedly. Sleep tugged at her mind, luring her back into that place of no pain, no worries.

Something hard nudged her buttocks. Crista frowned and shifted to get away from it. That's when she felt a hand on her stomach, beneath her shirt.

Her eyes popped open. Jeff. That meant the hard thing against her buttocks…

Crista lay still, trying to breathe normally so she wouldn't disturb him. It had been eight months since she'd awakened with a man in her bed. That warmth, that feeling of closeness…she wanted to savor it for a few more minutes.

Groaning softly, Jeff thrust his erection against her buttocks. Crista had to bite her lip to keep from groaning too. So many times she'd awakened with Joe pressed up against her just like this. He'd lift her top leg and slide his cock inside her, or pull her over on top of him. He'd loved for her to be on top so he could play with her breasts and buttocks.

I want that again.

Crista slowly rolled her head toward Jeff. He still slept soundly. His tousled hair drew her attention. Lifting one hand, she touched a tendril that curled over his forehead. Soft, as she suspected.

He shifted again. His hand moved, dipping beneath the waistband of her sweats. Crista quickly pulled her hand back. She didn't want him to wake up yet. It felt too good being in his arms.

Jeff's hand flattened on her abdomen, then slowly inched upward underneath her shirt. Her breath hitched when he cupped her breast.

He plucked at her nipple with his thumb and forefinger. Closing her eyes again, Crista tilted back her head. Warm, moist lips touched her neck, the sensitive skin below her ear. A gentle tug on her earlobe with his teeth made goose bumps erupt over her skin.

"Crista," he whispered.

In the next instant, Jeff froze. His entire body tensed. "Crista?"

Before she could say anything, Jeff jerked his hand away from her and scooted back, putting several inches between them.

"Damn it, Crista, I'm sorry. I wasn't… I didn't mean to…" He ran his hand over his face. "Shit."

Crista rolled over to face him. "You were asleep."

"That's no excuse for touching you."

The covers bunched around his waist. She'd been too upset last night to notice the way he looked. She wasn't upset now. Crista's gaze traveled over his broad shoulders, wide chest, and strong arms. A generous sprinkling of blond hair spread across his chest and down his stomach. Warmth flowed through her body and settled between her thighs. The man was gorgeous.

"Jeff, I'm not angry with you. In fact, I…"

She stopped, unsure if she should admit her feelings. She didn't want to sound like a desperate, sex-starved widow.

"You what?"

"I enjoyed it. It's been a long time since a man has held me, touched me."

Jeff propped up on one elbow. "You're a beautiful woman, Crista. I can't imagine there's a man alive who wouldn't want to touch you."

"Do you?"

"Yeah," he said, his voice husky. "I won't lie to you. I very much want to make love to you. I've wanted that since I opened my door and saw you on my porch."

He reached over and drew one finger down her cheek. "We hardly know each other. I don't want you to do anything you don't want to."

The dim light from the fire barely lit up the room, but she could clearly see the desire in Jeff's eyes. It had been so long since a man had looked at her the way Jeff did now. Yes, they hardly knew each other, but something definitely existed between them. Talking to him, being comfortable with him, had been easy right away.

That had never happened to her with any other man but Joe.

Crista touched his cheek and ran her thumb over his lips. "I want you, Jeff. Make love to me."

Chapter Five

Jeff kissed Crista's thumb. He'd like to believe her. He ached to hold her, be inside her, but he had to be sure before he ever touched her.

He lowered his head and covered her lips with his own. Those full lips had beckoned to him since he'd opened his door and saw her standing on his porch. If she wanted him, *truly* wanted him, her kiss would tell him.

Crista tilted her head and parted her lips.

Desire surged through Jeff at the touch of her tongue against his. She wiggled it over and around his tongue, then withdrew. Jeff followed it back into her mouth. A deep moan erupted from her throat. Tunneling her fingers into his hair, she held his head in place while she kissed him hungrily.

Hot. That's the word that popped into Jeff's mind to describe her mouth, her kisses. It's also the way she made him feel. Her touch drove up his desire another notch.

He needed even more. He needed her naked as soon as possible.

Rising to his knees, Jeff tugged Crista to a sitting position. He grasped the hem of her sweatshirt, pulled it over her head, and tossed it to the floor.

"My God," he muttered. Her breasts were incredible—round, large, with dark pink nipples and areolas the size of half dollars. He cradled both of them in his hands, lifting and massaging the heavy globes while rubbing the nipples with his thumbs.

Crista arched her back. "That feels good."

"I want to make you feel good. I want to make you feel *so* good."

Jeff drew one nipple deep into his mouth. Delicious. He suckled harder, taking as much of her breast into his mouth as he could while thumbing her other nipple. The sound of her soft gasp traveled straight to his groin. His cock grew harder, his balls tighter.

Crista slid her hands inside his sweat pants. One hand wrapped around his cock, one slipped beneath his balls. She tightened both hands.

Jeff groaned. "Easy, baby."

"I need you inside me, please."

His lungs burned from breathing so heavy. Still, he had to be sure she wouldn't have any regrets if they made love. "Crista, we need to slow down—"

"I don't want to slow down." Grabbing the waistband of his pants, she jerked them past his hips. "*Now.*"

He'd been raised to never argue with a lady.

Crista lay back and pushed her pants over her hips. Jeff tugged them the rest of the way off her legs. He tossed them to the floor, then rose from the bed and shucked off his own sweat pants.

When he returned to the bed, Crista opened her arms and legs to him. Jeff stretched out on top of her and kissed her again while sliding one hand between her legs. Warm, liquid silk coated his fingertips.

Jeff preferred long, easy lovemaking. He liked to take his partner up gently, make her desire build slowly, until she couldn't wait one more second to be joined with him. He wanted Crista too much for an easy build-up this time. The hungry way she kissed him, touched him, proved she wanted him just as much.

Hooking his arms under her knees, he thrust inside her.

Crista arched her back and gasped. Immediately, Jeff stilled.

"Did I hurt you?"

"No. No, it's all right. It's just…been awhile for me."

"You're wet. I thought you were ready."

"I am. Don't stop. Please."

Crista wrapped her arms around his neck. Jeff stared into her eyes as he pulled back until only the head remained inside her, then thrust again. And again.

"Oh, God, Jeff, that feels good. It's been so long since…" Her breath hitched. She bit her bottom lip and squeezed her eyes shut. "Harder. Please, harder."

He increased the speed and depth of his thrusts. Her slick walls gripped him as he pumped. It felt so good, he knew he wouldn't be able to last very long. His orgasm began to build in his balls. Jeff fought it. He didn't want to come until Crista did, but he didn't want to stop either.

A moment later, she trembled and cried out.

Crista's climax brought on Jeff's release. He continued to pump inside her until the last spasm eased. He lay still, not wanting to move away from her warmth yet.

The gentle touch of her hands on his back made Jeff raise his head. He didn't have the words to tell her how powerful that had been for him. Instead, he kissed her, gently this time.

Crista smiled tenderly. "Hi."

Jeff returned her smile. "Hi."

"Quite a way to say good morning, isn't it?"

"A *wonderful* way to say good morning." He kissed the tip of her nose. "Are you sure I didn't hurt you? You were very tight."

"I'm sure. And I thought guys liked for gals to be tight."

He grinned along with her. He liked her spunk. "Tight is good. So is wet. You were both."

She slid her hands over his shoulders and up into his hair. "Hard and big is good too. You were both."

"Hmm, so you like hard and big, huh?"

"Better than soft and little."

Jeff snorted with laughter. He liked that she felt comfortable talking about sex, and what she wanted during sex. "Well, I'll do my best *not* to give you anything soft and little."

Crista ran one finger over his lips and down his chin. "Think you could give me hard and big again soon?"

"Oh, yeah. That won't be a problem at all." He nipped at her finger. "How about if we take a shower and I'll make us some breakfast?"

"Can I help?"

"You can wash my back."

"I meant help with breakfast."

"Oh. Well, you can't blame a guy for trying."

Jeff reluctantly withdrew from her body. He rose to his knees again and simply looked at her. Her body was exquisite. Ivory skin, large breasts, wide hips, firm thighs, rounded stomach…they all combined to make her lovely.

"You're beautiful, Crista."

She smiled. "Thank you." He watched her gaze travel over him. "So are you."

Jeff rubbed his chin. "I don't think anyone's ever called me beautiful."

"So, I'm the first."

"That you are." Climbing from the bed, he held out a hand to her. "Shower time."

Crista took his hand and let him lead her to the small bathroom. She stood next to the sink while he pulled back the shower curtain that surrounded the deep claw-footed bathtub and turned on the taps. She took a deep breath and let it out slowly. Wow. She hadn't experienced such an intense orgasm in a long time. Sex with Joe had been wonderful, but what she'd experienced with Jeff… She didn't know how to describe it.

The view of his firm buttocks as he bent over the tub made her tummy flutter. Looks had always been way down the list for Crista. But she was human, and couldn't help noticing how good Jeff looked. And felt.

He turned to face her. He looked even better from the front. Broad shoulders, a wide chest sprinkled with dark blond hair that tapered down his flat stomach to form a thick nest for his flaccid cock. Muscular arms, strong legs. Even his feet were sexy.

"Nice and warm," he said, once again holding his hand out to her.

With Jeff's help, Crista climbed into the tub first. Jeff followed and pulled the curtain shut, enclosing them in their own private sauna.

"Ladies first."

Stepping under the spray, Crista tilted her head back and let it flow over her hair. She stood still for several moments, enjoying the feel of the warm water. When her hair was completely wet, she opened her eyes and looked at Jeff. His gaze focused on her breasts.

Crista left her hands in her hair, knowing that having her arms raised also lifted her breasts. If he wanted to look at her, she'd give him a show. "You're staring, Jeff."

"I can't help it." He flicked his thumb over one hard nipple. "You have an incredible body."

"Thank you." Glancing over her shoulder, she noticed the wire caddy hanging over the shower head. She picked up the bar of soap and offered it to him. "Would you like to wash my back?"

He grinned wickedly. "I'd love to."

Crista turned her back to Jeff. She waited for him to touch her with a wash cloth. Instead, his soapy hands began caressing her shoulders. Crista let her head drop forward when he pressed his thumbs into the base of her neck.

"Feel good?" he asked before kissing her neck.

"*Very* good."

His hands drifted lower, his thumbs rubbing her shoulder blades. "I give a great massage."

"I can tell."

"This is nothing. Wait until I get you on the bed with a big bottle of lotion."

"Mmm, that sounds good."

His hands drifted even lower, until he cupped her buttocks. He massaged them for a few moments before gripping them and pulling them apart. Crista drew in a quick breath when she felt his hardening cock between her cheeks.

Jeff held her hips tightly as he rubbed his cock up and down the cleft. "You're a very sensual woman. You like to be touched." He slid his hands over her hips to her stomach. Slowly, they inched upward to her breasts. "Don't you?"

He pinched both nipples, and Crista groaned. "Yes."

"What do you want me to do to you?" he whispered directly into her ear.

His warm breath caused goose bumps to scatter over her skin. Crista closed her eyes and rested her head on his shoulder. He continued to roll her nipples between his soapy fingers. Each tug made her clit throb.

"Do you want me to tell you what I'd like to do? Explicitly?"

"Yes, please."

"I'd like to suck your nipples. They're nice and hard now, and getting bigger. I want to lick your pussy all the way from your clit to your ass and back again." He dipped his tongue in her ear. Crista shivered. "Would you like that?"

"Yessss."

His hand drifted down her stomach and slid between her legs. "I'd like to be inside this sweet pussy again. Maybe I should fuck you right here."

She didn't care what he did, as long as he did something *now.* "*Yes!*"

"Lean forward."

Crista braced her hands on the wall and bent her neck. The warm water beat on the middle of her back and trickled down her sides. She barely had time to inhale before Jeff thrust his cock inside her.

"Mmm, tight and creamy. I like that."

She hoped he didn't expect her to respond. Conversation wasn't even remotely possible right now.

"Spread your legs. Yeah, like that." He gripped her hips and began pumping slowly. "Arch your back more. I want that ass high. Good."

His thrusts picked up speed. Crista bit her bottom lip and squeezed her eyes shut. His cock was thick, long, and big enough to fill her completely. He gave her short, quick strokes, then long, slow ones. He'd stop completely for several seconds, circle his hips so his balls rubbed her clit, then start thrusting again.

Crista clenched her hands into fists. She'd never been fond of this position because she couldn't hold or touch her partner. The depth of Jeff's thrusts quickly changed her mind. She couldn't believe the incredible sensation of having him fuck her this way. The tension built inside of her, traveling higher and higher.

It broke when Jeff pushed a finger into her anus.

Throwing her head back, Crista cried out as the waves of pleasure washed over her. Jeff continued to grip her hips and thrust for several more moments before he, too, cried out from his climax.

He gathered her close to him, one arm around her waist and one arm across her breasts. "That was incredible," he rasped.

"Yes, it was."

"Do you realize the water is cold?"

"What water?"

She felt his chuckle against her back. "How about if we get out?"

"I don't think I can move."

He kissed her shoulder. "I'll help you. As soon as my legs work again."

Despite the water turning cold, Crista stepped under the spray once again to rinse off the last residue of soap. She moved to the side to allow Jeff to rinse also. The sight of him running his hands over his own body looked so incredibly sexy.

Jeff turned off the water and faced her. "Are you ready for breakfast?"

"I'm past ready."

Tilting up her chin, he dropped a soft kiss on her lips. "Then let's get dressed and fix breakfast."

Chapter Six

Jeff propped his elbow on the table and rested his jaw on his fist. He liked watching Crista eat. She obviously enjoyed food very much. She didn't take dainty little bites that she wouldn't even have to chew, but ate heartily. When he'd offered her seconds of hash browns and scrambled eggs, she hasn't hesitated to accept.

Becky had barely eaten anything. Her entire meal would've fit on a small saucer instead of a plate. She'd been obsessed about staying so thin, she'd almost looked anorexic. She definitely didn't have all the soft, womanly curves that Crista possessed.

He preferred the womanly curves.

Crista looked at him as she popped the last bite of toast in her mouth. "What?"

"Nothing. I'm just watching you."

She chewed and swallowed while wiping her hands on a paper towel. "You like watching me stuff my face?"

"I like watching you enjoy your food. That isn't stuffing your face."

"I definitely enjoy food. That's why I need to lose another fifteen pounds." She laid the paper towel next to her plate. "I had a lot of trouble eating after Joe died. I dropped twenty-five pounds. I'd like to lose another fifteen, but my appetite seems to have come back in full force."

"What's wrong with that? You look beautiful."

"You're sweet."

"I'm not sweet, I'm honest. Are you forgetting I saw you naked in the shower?"

A becoming blush spread across her cheeks. "No," she said softly. "I'm not forgetting that."

Jeff rested his forearms on the table. "I'll never understand why women feel like they have to punish themselves if they believe they're five pounds over some chart that's supposed to be 'perfect'. Men like curves, Crista. Personally, I like a lot of curves." His gaze passed over her breasts before he looked in her eyes again. "Becky is very thin. That didn't stop us from having great sex. But if I could choose the woman I'd want in my bed, I'd choose a woman who's built like you. In fact, I'd choose a woman who was built like you were before you lost those twenty-five pounds."

"Are you serious?"

"Totally." Reaching across the table, he laid his hand over hers. "Don't you know how beautiful you are?"

Her blush deepened, showing him more than words that she had no idea of the way she affected him. "I had…relationships with a few women before Becky and I got together. Every one of them was built like you." He leaned closer to her and lowered his voice. "Full-figured women are sexy, Crista. *Very* sexy."

She pulled her hand away from his and pushed her hair behind her ears. He loved that sign of her shyness.

Determined to convince her that he found her *very* attractive, Jeff took both her hands in his. "I can't speak for every man. I'm sure there are a lot of men who prefer their women to be thin. I'm not one of them." He rubbed his thumbs over the back of her hands. "I like running my hands over a curvy ass, wide hips, full breasts. You're perfect."

"I'm hardly perfect, Jeff. And I've had enough of being embarrassed. Let's change the subject."

"Deal." He squeezed her hands. "What about you? What kind of man do you find attractive?"

"You."

Jeff chuckled. "That didn't answer my question."

Crista turned her hands over so their palms touched. "I always thought Joe was the perfect man."

"What did he look like?"

"He had auburn hair and dark brown eyes. He was slim and in good shape. He wasn't drop-dead gorgeous, but good looking." She entwined her fingers with Jeff's. "He loved all kinds of outdoor sports, especially skiing. He wasn't a very good skier, but he liked it."

"Then Joe and I had something in common. I like skiing too, but I'm a long way from an expert."

"I'll teach you."

Jeff laughed while Crista grinned impishly. "Are you that good?"

"I grew up in the mountains of New York. Of course I'm that good."

"Well, you may get the chance while we're here. Have you looked out the window? We may have to wear skis to get out of here. There's almost two feet of snow on the ground."

"There is?" Crista hurried over to the window and pulled aside the curtain. "Wow."

Stepping up behind her, Jeff slipped his arms around Crista's waist and looked over her head at the blanket of white. "Quite a sight, isn't it?"

"It's beautiful," she whispered. "The trees... Oh, Jeff, the trees are so pretty."

"Yes, they are."

He hooked his fingers over her waist. She leaned back against him and laid her hands over his. He'd always enjoyed seeing snow on the trees and landscape. Seeing them with Crista made everything even more beautiful.

She turned in his arms. Her eyes glowed with pleasure. "Let's build a snowman."

"Didn't you hear what I said? There's two feet of snow on the ground, maybe more. *Probably* more. You'll sink in up to your knees if you go out there."

"I don't care. It'll be fun."

He didn't want to deny her anything she wanted, especially something that would make her happy, but he had to be practical. "You don't have any heavy clothes."

"I have a warm coat and lined boots. That's all I need."

"Do you have any gloves?"

She bit her bottom lip. "Oops."

"Your hands will freeze within minutes if you try to build a snowman without wearing gloves."

Her crestfallen expression tugged at his heart. He felt like he'd just told a six-year-old that Santa didn't exist. Disappointing her simply wasn't an option. "I probably have an extra pair you can wear."

She released a squeal of excitement and clapped her hands. "Really?"

"Yeah, really."

Crista threw her arms around his neck and hugged him fiercely. "I'll do the dishes while you look for the gloves. Deal?"

"Deal."

* * * * *

Crista hit Jeff right in the face with a snowball. Knowing he wouldn't possibly let her get away with that, she quickly ducked behind the snowman.

"Don't think hiding will do you any good, Crista."

She peeked around the snowman to see what Jeff was doing. He stood ten feet away, slowly packing snow into a large ball…one a lot larger than the one she'd thrown at him. "Hey, it was a lucky shot."

"Like hell. You've hit me a dozen times already. I've been a gentleman so far, but I think it's time I retaliate."

Crista gulped. *Oh, shit. I'm in trouble.* She couldn't run in the deep snow. They'd made paths while building the snowman, but those paths didn't go very far. If she could make it back to the house, she'd be safe.

Jeff came after her. Crista waited until he began to circle the snowman before she darted around the other side. She made it three steps before the snowball hit the back of her head. Crista yelped, but didn't stop. The back porch loomed closer. Just a few more steps…

Crista came to an abrupt stop when Jeff grabbed her jacket. She tried to jerk away from him, but his hold was too strong. He encircled her waist, holding her arms tightly to her sides.

Her years of self-defense training kicked in. Crista went limp and dropped to her knees. Jeff's hold on her loosened enough for her to move her arms. Leaning to the side, Crista gripped his wrist and flipped Jeff over her shoulder.

He landed on his back, mouth open and eyes wide. Afraid she may have hurt him, Crista quickly scrambled to his side. "Jeff! I'm so sorry. Are you okay?"

"What…" His voice sounded strangled. He cleared his throat before speaking again. "What the hell was that?"

"Aikido. I have a black belt."

"Apparently."

"I didn't think about what I was doing, I just reacted. I'm sorry."

Jeff slowly sat up. "I guess I don't have to worry about you taking care of yourself."

"No, you don't have to worry about that. Besides the black belt, I'm an expert marksman. I have a .22 Jennings in my purse. And a concealed weapon permit, of course."

"Of course." He rose to his knees and began brushing snow off his clothes. "What other surprises do you have for me?"

"Well, I—"

She got no further before he tackled her.

One moment, Crista was trying to apologize to Jeff for flipping him. The next moment, she lay on her back with him leaning over her. He held both her wrists to the ground with his hands, both her legs with one of his. Crista instinctively arched her back, trying to get free. Jeff's hold on her tightened.

He grinned down at her. "Gotcha."

The bum had tricked her! Oh, he was going to pay. As soon as she could get loose from him, he was going to pay big time.

"Let go of me."

"I don't think so. You've been a very bad girl. Bad girls get punished."

Crista stopped struggling. "How do they get punished?"

"Well, now, I have to think about that. What's the best way to punish you?"

"Lying on top of me in the snow is a good way. I'm freezing my buns off."

"Since I happen to like those buns very much, I certainly don't want them frozen off." Jeff rose and held out his hands to her. "How about we give up the snow for some hot chocolate?"

"Hot chocolate sounds *wonderful*."

Placing her hands in his, Crista let him pull her to her feet. He continued to hold one hand while he led her to the back door. Crista liked that. The feel of her hand in his seemed right.

The heat of the cabin hit her face as soon as she stepped inside. Without pausing, she crossed the floor and stopped in front of the fireplace. Her gloves hit the hearth and she held her hands up to the fire. They began to tingle as the warmth seeped into her skin.

Jeff stepped up beside her, removed his own gloves, and held his hands toward the fire. "I didn't think those gloves would keep your hands warm. They're too big for you."

"I didn't mind. I enjoyed being outside. I love the snow."

"Me too, but you need to get out of those wet clothes."

Crista pressed her lips together to keep from smiling. He sounded all concerned for her health, but she could see the twinkle of devilment in his eyes. "Wet clothes are definitely uncomfortable." Slowly, she slipped her jacket from her shoulders and let it drop to the floor. "Wanna help me?"

Jeff grinned. "I'm always willing to help a lady."

Chapter Seven

Jeff let his own jacket fall to the floor. It would be easy to quickly shed his clothes, remove Crista's, and throw her to the floor. He didn't want that. They'd had incredible sex twice, but it had been *sex*—fast, hard, and far from gentle.

This time, he wanted to make love to her, right here in front of the fire.

"Will you grab the quilt off the bed?" Jeff asked.

A puzzled expression crossed her face, but Crista didn't argue with him. "Sure."

The quilt he had given Crista last night lay on the couch. Jeff picked it up and spread it out on the thick rag rug before the hearth. Still on his knees, he watched Crista gather up the quilt from the bed and walk back to him. Taking it from her, he spread it on top of the first one and made a soft pallet for them.

"Take off your clothes," he said. "Slowly."

She started with her boots, removing one at a time and setting them next to the hearth. The socks he had loaned her came off next, again one at a time. She pushed her sweatpants down to her hips. Jeff waited for them to slide down her legs and fall to the floor. They stubbornly remained perched on her hips. She grasped the hem of her sweatshirt and inched it up until it was under her breasts. She held it there as she looked into his eyes.

"Don't stop," Jeff said thickly.

"You told me to undress slowly."

"I didn't tell you to drive me crazy."

"Is this driving you crazy?" She pushed on the waistband of her pants until it rested at the top of her pubic hair. Jeff drew in a sharp breath at the site of her ivory skin. He wanted to press his lips against her stomach, trail his tongue around her navel, nibble on her hipbones. Blood rushed to his cock. He shifted, trying to get in a more comfortable position.

Crista raised her sweatshirt another inch. Now he could see the bottom curves of her breasts. His cock stiffened further. "More."

Another inch higher, another inch of curves. Jeff tugged on the crotch of his jeans. Things were getting mighty crowded in the tight denim.

"Maybe you should take off your jeans," Crista said. "You look…uncomfortable."

"I'll take off my clothes after you take off yours. I want to see your body in nothing but firelight."

"In that case…" Crista crossed her arms, grabbed her sweatshirt hem, and pulled it over her head. Before it hit the floor, she tugged her sweatpants off her legs. Now she stood before him wearing nothing but firelight, just like he wanted.

"God, you're gorgeous." He held out one hand to her. "Come here."

Crista took his hand and dropped to her knees before him. There was something wicked about being nude while he still wore all his clothes. He lifted her hand and entwined their fingers, then repeated the action with their other hands. Holding them at shoulder height, he leaned toward her and kissed her.

Such a simple thing, a kiss, but what an impact it made. Crista sighed as Jeff's lips gently moved over hers. She'd never kissed a man who had a mustache. She loved the way it brushed her skin. He squeezed her hands while he sipped at her lips. His teeth nipped lightly, his tongue soothed, then his lips covered hers again. He didn't touch her anywhere else but her hands and her lips.

It was the most erotic thing she'd ever experienced.

Time passed; she had no idea how much, as they continued to kiss. When Jeff finally lifted his mouth from hers, Crista had to struggle to open her eyes. Jeff's face was only inches away, his eyes dark with passion. He hadn't shaved this morning. The day-old beard made him look even more rugged.

"You're wearing way too many clothes," she whispered.

The corners of his mouth twitched slightly. "I like having you naked while I'm dressed."

"I think you'd like it a lot more if you were naked too. I know *I'd* like it a lot more."

"How about if we kiss some more first?"

Still holding her hands, Jeff kissed her again, parting her lips with his tongue. His tongue dueled with hers…dipping inside her mouth, withdrawing, and dipping inside again. He tilted his head one way, then the other, as he made love to her mouth with his lips and tongue.

Crista was ready to start tearing off his clothes when he pulled away from her and jerked his sweatshirt over his head. Cradling her face in his hands, he kissed her once more before rising. She watched him struggle to lower his zipper over his erection. His jeans, boots, and socks came off in one bundle.

He hadn't bothered with underwear.

When he started to return to the pallet, Crista held up one hand to stop him. "Let me look at you."

Even though it had stopped snowing, the sky remained overcast. It gave the cabin a gray, dreary appearance. Only the firelight broke the gloom. Crista's gaze leisurely traveled over Jeff's body as he stood still, his arms at his sides. Light and shadow bathed his body. His fully erect cock jutted forward. She wanted to touch it. She wanted to touch every part of him.

"Turn around."

He did as she requested, turning in a slow circle. She got the chance to admire all of him before he faced her again.

"Come here."

Once again, Jeff started to kneel on the pallet. Crista shook her head. "No. Keep standing, but move closer."

He took two steps toward her. Crista rose to her knees. "Closer."

"Crista, I want to touch you."

"Me first."

He moved forward until his cock was less than six inches from her mouth. Reaching out, she ran one finger over the head and down to the base.

"You're magnificent, Jeff. Long and thick and straight." She wrapped both hands around him and began to slowly move them up and down. Jeff's hips jerked. His cock jerked and swelled even more in her hands.

"Crista," he growled.

Her thumb tickled the slit. A pearl of moisture beaded the tip. Crista swiped it off with her tongue.

With a loud moan, Jeff clasped her face and tilted his hips forward.

Crista bathed the entire head with her tongue before taking it in her mouth. She slid her mouth an inch down his cock, back up, then an inch farther down. She repeated the action until she had all of him in her mouth.

Jeff groaned. "That feels so good." This isn't what he'd planned. He'd planned to make love to her, to bring her to a climax over and over before he ever took his own pleasure. The warmth and wetness of her mouth made it impossible for him to pull away.

She dragged her tongue down to his balls, licking both orbs as she caressed the sensitive skin between them and his anus. He wouldn't be able to hold off a climax for long if she kept…

Jeff drew in a sharp breath when she pushed one finger inside his ass.

"My God, Crista."

"Do you like this?" Crista looked up at him while she circled her tongue around the head again.

"Very much."

"So do I."

She took him even farther in her mouth this time, until her lips touched his groin. Jeff couldn't hold back; he had to pump. Gently holding her face still, he slowly fucked her mouth.

Jeff loved the intimacy of oral sex, both giving and receiving. To find a woman who apparently enjoyed it as much as he made the act even more intimate, more special. He caressed her face as he moved, telling her without words how good her mouth felt on his skin.

The pleasure built higher. "Crista, if you don't stop soon, I'm going to come."

She didn't stop.

"Crista, I mean it. I… *Shit!*"

Pleasure crested and overflowed. Closing his eyes, Jeff threw back his head and groaned loudly.

When he was able to think clearly again, he opened his eyes and looked into Crista's face. She sat on her heels, gazing up at him. The firelight turned her creamy skin golden. His chest tightened, as if something were squeezing his heart.

Falling in love with her wouldn't be at all difficult.

He still cradled her face. Leaning over, he kissed her tenderly. "Thank you," he whispered.

She smiled. "You're very welcome."

Jeff dropped to his knees before her and took her hands in his. "That was incredible."

"For me too."

"You realize you spoiled my plans."

She tilted her head. "I did?"

Jeff nodded. "I planned to thoroughly make love to you before you ever touched me."

Her eyes narrowed and turned sultry. "Define 'thoroughly'."

"I thought I'd…" He kissed her left palm. "…lick your nipples until they got nice and hard. Then I'd…" He kissed the back of her right hand. "…bite them. Gently. I wouldn't want to hurt you."

"Of course not," she said, her voice sounding strangled.

"There'd be some sucking in there too, in case you're curious."

"Sucking is good."

Turning over her hand, he trailed his tongue across her palm and down to her wrist. "And a lot of caressing. I really like…" He nipped her wrist. "…caressing."

"Caressing is good too."

"How about…" His mouth moved up her arm. "…licking?"

"Oh, yes. Licking is *definitely* good."

He tickled the inside of her elbow with the tip of his tongue. "Any particular place on your body you want licked?"

"I'm sure I can think of a few… Oh!" She gasped when he moved farther up her body and bit the spot where her shoulder met her neck. "You have a thing about biting, don't you?"

"Maybe I was a vampire in my past life," he whispered into her ear.

Jeff smiled to himself when she shivered. He continued to gently nibble his way up her neck while he cradled one breast in his hand. He lifted and squeezed the heavy globe, caressing the nipple with his thumb until it felt as hard as a diamond.

Crista grabbed his head and brought his lips to hers for a voracious kiss. "I want your mouth on me."

"Where?" he asked against her lips.

"Anywhere. Everywhere."

"Whatever the lady wants."

Chapter Eight

Jeff swiped his tongue across her right nipple. "How's this?"

"Wonderful," Crista breathed. "More."

"Hmm, being greedy, huh?"

She tunneled her fingers into his hair and held his head close to her breast. "Yes, I'm greedy. *More*."

"I love when a woman knows what she wants." He swiped his tongue across her nipple again before drawing it into his mouth. He suckled gently, not increasing the pull until Crista arched her back. Still he remained gentle, wanting to drive up her desire slowly until she couldn't wait to be joined with him.

"I know what I want now." Crista tightened her hold on his head. "Harder."

He cradled her other breast and flicked the nipple with his thumb while he tongued the first one. "Don't you want slow and easy?"

Raising his head, Jeff looked into her desire-filled eyes as he slid one hand between her legs. His fingertips dipped into her thick cream. He had no doubt he could bring her to a climax quickly with his hand. That wasn't enough. He wanted to take her higher than she'd ever been.

"Lie back, Crista."

She did as he said with no argument, her legs spread. Jeff struggled to hold back a smile. She obviously thought he planned to fuck her now. Not yet. He had other plans for her first.

Jeff pushed her legs apart and moved between them. He cupped her breasts and began kneading them...softly at first, then more firmly. Crista's eyes drifted closed. Jeff rubbed his thumbs over the hard nipples until he heard her moan. Leaning forward, he dropped a kiss on each hard peak, then between her breasts. Soft kisses landed on her skin to her navel. The tip of his tongue dipped inside the sensitive area.

Crista arched her back. "Jeff," she rasped.

"Your skin is so soft." He continued down her body, dropping kisses on the nest of dark curls. He nuzzled her as he pushed her legs farther apart. "I love the way you smell." One swipe of his tongue across her clit made him growl softly. "I love the way you taste."

Jeff licked her again, gently. She grabbed his head and tried to push him closer to her. He pulled back.

"Uh-uh. No rushing. Put your arms back over your head."

He didn't touch her again until she did as he said. Lowering his head, he circled her clit with the tip of his tongue. When she lifted her hips, he moved his tongue between her feminine lips. Over, around, back and forth…he covered every bit of the moist, velvety flesh between her legs.

She began to shift her hips in rhythm with his stroking. "Oh, that feels good."

"That's what I want—to make you feel good." Using his thumbs, Jeff parted her lips so he could delve between them. "You're so delicious." He licked her from her clit to her anus and back again. He enjoyed it so much, he repeated the action.

Crista spread her legs even farther apart.

"Mmm," Jeff hummed against her clit. The gentle vibration made Crista gasp. She wanted to hold his head close to her, but he'd told her to leave her arms over her head. She could easily disobey him. That thought lasted only a moment. The anticipation of what he would do next outweighed her desire to disobey.

His tongue circled her anus twice before darting inside. Crista closed her eyes. The gentle rasp of his tongue, the warm touch of his breath, the slight abrasion of his mustache and beard…they all combined to send her desire soaring.

When he started tickling her clit with the tip of his tongue again, her desire peeked. Crista bit her bottom lip to keep from screaming. Her pleasure built and built, until it crested in an intense orgasm. No longer able to lie still, she grabbed his head while the sensation shook her body.

Crista opened her eyes to see Jeff leaning over her, his arms straight. She ran her hands up his arms and over his shoulders. "That was… I don't have any words to describe it."

He kissed her softly, his lips barely touching hers. Her own scent drifted to her nose from his skin, his mustache. Crista closed her eyes again when he deepened the kiss. His tongue slid along the seam, seeking entrance. She granted it as she plowed her fingers into his thick hair.

The kiss turned more passionate. Crista accepted the gentle thrust of his tongue, and returned it with her own. Jeff stretched out on top of her and slipped his hands beneath her buttocks. She inhaled sharply at the feel of his erection pressed against her stomach. His tongue between her legs had been wonderful, but she wanted that hard cock inside her.

Before she had the chance to tell him, he lifted her buttocks and entered her with one long, lazy thrust.

Crista arched her neck as he began to pump his hips. His teeth nipped the pounding pulse in her neck, but he didn't increase the speed or intensity of his thrusts. Instead, his movements remained unhurried and easy, building her desire slowly.

"I love being inside you," Jeff whispered in her ear.

He nipped her pulse again, and Crista shivered. Goose bumps skittered across her skin. She tightened her arms around his neck. His thrusts picked up in speed, but still remained slow and easy. He'd pump for several moments, then stop completely before starting over again. Each time he started over, her desire rose another notch. Her climax was right *there*, so close…

It crested a moment before she felt Jeff's body tense. A low groan came from deep in his throat. He squeezed her buttocks hard, thrust twice more, then lay still.

Crista caressed his back while her breathing slowed. She could feel his warm, damp breath against her neck and his heart pound against her breasts. A feeling of contentment washed over her. It wasn't because she'd had two incredible orgasms, but from the man she held in her arms. Being with Jeff just seemed…right.

This intense feeling was wonderful…and terrifying. She shouldn't be feeling so much so quickly. She hadn't even known Jeff two days ago. Surely this wasn't a case of her being grateful that some man showed her attention.

No. It had to be more than that. She'd never make love with a man who simply showed her attention.

Jeff raised his head. "Hi," he said with a smile.

"Hi, back."

He kissed her softly, then withdrew from her body and rolled to his back. "You're right. Sometimes words can't describe it." He lifted one arm. "C'mere. I want to hold you."

She cuddled up to his side and laid her arm over his waist. Closing her eyes, she took a deep breath and let her body relax.

Several moments passed before Jeff spoke again. "Crista?"

Almost asleep, she mumbled, "Hmm?"

"I know it's late for me to say this, but we didn't use any protection."

She tilted her head on his shoulder so she could look in his eyes.

"I don't have any condoms here. I always come here alone, so I've never needed any. And to be honest, I didn't think about them." He touched her hair, his fingers sifting through the strands. "I know this isn't exactly a romantic thing to talk about, but I want you to know I always wore a condom with Becky." A hint of a smile touched his lips. "She didn't like the mess."

Crista chuckled.

"I was involved with her for a long time, and haven't been with another woman since. I had my yearly physical a month ago. I'm clean."

She propped up on one elbow. "You're my first lover since Joe died."

"I know that, but what about…" He stopped.

"Birth control?"

Jeff nodded. "Yeah."

"I'm on the Pill. I've been on it for years to regulate my cycle."

"You have them with you?"

Crista nodded. "They're in my purse. I take one every day at lunch."

"Oh."

His disappointed tone surprised her. She touched his chest. "You almost sound sad."

"No, of course not. We barely know each other. An unplanned pregnancy wouldn't be a good thing."

But Jeff couldn't deny the idea of Crista carrying his child intrigued him.

He cradled her cheek in his hand. She tilted her head and rubbed her cheek against it. Such a sensual, caring woman would be a wonderful mother.

She laid her hand over his. "Where is this going, Jeff? Is this just two stranded people having sex, or is it something more?"

He wanted to say it was something more, at least for him. He had no doubt his feelings went far beyond sex. A relationship with Crista would be wonderful. Taking her out to dinner and a movie, going for a walk in the woods, spending a day on Puget Sound in his boat…he wanted all those things with her. He definitely had strong feelings for her, feelings he wanted to explore further. Crista was warm, caring, sensitive, funny, beautiful, sexy…all the traits a man wanted in a woman.

She was also a woman still grieving for her lost husband.

Jeff's gaze fell to her hand clasping his—her left hand. Her gold wedding band rested there. Despite making love with him more than once, she still wore the ring another man had given her.

She wasn't ready to give up her husband yet. As long as she wore that ring, Jeff knew she had no room in her heart for him.

"I think it's too soon for us to know anything for sure, Crista," he said softly. "We can't help being here. We were thrown together due to circumstances we had no control over, and things have been…intense between us. We can't base our feelings on one day."

"No," she whispered, "I guess we can't."

He propped up on his free hand so he could kiss her. "I don't regret what we've shared."

"Neither do I."

Maybe not now, but he couldn't help wondering how she'd feel once they left this cabin and went back to the real world. He didn't believe Crista was the kind of woman who would've fallen in bed with any man who'd been here in this cabin, but it'd been a long time since she'd had sex. Her reaction to him proved how much passion existed inside her. She was an intelligent woman. Even intelligent people mistook passion for love.

Once he managed to get them out of here, he had to let her go. She had to build a life for herself before she could become involved with another man.

Jeff pulled her left hand to his mouth and kissed her palm. "I could use a cup of coffee and a sandwich. How about you?"

She smiled, but the smile didn't reach her eyes. "Sure."

Chapter Nine

Crista stood at the bedroom window, mug of coffee in her hand, and watched Jeff shoveling snow from the driveway. She'd offered to help him, but he'd refused, saying he only had one shovel. Not wanting to simply sit around and do nothing while he worked so hard, she'd baked a cinnamon coffee cake. It sat on a plate in the center of the small table, ready to be sliced when he decided to take a break.

The smell of the cinnamon coffee cake reminded her of all the baking Gram had done. She'd taught each of them to cook and bake. There'd been quite a few batches of burned cookies while they were learning. Gram had never gotten mad, but had simply thrown out the burned ones and baked a new batch.

Cookies at Christmas were the most special. Gram assigned a different kind to each girl while she made fudge and divinity. Crista made peanut butter. Gram had known they were her favorite, so made sure she always assigned them to Crista.

Later, they'd eat their cookies with glasses of milk while opening presents beneath the Christmas tree. That tradition continued to adulthood. Whenever Crista got together with her sisters, they always baked cookies in memory of Gram and those special Christmases together.

Crista had hoped to continue that tradition with her own daughters.

Closing her eyes, she rested her forehead on the cool glass. Today was Christmas Eve. She'd never expected to celebrate Christmas without Joe. This special holiday meant being with family and friends. It wasn't a time to be alone.

The sharp, piercing pain she expected to feel didn't materialize. Opening her eyes again, she looked out at the tall, handsome man working so hard. He was the reason for her lack of pain. Jeff had brought passion back into her life.

And love.

Her sisters would tell her she couldn't possibly be sure of her feelings after only one day with Jeff. She'd known after one *date* how she felt about Joe. When Crista fell in love, she had no doubt of her feelings.

If only Jeff felt the same way.

His gentle rejection yesterday after they'd made love in front of the fire had stripped the golden haze from in front of her eyes. He didn't feel the same for her as she did for him. Maybe she'd been rebound sex. After all, he'd recently broken up with a woman whom he'd slept with for years. Jeff was a virile man, and she'd practically thrown herself at him. She couldn't blame him for being human.

"I wish it could be different," she whispered. "I wish he loved me too."

She wrapped both hands around her mug. A clinking sound drew her attention. Crista set her mug on the windowsill and looked at her hands. The sound came from her wedding ring touching the mug.

Crista twirled the plain gold band that was a symbol of the vows she'd taken with Joe on her wedding day. It had never been off her finger since he put it there two years ago. He'd wanted to buy her a diamond ring too, but she'd insisted on only the simple gold band.

Joe's matching band rested in her jewelry box at home.

Taking off the ring had never entered her mind, not even when she and Jeff were making love.

Slowly, she tugged the ring off her finger. Tears sprang to her eyes, but she blinked them away. It was time to take it off, even though it hurt to do so. Joe would want her to go on, to find someone else to love.

She kissed the ring, then wrapped her hand tightly around it. *I'll always love you, Joe. I promise you that.*

Looking back out the window, she saw Jeff heading for the cabin. Quickly, she grabbed her purse from the top of the cedar chest and dropped her ring in it as he came through the front door.

His gaze swept the small room until it landed on her. "Hi."

"Hi. Did you finish the driveway?"

"Yeah." He pushed his damp hair back from his forehead. "Now if I could get my truck started, we could get out of here."

"The main road is still covered with snow."

"Not for long. A snow plow is up the hill heading this way."

"Oh." One way or another, their time together would be over soon. "Maybe the phone is working too."

"Maybe. I haven't tried it yet today." He crossed the room and picked up the telephone receiver. "Still no dial tone."

He seemed…distant, even more so than last night. They hadn't made love again after being together in front of the fire. He'd held her close to him when they went to bed, but hadn't initiated sex. After the way she'd botched things with him by asking if there could be anything between them, she didn't feel right initiating anything either. It had taken her a long time to fall asleep. The tenseness in Jeff's body proved it had been difficult for him to fall asleep too.

His cock had been awake this morning and pressed firmly against her bare buttocks. He still made no move toward her. Instead, he'd risen from the bed and gone into the bathroom without saying anything.

She hadn't left the cabin yet, but it had already ended for them.

Crista watched Jeff hang his jacket on the coat tree. "I have fresh coffee."

"I could use a cup." He turned to face her and sniffed the air. "What smells so good?"

"I made a coffee cake."

He smiled. "You did?"

"I couldn't sit around and do nothing while you were working so hard. It's a simple recipe. I make it a lot to take to my salon, so I have the recipe memorized." She shrugged, unsure what else to say. Despite his warm smile, she could still sense the distance between them.

She didn't know what to do to bridge that distance.

"I worked up quite a sweat out there," Jeff said. "I'm gonna take a quick shower, okay?"

"Sure. I'll get everything ready in the kitchen."

He touched her cheek with one fingertip. Crista longed to tilt her head and deepen that caress. Instead, she gave him a shaky smile and turned toward the kitchen.

* * * * *

He'd hurt her and that's the last thing he wanted to do. Jeff turned off the water taps and pushed aside the shower curtain. She'd tried to mask it, but he'd seen the sadness in her eyes both yesterday and a few minutes ago.

Sighing heavily, he reached for a towel. He thought about last night as he wiped the water from his body. How he'd wanted to make love to Crista when they went to bed. Cuddling up next to her naked body and not slipping inside her had been agony.

Being noble sucked big time.

Jeff strongly believed a plan existed for everyone. If he and Crista were meant to be together, they would be. But he couldn't be the one to decide that. It had to be her choice. Only *she* knew for sure when she was truly over her husband and ready to start a new life with another man. Mind-boggling sex with a stranger in a cabin couldn't decide it for her.

He'd planned to spend the rest of the Christmas holiday here. His parents had wanted him at their house on Christmas Day, but he told them no, that he needed the time to himself after his breakup with Becky.

It wouldn't be Becky on his mind now.

Donning a clean pair of gray sweats, Jeff left the bathroom and headed for the kitchen. Crista stood at the back door, looking out the glass. She stood at an angle, so he could see her profile. Even in a pair of his baggy sweats, she looked beautiful.

The tightness in his chest almost made him change his mind about admitting his feelings to her. Ignoring that tightness, he stepped closer to her.

"Where's this famous coffee cake?"

She turned to him and smiled softly. "On the table. Sit down. I'll get your coffee."

"You don't have to wait on me."

"You've been waiting on me for two days. It's my turn."

Jeff nodded his acceptance and took a chair at the table. She'd already cut the coffee cake and placed a large slice on a saucer for him. He pinched off a piece and popped it in his mouth. "Very good," he said after he swallowed.

"Thanks." Crista set his coffee next to the saucer and took the chair opposite him. "It was my grandmother's recipe. She was a wonderful cook."

Her eyes always shone with happiness when she spoke of her grandmother. "You loved her a lot."

"Yes, I did. Gram was the best." She pinched off a piece of her own slice and ate it. "Would you like a fork?"

"Nah. Fingers are better." He took another large bite and washed it down with coffee. They'd talked about her grandmother and how good the coffee cake tasted. Jeff didn't know what to say next. The tension between them felt thicker than the twenty inches of snow he'd shoveled off the driveway, but he didn't know what to do to ease it.

"You know, we aren't very smart," Crista said.

"Why do you say that?"

"You said a snow plow was heading this way. We could've walked down to the road and asked for help."

Yes, they could've, and Jeff had thought about doing that. He hadn't because he didn't want to leave yet. Once Crista left this cabin, she'd be out of his life forever. "He's probably already gone past here, but I can check for sure—"

"Don't bother. I'm sure he's left already."

"Yeah."

End of conversation. Inwardly, Jeff sighed. He liked it much better when they actually *talked* instead of struggling for something to say.

"My salon is closed until January second. Do you have to go back to work before the first?"

Jeff paused in the act of slicing another piece of coffee cake and looked up sharply. He'd avoided talking about his job other than a vague reference to pushing paper. He didn't want to talk about it now. "No, I'm off until the sixth."

"How nice. You work for a very generous boss." She rested her forearms on the table. "Who do you work for?"

Scrambling for an answer that wouldn't give him away, he drained his mug. "May I have some more coffee?"

Crista's brows drew together, but she didn't question him further. "Sure."

His reprieve didn't last long. As soon as Crista refilled their cups, she said, "Why won't you tell me who you work for?"

Jeff rubbed his mustache. He wouldn't be able to get out of this. "I never said I wouldn't tell you who I work for."

"But you haven't, and I've asked you twice."

"I told you I crunch numbers at a paper company."

"And you said you're 'sort of' an accountant." She frowned. "Are you ashamed of what you do?"

"No, of course not."

"I've told you all about my job. It's only fair you tell me about yours."

Maybe I should tell her the truth, even add to it a bit. If she's angry with me, she won't want anything to do with me.

Pushing his half empty saucer away, Jeff leaned back in his chair. "I work for Bower Paper and Lumber."

Her frown remained. "So? What's the big secret about that?"

"You've heard of it?"

"Of course I've heard of it. It's a huge company. It…"

She stopped, and her eyes widened. That's when Jeff knew she realized his true identify.

"It's no coincidence that my last name is Bower and I work for Bower Paper and Lumber."

"You *own* the company?"

"Technically, my parents own it, but it'll be mine someday. Right now, I'm in charge of research and development in the paper division."

"Why didn't you tell me the truth?"

Jeff released a heavy breath. "Because I'd see dollar signs in your eyes, like I have with so many other women when they find out who I am. That's why I went with Becky for so long, because she comes from money too."

He knew the moment his words sunk in. He saw the pain in her eyes, and the sheen of tears. They lasted only a moment before she blinked them away.

Now he saw anger.

"I don't believe what you just said. How arrogant can you be? Not every woman is interested in how much money a man has in the bank."

"I know that—"

"No, you don't. You automatically assumed I'd fall into bed with you as soon as I found out you have money. In case you didn't notice, I fucked you long before I knew anything about your money."

Crista didn't normally use coarse language, except when joking around with her sisters, or when she was really angry…like now.

She stood, placed her palms flat on the table, and leaned forward so Jeff would hear her clearly. "For your information, I make a *very* nice living at my salon. I received a large settlement when my husband died, plus his life insurance. I don't need or want your money, Mr. Bower."

Jeff opened his mouth as if to speak, but stopped when a knock sounded on the front door. He looked at her another moment before rising and crossing the room. Crista didn't bother to watch him or to see who stood on the other side of the door. But she recognized S.C.'s voice as soon as he spoke.

"Hi. I was wondering if the little lady is still here."

Crista walked toward the door on legs shaking from anger. "Yes, I'm here."

He looked relieved to see her. "I'm sorry for running off like that, but I had an emergency. Then the storm got worse and—"

Crista stopped his apology with a wave of her hand. She didn't care why he'd left her, as long as he was back now. "It doesn't matter." Looking past him to the driveway, she saw her Nissan hooked up to his tow truck. "You have my car."

"Yes, ma'am. I can take you wherever you want to go, if you're ready to leave."

She looked up at the man she'd fallen in love with, the man she really didn't know at all. "Yes, I'm definitely ready to leave."

Chapter Ten

Jeff watched Crista go into the bathroom and close the door. He'd definitely made her angry. It had to be that way for her to leave him and get on with her life. That didn't mean he had to like it.

He had to try and smooth things over with her before she left. He faced S.C. again. "Would you excuse us a moment?"

"Certainly." He motioned over his shoulder with his thumb. "I'll wait in the truck."

Jeff shut the front door. The sound of the bathroom door opening made him turn around. Crista came out wearing her jeans and maroon sweater and carrying a small plastic bag. He assumed the bag held her underwear. The way her breasts swayed when she moved proved she hadn't put on her bra.

Walking past him without giving him a glance, she picked up her boots from the hearth and sat on the couch. "I left your sweats in the bathroom," she said as she slipped on her boots. "I'm sorry I kept your socks, but I'll get blisters on my heels if I wear these boots without socks. I'm sure with all your millions, you can afford to lose one pair of socks."

"Crista, let me explain—"

"You explained yourself just fine. I was good enough for sex, but not good enough for honesty. That's something I insist on, Jeff. I want *nothing* to do with a man who can't be totally honest with me." She stood and looked at him. It tore at his heart to see tears in her eyes. "And I was stupid enough to believe you care about me."

"I *do* care, Crista."

"You have a strange way of showing that."

She walked to the coat tree and retrieved her jacket. In the process of slipping it on, she dropped her bag. Jeff hurried to pick it up for her at the same time that she reached for it. Their hands touched. Crista quickly pulled back as if he'd shocked her. He picked up the bag and held it out for her. When she took it from him, he noticed her bare ring finger.

She'd removed her wedding band.

"You took off your ring," he said softly.

"I thought it was time."

"When did you do it?"

"This morning, when you were shoveling the driveway."

She'd taken off her wedding ring before they had an argument. That had to mean she'd truly put her husband to rest and was ready to move on with her life. Jeff's heart began to pound. She cared for him, or she never would've removed her ring.

He had to make her understand how much he cared for her.

"Crista, I made a mistake and I'm sorry. Please let me explain."

Tears welled up in her eyes again. "You can't explain, Jeff. I'm really hurting right now and want nothing to do with you. Just…just leave me alone."

She swept past him and out the door. Jeff followed her as far as the front porch. He watched her climb into S.C.'s tow truck, but she never looked at him again.

You blew it, Bower. You blew it big time.

* * * * *

Crista huddled close to the door, her arms crossed over her stomach. S.C. had the heater running, but the warmth couldn't penetrate the pain in her heart. She thought she'd found a wonderful, caring man to love, a man who might possibly return her feelings. Instead, she'd had her heart broken.

She looked up at the gray, cloud-filled sky. *I don't ask for much from You. I just want to love someone and have him love me. Why is that too much to ask?*

"Wanna talk about it?" S.C. asked softly.

Crista shook her head.

He remained silent for several moments, so long that it startled Crista when he spoke again. "Mrs. C and I have been married a long time. We have our spats now and then, like every other couple does. Just because you love someone doesn't mean you won't disagree with him or her now and then."

"Jeff doesn't love me."

"I think that young man cares more than you know."

Crista turned her head and looked at S.C. "I thought he cared. He was so nice, and funny, and considerate, and loving…" She stopped and bit her lip. Warmth flooded her cheeks at admitting something so private to S.C.

Chuckling, he reached over and patted her knee. "Don't be embarrassed, Crista. I'd be surprised if you told me the two of you *didn't* make love while you were stranded. I may have white hair, but I know how powerful desire can be." He returned his hand to the steering wheel. "Whatever you two fought about can't be so bad that it can't be forgiven."

"He accused me of being a gold digger. How am I supposed to forgive that?"

S.C. rubbed his beard. "Did he actually accuse *you*, or women in general?"

"He lumped me in the same category with other women who wanted his money."

"But he didn't accuse *you*." He glanced at her. "Don't you think you jumped the gun a bit?"

"He doesn't feel for me what I feel for him. I asked him yesterday where we were going. He said we were thrown together under unusual circumstances and couldn't base our feelings on our situation."

"Sounds like he's being considerate."

Crista frowned. "And it sounds like you're taking up for a member of your sex."

"I'm only trying to make you see his side of this. Sure, he made a mistake. We *all* make mistakes. That doesn't mean you love him any less, or he loves you any less."

"Jeff never said he loves me."

"You never said it to him either, did you?"

"No. I thought it was too soon. We knew each other less than two days."

"The heart doesn't look at a clock, Crista."

No, it didn't. She'd learned that when she'd fallen so quickly for Joe. "This whole conversation is pointless. Jeff and I were stranded in his cabin for almost two days. We were…close during that time. That's all it was."

"It could be more. I can turn around right now and—"

"No. I want to go home. Please take me home."

Turning her head back toward the window, Crista stared at the passing scenery. Snow and ice still covered the trees and ground, but the roads had been cleared. In another few days, the snow would be gone, wiped away by sun or rain as if it never existed. Life would return to normal. She'd go back to her lonely existence and keep wishing to share her life with someone.

How pathetic.

She'd call her sisters tonight. That would make her feel better. Then tomorrow, she'd spend Christmas Day with Joe's parents. They'd invited her weeks ago, and Crista knew it'd be easier on them to spend their first Christmas without their youngest son if she were there with them. It would be easier on her too, to be with family. Spending time with people who loved her would help her forget about Jeff.

* * * * *

Crista opened her eyes and blinked. She didn't remember closing her eyes, but she must have fallen asleep. Turning her head, she saw S.C. smiling at her.

"You're home."

"Home?" She sat up straighter in the seat and looked around. They sat in the driveway of her small house, facing the street. She looked behind her to see S.C. had unhooked her Nissan in front of the closed garage door.

"You said to take you home, so I did. Would you rather I take your car to a repair shop?"

"No. I'll call my brother-in-law to come over and look at it. He's a great mechanic." Crista covered her mouth to hide a yawn. "Excuse me. I didn't mean to fall asleep on you."

"No problem. I'm used to it. Mrs. C often falls asleep when I'm talking to her."

She chuckled. "What do I owe you for the tow?"

"Nothing. Consider it a Christmas present."

"I can't let you do that—"

"It's already done."

His kindness touched her heart. Crista smiled. "That's very sweet. Thank you."

"My pleasure."

She opened the door and climbed down from the truck. After shutting the door, she waved to S.C. Instead of driving away, he lowered the passenger window.

"Wishes are special things, Crista, especially at Christmas. You wished for Jeff to love you too. I believe he does. All you have to do is give him another chance. It's the season of love and forgiveness. Don't forget that."

He raised the window again before she could respond and drove away. Thinking about what S.C. had said, Crista watched the truck until it disappeared around the bend of the road. Yes, Christmas was a time for love and forgiveness. She had never been one to hold a grudge, especially when she cared about someone. And she cared deeply for Jeff.

But he didn't return her feelings. If he did, he wouldn't have said they couldn't base their feelings on one day of being together. He would've asked to see her once they left the cabin. She didn't know where he lived, but it had to be somewhere in Washington. Wherever he lived wasn't so far away that they couldn't see each other. She'd drive all the way to Spokane to be in his arms again.

Apparently, Jeff didn't feel the same way.

A light mist began to fall. Hugging her jacket tightly around her, Crista turned and walked toward the front door of her house. As she dug through her purse for the keys, she thought again about what S.C. had said. Her hand stilled. He'd known about the wish she'd made this morning. And he'd known where she lived without her giving him an address or any directions.

He got my address off my car registration. No big deal.

Except her registration and insurance card listed only her post office box.

Crista glanced at her car. Following a hunch, she strode to it and slid inside. A single turn of the key started it with no problem.

A shiver ran through her body, one having nothing to do with the damp or cold. She would swear she could hear Gram telling her to believe in miracles, especially at Christmas. Crista wanted to. She wanted so much to believe in miracles, and in the power of love.

Her cell phone rang. Crista dug it out of her purse and flipped it open. She smiled when she saw Lindsey's phone number. "Hi, sis."

"Hi! What's up?"

"Oh, nothing much. What's up with you?"

"I'm wondering what you're doing for Christmas."

"I'm going to Joe's parents' house."

She could hear Lindsey's sharply indrawn breath. "Are you sure you're ready for that, Crista? That'll be really hard on you."

"Yeah, it'll be hard, but they need me as much as I need them. This will be their first Christmas without Joe too. We should be together."

"So, what about after that? Do you have any special plans?"

Jeff's face flashed through her mind. A quiet dinner with candlelight, soft music, lovemaking in front of the fire...

Crista swallowed hard. "No, I don't have any special plans."

Chapter Eleven

Jeff frowned when his private line rang. The entire Bower building was deserted, other than Security, meaning he had peace and quiet to get some work done. He couldn't think of anyone who would call him at his office on New Year's Eve, except his mother.

He loved his mother dearly, but he knew the reason for her call. She didn't want him to be alone at midnight and would insist he go over to his parents' house to bring in the new year.

The third ring made him reach for the receiver. "Jeff Bower."

"Why are you working on New Year's Eve?"

Jeff ran one hand through his hair. "Hi, Mom."

"You didn't answer my question."

"I'm working because I have work to do."

"Don't use that tone with me, Jeffrey." Her voice softened. "I'm worried about you. You've been so sad since you came back from your cabin, but you won't tell me why. Come over and spend the evening with us."

After thirty-five years of marriage, his parents were still deeply in love. Watching them touching and kissing all evening would drive the knife deeper into his heart.

He missed Crista so much.

"Ida is preparing prime rib for dinner."

Jeff chuckled. His mother always bribed him with his favorite foods. "That's blackmail, Mom."

"Yes, I know," she said smugly. "So, will you come over?"

"I'll be there about seven-thirty."

"Perfect."

He replaced the receiver and returned to the mound of paperwork on his desk. Several minutes of shuffling the papers made him realize he couldn't concentrate. Jeff threw down his pen and sighed heavily. Trying to get any work done was a waste of time. He'd go home, take a shower, and go to his parents' house.

After letting Security know he was leaving the building, Jeff headed for the elevator that would take him to the parking garage. His SUV sat alone ten feet from the elevator. It ran perfectly again, just like it had before the storm at his cabin. He'd tried the ignition after Crista left with S.C. The motor had turned over on the first try. He hadn't had any problems with it starting since then.

His good luck ran out. Jeff turned the key…and nothing. He tried again. Still nothing.

"Shit," he muttered. He should've taken it to his mechanic and had it checked out, like he'd planned to in the first place. Instead, he sat in a deserted garage on New Year's Eve. "Shit, shit, shit."

Sitting here cursing wouldn't get the thing started. Maybe one of the Security guys could give him a jump.

Jeff opened his door and froze. S.C. stood next to his tow truck less than fifteen feet away.

"Truck won't start?" he asked.

That tow truck had not been there when he came out of the elevator. Even though his windows were up in his SUV, Jeff would've heard the rattle of a tow truck. "How… Where did you come from?"

"I figured you needed some help."

Jeff climbed out of his SUV and shut the door. "You just happened to drive up to the fifth floor of this parking garage on New Year's Eve on the slight chance that someone would need a tow?"

"Not someone, Jeff. You."

"And how did you know I'd need a tow?"

"I have my ways."

The theme from "The Twilight Zone" ran through Jeff's head. S.C. appearing out of nowhere was creepy. "Who are you?"

"A friend who wants to help you and Crista get together."

Jeff slipped his hands in the pockets of his jacket and leaned back against his vehicle. "That's not possible. She very clearly told me she wants nothing to do with me."

"She was hurt. Her pride wouldn't let her forgive you. A week has passed. Go to her."

He wanted to. God, how he wanted to! He wanted to take her in his arms, hold her tightly, tell her he loved her.

"She loves you, Jeff. Go to her." S.C. walked over and handed Jeff a piece of paper. "There's her address and the directions to get to her house."

Jeff studied the directions. He could be at her house in an hour. "So now that I know where Crista lives, I have no excuse not to go to her, right?"

"None whatsoever."

"Fear won't work?"

"Are you afraid she'll turn you away?"

"Terrified."

"Don't be. I promise you, she won't turn you away."

S.C. returned to his tow truck. After starting the engine, he leaned out the open driver's window. "While you're there, you can pay her that $98.36 you owe her from your gin rummy games."

"The Twilight Zone" theme flashed through Jeff's mind again. He watched, open-mouthed, as S.C. waved and pulled away.

"Hey, wait!" Jeff called. "What about my truck?"

"Try the key," S.C. called back and kept going.

After S.C. was gone, Jeff climbed back into his vehicle and turned the key. The truck started on the first try.

Jeff chuckled. "Thanks, S.C. You've just given me the best belated Christmas gift I've ever received."

After turning on the heater, he pulled his cell phone from his pocket and dialed his parents' number.

"Change of plans, Mom. I won't be there for dinner."

* * * * *

Crista shifted on the couch and pulled the afghan up to her breasts. Sipping her coffee, she stared into the flames in the fireplace. Although she loved sitting before the fire in the evening, she'd built a fire for the first time tonight since Christmas Eve. Looking at the dancing flames reminded her too much of Jeff and when they'd made love in his cabin.

The pain hadn't dulled yet. She knew from experience that it wouldn't dull for a long, long time.

Her phone rang. Crista glanced at the cordless on the coffee table. She could let the answering machine pick up the call. If she answered, she'd have to stop wallowing in self-pity.

She snatched up the receiver on the fourth ring, before the answering machine picked up. "Hello?"

"Happy New Year!"

Crista chuckled. "Happy New Year, Jade, even though it's only nine o'clock here."

"Well, it's midnight on the east coast. What are you doing to celebrate?"

Feeling sorry for myself. "Nothing special."

"Are you okay?" Jade asked softly.

"I'm fine."

"That sad tone in your voice isn't very convincing, little sister."

"I promise I'm *fine*."

"Are you alone?"

"Yes, and I don't mind being alone on New Year's Eve. I like my alone time."

"Has Lindsey called you lately?"

"Yes, she called about two hours ago to check on me too."

"We aren't checking on you—"

"Yes, you are, and I love you for your concern, but I promise I'm all right. I…"

Crista stopped when her doorbell rang. She wasn't expecting anyone, especially not this late.

"Someone's at the door, Jade."

"Who is it?"

"I won't know who it is until I answer the door. I'll call you tomorrow. Love you."

Crista rose from the couch and tugged down her sweatshirt. Visitors at this time of night normally didn't happen. She lived in the outskirts of Tumwater in an area that hadn't seen a developer's hand yet. Her nearest neighbor lived two miles away.

The bell rang again. Debating for a moment whether or not to get her pistol, she decided to check first and see who stood on her porch.

She flipped on the porch light, looked through the peephole, and gasped. "Jeff," she whispered.

Hesitating didn't even enter her mind. Crista quickly unlocked the door and swung it open.

Jeff held up a small white envelope. "I never paid you your gin rummy winnings."

Crista laughed, even though tears clogged her throat. "No, you didn't." She took the envelope from him and clasped it in both hands. "Is that the only reason you came, to clear up your gambling debt?"

"No," he said gently. "I came for a lot more than that." He hunched his shoulders. "It's pretty cold out here. May I come in?"

Silently, Crista stood aside and let Jeff enter. She watched him shrug out of his brown leather jacket. Her gaze quickly passed over him before he turned to face her, jacket in hand. He wore a thick, natural-colored sweater, baggy brown trousers, and brown boots. Other than for his hair being mussed from the wind, he looked as if he stepped from the pages of *GQ*.

Her heart galloped.

"Do I smell coffee?" Jeff asked.

His question snapped her back to reality. "Yes, I just made a pot." She opened the coat closet and hung his jacket inside. "Would you like some?"

"Please."

She led the way to her small kitchen. Jeff stood close by while she got a mug from the cabinet and filled it with the hot brew. He was near enough for her to smell the clean scent of his skin. He must've showered before he came here. Thinking of the hot water running over his nude body made her stomach clench.

She held the full mug out to him. Their fingers touched. Crista's gaze flew to his face.

She heard him release a heavy breath as he took the mug and set it on the cabinet. "Crista, I'm sorry." He looked back at her, his eyes full of regret. "I'm sorry I wasn't honest with you about my feelings. I was trying to be noble, but it backfired." He took her hands in his. "Our lovemaking was incredible. I've *never* felt that way with a woman. What we shared… It was more than our bodies." His eyes twinkled wickedly. "Although I *really* like what we did with our bodies."

Crista couldn't help chuckling at his joke.

Jeff sobered. "I knew you were still hurting from losing your husband. It would've been easy for you to mistake passion for love. I didn't want you to be hurt if you didn't feel for me what I feel for you." Raising her hands to his mouth, he kissed each palm. "I fell so hard and so fast for you, Crista. I wanted to be with you, but only if you were truly ready to become involved with another man. That's why I let you believe I thought you might be a gold digger. I was trying to drive you away to protect you. I didn't want to hurt you."

"Shh." Crista drew one hand away from him and touched his mouth. "I know you didn't mean to hurt me."

Jeff took her hand back in his and gripped it tightly. "God, no. I wouldn't hurt you for *anything*. I love you, Crista."

"I love you too."

Standing on her tiptoes, she kissed him softly. One kiss led to another, then another, then another even more passionate. Soon, she had her arms wrapped around his neck while his arms encircled her waist.

"I've missed you," she whispered in his ear.

"I've missed you too. We have a lot to talk about."

She pulled back so she could see his face. "Talk later. Make love to me now."

His hands slid down to her buttocks. "Where?"

"In front of the fire."

Chapter Twelve

Lifting Crista in his arms, Jeff carried her back into the living room and laid her on the carpet in front of the fireplace. He took the time to pull his sweater over his head and toss it aside before lying beside her.

Her skin glowed golden in the firelight. "You're so beautiful, Crista." He touched her hair, her cheek, her jaw. He had to touch her to be sure he wasn't dreaming, that he was truly here with her. "Everything about you is beautiful. I love you."

"I love you too."

Her voice was barely a whisper, but he heard her clearly…with his ears and his heart. He kissed her gently, telling her without words how very much she meant to him. He wanted their lovemaking to be slow and tender, the build-up to orgasm easy.

Crista's tongue pushing past his lips destroyed that notion.

Lust consumed him. His hormones roared to life. The urge to mount her, claim her for his mate, filled every fiber of his being.

To try and curb the caveman urge, he moved his mouth to her neck. He nipped her lightly, then soothed the bite with his tongue. Arching her neck, she clasped his head and pulled it closer to her. Jeff nipped her skin again, harder this time.

"More," she breathed.

Her husky request destroyed his good intentions. Jeff rose to his knees and pulled Crista into a sitting position. One tug and her sweatshirt fell to the floor, quickly followed by her bra. He filled his hands with her breasts as he kissed her again.

Crista moaned deep in her throat and shifted to her knees. She pressed her breasts against his chest as she kissed him again. Jeff ran his hands down her back to her buttocks. Holding them firmly, he rocked his hips back and forth, rubbing her pelvis with his erection.

Twenty seconds of that action had him panting for breath.

Jeff stopped their kiss, but continued to caress her buttocks. "Crista, I want you."

"I want you too."

She tunneled her fingers into his hair and tried to pull his mouth back to hers. Jeff resisted.

"Kiss me," she begged, her voice husky.

"Crista, you don't understand. This should be *lovemaking*, not a quick fuck. But that's what I want. I want you on your hands and knees while I fuck you hard and fast. I have to slow down a bit before I..." He took a breath. "I have to slow down."

She slid one hand between his legs and squeezed his balls. "I don't want you to slow down."

Crista rose to her feet. He watched her push her jeans and panties past her hips. They joined the pile of her clothing on the floor. Once she was naked, she dropped to her hands and knees and looked at him over her shoulder.

"Fuck me hard and fast."

Jeff swallowed when Crista spread her knees, bent over, and rested her elbows on the carpet. Her pussy glistened with her juices, the lips red and swollen. He could smell her arousal.

He had to get inside her.

Taking off the rest of his clothes would take too much time. Jeff unfastened his belt and slacks and pulled his cock from his shorts. One hard thrust and he was inside her.

Wet heat surrounded his cock. Her pussy gripped him like a silk-lined glove. Jeff held her hips and pushed until his balls touched her. He stayed that way for several seconds, simply absorbing the feeling of being inside her again, then he began to move. His thrusts gained speed quickly, until the sound of his flesh slapping her buttocks filled the air.

"Spread your legs more, Crista. Yeah, like that. Arch your back. More. Yeah. Oh, yeah."

Crista bit her bottom lip and closed her eyes. There was definitely a time for lovemaking and a time for fucking. Right now, Jeff wanted fucking, and so did she. He gripped her hips and pounded into her, over and over. She'd experienced this wild, animalistic side of him once, when they showered together at his cabin.

She loved it.

He stopped pumping and leaned over her body. His skin felt hot and damp next to hers. "I don't want to come yet," he breathed into her ear. "I want *you* to. What do you need me to do?" He slid one hand between her thighs. "Is this what you need?"

His touch sent shivers up her spine. "Yessss."

"Mmm, your clit is hard. I think it likes my touch."

"It does. *I* do."

"Do you want me to rub it fast? Easy?" He drew little circles with one finger. "Do you like it this way, or back and forth?"

He couldn't expect her to answer when her blood pounded through her body. Crista couldn't think; she could only feel.

"How about if I pinch it?"

He did, and she flew apart. Crista threw back her head. "Oh, God, yes!" She bucked against him as her orgasm took over her mind and body. She could feel her pussy grabbing his cock with each contraction, trying to draw it even farther into her body.

The contractions slowly faded. Crista lay with her forehead on the carpet, trying to draw in a deep breath. It didn't work. She'd never be able to breathe normally again.

"Where's your lotion?" Jeff asked.

"There's some under the sink in the kitchen."

He squeezed her buttocks. "I'll be right back."

Crista moaned when he pulled his still-hard cock out of her. Needing to straighten her legs, she lay flat on her stomach and rested her head on her folded arms. That's when she realized he'd asked her for lotion.

She didn't get the chance to wonder why he wanted it before he came back. Sliding his arm under her waist, he raised her enough to slip two of the pillows from the couch beneath her stomach.

"This'll make it easier on your knees."

She would've thanked him for his consideration, but the words stopped in her throat when he thrust his cock inside her pussy again. She clenched her fists and squeezed her eyes shut when he began to move. He pumped slowly, lazily, as if he had all the time in the world to reach a climax.

His hands, slick with lotion, caressed her lower back. Crista sighed.

"Like that?" he asked.

"Mmm-hmm. I love having my back massaged."

"What else do you like massaged?" His hands slid over her buttocks while he continued to pump. "How about here?"

"That's nice too."

"Here?" He flattened one hand over her cleft and pressed his thumb against her anus.

Crista inhaled sharply. Jeff drew small circles, then dipped inside her ass. He did it again and again, until she was raising her hips each time to take his thumb deeper.

"I love how hot you are," Jeff growled. "How free you are with me." He pushed his thumb all the way inside her ass and began pumping faster. He'd fought his climax for so long his balls ached, but he kept fighting it, wanting Crista to come again first.

He pulled his thumb from her ass. Spying the bottle of lotion on the floor, he picked it up and drizzled more over his hand. He smoothed the creamy liquid around her anus, then pushed two fingers inside her. Crista moaned loudly, but didn't pull away.

"Are you okay with this?" he asked, working his fingers deeper.

"Yessss."

Jeff couldn't help grinning. She always put extra emphasis on her "yes" when she really liked what he did.

His grin faded as his lust grew. He wanted Crista to come again, but his own body demanded release. Picking up speed, he pumped his cock harder into her pussy while he drilled her ass with his fingers. His balls tightened, his cock twitched.

Crista arched her back. "Harder, please. Like that. Oh, yes, like that. Yes, yes, *yessss*!"

Her walls milked him as she came. Her climax pushed Jeff over the edge. Slamming his cock hard into her, he groaned out his own orgasm.

It took a moment for Jeff to think clearly again. He slowly withdrew from Crista's body and lay beside her. Pulling her into his arms, he held her with her back to his chest. His arm rested over her breasts. He could feel her heart pounding.

"You okay?" he whispered.

"I'm wonderful."

"I'll say," he growled softly before nipping her earlobe.

Crista giggled and hunched her shoulder. "That tickles."

"Ah, so you're ticklish. I didn't know that."

"There's a lot about me you don't know."

"True, but I'm going to have a long time with you to learn."

He tightened his arm around her and sighed in contentment. There was no place he'd rather be than in front of the fire with the woman he loved.

Several moments passed in silence. Jeff wondered if Crista had fallen asleep, when she spoke.

"How did you find me?"

"S.C."

Crista looked at him over her shoulder. "Are you serious?"

"Yeah. He came to see me tonight." Jeff propped up on his elbow. "My truck wouldn't start. He conveniently showed up to help me."

She looked confused. "How did he know you needed help?"

"Now that's a question I can't answer. I also don't know how he knew about the money you won from our gin rummy games, but he did, and to the penny."

Crista shivered slightly. "That's too weird. You don't think he really is Santa, do you?"

"I think there are a lot of things that happen which can't be explained. Something magical happened between us, Crista, and S.C. helped. He gave me the directions to your house and convinced me you'd welcome me if I came to see you."

"He was right."

She rolled to her back and reached for him. Jeff gladly went into her arms and kissed her. With his lips pressed to hers, he slipped between her spread legs and lay on top of her.

Crista slid her hands up and down his spine. "Remind me to send S.C. a thank you card."

"First thing in the morning." He kissed her shoulder, her neck, her lips. "I want to marry you, Crista."

She smiled, her eyes glowing with love. "I want that too."

He kissed her again, longer this time. "How long will it take to plan our wedding?"

"My sisters will help, but I don't want to be rushed. How about June? That'll give Lindsey and Jade plenty of time to work around their schedules so they can be here. And I'd love to have an outdoor wedding."

"I can help with that. My mother has an incredible garden, lots of roses and rhodies and other flowers I don't know the name of. She'll be ecstatic if we have our wedding in her garden."

Crista smiled. "Sounds perfect."

"We're talking *early* June, right? The sooner you become Mrs. Jeffrey Bower, the better I'll like it."

"Mrs. Jeffrey Bower." Crista wrapped her arms around his neck. "*I* like the sound of *that*."

The End

About the author:

Lynn LaFleur was born and raised in a small town in Texas close to the Dallas/Fort Worth area. Writing has been in her blood since she was eight years old and wrote her first "story" for an English assignment.

Besides writing at every possible moment, Lynn loves reading, sewing, gardening, and learning new things on the computer. (She is determined to master Paint Shop Pro and Photoshop!) After living in various places on the West Coast for 21 years, she is back in Texas, 17 miles from her hometown.

Lynn would love to hear from her readers about her writing, her books, the look of her website…whatever! Comments, praise, and criticism all equally welcome.

Lynn LaFleur welcomes mail from readers. You can write to her c/o Ellora's Cave Publishing at 1056 Home Ave. Akron, Oh. 44310-3502.

Also by Lynn LaFleur:

Jade

Jan Springer

Prologue

The third candle flared for Lindsey almost a week before Christmas the next year. She was in the midst of a delicate negotiation between the state government and her biggest corporate client over some back taxes the state insisted were owed. She really didn't have time to pursue it.

But she couldn't afford not to. Not when she saw Jade's bleak face in the vision turn gradually to happiness. Jade had suffered so much. Lindsey would do almost anything to help her sister gain her heart's desire.

Previous visions had asked her to do strange and risky things, but nothing like this. Nothing remotely like this.

Kidnap Fantasies, Inc.? The name rang a faint bell. She was pretty sure she'd seen the name on something in Gram's papers. It had struck her because it was such an odd thing for Gram to have.

And what did that have to do with Jade anyway? It sounded…kind of exciting, but dangerous, too. This would be far riskier than rescuing a dog for Joanna or making a phone call to the North Pole for Crista. This could actually be dangerous.

Wait for them to show you their message, Gram had said, *and then act boldly on what you see.*

It had worked out well before.

When the light faded and the vision ended, Lindsey went to the closet where she'd stored the box with Gram's papers, pulled it out, and began to go through them.

Chapter One

Tampa Bay, Florida USA

Four days before Christmas…

"It's really called Kidnap Fantasies?" Jade asked her two sisters, as she poured each of them another glass of iced tea, and sliced some more strawberry cheesecake.

"That's what it's called," Lindsey replied. "Kidnap Fantasies, Inc."

Lindsey and Crista had flown into town unexpectedly yesterday to give her the fascinating news that Crista was about one month pregnant and Jade and Lindsey would become aunts in the summer.

The baby would be their first niece or nephew and Jade was ecstatic.

Yesterday the three of them had gone on a shopping spree for baby stuff and Christmas presents until they'd dropped from exhaustion and then watched movies into the wee hours last night just like when they'd been teenagers. Now they sat at the table on the upper deck of Jade's yacht discussing Lindsey's idea of indulging in some sort of sexual tryst with a stranger.

In a matter of minutes they would be leaving to go home and Jade wanted to get the scoop about this Kidnap Fantasies, Inc., before they left.

"How'd you hear about it?" Jade prodded.

An odd gleam sparkled Lindsey's blue eyes. "From an acquaintance."

"You're seriously considering hiring a strange man to have sex with you?"

"Why not? Isn't it every woman's fantasy to be swept off her feet by a completely gorgeous stranger and have her deepest sexual desires fulfilled by him over and over again?"

"I know I was swept off my feet by my stranger." Crista chimed in.

"You mean by Jeff's hunky body and all those nice muscles," Lindsey chuckled.

"A man only needs one very well working muscle to satisfy a woman." Crista leaned back in the deck chair. Her shoulder-length brown hair fluttered in the Florida breeze. She inhaled and smiled dreamily. "And his big muscle most certainly does the job quite well."

Oh God! Her sisters were at it again—talking about sex.

Jade could feel her face heat up with embarrassment. She'd never been particularly comfortable talking about the subject but this Kidnap Fantasies, Inc., had piqued her interest and was forcing her to overcome her shyness.

"But to have yourself kidnapped? I mean what if he…"

What if he did all the naughty things you've always dreamed of, a little voice purred in her ear.

"Don't look so shocked, sweetie." Lindsey laughed, "Some women love to be sexually dominated in the bedroom."

"Yeah, but is it legal?"

"What? Being dominated in the bedroom?" Lindsey winked at Crista. Both sisters seemed to be trying to keep a straight face. Obviously, they still enjoyed teasing her about sex. Some things never changed.

Jade exhaled in frustration. "C'mon, I mean Kidnap Fantasies."

"Oh! Well, let's just say they prefer not to advertise to the public. Only a select group of the rich and famous knows about it." Lindsey picked up last week's edition of *People* magazine with the recent picture of Jade holding her newly released autobiography about her life as a professional downhill skier.

"And you're famous, sis. So I've just let you in on the secret club, but don't tell anyone about this organization."

Jade's excitement plunged. "So it isn't legal."

"How can something be illegal if it doesn't exist?" Crista winked.

"You sound intrigued, and a little nervous." Lindsey leaned forward, her face suddenly very serious. It made Jade a tad uneasy. "You wouldn't by any chance be interested in checking out this Kidnap Fantasies for yourself would you?" she asked.

"Oh no, I couldn't!" Jade said it so fast that both her sisters smiled knowingly.

"Nice reaction, Jade." Crista chuckled, her ice blue eyes flashing with amusement. "Exactly how long has it been since you've been properly fucked by a man?"

She couldn't stop the heated flush from giving her away at Crista's bold question. Twenty-eight years old and her face still flamed with embarrassment over the subject of sex. She took a quick gulp of her cold drink but it did nothing to cool her uneasiness.

"That long, huh?" Lindsey replied.

"It's not that I haven't wanted to…it's just since the accident."

Lindsey winced. Her gaze quickly strayed to Jade's cane where she'd hung it earlier from the back of her lounge chair.

"The accident was a year ago. You said your therapists are happy with your progress and you sure are walking a heck of a lot better since the last time we saw you. So what's preventing you from going after a man?"

Jade shrugged, "My scars for one thing."

"Oh please, the scars on your leg are barely visible. Any guy would be thrilled to go out with you. You are beautiful, Jade," Lindsey said in a reassuring voice.

"I've packed on twenty pounds…"

"Cut the crap," Crista interjected. "You were too skinny before anyway. Tell me this, does it have something to do with Beau?" The earlier amusement had disappeared from Crista's voice replaced by one of contempt as she spoke about Jade's ex-fiancé.

Again, Jade shrugged.

"You're better off without that rotten scoundrel," Crista continued. "Besides not all men are like that. Look at Jeff. He's absolutely adorable. You said so yourself."

That was true. Crista and Jeff were so much in love. Jade had met him a couple of times before their June wedding and she couldn't help but wish for a sexy blue-eyed guy like Jeff for her very own. Husky body. Lots of nice muscles. And the love that shone in his eyes for her sister almost took Jade's breath away. She'd do anything to have a guy look at her the way Jeff looked at Crista but it didn't mean she had to trust one of them again.

"I'm not ready for a relationship," she admitted.

"Okay, so what you're saying is you're ready for some good old-fashioned sex without the strings of a relationship. Kidnap Fantasies is perfect for you. Here…" Lindsey slid the brochure across the table at Jade. "It sounds like you're the one who needs Kidnap Fantasies more than I do. Take a look at it. It's their latest catalogue and there's even a questionnaire in there. Why don't you fill out it out tonight for fun?"

Jade slipped on her reading glasses and slid her fingers across the velvety softness of the thick brochure with the dark blue cover and sharp pink lettering. She found herself trying hard to resist the urge to start flipping through the catalogue right then, and there.

The idea of having sex with a complete stranger without strings attached made her pulse race with excitement. She'd had fantasies about how a man would use sex toys on her and tease her until she screamed for mercy but she'd never actually had the nerve to walk into one of those shops and get a toy or ask her ex-fiancé Beau if he might want to explore that angle in their stagnant sex life.

He'd been a missionary man.

Slam. Bam. Thank you, ma'am.

This Kidnap Fantasies just might be a nice way to live out some of her fantasies. The best thing was she wouldn't have to be embarrassed because she'd never see the guy again.

"These men...who do this type of thing," Jade asked. "Are they safe?"

"I believe you're talking of STDs and stuff. The men and women are screened with great care. From what I've learned the participants are rich and famous themselves and are looking for a little casual sex in between relationships but don't want any media attention or paparazzi around so they go to KF. Everything is understood to be confidential. It's a tight little group. Call it a club. Everyone knows everyone. Besides, KF, Inc., wouldn't be in business long if they didn't make sure their people were safe and happy, right? It's all there in the brochure." Lindsey glanced at her watch and frowned. "Well, it's time to meet our flights, Crista. We're both going to have to get a move on."

"Can't you guys stay an extra night? Just this once? I miss you both so much."

"Sorry Jade, I promised Jeff I'd only be a couple of days and that I'd be back in time to do some serious last-minute Christmas shopping with him." Crista replied.

"And I've got important meetings scheduled all the way through to Christmas Eve that I can't cancel," Lindsey said quickly hugging her so tightly she thought they'd squeeze her to death.

"Merry Christmas, Jade." Lindsey whispered into her ear.

"And you take care of yourself, sis. Merry Christmas, sweetie," Crista said as she kissed Jade on the cheek.

"Thanks for all the Christmas presents, you guys," Jade replied as she hugged them back. "And Crista, take care of yourself. No stress. It's not good for the baby."

When they let go of her, she didn't miss the tears sparkling in both her sisters' eyes. Before she could question why they suddenly looked so...conflicted, both were waving to her and heading down the stairs to the main deck.

If she could walk as fast as they could, she would have sprinted after them and asked what was going on but right now she was pretty much useless. Her hip had stiffened up as it always did from sitting for too long in one stretch.

The familiar shard of sadness tugged at her emotions as she watched her two sisters wave yet again and then they disappeared behind another docked boat.

Her sisters were so lucky. Both were confident women. Knew what they wanted and went after it. Not like her. Her whole life had been her passion for skiing. That was gone now thanks to her accident. All she had left was lots of money, a crippled body and no man to love her or call her own...not that she wanted one...but it would have been nice if men weren't such no-good louses and so untrustworthy.

Her sadness quickly disintegrated as she settled her attention to the snappy-looking Kidnap Fantasies brochure Lindsey had left behind.

Too bad she had a meeting with her agent this afternoon. The woman was trying to talk Jade into agreeing to a meeting with a prominent talk show host who wanted her on his show to talk about her autobiography.

If Jade agreed to the appearance, it would get her book more exposure. Exposure she really didn't want.

However, hindsight was twenty-twenty. It had been a silly thing to write her life story. She knew it now but after her accident, she'd needed something to do besides feeling sorry for herself. Writing the book had helped her a lot. Unfortunately, since it had released the paparazzi had been coming out of the woodwork back in Los Angeles. She'd even found one of them sitting on top of the security wall surrounding her home. He'd had a camera with the longest zoom lens she'd ever seen. To her embarrassment, he'd been taking pictures of her sunbathing topless.

The next day her picture had been plastered over all the gossip rags. That had been the last straw. She'd packed up her bags, dressed incognito and taken refuge here under the warm Tampa Bay sun in her yacht just in time for her sisters' surprise meeting.

Boy was she ever glad they'd mentioned Kidnap Fantasies. Throwing a longing look at the catalog, she grabbed her cane and hobbled toward her bedroom just inside the glass door. Barely able to contain the tingles of excitement and the cheerful giggles at the thought that she was actually thinking she might hire a man to satisfy her sexual fantasies, Jade reluctantly got ready for her appointment with her agent.

* * * * *

It wasn't until late that night when Jade had snuggled herself into her cozy king-sized bed in her yacht bedroom, thrown a light sheet over her nude body, propped herself up on an elbow and slipped on her glasses that she dare examine the Kidnap Fantasies brochure Lindsey had given her.

The minute she flipped it open her mouth dropped in surprise at the words splashed across the first page.

Ménage a Trois. BDSM. Sex Slave Training. Kidnap Fantasies. Whatever your sexual wish we'll fill your desires. Complete the questionnaire and let our discreet Kidnap Fantasies, Inc., set you free.

Sweet heavens! What had she gotten herself into?

Well, she hadn't gotten into anything yet but by the delicious way her cunt muscles were clenching with excitement Jade knew she already liked what she saw.

As she turned the pages and read the vivid descriptions, her heart picked up speed and a hand slipped over one of her breasts. She found herself plucking and toying with her plump nipples wondering how it would feel to have a gorgeous man touching her breasts as she was doing now.

Beau hadn't really bothered priming her for sex. So, she had little experience being intimately touched by a man.

Would her nipples harden beneath a man's calloused fingers in the same way they were hardening now? Or would if feel different? Would her breasts swell with need as he gazed upon her nakedness, lust shining brightly in his eyes?

Jade inhaled an aroused breath and forced her globes to puff outwards. Her fantasy man's hands would be big enough to cup her breasts, his fingers long and thick enough to do some heavy duty massaging on her clit and to slide deep inside her cunt so he could finger-fuck her.

Her pussy moistened at that idea.

Wow! She definitely needed some woman to man, hot flesh-to-flesh contact.

Her gaze flickered back to the brochure. If she went with the Ménage á Trois Special, she'd have to give Kidnap Fantasies permission to have her kidnapped by two strange men who would sexually satisfy her for one glorious weekend. In the Sex Slave Fantasy, she could order herself to be kidnapped and trained in a dungeon as a sex slave for a month. Then there was an Emerald City fantasy. A woman would give the organization permission to allow herself to be whisked away to a fantasyland where she could experience multiple ménages with the Scarecrow, Tin Man, Cowardly Lion and the Wizard of Oz.

And there were other exciting options that quite literally left Jade breathless as she tried to decide which one she'd like to try.

What finally caught her eye was the kidnap fantasy with one man who would fulfill her every sexual wish for a weekend.

She'd fill out the questionnaire.

Grabbing a pen, she ripped the forms out of the brochure and began to answer the questions.

Name: Jade Hart.

Age: 28.

Sex: Female.

Sexual preference: Hot-blooded Male.

Sexual experience?

Jade laughed and wrote—not much...*actually only one man. Missionary style. Vanilla sex. Boring.*

She continued down the list answering more questions and then hesitated at one in particular—How well-hung do you want your man to be?

She inhaled softly at that question. Dropping her pen she flopped onto her back, closed her eyes and began a slow massage on her nipples. She relished the idea of how big her dream man would be and how he'd fill the lovely ache beginning to erupt between her legs.

Beau's cock had been rather on the small and short side never quite reaching the ache deep within. In other words, he'd always left her sexually hungry and craving for more.

What she wanted was a man who'd make her scream lustily like those heroines did at the hands of their well-endowed heroes in the erotic-romance electronic books she downloaded into her handy electronic book reader.

She kneaded her breasts harder inhaling at the wonderful way her nipples stiffened beneath her fingers.

What she craved was intense sexual satisfaction at a man's expert hands. What she wanted was a man's hard calloused fingers gliding over her passion-swelled breasts. A man with wide strong shoulders she could grab onto as he slid his thick, giant cock into her, stretching her open wide. A giant velvet rock-hard cock with pulsing veins that she could wrap her mouth around and suck and taste and just feel a man's power.

Jade's eyes snapped open. Her hands left her breasts. She rolled to her side and grabbed her pen again.

Very well-hung, she giggled as she continued to write. *The bigger, the better.*

Oh, don't be shy!

The biggest cock you've got in stock.

With each question, Jade's boldness grew and her arousal blossomed. Gosh, some of these questions sounded downright delicious while others turned her right off.

But that was the whole point, wasn't it? To give the well-hung man of her dreams a bird's-eye view of what she wanted.

Completing the questionnaire, Jade couldn't help but sigh wistfully.

Wouldn't it be something if she actually had the nerve to send the questionnaire to Kidnap Fantasies?

No, she couldn't do that. Having a strange man make love to her wasn't romantic. But she wasn't looking for romance. She just wanted to be fucked by a big strong man. Wanted to dull the ache between her legs. Wished for a man's long, thick cock to slide into her body and claim her pussy.

Jade bit her bottom lip thoughtfully.

Lindsey did say the medical histories of those men were checked out. Wouldn't it be wild to have a well-hung, good-looking man fucking her senseless?

A man who would spread her legs far apart.

Jade pushed the sheets aside, lifted her knees and spread her legs wide, trying not to wince at the dull ache deep inside her injured hip.

He would be a man who would not be afraid to touch a woman where she needed to be touched.

She slid a hand between her legs and slipped a finger between her now drenched, puffed labia.

Gosh, her cunt felt as if it were on fire.

Actually, her entire body burned at the thought of a man standing right here in front of her. A man with muscles gleaming with perspiration, his massive cock stretching straight out in front of him, rigid and solid and wanting to fuck her so bad he could barely stand.

Jade smiled and teased her sensitive pleasure nub with torturous slow strokes.

She liked the thought of a man wanting her that bad. A man who couldn't keep his hands off her. A man who would feel comfortable enough for both of them to persuade her into experimenting with the fantasies she'd just written down on the questionnaire.

She slipped a finger inside her wet swollen vagina and collected some moisture withdrawing and massaging her pleasure nub once again.

Her other hand settled back on her breast and she kneaded her sensitive pink nipple watching it elongate with arousal. She continued to massage her clitoris, tightening her abdominal muscles dipping inside her soaked vagina collecting more juices to rub against her slippery pearl.

Her well-hung man would be honest. Trustworthy. Good-looking.

A man who liked to surprise her with presents and flowers and…sex toys.

Definitely sex toys.

Her finger slipped inside her wet vagina. Her other hand continued to stroke her breast and her stiff nipples. She could feel the stirrings of the orgasm.

Her breathing quickened.

She closed her eyes as the slow burn began to unravel.

Another finger slipped inside her slit and she slid in and out of herself in quick experienced strokes. Her other hand flew away from her breast and she rubbed her clit in strong firm movements.

Her man would plunge deep into her pussy in hard, pounding thrusts. His groans of arousal would rip through the air and join her whimpers of pleasure.

Jade smiled as she envisioned their two perspiration-drenched bodies writhing on her bed, the sharp sound of their bodies slamming into each other, the sexy scent of their passion seeping deep into her lungs.

Fire erupted deep in the pit of her belly and in a second, she was lost in the orgasm. She rode the pleasure waves that ripped through her belly.

Her nerve endings sizzled. Her mouth dropped open as she cried out her release.

Opening her eyes she watched her legs tremble and her hips gyrate beneath the powerful orgasm as her hands moved masterfully between her legs. Her pink nipples stabbed into the air. Her breasts jiggled sensuously with her every breath.

Oh God! She needed a man to do this to her!

Too soon, the orgasm slithered away leaving Jade panting and alone on her bed.

She eyed the questionnaire sheets and frowned.

She'd poured her heart into that questionnaire and yet it would never be seen by anyone other than herself because no matter how much she wanted to have a strange man doing delightful things to her body she knew she was just too chicken to mail it in.

Chapter Two

Three days before Christmas…

"Hello! Jade, honey!" Lindsey's voice echoed through the early morning ocean mist as she and Crista stepped onto Jade's yacht.

No answer.

Lindsey smiled.

She and Crista had watched from behind a nearby building as Jade ambled down the dock with her cane and gotten into a waiting limo.

"Where do you think she put it?" Crista asked from behind her.

Remembering Jade's bedroom being toward the end of her yacht, Lindsey motioned Crista to follow. A moment later, they were peeking into the bedroom windows.

Lindsey smiled when she spotted the Kidnap Fantasies brochure lying smack in the middle of the rumpled sheets of Jade's bed.

"I see the questionnaire," Crista giggled. "Right over there on her night table. Do you really think she filled it out?"

"If I know our middle sister, she's fantasized and filled it out…however, mailing it would be the problem. And that's what the good Lord created helpful sisters for. To keep an eye on her and make sure we honor those visions I saw."

A moment later Lindsey was not surprised to discover Jade's bedroom door unlocked. Her sister had always been that way. Too trusting of everyone around her. That's why that no good fiancé of hers had so easily broken Jade's heart.

Well, it wouldn't happen this time.

"You think she'll realize it's missing?" Crista asked as Lindsey slipped the questionnaire into her purse.

The urge to read it was great but she valued her sister's privacy. There would only be one person who would see it and it wasn't her.

"Hopefully she'll think she misplaced it," Lindsey replied as they quickly left the bedroom and headed off the yacht. "Besides, that hundred I flipped the security guard should take care of her having no clue we're still in town."

"You're sure we have to be so sneaky, Lindsey?"

"It's out of our hands now. We have to do what he says if we expect this to work for Jade."

Crista nodded.

Lindsey sighed with relief.

Thankfully, her sister understood why it had to be done this way and if everything went according to plan then their sister Jade would be experiencing some much-needed happiness in her life.

Chapter Three

Two days before Christmas…

Chestnuts roasting over an open fire, Jack Frost nipping at your nose…

The song blared from the nearest marina speaker set high on a pole right beside Jade's yacht.

Silly Christmas music! Why couldn't they shut it off, for crying out loud? With Christmas fast approaching most of the nearby yachts and the marina was practically deserted. Except for the jolly female security guard at the marina entrance, no one else seemed to be around for the holiday season.

So, who in the world were they playing these Christmas tunes for?

If she wasn't enjoying the heat from the warm sunshine washing over her skimpy thong and caressing her naked breasts she'd have given the marina guard a call by now and told her where to shove that racket!

Jade frowned.

She knew why she was in such a rotten mood. It was exactly one year ago today that Beau had become engaged to that other woman. The last thing she felt like doing today was listening to bright season's carols. Even yesterday's second round of meetings with her agent and then again this morning when she'd hit the shopping malls to hunt for more cute baby clothes for her upcoming niece or nephew she'd been bombarded with cheerful salespeople wishing her season's greetings.

Pooh! She just couldn't get away from Christmas.

She frowned and sipped on her tequila. The warm liquid almost made her gag. She hated warm drinks!

Plopping the tequila glass onto the nearby table she grabbed the Kidnap Fantasies brochure and slid her glasses on trying her darnedest to tune out the music.

The words in the brochure grabbed her attention yet again and her heart picked up a quick pace as she read.

Sex slave training.

BDSM specials. Bondage. Kidnap fantasies.

Sexual adventures including being kidnapped and taken to a nudist colony, outdoor adventures such as being hunted down by a man in the woods, or having sex in public places or in front of other people.

If she hadn't misplaced that questionnaire she just might have gotten up the nerve to send it in. Last night her body had burned bright with fevered lust just thinking about a strange man fucking her senseless.

This afternoon when she'd come back from shopping she'd been on the edge of mailing the questionnaire. Unfortunately, she couldn't remember where she'd put it. That just wouldn't do. It would be quite embarrassing if the housekeeper found it next week.

Jade would have to do a thorough search of her bedroom before that happened. But right now, she wanted to suck up some rays and just think about nothing.

The song on the marina speakers switched over to "I'll Be Home For Christmas". Sadness tugged at her heart. No one would be coming home for Christmas for her this year. No big deal, though. She'd get used to being alone through the holidays.

She'd done it last year.

Crista had spent it trapped in a snowbound cabin with a sexy stranger who she was now married to and Lindsey hadn't been able to get away because the airports had been shut down due to bad weather.

Even when Crista had called a couple of weeks ago to ask if she'd like to join her and Jeff over Christmas, Jade had lied and said she was throwing a big Christmas yacht party for her friends.

Truth was she'd wanted to hunker down here and sob into her tequila over her crushed dreams with Beau. Not that the creep deserved one shed of her tears but still it hurt to think he could drop her so easily and move onto another woman. She thought she'd been in love with him. Now she knew better.

Besides, she hadn't wanted to intrude on Crista and Jeff. After all, it was their first Christmas together after being married and next year they'd have a gorgeous baby.

The marina music drifted off to a Frosty the Snowman tune when Jade got the strangest fluttery feeling deep in the pit of her belly and the wildest feeling she was being watched.

Even before she could raise her head to look around and investigate, the sound of his deep voice sent shimmers of pleasure sliding over her flesh.

"Miss Jade Hart?"

She swallowed at the sound of his husky voice and looked up.

He stood on her gangplank.

All six feet plus of gorgeous, testosterone male.

Tight blue jeans were wrapped snugly around a nice torso and swaddled quite an impressive bulge between a set of powerful-looking legs.

His arms bulged with sleek muscles as he held onto a battered-looking tool case. He wore a simple white short-sleeved cotton shirt with the first few buttons undone to reveal a healthy dusting of curly dark chest hair. Equally dark brown hair fluttered over a nice forehead, feathered loosely against his sides and curled over his shoulders. A gorgeous five o'clock beard shadowed his face. Full kissable lips were upturned into a heart-clenching smile complete with bursting dimples in his cheeks and quite a deep cleft in his square chin.

At the delicious sight, a carnal tremor shimmered through her entire body making her blood heat and her cunt scream in sexual awareness.

Wow! Hello handsome! Please fuck me now!

The hottest-looking pair of denim blue eyes squinted against the late afternoon sunshine, as he stared straight at her, well no, not at her exactly.

At her bare breasts!

Oh, shit!

She resisted the urge to cover herself and watched the pink tip of his tongue peek out from between his sensually shaped lips as he continued to watch her.

Gosh what she wouldn't do to feel this guy's hot mouth and wet tongue roaming over her breasts, lapping her nipples and licking the rest of her sex-deprived body.

At those delicious thoughts her cunt moistened and Jade realized that in the way she was lying on the chaise, with both her legs pulled up and slightly parted he was probably getting a great view of her skimpy cloth-covered pussy.

Okay, just act natural. Act as if it was an everyday occurrence that she allowed a strange man to see her practically naked.

By golly, why wasn't she the least embarrassed by his appreciative gaze?

"Hi! I'm Jade Hart. May I help you?" she managed to squeak and quickly cleared her throat.

He blinked at the sound of her voice and she didn't miss the sweet pink flush that rushed over his cheekbones.

How cute! The man was embarrassed!

And she wasn't!

Wasn't this a lovely turn of events?

"Um… I um…" he stammered.

Jade's gaze zeroed in on the toolbox.

"You're the mechanic? To fix my engines?"

She'd called the marina asking them if they would send someone reliable over to fix the intermittent stalling problems the yacht had encountered when she'd taken her sisters out for a spin the other day.

The handyman cleared his throat.

"Yes ma'am. My name is Caydon. Caydon Minnelli. Um… If you'll just tell me where your engine room is…"

She really should send him away until she could verify his credentials. Or at the very least, she should cover her breasts.

It was too dangerous to be alone with a strange man and her lying around half-naked. He might get the wrong idea.

But the cute way he kept glancing at her breasts was really turning her on.

Her stomach fell as his gaze dropped to where she'd hung her cane off a nearby deck table.

Who was she kidding? The man wouldn't even bother with her! She was practically handicapped. Her hip and leg were full of hideous scars from the surgeries. No man in his right mind would find her sexy.

Besides, since the accident, she'd packed on a good twenty pounds and here she was showing off her body. The only thing she'd get from this guy was him feeling sorry for her.

That's probably why she wasn't embarrassed at having him seeing her…because she was too busy feeling sorry for herself.

Loser girl!

Get a grip. The guy is here to fix the engines and nothing more.

Jade pointed to the cabin behind her and immediately noticed how her breasts jiggled wantonly at him.

Hmm. Maybe there was something good about her packing on those extra pounds after her accident. Her boobs weren't so small anymore. She hadn't realized it until just now.

Smiling inwardly at the way his Adam's apple bobbed when he swallowed, she kept her voice cool and professional as she spoke, "The stairs to the engine room are through those doors, through the kitchen, through the bedroom. You'll find the door to your right at the end of the hall."

He stood there for a moment, his gaze transfixed to her cane, an odd little frown on his cute face.

Her stomach plummeted.

See? He was already feeling sorry for her.

"When you're finished you can just send the bill to the marina…they'll forward it to me, if that's okay?"

He nodded, stepped onto her deck and quickly slipped past her without looking her way.

It gave her the encouragement to watch his long strides as he strolled across her cherry wood-paneled deck.

Despite her best efforts to still the sexual hunger flowing through her heated veins, her pulse went haywire at the sensual outline of his plump ass cheeks cupped by his jeans.

Wowsie! Nice ass.

When he disappeared through the door, Jade let out a long slow whistle.

She wouldn't mind running an exploring tongue along that butt or get a taste of his cock.

She let out a quick breath and wiped away the perspiration sprinkling across her forehead.

The man was one juicy-looking fellow!

Jade rolled her eyes in disappointment. A man built like him wouldn't be interested in her. It was best she just resign herself to the fact that the only reason he'd pay attention to her was because he thought she was loaded and she was paying his handyman bill.

Jade shook her head.

Sometimes having lots of money sucked.

As a child, she'd craved it. As a teenager, she'd trained for it. Now as an adult, she had it.

Unfortunately, having money produced lots of admirers. Admirers for her money, that is. That's the harsh lesson she'd learned from Beau.

Settling herself more comfortably in her white vinyl lounge chair, Jade resisted the urge to cover her breasts with her beach towel. She'd allow the sun to bathe her just like she'd been planning to do and when she heard him coming back she'd cover herself then.

She smiled to herself.

It sure had felt fantastic to have him looking at her the way he had. The hungry look in his eyes, the cute way his tongue had licked his lips as if he'd wanted to feast on her nipples, maybe even taste her wet cunt?

She felt herself blushing at that thought.

Her sisters were right. It was time she got herself laid.

Maybe she should phone Lindsey and ask her to express-courier another questionnaire?

Wouldn't that shock her sisters silly if shy Jade actually did mail a questionnaire to Kidnap Fantasies, Inc., and had herself a lovely fuck-fest with a stranger?

A burst of hammering from below deck shattered her thoughts.

It was quickly followed by silence.

The handyman was busy with his job and thankfully someone had finally shut off that blasted Christmas music.

Halleluiah!

Peace and quiet.

Jade closed her eyes and relaxed.

Her fingers let go of the Kidnap Fantasies brochure and it dropped with a plop to the deck.

A moment later an easygoing whistling tune from the handyman drifted through the air.

Gosh, she hadn't heard a man whistle so softly before in her life.

Thankfully, it wasn't a Christmas song but an old Frank Sinatra song she hadn't heard in ages.

Her grandmother loved listening to Frank Sinatra.

Warm memories of Gram bustling in her kitchen filtered into her mind. She could still remember the cinnamon and allspice scents of her hot apple pies baking in the oven. The peppery sound of ice crystals and snow snapping against the windows of their home during the snowstorms they'd experience in upper New York state. Most of all she remembered how every Sunday afternoon Gram would put on the record player and play her favorite records.

Jade smiled into the memories. Gram was the sweetest woman in the world who'd always made her and her sisters feel so loved. So safe and secure.

The handyman's calm whistling slowly intermingled into her thoughts of Gram. She could practically hear dear Gram's soft voice, "It doesn't matter how rich or how poor the man is, base your decision on what your heart tells you. Nothing else matters…"

The gentle breeze tinged with the salty aroma of the ocean and the warm sunshine splashing over her practically nude body made her mind drift into a peaceful place she hadn't experienced in a very long time.

Before she knew it, she'd been lulled to sleep.

* * * * *

Caydon Minnelli smacked the hammer against the engine room's wooden floor one more time just for good measure. He had to make it sound like he was fixing her engines, didn't he?

Even if he was here for a totally different reason.

From what the team at Kidnap Fantasies had found out, Jade Hart was rich and a celebrity of sorts.

She'd won several gold medals at the Olympics and won a few Downhill Skiing World Cup Championships. Up until last year's tragic skiing mishap in Cortina d'Ampezzo, Italy, an accident many blamed on her coach, she'd been roaring toward the world's best professional skier position.

Gaining an impressive financial situation due to appearances in various commercials, she also had a signature jewelry line that a conglomerate ran for her and with some good sound investments, she was now a wealthy woman who didn't want for money.

Over the past year while she'd recuperated from her wipeout on a mountain slope, she'd written a tell-all tale about her childhood including the death of her parents at an early age and the tumultuous relationship with her ski coach of ten years.

A coach who'd pushed her mercilessly, conditioning her for the number one position in the skiing world. A coach who'd let her go out onto an icy slope for a trial run even when the authorities had warned everyone to stay off the slopes.

A disgusting coach who'd finagled his way into becoming her fiancé and who'd left her shortly after the tragic accident last year and moved on to coach and marry another famous millionaire skier.

Jade's autobiography titled *Skiing in the Rain*, released not too long ago, had once again put her in the spotlight.

Caydon's grip tightened on the hammer as remembered seeing her cane. Conflicting emotions had bombarded him. Anger, at wanting her ex-fiancé dead. Inkles of fear that she'd reject him at what he was planning to do with her. Most of all though he experienced a nice warm fuzzy feeling whenever he thought about her.

She'd looked so vulnerable lying there in the bright sunshine reading the Kidnap Fantasies brochure he'd given her sister to give to Jade.

His hungry gaze had roved over every inch of her body in mere seconds.

The instant he'd seen her tanned globes with the large suckable pink nipples nestled in large areolas, his mouth had watered at the thought of taking her flesh into his mouth and making her moan with erotic pleasure.

To his horror, his face had flushed with embarrassment when her gorgeous eyes had latched onto him and seen him ogling her. By golly, he hadn't been this shy near a woman since high school. Not to mention his cock hadn't reacted so powerfully since he was a teenager.

He'd felt his equipment harden, swell and pulse painfully against the tight restraints of his jeans, aching to burst through the zipper and slam into her hot juicy cunt.

And he hadn't missed her reaction either as he'd spied the wet spot of her arousal dotting her thong swim bottoms.

By god! The woman was even prettier than the pictures he'd seen of her.

He could tell she was tall by those long powerful-looking legs. And her hips were nice and wide enough so he could grab onto her while he fucked her good and hard.

Her hair was a shoulder-length sandy brown with golden highlights, her lips were a ripe red. She had a perfect nose, cheeks with a pretty dusting of freckles and delicious-looking naked earlobes he could nibble on all night.

Not to mention those gorgeous jade-colored eyes that had looked at him from behind a pair of sexy gold-rimmed glasses. It made his breath slam up in his lungs making it hard for him to breathe.

Jade Hart was an elegant piece of work. Nice and curvy in all the right places just like her boat, *Jewel of the Sea*.

When he'd walked along the docks with the smell of fish drifting through the air he'd been impressed by the gleaming black and white fiberglass hull and the shiny silver-colored railings of her yacht. He couldn't help but admire the elegant mix of wood decorating the interior as he'd walked through the kitchen. Teak walls with mahogany trim and red cherry planked floors gave it a nautical air but the cotton canvas blinds that dressed the windows, the cherry curved countertops, the stainless steel pots hanging from the low ceiling and the denim blue slipcovers on the benches gave the boat a homey lived-in feel.

And then he'd seen her snug bedroom. Well maybe bedroom wasn't quite the word for it.

A seductress' haven sounded more appropriate. The walls golden pine wood planks with tongue-and-groove white-planked ceilings. Lots of windows framed by delicate white lace gave for a great view of the marina loaded with stylish yachts, the turquoise-colored ocean and the handful of boats with billowing sails dotting the horizon.

Best of all her bed was big enough for the two of them to tumble around freely while he made mad passionate love to her.

Caydon's lips tilted in a smile.

He sure was going to enjoy living in such close quarters with the pretty Jade Hart.

His smile quickly faded.

Now, if only he could get up enough nerve to carry out the rest of his plan.

Doubts crept into his thoughts and he gave a nearby pipe a frustrated whack.

Dammit! He'd never done something like this before.

Was he nuts coming here to seduce a virtual stranger?

Shit!

The answer was simple.

Yes. He was nuts.

Throwing the hammer down into the toolbox, he withdrew Jade Hart's Kidnap Fantasies questionnaire and began to read it for the umpteenth time.

The written words made his cock thicken and elongate. Within seconds his flesh pressed agonizingly against his pants, throbbing wildly, anticipating what was to come.

He inhaled a deep steadying breath and nodded to himself.

It was high time to gather his nerves, put his ass into gear and kidnap himself a woman.

Chapter Four

It wasn't the sound of the waves smacking against the hull of her yacht that drifted through Jade's many layers of sleep and alerted her to the fact something wasn't quite right. Nor was it the salty smell of cool ocean air that sent a shiver of alarm racing up her spine.

It was the lack of bell buoys clanging, the gentle rocking of her craft in obvious movement and the unmistakable zesty scent of tomato sauce drifting into her lungs that warned her something wasn't as it should be.

But how could that be? She was alone on her boat.

Alone…except for that handyman she'd let on board.

She forced her eyes open and blinked at the rosy-colored clouds sailing through the late afternoon blue sky unable to figure out where she was.

And then it hit her.

Sweet mercy! She'd fallen asleep. Drifted off while listening to that handyman whistling those Frank Sinatra melodies.

She noticed a beach towel had been draped over her naked breasts and a shiver of unease zipped through her.

Oh dear. She didn't remember doing that.

Shooting a glance at the railing and beyond she saw nothing but miles and miles of endless green ocean waves.

Not good!

A shot of adrenalin made her bolt upright into a seated position and she looked around.

There was no sign of him.

Heart hammering against her naked chest she grabbed her nearby white silky swim cover-up and quickly shrugged into its softness. Tying the sash, she grabbed her cane and ignored the stiffness in her hip as she wrestled out of her chaise.

Where was that handyman? Had he left? Had the yacht somehow become disentangled from the security lines and drifted out of the marina? That would explain why she didn't hear the sound of engines.

How in the world did the boat get free? She always made sure the lines were secure. She'd need to get up to the pilothouse and swing the yacht around and head back to shore.

"Good evening!"

Shit!

The sound of the handyman's deep, masculine voice sent a shiver of nervousness racing up her back. Shielding her eyes against the late afternoon sunshine, she caught sight of his head poking out one of the kitchen windows. He leaned further out the window and waved at her.

Her pulse picked up speed as she noted his shirtless, tanned chest dotted with sparse dark chest hair.

"What happened? Why are we out here?" she called to him praying he'd give her a perfectly reasonable explanation.

"I didn't want to wake you so I took her out to see if I fixed the problem and…it died."

"It died?"

Her grip tightened on her cane. *Oh! Please don't tell me this.*

He elaborated by slicing a finger across his neck in a cutting his throat motion.

"Like in dead," he called out. "Looks like we're stranded out here for a little while. At least until after dinner."

Dinner? Was he nuts? She couldn't be stranded out here in the middle of the ocean with a stranger.

"I can radio for help!" Yes, that's what she'd do.

"I already did. The Coast Guard is tied up with a missing boat. I told them not to worry about us. It isn't an emergency. I can fix the problem...I think."

He thinks?

Those cute dimples burst into his cheeks making her pulse quicken despite her fear of being alone with a complete stranger in the middle of the ocean.

"They know where we are. In the meantime, come on over. Dinner is just about ready. You are hungry, aren't you? I hate eating alone."

Dinner was almost ready? He hated eating alone?

Bold fellow, wasn't he? A complete turnaround from the shy guy with the pink-tinged cheeks as he'd avoided looking at her breasts earlier.

"While you slept I took the liberty of whipping up some dinner for us. I hope you don't mind?"

God, yes she did mind. The man had her scared witless for heaven's sake.

"Um, that's fine," she said meekly.

"Come on!" He waved his arm again and Jade's mouth went dry at the sight of muscles rippling across his bare chest.

Is this guy for real?

Before she could protest, he poked his head back inside the cabin and was gone.

Now what should she do? It certainly would be highly embarrassing if she called for help and this guy was legit. Besides, if he were a killer or a rapist he sure wouldn't be cooking dinner for her. Would he?

The soft sound of his whistling "Rudolph the Red-Nosed Reindeer" reached her ears.

She nodded to herself and squared her shoulders. Okay! She could handle this. Truly, she could.

Tightening her hold on her cane, Jade hobbled precariously until her stiff hip loosened and then she picked up her pace.

She'd march right into the galley and make him take her back to shore.

Well, that wouldn't work, would it? He'd just said the engines had died. Or had they? Could she trust him? Maybe he'd only told her that so he could…what?

Jump her bones?

As if he would want to screw a cripple, Jade thought wryly.

Don't be melodramatic woman! He isn't the least bit interested in you.

Cautiously she headed toward the kitchen. The mouth-watering smell of tomato sauce teased her into the room

Yes, she could definitely handle this guy. He was just a handyman. He had no ulterior motives. She was the one who kept thinking about him wanting to have sex with her. Not that she wouldn't mind jumping his bones and pulling down those tight jeans to get a good look at that lovely sized bulge he had hidden in there.

Jade shook her head.

This is what happens when you go too long without a man, she chided herself.

Gathering a breath, she pushed open the door and to her surprise found the small kitchen empty.

Where the heck did he go?

The mouth-watering smell of the tomato sauce teased her into the room. Passing the scaled-down marine fridge she found a pot of boiling water and in another pot, sauce splashing all around the stainless steel stovetop.

She groaned inwardly. Not at the mess but at the yummy mouth-watering aroma.

She hadn't smelled something this delicious since before Gram had died.

Jade couldn't stop the smile from lifting her lips at the memory of her grandmother and at the way she'd enjoyed slaving over a hot stove on a cold winter day getting supper ready for her two sisters and herself after they'd spent a day of skiing.

"You like?"

She jumped in surprise at his voice and froze at the unmistakable bulge pressing ever so slightly against her ass.

Have mercy! The bulge felt exceptionally big and oh so hot and wonderfully hard. She felt a rush of moisture cream her pussy and her swimsuit bottom suddenly felt wet.

"Sorry, I didn't mean to scare you," he whispered and stepped around her.

Was he talking about the size of his cock frightening her?

No, he couldn't be. He was acting way too casual. As cool as a cucumber. Acting as if he hadn't just teased her with that hot swell pressed so lightly against her butt.

Or maybe that bulge had been her imagination?

As he stirred the sauce, her eyes drifted to the front of his jeans.

Jade groaned inwardly.

Oh dear!

The front of his jeans swelled wonderfully and she fought the impulse to slip her fingers into his jeans and bring out what must be a magnificent-sized cock.

Anticipation weakened her legs.

She lifted her gaze to his naked chest.

God! What she wouldn't do to smooth her hands over those lovely rippling muscles or take his plump nipples into her mouth and bite those bronze pebbles.

Oh yes, and she wouldn't mind having this man go down on her.

As he stirred the sauce, she watched those long masculine fingers curl around the wooden stir stick and her ass ached to have his large hands smacking her sensitive bottom until her flesh blazed. She wanted to have those long fingers spreading her cheeks apart and welcoming his thick long cock into her tiny back hole.

Heavens!

It suddenly seemed a wee bit too warm in here. She needed an excuse to pop outside and suck in some cool ocean air.

"Why don't you head out to the back deck? Everything's ready."

Gosh! Was he reading her mind or what's the story?

"Why are you doing this?" The words were out of her mouth before she could stop them.

He cocked a puzzled eyebrow at her. "Doing what? Cooking?"

No, making my hormones go haywire. Making me want you. Making me yearn for your hard cock plunging deep inside my cunt until I scream from orgasm after orgasm.

Oh boy.

She nodded, wishing away the flush of heat flooding her cheeks and trying to still the fear of an answer she didn't want to hear. Like maybe, he was a serial killer. Like maybe, he wanted to fatten her up before he killed her.

"I like to cook."

Simple enough answer.

So why didn't she believe him?

"Why?" he asked softly. "Did you think I kidnapped you?"

His words hung heavy in the air as he awaited her answer. Obviously, he'd seen the Kidnap Fantasies brochure that she'd dropped onto the deck before nodding off.

Had he read it while she'd slept? Had that brochure given him some naughty ideas?

Oh, my gosh! Wouldn't that be something? Kidnapped by the handyman.

"No, of course not, don't be silly," she lied.

Have mercy but if she hadn't misplaced that questionnaire she would have asked for a guy just like this one.

He smiled, broke eye contact and returned his attention to his sauce.

"Grub's just about ready. Have yourself a seat on the back deck."

The guy was making himself quite at home, wasn't he? Cooking supper without a shirt. Wrecking her boat's engines. Stranding them out here in the middle of nowhere. Looking hot and sexy in a tight pair of jeans. Pressing his gorgeous cock against the crack of her ass. Making her crave him.

Jade found herself doing what he suggested. On rather shaky legs, she made her way out of the kitchen and past her bedroom with the ominous cane clicking loudly against the polished cherry planked floor.

When she emerged outside, the warm salty ocean air kissed her face, but it did nothing to dampen the heat uncurling deep in her ass where he'd pressed ever so slightly against her, nor did it stop the fire that had unraveled deep inside her pussy.

She blinked in surprise at the sight in front of her.

He'd set the small deck table with her nicest tablecloth complete with the white linen napkins and the silver cutlery she'd inherited from Gram.

A lone candle perched inside a candleholder flickered in the middle of the table. Chilling inside the ice bucket sat a bottle of wine.

What in the world? If she didn't know any better she'd think he'd prepared this romantic dinner to set a scene for a seduction.

Jade's pulse hammered at that thought.

Could this handyman actually want to have sex with her?

This time she smelled his clean male scent even before she felt his masculine heat caress her back as he came up behind her.

"You like?" His blue eyes seemed to shine with lust as he held a large dish full of tomato sauce-laden spaghetti.

Her pulse skittered.

"Yes, it's very pretty." No way was she going to say it was a romantic scene for a seduction. After all, she could be reading this all wrong.

He set the dish onto the table and to her surprise he pulled out a deck chair. "Have a seat."

Quite aware that she was topless beneath her cover-up, she hesitated.

"Um, maybe I should go and get dressed for dinner."

"You're perfect the way you are. Please, sit. Enjoy the view while I get us the rest."

Oh, she was enjoying the view all right, she thought as she sat down and watched his cute ass sway against his tight jeans as he went back inside.

When he disappeared, she shook her head.

What in the world was she going to do? What if he was setting a scene for a seduction? Could she go through with it?

But what if the way he'd pressed his cock against her backside had been a mistake? Maybe he'd accidentally brushed against her and he hadn't even noticed?

Jade swallowed her nervousness. She'd noticed and she wanted more.

Much more.

A moment later, he showed up with a large dish of raw vegetables.

Obviously, he'd raided the pantry.

As her gaze raked over the phallus-shaped raw eggplant, the thick short carrots, and the long slender cucumbers, a hot blade of lust shimmered up her channel. She'd thought about doing it with vegetables but truly never had the nerve.

Her momentary excitement plummeted when she spotted a peeler and the vegetable dip set in the middle of the dish.

"I know some women prefer their vegetables raw," he said as he set the dish on the table.

He nodded to the steaming bowl of spaghetti. "So? What do you think? You like my culinary expertise?"

"I must have been asleep for quite some time for you to whip all this up."

He winked at her. "By the way you were smiling in your sleep I didn't want to disturb you."

To her shock, her face heated up at the thought of his hot gaze roving over her naked breasts while she'd slept.

His silky-looking chest muscles jerked wonderfully as he scooped a couple of healthy helpings of the delicious-looking spaghetti onto her plate.

"Dig in. Tell me what you think."

Gosh, she was sitting here beside a gorgeous hunk who was feeding her spaghetti and all she could do was blush?

Fuck me! her mind shouted at him.

On the other hand, her mouth didn't participate with her thoughts and she shoved a forkful of spaghetti past her lips. Scrumptious flavor burst against her taste buds. She closed her eyes and moaned her approval.

"Sounds good," his voice sounded husky.

Was he talking about the way she'd just moaned? Or the way she'd just…moaned…like in a sexual way?

She snapped her eyes open to catch him watching her in such a way that made her feel vulnerable and scared.

Vulnerable because she could easily fall for a guy who'd actually cook supper for her and scared that she was reading way too much into this.

"C'mon, eat it all up."

You can eat me anytime, Jade thought as she swallowed the food and tried to act natural.

"I haven't had spaghetti this good since before my grandmother died. You must give me your recipe." She would have her cook whip up a batch for her when she got back to Los Angeles.

"Actually it is a secret family recipe but I'll tell it to you. Wine. A healthy dose of wine to canned tomatoes and spices. Lots of basil, sage, thyme."

He shoved a healthy forkful into his mouth.

"Mmm, very good if I do say so myself." He wiggled his dark eyebrows at her in Groucho Marx style and she couldn't help but laugh and relax a little.

She had to be reading too much into this guy. He wasn't interested in her. He was probably feeling guilty for stranding them out here, had simply cooked up a meal because he was hungry and she'd been asleep.

Twirling her fork, she gathered up more of the delicious spaghetti and continued to eat. Each bite seemed more succulent than the previous one. Before she knew it, she'd totally relaxed and helped herself to seconds.

"Is there anyone you should contact? Anyone waiting for you at home? I mean it'll be Christmas Eve tomorrow…" she said trying hard to appear casual as she dabbed sauce from the corners of her lips with one of her grandmother's linen napkins.

"You're asking if I'm married or have a girlfriend. The answer is no. Not at the moment. And no one is expecting me this year for Christmas festivities. Unless you consider a fern that my mom gave me because she thought I'd need some oxygen in the big stuffy house I live in. Wine?" he asked as his big hand picked up the bottle.

She couldn't help but once again admire the length of his fingers as they curled around the stem of a glass. Oh yes, nice long thick fingers. Perfect for fucking her aching cunt.

"What about your family?"

"A toast," he suddenly said and handed her the glass and then held his up. "To…a very Merry Christmas and a Happy New Year."

"A Merry Christmas," Jade found herself whispering as his warm gaze held hers.

Their glasses clinked together.

It was a happy sound. A sound she hadn't heard in quite some time.

"My family can survive without me this year," he grinned.

She sipped her wine trying hard not to read too much into his comment or that gorgeous smile that was making her toes curl as she watched the sexual way his lips arched over his glass as he drank the ruby liquid. She wouldn't mind tasting the sensual curves of his mouth. Wouldn't mind having his hot lips sucking on her clit the way he was doing that glass.

Oh dear, she needed to get her thoughts onto something else.

"You said your last name is Minnelli?"

He nodded.

"Italian?"

"My grandparents are from northern Italy."

Northern Italy.

A cold familiar tightness clamped over her chest. That's where she'd taken the horrible fall on the icy slope during last year's training run.

"You're not smiling anymore. Something I said?"

Concern etched his features and he placed his wineglass upon the table.

"No, it's nothing."

"Tell me," the softness in his voice soothed her. Made her want to share what she'd gone through over the past year.

"It was in Italy where I broke my hip and leg."

"Ah yes, your skiing accident."

Jade blinked in shock. "You know about that?"

"I've seen your pictures in the magazines. I recognized your name."

"Oh." So he knew she was rich, too. Was that why he was interested in her? Was he like Beau? Looking for an easy buck?

His toe nudged against her bare foot. "You're still frowning."

She looked down and realized he'd slipped his shoes off.

He had big feet.

Big feet.

Big cock.

Oh boy! Her thoughts were turning to *that* again. Was it any wonder? With a gorgeous, bare-chested man sitting right beside her.

"So why were you out on the slope that day? I'd read everyone had been told to stay off of it."

"Apparently someone forgot to tell me."

"Meaning your coach…your fiancé."

"Ex-fiancé," she said coldly, the familiar anger churning up inside her. "It wasn't really his fault. He was too busy kissing up to a new blonde bombshell ski supplier that morning. When I asked him if it was okay to go out on the slopes he merely nodded. Thinking back on it I don't think he'd heard a word I'd said. I should have checked the conditions myself before going out."

"But your coach did that stuff for you. So you had no way of knowing about it."

"Why are we talking about this? How do you know about what my coach's responsibilities are?"

"I read your book."

Shit!

"So you pretty much know everything about me then." She fingered the moisture droplets forming on her wineglass.

Wondered if maybe he just might be one of those paparazzi who'd tracked her down.

"Not everything. But I'd like to find out."

Her head snapped up at the soft way he said it.

She caught that sexy smile that made her toes curl.

"For instance?"

He grabbed the biggest carrot from the vegetable tray and examined it carefully.

"I remember reading you eat vegetables from your own vegetable garden."

Her throat went dry at the way his finger tenderly stroked the long thick carrot.

"That's right."

"And you enjoy physical labor."

Her heart was beating so loud now that she was sure he could hear it too.

"Depends on what type," she whispered.

His smile widened and he nodded to the quickly darkening horizon. "Looks like a good night to spend out on the ocean."

Was that an invitation? Or merely an observation?

She followed his gaze and inhaled at the pale pink blooming clouds tinting the baby blue skyline.

"I haven't seen something this breathtaking in a very long time," she agreed as she fought to find some sort of neutral ground.

"Neither have I." His voice sounded too husky for her not to catch his meaning.

She looked over at him.

Lust shone in his eyes. "I've been wanting to taste you from the moment I saw you, Jade Hart. Taste all of you," he whispered.

All of her?

Her pulse skittered and her cunt quivered in anticipation.

His words stunned her. The intense way he looked at her shocked her.

He leaned closer. His rich masculine scent devoured her senses. A mental image popped into her head. An image of her handyman lowering himself between her legs, the heavy weight of her body pinned beneath him, his strong muscles flattening against her softness, his engorged cock plunging into her.

If that bulge she'd felt pressed against her backside was an indication she was in for quite a ride. Her vaginal muscles spasmed with excitement and she swallowed at a tinge of nervousness of maybe not being able to accommodate his size.

Her gaze became magnetized to his face, to his succulent-looking mouth that was now opening.

Her lips tingled in anticipation.

Oh, my gosh! She'd been right.

He *had* pushed his cock up against her backside on purpose.

He'd been checking for her reaction. Checking to see if his size would frighten her.

Her eyes closed the instant his mouth touched hers. Any and all coherent thoughts flew into the ocean breeze.

Fire puffed through her mouth as hot lips brushed against hers. He tasted of ice-wine, tomato sauce and raw man.

What a magnificent combination!

She could hear his harsh breathing. Could feel his lips tightening over hers, holding her captive.

A little growl of pleasure escaped his throat. It was a sound she'd never heard before from a man. A sexy sound that made her vaginal muscles tremble wonderfully.

Suddenly she couldn't get close enough to him. Her hands slipped around his neck pulling him deeper into the kiss.

Eager masculine fingers fought with the sash on her cover-up. Mild ocean air brushed against her bare shoulders as the robe slipped away.

Warm calloused hands palmed her breasts.

Oh gosh, that feels so good.

She pressed herself into his hands. Her breasts swelled beneath his fingers as he began a slow erotic massage. She hadn't had a man touch her like this in so long. Hadn't ever had a man kiss her so hard and with such confidence.

His moist mouth slid against hers, licking at her bottom lip, biting sweetly until she couldn't resist but to open to him.

He came in hard and he came in fast.

Teeth scraped against teeth. His scorching tongue slid quickly over the upper row of her teeth and gums, exploring every detail before pushing into her to tangle mercilessly with her tongue.

He kissed her like a man possessed. His quick tongue shooting deep thrusts into her mouth, keeping her mind off balance and preparing her body for sex.

His fingers squeezed at her nipples.

Sweet pain seared through her breasts and he caught her cry in his mouth. Fevered heat spread outward from her lower abdomen.

It felt incredible.

Suddenly he pulled away.

In the sunset his eyes were dark, his mouth shone red and gleamed wet from their kiss.

Heat brewed in his eyes and she became magnetized to the sweetly dangerous expression on his face as he stared at her bared breasts.

"Your breasts are breathtaking. Nipples so large that a man's mouth would have a feast making love to them."

Oh my gosh! No guy had ever said that to her before.

She found it hard to draw in a breath as she watched his large hands tighten around her breasts making them appear bigger and more swollen.

"Absolutely beautiful," he whispered.

She felt her eyes widen with surprise as his head lowered. His mouth opened and his moist lips greedily latched onto her plump nipple.

A soft moan escaped her throat as spirals of pleasure zipped along her flesh. He sucked her bud into the hot interior of his mouth as if it were a delicious red cherry.

Beneath his ministrations her body trembled. His teeth nibbled on her quivering bud. She found herself lifting her hands from his neck and placing them on both sides of his head, sifting her fingers through his feathery hair and inhaling the sexy scent of man.

Arching her back, she pressed her swollen breast into his face. The five o'clock stubble surrounding his lips scraped her flesh. Erotic fervor shifted wonderful warmth through her lower belly. Her cunt reacted immediately, tightening into a wild burn.

He drank at her nipple. His tongue swirled around her areole, lighting her flesh on fire. Firm masculine hands trailed along her sides to caress the curves of her hips. Sweet sucking sounds drifted through the air. The sensual movements of his tongue laved her nipple igniting shards of lust deep inside her pussy.

Heated moisture of her arousal pooled into her swimsuit panties.

Drawing away from her swollen nipple, he attached his moist eager mouth to the other quivering bud. He sucked with so much enthusiasm Jade couldn't stop herself from throwing her head back and moaning her pleasure.

The man was good. Very good.

She could smell the scent of her arousal drifting up from between her legs and mingling with the salty scent of sea air. It was an aroma that blended deliciously together.

She wondered what he was thinking as he smelled her arousal. Wondered how far he wanted to go. Wondered how far she would allow him to go.

Desire raged at the idea she wanted him to go all the way.

A one-night stand.

She could free herself in his arms tonight. She could get him to do things to her that she'd always wanted done.

And she'd never have to see him again. She'd never have to be embarrassed.

She eyed the bowl of vegetables with longing, her anticipation mounting.

With a pop, he let go of her nipple and buried his face in the valley between her breasts.

His breath came hard and fast.

Aroused.

Shaky.

Like hers.

"Don't stop," she found herself whispering.

She wanted more from him.

Wanted him to unleash her carnal side.

God! Her sisters had been right. She needed a good stiff fucking. And she needed it bad.

His hands slid away from her hips.

A moment later burning fingers curled over her knees.

"Open." His word was muffled and he kissed her valley.

She hesitated.

Fantasies were fantasies. This man was real. Could she open her legs to a complete stranger?

"Open wide, Jade," he prodded.

This time he spoke with a sweet firmness that sent a tingle of fear skittering up her spine. What would he do to her if she protested? Would he tie her down? Would he take her against her will?

Her cunt clenched wonderfully at those thoughts.

She was so tempted to find out. So tempted to live dangerously.

But what if she denied him and he stopped doing what he was doing?

She didn't want him to stop. She'd never had a man touch her with such heat in his hands.

He made her feel like a woman.

Heart beating rapidly against her chest she opened her legs wide to him.

He pulled his head away from her breasts. Within a split second, he sank onto his knees in front of her.

His gaze scorched her pussy as he stared between her legs. His hot look made her pulse race.

Oh God!

"You're soaked," his voice sounded strangled.

"Happens when a man kisses me," she replied unsure if she was saying the right thing.

His eyes narrowed at her words. A brief flash of anger zipped through his eyes.

Did she detect a hint of jealousy? It made her tremble with excitement.

"I bet many men have kissed you but not where I'm going to."

His voice had lost the softness. His gaze had a determined hard edge to it. That tingle of fear slithered into her again. This time she got the feeling if she protested he wouldn't stop.

Her thoughts spun.

This was happening way too fast.

But there was no denying the heat searing her pussy. No denying she wanted him between her legs anyway she could get him.

Long masculine fingers slid along the curve of her generous hips, curling beneath her thong bottom. As he drew the thin material down over her hips, she eagerly lifted her ass allowing him to pull the thong off.

"Touch your breasts," he whispered.

His eyes were intent, his voice a strong command.

Feeling a bit clumsy and suddenly shy, she cupped her hands over her breasts and began to massage herself the way she did when she masturbated.

"Watch me while you do it, Jade."

A scorching quiver of excitement rocked her. She did what he asked and kept her eyes drawn to his face.

"Pinch your nipples. Like the way I did to you earlier. Nice and hard. I want to see the pain flash in your eyes."

She did as he asked loving the fierce way he watched her every move.

Plucking her hard buds until her nipples ached, she grimaced at the pleasure-pain.

His blue eyes sparkled with approval when she finally cried out.

"That's it, Jade. Keep doing it while I tend to other business."

Before she could comprehend his meaning, his head lowered to the area between her legs.

Oh God! She couldn't believe this was happening. A man was actually going down on her!

The heat of his hands seeped into her flesh as he clasped her hips tighter. His face burrowed between her legs and a hot whisper of his breath teased her clit. The heated warmth of his breath was fantastic and the sight of a man's head between her legs was enough to almost make her climax on the spot.

His mouth covered her entire clit making her jolt against him. Her fingers, momentarily having forgotten her breasts, began a fast rub kneading her flesh.

His hot tongue split her plump lips apart and flitted around her engorged pleasure nub in tiny circles, not quite touching it but stoking the sensations, building a hungry sexual tension that made her moan out loud.

Her body throbbed. Her cunt pulsed. Her nipples poked hard against her hands.

Jade could feel the magnificent quivering of an oncoming climax and she forced herself not to go over the edge.

She wanted to savor his gift to her. Wanted to make it last as long as possible.

A hot tongue slid into her drenched channel, stretching her.

She could feel the heated length of his tongue burrowing into her straining cunt like a stick of molten steel.

Her legs trembled. Her bad hip ached but it was a good ache.

Her thighs tightened around his head and she squeezed.

Hard.

His tongue found her G-spot, hitting the sensitive area making her body shudder.

A wonderful euphoric haze seeped against her senses.

Jade gasped.

The orgasm was gaining momentum.

Her swollen breasts jiggled beneath her warm hands. Her nipples ached and throbbed as she continued to pinch herself keeping the pain to a wild soreness. The gratifying pain shot lightning arrows between her legs adding pleasure there.

His tongue came out of her vagina and he vigorously lapped against her sensitive love button. Sucking sounds sang through the cool ocean air.

Blood roared in her ears and she wiggled against his torturous movements bringing herself close to release.

God help her but having a man's head between her legs, the tension of a tongue spearing her cunt, the frantic touch of a man's lips suckling her labia was better than any fantasy she could have dreamed.

He sucked her clit harder obviously trying to push her over the edge.

Her breathing became labored.

She continued to plump her aching nipples, knead her puffy breasts, held her breath.

His tongue slid inside her again and impaled her.

The orgasm hit hard and it hit with a vengeance.

She cried out at the onslaught. Heard him purr from somewhere deep in his chest as his tongue speared in and out of her hot channel lapping her of her cream.

Throwing her head back, she gritted her teeth allowing the scorching spasms to wash around her.

Breathing through her clenched teeth, she let go of her breasts blindly grabbing onto his massive shoulders grinding her hips against him.

Sharp white-hot fragments of pleasure scorched her body keeping her gasping for air, keeping her hips slamming into his face as her inner muscles clutched frantically at his tongue.

The orgasm rocked her. Tortured her. Relieved her.

In the end, she slumped against the chair, perspiration dotting her flaming skin.

Her breasts felt swollen. Her cunt pulsed with tiny aftereffect spasms.

Her eyes stayed closed.

Her breaths came harsh and shallow.

He picked her up in his strong arms.

She didn't care where he was taking her. All she wanted was to bask in her sexual exhaustion.

Cool vinyl pressed against her back. Soft material of a beach towel drifted over her warm body.

"That was just the appetizer. I'll be back soon," he promised.

Oh God!

She nodded. At least she thought she nodded.

Then she found herself drifting away into blissful nothingness.

Chapter Five

He'd done it! He'd actually seduced her!

It had been so easy. Of course, it helped to be sexually attracted to her.

And now as he stood at the railing of her yacht looking out at the pristine mirror-like ocean, his legs trembled and his body screamed with sexual tension.

Reaching down he unzipped his jeans, slid open his briefs and allowed his sore cock to spring free. The entire length burst forward, angry and raw, long and thick, heavy and hurting.

Damn, his cock had never ached so badly. Had never throbbed so much that he swore his balls would burst.

Reaching down he tenderly stroked his erection and felt the veins throb beneath his fingertips.

Unfortunately, his gentle stroking didn't ease him at all. It just aroused him more.

Gritting his teeth in frustration he let go of his hard shaft and curled his hands around the metal railing allowing the cool ocean air to wash against his flaming shaft.

He knew he could bring himself relief in a mere few seconds. That's how primed and ready he was. He'd done it numerous times in the recent past but now he had Jade.

Beautiful.

Soft.

Sexy Jade.

If he went to her now, with this fiery need to fuck her with uncontrollable thrusts, he would most likely hurt her with his size.

Her channel was tight. Maybe too tight.

That's why he'd tongue-fucked her first. So he could explore her silky wetness to see if he'd fit. He'd savored the way her vaginal muscles had frantically gripped him.

His mind had screamed for him to pull out his burning cock and ram into her slit. But the fear of hurting her had stopped him.

Besides, her sweet cream had been intoxicating as he sipped from her cunt. The velvety flesh of her inner thighs had pressed against his head keeping him a willing captive between her luscious legs.

He smiled as he remembered the events leading up to his tongue-fucking Jade.

When he'd finally gathered the nerve to come out of the hold, he'd found her fast asleep on the lounge chair, a very pretty smile curving her lips.

Raking over her fully exposed plump breasts, his mouth had watered at the cherry sized nipples. Heated blood had rushed straight into his shaft, hardening his flesh until it seared like a long tight piece of molten steel making him cry out from the pleasurable sensations.

At the sound of his voice she'd moved in her sleep, her legs widening as if she knew he was there standing over her. As if she'd wanted him to do her while she slept.

His blood had pumped feverishly through his entire body as he'd once again spotted the wetness dotting the thong.

He'd wanted to rip the tiny garment off her right then and there while she'd slept. Had wanted to push his heavy cock into her soaked pussy and then wake her so she'd find out she'd just been impaled.

He wanted to fuck her brains out.

But first, he wanted to romance her. Wine and dine her and not just have the wild sex she'd so liberally filled out in the Kidnap Fantasies questionnaire.

Instead of following his cravings, he'd draped the protection of the beach towel over her body and headed into the yacht's pilothouse.

He'd found the key on a hook beneath the console exactly where he'd been told it would be. He'd jammed the key into the ignition and looked out the crystal-clear windows down onto the gleaming cherry wood main deck where she lay stretched out on the chaise.

He'd twisted the key and the engines had roared to life.

She hadn't moved.

Pushing the throttle forward, he'd slowly eased the yacht out of the marina and headed for open water.

She still hadn't budged.

She was sleeping through her own kidnapping!

He'd almost laughed out loud at that thought.

Now he had himself a sexual captive and free rein of a delicious-looking sex-starved woman with the ocean as their playground.

He should be enjoying himself.

Yet, instead of telling her he'd just kidnapped her and was going to make all her fantasies come true, he'd chickened out.

Instead, he'd cooked her dinner and tongue-fucked her.

Shit!

He should tell her the real reason he was here. Tell her about Kidnap Fantasies. Tell her he'd come here because of the questionnaire he'd been given.

Peering over his shoulder, Caydon gazed at Jade who lay where he'd left her on the lounge, her luscious body hidden beneath a beach towel.

Apparently, she'd awakened from her sexual stupor.

Her eyes were open as she stared into the now dark sky. Beneath the beach towel, he could tell her knees were lifted and he wondered if she was touching herself, toying with that plump clit, squeezing her puffy labia, sliding her fingers into her tight channel.

A blade of lust clenched his rock-hard balls and cock as he watched her. The blade twisted beautifully, making him want to show her exactly what she did to him.

From the moment he'd seen her picture and read her autobiography, he knew Jade was special.

A giving, trusting person.

Innocent in sex.

According to quick research through Kidnap Fantasies, she'd been intimate with one man. Her ski coach who'd managed to become her fiancé.

Caydon intended to amend that situation. He planned to show her just how special she was but he hadn't missed the fear burst in her eyes a split second before he'd kissed her. The fear of getting hurt—fear of trusting him.

Then again, it would be natural for her to be afraid of him. He was a stranger, a man who'd made her dinner and taken her delicious nipples and her hot quivering cunt into his mouth for desert.

And he'd barely gotten started.

His heart crashed in his ears as he quietly approached her.

Her lush naked body looked relaxed in the moon glow. Her plump breasts moved up and down in a steady rhythm as she breathed. He could tell she was fingering herself, toying with her plump little clit. Maybe wanting another mouth-induced orgasm.

He should tell her right now about Kidnap Fantasies. That he had her questionnaire.

And when he did tell her?

Would she still enjoy the pleasures he'd bring to her? Or would she insist she wasn't interested in any more sex with him?

Without warning her hand flew out from beneath the beach towel giving him a cock-clenching view of her generous breast and hardened nipple as she pointed to the sky.

"Falling star!" she cried out. "Make a wish!"

It only took him a split second to see the silver streak flash in the darkness and he quickly made his wish. The star disintegrated and Jade grew quiet again.

He noted the wistful smile playing on her sensually shaped lips. Lips meant for kissing. Lips meant for sucking cock.

His shaft tightened making him groan.

His breathing sounded harsh and fast in the semi-darkness.

He saw her body tense ever so slightly as he drew closer. She'd heard him, but she didn't look his way. Didn't see his angry cock sticking out of his pants wanting her so bad it trembled in anticipation of sinking into her.

"Let me look at your body, Jade," he whispered.

He saw her throat move as she swallowed, watched her pull the beach towel off her body and let it drop to the floor.

Her nipples were still peaked, aroused. Her breasts swollen and full.

"Touch yourself, Jade. I want to watch."

A hand slid up her slightly rounded belly to her breast. Her fingers tweaked at her nipple. Her other hand slid between her legs moving slowly as she stroked her clit.

"What did you wish for?" he asked.

"I can't tell you."

"Don't tell me you believe in that silly old wives' tale where if you tell someone your wish it won't come true, do you?"

She nodded. "You can tell me your wish if you want but I still won't tell you mine...unless it comes true."

"You sound doubtful it will."

She frowned and his heart tightened with sadness.

"My grandmother always said wishing upon a star would bring magic into my life. I always believed what she said was true. When I first bought this boat a couple of years back I used to sit out here in the dark and make lots of wishes but now I don't make them anymore."

"You just did. What's changed?"

She shrugged her bare shoulders and he noticed the wetness on her fingers as she slid her hand away from between her legs.

"Don't stop touching yourself."

Her eyes widened with shyness at his remark yet her hand slid between her legs again and he could see her fingering her pleasure nub.

"The scars don't bother you?" she whispered.

He hadn't really noticed them but now that she mentioned it he could see several long lines along her thigh and hip areas. Obviously, she was self-conscious about them.

"Why? Should they bother me?"

"They're ugly. I thought about plastic surgery but I really don't want any more surgeries for awhile."

"Your scars are a part of you, Jade. At least they are for now. And I like everything I see about you."

"And so far I like everything about you, too," she said timidly.

"Look at me, Jade," he instructed. It was time to introduce her to another one of her fantasies.

Her head swung around to look at him and she blinked in surprise. The surprise quickly turned to shock, which quickly followed by fear when she discovered the mushroom-shaped head of his long, thick ten-inch cock a foot away from her mouth.

"You don't have to if you don't want to." His voice sounded strangled and hopeful.

"I…do want to. Very much."

He noticed the tremble in her voice. Saw a pretty pink blush breeze across her cheeks. The fear in her eyes was gone, replaced by interest.

And desire.

Suddenly he felt nervous. Nervous at the things he'd planned for her, things that when she'd written them on paper might sound better to her than when she actually experienced it.

His anxiety quickly disappeared when she parted her sensually shaped lips. Lips still red and swollen from their earlier kiss.

With both hands, he held onto the base of his cock and could barely push the tip of his bulging flesh into her eager mouth before her lips clamped around his flesh.

Heated moisture sizzled around his cock and shot down his shaft straight into his tight balls.

His knees weakened at the impact and he almost exploded right then and there.

Gritting his teeth he stifled a groan and held his ground.

Damn! Her mouth felt so good.

So tight.

So velvety hot.

His entire body stiffened as the hot tip of her tongue poked tenderly at the slit in his cock-head.

Her hands began to move away from their respective places on her body but he didn't want that.

"No, Jade. I want you to keep touching yourself."

He wanted her to stay aroused while she tended to him. Wanted her wet and ready for him.

She did as he instructed, her fingers toying with her plump nipples, her other hand remaining between her velvety legs, moving slowly back and forth as she massaged her clit. Her breasts looked big and hard beneath the moonlight, her chest heaving with her heavy excited breaths.

With not even a quarter of his engorged cock disappearing between her luscious lips, her brown hair all tangled and messed up, eyes bright with lust, she looked like a sweet sexy angel.

His erection throbbed madly at the sight.

"Suck me, Jade. Suck me hard."

Her heated lips squeezed his cock as if it were in a vise and she began a slow caress around his engorged flesh, her hot little tongue laving his aching head making his balls constrict painfully.

A razor blade of pleasure zipped up his shaft making his breath catch.

He thrust his hips forward, pushing himself deeper into her mouth, wanting more of this agonizing joy.

She whimpered as his cock hit the back of her throat.

He withdrew slightly and curled his hand around his cock making sure not to go beyond that point.

The last thing he wanted to do was hurt her when he lost control.

Velvety cheeks slid against his hard rod. Sucking sounds split the air.

The pressure of her moist mouth sucking on his rigid flesh overwhelmed him, made him desperate for release. When her tongue began a mad circling around the head of his cock, he couldn't stop the groan of pleasure.

She whimpered in answer.

It was a beautiful sound that made his heart leap with warmth.

Pleasure rushed along his shaft. His hand clenched tighter around the base of his cock as he watched her continue to toy with her breast, rolling her nipple between her fingers until he saw the beautiful flash of pain in her eyes.

Her other hand moved quicker between her legs as she rubbed her clit. He could hear the slurping sounds of her fingers sliding in and out of her cunt.

Heat consumed his flesh as his orgasm built.

Closing his eyes, he remembered how she tasted when he'd taken her orally. Her hot, pulsing pleasure button had been stiff in his mouth. Her cum tasting sweet and innocent. Her throaty cries had sifted through the air warming his heart.

Now it was his turn to cry out as her mouth worked its wondrous magic.

Her lips gave his cock a hard squeeze, and Caydon's shaft rippled in ecstasy making him inhale sharply.

His heart thundered in his ears. His body screamed for relief. His self-control washed away in the lusty sensations.

The orgasm took over.

He groaned at the onslaught of pleasure.

"I'm coming!" he cried out as lusty lightning blades shimmered along his shaft and slammed into his heavy scrotum.

His balls burst.

Spurt after spurt he shot his sperm down her throat. Her lips tightened around his swollen cock sealing him as if she wanted to make sure he wouldn't withdraw or that she didn't miss a drop.

She sucked harder. The vibrations racing through his cock were unbelievable.

He cried out as she continued to milk him with her mouth.

Finally, when his cock went somewhat limp he withdrew and stared down at her.

She was a beautiful creature.

Eyes sparkled with passion. Her heart-shaped face was flushed, her parted lips swollen.

His body shuddered at the erotic sight.

Without a doubt, he knew what he wanted to do next.

* * * * *

"You give head beautifully."

"Thank you," Jade whispered.

Her face flamed in the darkness as he nestled onto the chaise beside her.

What had just happened between them was making her thoughts wobble all over the place and her body yearn for more sex. Taking a strange man's powerful cock into her mouth had always been one of her fantasies. She'd even wanted to take Beau orally but he'd pushed her away from him as if her wanting to suckle his cock was a disgusting act. She'd never tried again.

But the instant she'd spotted Caydon's large cock hovering like a stiff pole in front of her face, the intricate weave of angry veins pulsing along a thick shaft begging for relief she'd wanted him so bad she would have begged him to allow her to take him into her mouth.

She'd felt surprise that she hadn't noticed him standing so close with his erection sticking out of his pants pleading for her attention. Fear had quickly followed at the sight of his shaft. Fear that maybe he wouldn't enjoy what she wanted to do to his cock. But that had quickly vanished, followed by an intense need to have him in her mouth.

Gosh!

He'd felt awesome. His blistering heated length had sunk deep into her, banging against her tonsils making her gag and she'd panicked.

When he'd retreated and allowed her full rein she'd relaxed.

Allowing her lips to wrap around his hard velvety cock, she tightened her hold on him. Her tongue had laved and explored the mushroom-shaped head.

She'd tasted the salty pre-cum from his slit.

Had enjoyed it. Had wanted more.

And now her lips felt bruised, and swollen and oh so ready to suck him off again.

But what she wanted more was him driving his succulent cock deep into her wet pussy.

"You are beautiful woman, Jade. I can't get enough of looking at you." He nuzzled her earlobe with his firm lips sending sweet shivers racing down her spine.

"Despite my cane, you mean?" She couldn't keep the self-pity out of her voice. Couldn't stop herself from wanting him to reassure her that he truly did find her desirable as a woman.

"It gives you a damsel in distress quality. A quality I find enticing. It makes me want to protect you. Like I'm your knight in shining armor. Like you're vulnerable, totally at my mercy writhing beneath me as I fuck you long and hard."

Her breath caught at his seductive voice.

As he brushed his lips along her neck, she felt the hard outline of his fierce cock push against her naked hip.

Sweet heavens! The man was as hard as a rock already.

"You're such a sexy woman. I want you again."

She gasped in disappointment as he moved off the bench. The disappointment didn't last long as his warm hands slipped underneath her, one beneath her knees, the other under her waist.

Scooping her into his arms, he stood. His body felt solid and deliciously feverish against her flesh as he began to walk.

"Where...where are we going?"

He flicked his lusty gaze down at her. "To your bedroom."

Heated blood coursed through her veins as he held her tightly in his arms. His hard chest scraped against her left breast sparking renewed arousal.

When he stepped into the dark kitchen, she wondered how he could see anything in the unfamiliar surroundings. She couldn't stop herself from splaying her hands across the tight band of chest muscles, curling her fingers in the light mat of hair and holding tight just in case he fell over a chair or something.

Beneath her hands, his heart thumped just as wildly as hers.

As he kicked the kitchen door closed, a breeze caught a tangle of his hair blowing it over his forehead giving him a terribly sexy appeal she just couldn't resist. Lifting her head, she kissed him full on the mouth.

She tasted her cum on his lips. She'd never tasted it before. It was rather sweet and spicy, an interesting flavor.

He kissed her back eagerly, an untamed promise of delicious things to come. His tongue prodded deep into her cavern making her world tilt with pleasure.

She hadn't even realized they were in her bedroom until she felt cool sheets beneath her backside as he deposited her on her bed.

"Where's your pantyhose?" he whispered when he broke the kiss.

"My pantyhose?"

"Where do you keep them?"

"Why?"

"So I can tie you down and fuck you senseless."

Oh, my gosh!

Being tied down while a man made love to her had always been one of her fantasies and now that she was coming face to face with it, she hesitated.

She didn't even know this guy!

They'd only done oral sex on each other and now he was asking her to trust him by having him tie her down? To her surprise, the idea of a stranger taking her in such an intimate trusting way just about made her orgasm on the spot.

She couldn't stop the giggle from escaping her lips at the insanity of it.

Of wanting this man to fuck her for as long and as hard as he wanted while she lay on the bed totally helpless to stop him.

Besides, she shouldn't be afraid, he must have had cleared security. He was a handyman. A ship mechanic. People had sent him to her yacht. They knew he was here. He wouldn't try to would harm her.

"If you rather I don't..." his eyes sparkled down at her with a hope she couldn't resist.

"Top left drawer. And hurry!"

He hurried and found what he needed.

The sexy way his muscles played across his big chest and arms as he tied her wrists ignited a wild fire deep inside her woman's core.

Within a minute, he had her arms tied to her bedposts. He left her legs free.

Kissing her neck, his lips left a trail of wet fire as he teasingly moved over the swells of her breasts, along the rounded curve of her belly, circling her quivering clit like a vulture until she writhed helplessly on the bed.

When he stood, he flicked on a nearby light switch bathing them both with a warm buttery glow.

Jade's heart crashed against her chest like a jackhammer as he dropped his pants and climbed out of his underwear.

He straightened and Jade gulped at his awesome erection.

Outside in the moonlit darkness when she'd taken him orally she'd seen what a lovely size of a cock he possessed, but now here in her cozy bedroom with the pine paneled walls and dainty white curtains flowing behind him she could see his magnificent pulsing size was a heck of a lot bigger than she'd thought.

The mushroom-shaped head looked red and fierce.

Ready to impale her.

Her pussy quivered in anticipation.

Have mercy but the man was extremely well hung.

Large cock.

Nice manners.

Good-looking.

Sexy.

Everything she'd dreamed about her man being.

A nice fluttering feeling zipped through her lower belly. Her face flushed at the thought that this man could be *the* one.

"You're blushing," he smiled.

"I've never…never seen such a big cock before," she said truthfully.

"Before long I'll have your whole body blushing, Jade. Spread your legs for me."

She swallowed her excitement and did as he instructed.

This time it was his turn to exhale softly.

"Your clit is beautiful and puffy. Your cunt, soaking wet. Just the way I like it. Just the way I need you. You did good, keeping yourself aroused, Jade. You're almost ready for me. But first, I have to prepare you. I'll be back in a minute."

Before she could ask him where he was going, he'd vanished.

A couple of minutes later, he returned holding the bowl of raw vegetables in his hand.

"I saw the way you looked at them during dinner. It gave me some delicious ideas."

"What kind of ideas?" she could barely speak from all the excitement washing over her senses.

He grinned wickedly. "You'll see."

Instincts told her this man was going to do something to her with those vegetables.

Something wicked.

God help her she wanted him to do all sorts of things to her body.

Her senses exploded when he pulled a long thick carrot from the bowl.

Long male fingers stroked the orange object in the same tender way he'd done to it earlier after dinner. The carrot was about half the width of Caydon's cock and about half as long.

"Vegetables are called the poor man's sex toys, Jade. We'll have to use these until I can get us some proper ones."

Poor man's sex toys? Until he can get proper toys?

Exactly how long did he plan on staying? How long did he plan on having her tied up here?

The questions sat at the tip of her tongue but she didn't dare ask. To tell the truth she didn't want to know when he planned on leaving her. For now, she just wanted to pretend this man was hers, forever.

"Time to see how much you can take, Jade."

"I can take whatever you dish out, Minnelli," she threw back.

He inhaled sharply at her trembling words. His eyes darkened in the same way they'd done when he'd instructed her to pinch and pull at her nipples until the pleasure-pain had become so unbearable she'd cried out.

"We'll see how much you can take, Jade. Spread your legs wider for me, honey. I'm going to give you something you won't soon forget."

Moisture dripped from her pussy at the husky promise in his voice. The scorching look in his eyes turned her body into a slab of heat and her cunt into a quivering mess. Even her breasts reacted to his intense gaze by tightening, swelling, becoming hard and eager to be caressed.

He leaned over her, the warm head of his rigid cock poked deliciously into her belly button as he grabbed a nearby pillow. Fluffing it up he stuffed it beneath her hips, which allowed him to raise her up higher exposing her fully to him.

"There, that's much more comfortable. This will give me the perfect angle to enter you."

Jade swallowed a whimper of arousal.

She could barely breathe as she watched him guide the big, thick carrot between her legs.

When she felt the smooth rounded end of the vegetable rubbing gently at her sensitive pleasure nub, she sucked in a heated breath.

More of her aroused juices escaped her cunt and she could smell her sex permeate the air.

"I'll just get you back into the mood," he whispered.

"I'm already in the mood."

"Vegetables turn you on, do they?"

"Along with the man holding them," she admitted.

"I'm glad you approve of my abilities to arouse."

"That's an understatement," she breathed. "You're like magic when you touch me."

The sensual way the head of the carrot stroked her quivering clit was making Jade's body come alive with delicious sensations.

Her legs fell further apart.

Her cunt hummed. Her heart sang at the intense way he was looking at the area between her legs, the concentration twisting his lips while he worked her clitoris.

"Magical fingers can earn a man a decent living. A magical cock can earn a man a woman's love for life."

Jade swallowed at the sound of his husky voice.

Some lucky woman would have this gorgeous man and his throbbing cock one day. Oh! How she hoped what she'd wished on that falling star tonight would come true.

It had been a silly wish.

A wish about a man she knew nothing about.

But what he'd done to her and was doing was a good start.

She watched with wonder as his eyes slowly glazed. She felt her velvety folds of her labia part and he slid the thick item into her channel. Her vaginal muscles clenched tightly around the foreign object and she couldn't help but cry out at the delicious tremors as it stretched her sex hole.

"You're nice and tight, Jade. Tight and so deliciously wet."

Her hips moved in little thrusts and her body trembled as he slid the carrot in and out between the swollen tissues of her heated cunt.

"Harder?" he asked as she clenched her teeth and fought for release.

She nodded, totally transfixed by the wonderful way the muscles in his arms rippled as he pulled back and thrust the carrot into her pussy nice and hard this time. It surged deep into her, but not filling her to completion.

Giggling, she suddenly realized the carrot was about the same size as her ex, Beau.

Caydon grinned with curiosity. "What's so funny?"

"It's too small."

"Too small, huh? Well, we'll have to take care of that problem, won't we?"

Pulling the carrot back, it popped out with a big slurpy sound. Placing it into the bowl, he took out the slender English style cucumber and stroked it the same sensual way he'd done to the carrot.

My goodness! The cucumber looked almost twice as long as the carrot and twice as thick. But still not as big as Caydon's fierce-looking cock.

She held her breath as he directed the green item between her legs. It felt cool as he nudged it inside.

Slurpy sounds split the air as her hungry cunt enveloped the vegetable stretching her starving vagina wonderfully.

He sank it into her slowly, cautiously.

At the same time, his finger toyed with her sensitive clit igniting a flame.

She closed her eyes and moaned at the pleasurable sensations. He began in slow easy strokes, fucking into her eager pussy, dragging the vegetable out then probing deeper with each entry.

Pulling out the cucumber again he impaled her cunt with one delicious thrust that threw her fevered body right to the edge of a climax. Instinctively she arched her hips higher wanting a deeper penetration but groaned in frustration when he whispered, "I'm in all the way to the hilt, sweetie."

"You're a tease, Minnelli," she gasped trying hard to control her breathing.

She sobbed and tried hard not to yell and scream and demand him to satisfy her, this instant.

"So, you're looking for some heavier action, are you?"

"I want your cock, Caydon."

"You're that confident I'll fit, are you?" he breathed.

Her eyes snapped open and she read the uncertainty on his face.

Jade swallowed and suddenly realized why he was playing this game with the vegetables. He wanted to make sure he would fit her.

"I need a big man to fill the ache deep inside me. I've always craved one," she said truthfully.

She heard him groan in response yet the uncertainty remained in his gaze.

"I don't want to hurt you, Jade."

Frustration clawed at her cunt and she could feel her patience wane.

"I want you to fuck me, as hard as you can. I want to feel you deep inside me. I need it. I need you so bad."

Excitement exploded in his eyes. Her nipples responded to his hungry look.

Perspiration sheened his forehead, oiled his lovely muscular chest.

"I'm going to make love to you like you've never been made love to before, Jade Hart."

Shivering with anticipation she watched him stalk to the end of the bed, watched him saunter as if he were an animal in heat ready to claim his mate. Her blood pumped furiously through her veins in anticipation of being impaled with his rock-hard cock. Her breaths were heavy and labored, pushing her swollen breasts high. Her nipples felt puffy and stiff. Ready to be claimed by his masculine chest.

She widened her legs further and angled her hips upward giving him a great view of what awaited him.

Masculine muscles burst in his biceps as with hands and knees he climbed onto the bed between her legs.

Jade's heart crashed furiously against her chest as he came over her like a god. His naked body oiled by perspiration. His eyes glazed with lust. His wonderful cock hung like a molten piece of steel and to her delight it was aimed straight at her cunt. In the shadows of his pubic hair beneath his engorged cock she saw his balls nestled heavy and full, ready to burst.

Hot arms scalded against the sensitive side curves of her breasts, his hands came down tangling in the sheets beside her and his body descended upon hers with the tenderness of a soft downy blanket.

Powerful masculine legs aligned themselves on top of hers, his feet cradled side by side with hers.

She inhaled sharply as his huge cock sliced apart her drenched labia lips and he poised his heavy swollen flesh at the door of her wet pussy.

"You sure you want this? Do you want me to make love to you?" His breath brushed across her bangs and caressed her face.

Jade hesitated.

God! How could she be sure about anything?

It was all happening too fast.

Mere days ago she'd filled out a Kidnap Fantasies questionnaire asking for a well-hung man.

The biggest cock in stock, she'd written.

And she'd never mailed the questionnaire in.

Yet, here was exactly what she'd ordered.

A thick penis. So hard looking, so purple with arousal that she could barely contain the frustration at wanting him to slam into her over and over again.

And yet, he was so big.

Bigger than anything she'd created in her fantasies.

So wonderfully, blessedly huge.

Her cunt quivered with a need so immense she couldn't stop herself from whimpering every time she looked at his piece of raw pulsing flesh.

Oh yes! She wanted his shaft to satisfy that throbbing ache deep inside her womb.

But would his size hurt her?

She was willing to take that chance.

"I'm sure," she could barely speak now. Her body felt so tight, so ready for him she could just scream.

Caydon's nostrils flared in arousal. His eyes smoldered a deep lusty blue.

"You're so beautiful, sweetie. So damn beautiful. If only I'd known sooner…"

Before she had a chance to ask what he meant he rolled a bit to the side and using one arm to keep himself from coming fully down on top of her he lifted his other hand off the bed and it slipped between them settling his hot palm onto her stomach.

Such a huge palm.

A very gentle palm that slid warmly over her slightly rounded abdomen, through the tangle of the crisp curls covering her mons. She cried out her pleasure the instant he touched her juicy love button where he began to work his magic with his fingers.

While he massaged her shuddering clit, encouraging those wonderful sensations out of her, he sank his cock into her.

Slowly. Ever so agonizingly slow.

His large size pushed against her snug passage.

Vaginal muscles spasmed, contracted, gripped him.

He groaned.

It was a guttural sound as if he were in pain. But it was a beautiful sound too and it sent shivers up and down her arms.

"What did you wish for on that star?" he said hotly as his heat-seeking cock split her cunt wide open.

"What?" Jade could barely keep her eyes open. Could barely breathe. Could barely stem the quickly rising orgasm as his finger continued to slide over her sensitized clitoris.

"The falling star," he ground out between clenched teeth. "What did you wish for?"

"I'm...not...telling."

She found herself sinking into the pleasure taking hold of her cunt. Could feel her vaginal muscles quiver with excitement as he drove deeper into her. He stretched her like she'd never been stretched before. Expanded her vagina so much she wasn't sure she could take all of him in.

"Is this what you wished for? To get fucked by me?"

She tossed her head back and forth suddenly unable to speak.

"What does that mean? No? You didn't wish for me to fuck you? Or no, you aren't going to tell me?"

God! Why was he questioning her like this?

"No... I didn't wish for...this..." she groaned as his cock slid against sensitive spots. "It...sure comes...a close...second."

He grinned and shifted his hips slightly to allow for a deeper penetration.

Jade gasped at the sparkle of pleasure-pain zipping deep inside her channel.

He pushed his steely shaft deeper.

"Tell me your wish," he whispered as his lips sipped on the bottom curves of her mouth.

"Uh…uh not until it…comes true."

"Ah, there's confidence in that statement. Does it have something to do with me?"

A fantastic burst of pleasure zipped up her vagina as he pressed harder on her pleasure nub.

"Oh God!" she gasped and pulled frantically at her pantyhose restraints wanting desperately to curl her arms around his neck and pull him into a kiss.

He chuckled against her mouth.

"I love seeing you like this, sweetie. Love feeling the way your hips arch into me, the way your hot channel feels as its velvety sides grabs a hold of me and sucks me in. I want to fuck you so hard that you won't be able to escape me because you'll be too exhausted from all those orgasms I'm going to give you."

Oh God!

His mouth came down upon hers with such a mighty passion it took the breath clean out of her lungs.

His lips felt strong, powerful. His five o'clock shadow brushed erotically against her flesh. He kissed her so slowly and so deeply, she felt disoriented. If anyone would have asked her to give them her name at this point she wouldn't have been able to tell them. As for the heavenly sensations claiming her body… Whatever was happening, she loved it.

She barely realized he'd withdrawn his cock until she heard a suctioning sound as he left her and felt his cock reenter her soaked pussy in one smooth hard thrust.

As he buried his hot length deep inside her, Jade's body and mind came apart in the fiercest, wildest climax she'd ever experienced in her life.

Squeezing her eyes shut against the rich assault, she sunk into the pleasure.

He gave her exactly what she'd asked for.

Sliding his thick cock in and out of her in long, deep, torturous strokes he rode her hard, impaled her furiously.

Her body screamed with the arousal she'd always knew must exist but she'd never experienced with Beau.

Perspiration broke out on her flushed skin.

The smell of their sex swung past her nostrils intensifying her lust.

His primal mouth bruised hers with passion. His chest hairs sparked a blaze in her nipples. His rock-hard chest flattened her swollen breasts and his sexy throaty grunts encouraged Jade to meet his every thrust with a frantic enthusiasm of her own.

She found herself wrapping her legs around his hips, the soles of her feet digging into his firm ass cheeks allowing for an even deeper penetration.

His tongue plunged into her mouth over and over matching the strong confident thrusts of his cock as he impaled her again and again until they were moaning and gasping with pleasure.

He pumped hard, bringing her one wondrous release after another. Then he filled her cunt with his hot cum. Thick jets of heat spewed into her body. His cream claiming her vagina and branding her body with his sperm.

Afterwards, when he was finished, he withdrew his cock.

She could feel him moving his chest off hers and felt the restraints fall away from her wrists.

But she couldn't budge.

Sweet exhaustion claimed her limbs. Her body felt too weak from the fantastic fucking and all those exploding orgasms.

And she was even too tired to open her eyes.

She felt his semi-hard cock impale her again and she couldn't help but groan at the raw pleasure-pain sifting along her channel as he buried his thick length right to the hilt.

Instinctively she knew he was finished with her for the night. Knew that he wanted to lie this way with his body on top of hers and his thick gorgeous cock cradled safely inside her wet cunt.

His hard chest came down on her again, warming her breasts.

He leaned his bristly cheek against her damp one. She sighed contentedly and nuzzled against him.

Hot cum-scented breath flowed over her in delicious waves.

Before she fell asleep, she heard him whisper softly, "Tomorrow we'll have ourselves another fuck-fest you'll never forget."

Chapter Six

Christmas Eve morning…

Déjà vu, Jade thought as she awoke to the delicious scent of coffee sifting through her tiny bedroom.

Yesterday he'd made her dinner. Today, would it be breakfast?

Gosh, what had she done to get so lucky?

Her happiness however was short-lived.

Why was he being nice to her? Was he wheedling his way into her graces because she had money? Was Caydon like her ex?

No, please God, don't let him just be using me.

Okay, so maybe he might be using her. But she was using him too.

For great sex.

Using him to fulfill some of her wildest fantasies and she didn't even have to tell him what they were.

He already knew what she wanted.

He was perfect.

Too perfect.

Again a niggle of uneasiness zipped up her spine. A man like Caydon could have any woman he wanted. Why pick her?

She was a virtual cripple. A millionaire invalid.

Jade closed her eyes and bit the curve of her lower lip. It felt bruised and sensitive from his fierce kisses.

Kisses she'd thoroughly enjoyed.

Kisses she wouldn't mind experiencing for the rest of her life.

Stupid girl. You're getting yourself all tied up in knots over nothing! He didn't say he wanted to marry you. He didn't even say he was staying beyond today.

Besides tomorrow was Christmas.

Surely he had some family waiting for him somewhere.

A mother. Father.

Brothers? Sisters?

And he'd already said he wasn't married or had a girlfriend.

Besides, it was just casual hot sex between them. Something that occurred naturally between a hot-blooded gorgeous American male and a semi-attractive woman who sunbathed partially nude.

She shouldn't even be worried about him being after her money. She hadn't even spent a red cent on the man. And he hadn't asked her to.

She was reading way too much into this. Unfortunately since Beau dumped her she'd been jumping to conclusions about every single guy who'd even looked at her with interest.

Mutual sex was their only interest.

With that thought planted firmly in her mind, she pushed the sheets aside and sucked in a breath at the wonderful ache sparkling the entire length of her cunt.

Whoa!

The guy sure had filled her vagina with that excruciatingly beautiful sized cock.

She could feel the rawness, the sweet hurt deep inside her.

Jade smiled.

The rawness should produce some exceptionally delicious sex the next time he penetrated her.

Gosh, she couldn't wait until they had sex again.

She scooted out of bed and to her surprise her hip barely ached after all the fucking she'd experienced last night. And to her further surprise she found her cane settled right beside her bed. Her body filled with a warm happy glow. Bless that well-hung man's heart for thinking of bringing it to her.

Fifteen minutes later Jade had showered and dressed in a flowing white cotton knee-length skirt, a dark pink T-shirt and a light pink, long-sleeved cotton shirt to kick off the early morning chill from the ocean fog.

Grabbing her cane she limped along and followed the tantalizing trail of bacon and eggs to where she found Caydon slaving over a hot stove already fully dressed in the same sexy white shirt he'd worn yesterday and the same tight jeans that cupped a sensually shaped tush.

When he spied her standing in the doorway ogling his nice derriere, he grinned. Cute dimples burst wide open in his cheeks making Jade's breath back up all the way into her lungs.

"Hiya pretty lady, I've got flapjacks, bacon, eggs, toast is in the toaster and your coffee…straight black, is right here," he poured a cup of steaming black coffee for her and handed her the mug.

She accepted it with a grateful smile and eagerly took a sip of the hot liquid.

"It tastes wonderful. Thank you."

"Before we do anything else today I want you to wear these." He scooped something off a plate set on the counter. To her surprise he held up two, ping-pong sized balls that hung from a string.

"What are they?"

"Pleasure balls. They go inside you. Up your succulent vagina."

Her cheeks heated up with excitement.

A sex toy? This guy is unbelievable!

"In each of these devices is a small rotating bearing. Every time you move they give off a vibrating sensation."

"Where'd you get them?"

"While you were sleeping I fixed the engines and berthed us here." He nodded toward the nearby window where to her shock she noticed through the rising mist the masts of sailboats and shadowy silhouettes of unfamiliar cruisers and yachts.

"Where are we?"

"A town south of Tampa Bay. They've got a great sex shop in a private home I know about not far from the mall. I've been here before so you don't need to play guide. Now back to the pleasure balls. I've already lubricated them. Would you allow me to do the honors?"

The honors? *He* wanted to put them inside her?

Jade found herself nodding, her anticipation building to a tremendous roar. Gosh, she couldn't believe she was allowing a virtual stranger, a sexy hunk, to insert foreign objects into her vagina. She'd always considered herself shy yet this man was making her feel so at ease with his natural attitude toward sex she didn't even hesitate doing what the handyman ordered.

"Drop your skirt and underwear and sink that pretty little ass of yours onto the table."

Despite her sudden newfound freedom, she couldn't stop her face from flushing with heat.

Her heart quickened, her blood grew hot in her veins and she felt her vaginal muscles quiver with excitement.

He took her coffee mug and the cane from her and plopped them on the far side of the table.

An odd little noise sounded in his throat that made Jade smile as he watched her slip her skirt down her legs. She did the same with her panties gliding it off slowly and as sexy as she could.

Her breath felt heavy in her chest at the thought of him mounting her right here on the table. Wouldn't that be awesome if he did? Maybe she should ask him to do her. Maybe she should tease him into it?

Her pussy watered at that thought.

She looked into his eyes, the dark color of denim. There was a ripe expression sparkling in there, a cheerfulness that made her heart leap with curiosity. He was a stranger but instinctively she knew he was up to something and it was something she was sure she would love.

She dropped her gaze downward stifling a whimper. The heavenly bulge between his legs seemed to grow right before her eyes making a savage need ripple through her hungry body. She could barely stop herself from reaching out to yank down his zipper.

He was aroused.

Just as much as she was.

Obviously, he had better self-control than she did.

To her disappointment, he shook his head. "No time for fun right now, pretty lady. I've got plans for you."

Strong hot hands curled around her hips and she found herself being lifted off the floor as if she were as light as a feather. She gasped as her ass hit the cool table.

Gosh, he smelled really good this morning. His fresh male scent danced all around her. Combined with a hint of soap it was turning out to be the best smell in the world. And it was making her body feel hotter than ever. Hoisting her feet onto the table she once again noticed the tightness that had lingered in her hip over the past year wasn't as bad anymore.

Maybe last night's ferocious fucking had loosened her up?

To her surprise, she could spread her legs wide without too much trouble and held her breath as he crouched down between her legs.

Excitement coursed through her veins as he smiled with approval.

"Pink, puffy and wet. Just the way I want you."

She exhaled as the large palm of his hand blazed a line of heat along her inner thighs until his fingers met her crotch area.

"The balls are lubricated with some jelly for easy insertion," his voice sounded strangled, his hot gaze fixed directly at her trembling pussy.

Her cunt muscles spasmed wonderfully as he slid the pleasure ball between her throbbing labia lips and stuffed the first one up inside her tight wet channel. The second quickly followed.

"You're so perfectly tight I doubt I'll have to adjust it much during the day but maybe I'll have to make up any excuse to check."

Oh sweet heavens!

"The string dangles so I can remove it when I want to fuck you."

Jade sucked in an aroused breath.

"Wiggle your hips for me."

She did as he asked and sighed at the sultry sensations when the tiny erotic vibrations rippled inside her vagina.

"How's it feel?"

She couldn't stop her eager giggle. "Like I want to be fucked."

"Good, it'll keep you in a state of arousal while we shop."

Shop? The man wanted to shop when she wanted to be fucked? The only thing on her mind right now was to take him into her bedroom, or better yet writhe beneath him on this table, while he slid his yummy huge cock in and out of her like he'd done last night.

"Shopping? Exactly what are we shopping for?"

His dark gaze met hers with a flash of childish excitement she found irresistible.

"Christmas presents. I haven't finished shopping for presents. How about you?"

"Well…no," she lied.

She'd already given her two sisters their presents when they'd showed up unexpectedly but now that he mentioned Christmas shopping she wouldn't mind picking up a little something for him. A little thank you for last night.

"Great! We're going to shop till you drop." His warm hands sensuously cupped her naked hips as he hoisted her off the table and placed her feet firmly on the floor again.

"Don't put your underwear back on. Just the skirt. Are you wearing a bra?"

"No."

"Good, I have some surprises stored up for you today while we shop. Then we'll come back here and I'll fuck you till I drop."

Goodness, the man had a way with words.

Her pussy dripped with her cream.

He released her hips and headed back to the stove.

"Breakfast is ready. Let's eat. The sooner we leave, the sooner we get back."

* * * * *

With each and every step the pleasure balls vibrated teasingly inside her dripping vagina.

Thank goodness, she hadn't worn her panties. It would have been most uncomfortable plastered between her legs. As it was now she could feel her sticky juices sliding down the insides of her thighs.

They'd been here a little over three hours and the pleasure balls had made Jade so horny she was quite ready to head back to the boat to spend the rest of what was left of this day doing some good old hard fucking.

Yet, she still hadn't picked out a present for Caydon and she still had no idea what to get him. Whatever she picked though would have to be perfect.

Laughing and chattering with him as they moved from store to store, she'd been able to pry out some intimate details of his life.

Aside from his confession of loving to cook, she discovered he had a love for fishing. There were other things he dropped hints about, like he enjoyed the outdoors, loved swimming and craved to learn how to ski downhill. She kept all these tidbits stored in her mind waiting until they decided to separate and buy gifts for each other...that is if he wanted to buy gifts for each other.

She hadn't had the nerve to ask him about that yet.

However she found herself getting truly excited as she helped him pick out gifts for his mother, father and to her surprise he even asked her to help him pick out some things for his two sisters and two brothers.

All his siblings were younger than him. None of them were currently married and they didn't have any kids.

"So you really think the tea set I picked out is okay for your grandmother?"

He'd dragged her into an expensive little china boutique where he'd asked her to choose the pattern for an elegant tea set.

She'd picked a fancy shaped white teapot patterned with delicate pink forget-me-nots with a matching set of twelve teacups, saucers and cake plates.

Caydon had nodded his appreciation.

When she'd looked at the price tag however she'd just about balked. Caydon was a handyman. He couldn't afford her expensive tastes.

To her shock, he didn't even flinch at the price. He'd drawn out his credit card, made the purchase and asked for it to be gift-wrapped.

They'd lugged all the presents to a post office where he sent them off via courier laughing when she told him the presents would never be delivered on time. Apparently, it was a tradition that his presents were always late.

"My grandmother would have picked out the same pattern," he said. "She loves flowers and she loves delicate designs. The teapot she has right now is literally falling apart. It must be more than thirty years old."

He curled his arm around her elbow, and hugged her close to his body as they stepped away from the locker room and back out into the crowded mall complete with screaming kids, cheerful Christmas music and the smell of popcorn sifting through the air from a nearby vendor.

"Gram was the same way. She kept everything. When my sisters and I inherited her things we were really glad she hadn't thrown stuff away because everything has a memory attached to it."

"You think I shouldn't have gotten her a teapot?" He looked worried.

"Oh, I didn't mean that you shouldn't have. Gram had three sets of them. One was for family. One for company and the other was for Sundays. Grandmothers can never have too many tea sets hanging around the house."

Relief washed over Caydon's face and he nodded in agreement. "She'll probably need a bunch of them for when her future grandkids come over and start breaking things."

Jade laughed and said proudly, "My sister Crista and her husband are expecting their first baby sometime early this fall."

He looked down at her, a play of emotions she couldn't describe flashed in his eyes. "How about you? You want any kids?"

She shrugged. "I never really thought too much about it. My skiing career was my main priority in my life but now that I think about it I wouldn't mind having one or two."

"I want a lot of them. Maybe five kids just like my mom and pop had."

Jade's eyes widened in shock.

"My God! Five kids!"

"It was kind of nice being the oldest and helping my parents with the younger ones. I know how to change diapers, do the required burping, the whole shebang. Any woman would be lucky to snag me. She'd have herself a live-in babysitter."

"With a brood of five you could play Santa Claus too."

She nodded to the middle of the mall where a rumpled-looking man dressed in a red and black Santa Claus suit, complete with a curly white beard, sat on a gray throne with a sad-looking castle behind him.

On both knees, he bounced two bawling twin toddlers while shouting out a happy "Ho! Ho! Ho!". Curled in his arms were two sleeping babies who were also identical twins. A harried-looking man, who Jade figured was the father, stood to the side with an empty double-stroller while the cheerful female elf, dressed in shiny green garb, quickly snapped pictures of the fiasco.

From beside her, Caydon chuckled. "The dad looks beat."

"He looks like he's ready to crash and burn."

They left the scene behind as he suddenly pulled her into another store.

To her surprise, it was a lingerie boutique complete with frilly teddies and sexy panties with openings in the most intimate places.

An older saleslady quickly tracked them down.

"Merry Christmas!" she cooed. "May I help you?"

"We're looking for something really sexy for my honey bun."

Honey bun? Oh my God! Get serious!

Jade's face flushed as the saleslady winked at her.

"Did you have anything particular in mind?" she asked Caydon who was already eyeing a very pretty white lace see-through teddiette.

"I love this one. Do you have one in a jade color?"

"Oh you have fantastic taste. This design just came in yesterday. Yes, we do have it in that color. And I have a size that will fit her perfectly."

"I'll take it."

"Caydon!"

"Oh honey buns, you'll look fabulous in it. Can she put it on in the change room?"

My God! What was he doing?

"Of course, sir."

Jade's head whirled as the saleslady quickly shifted through the hangers and found a pretty jade-colored one.

"The teddiette has a Lycra back, underwire bra, adjustable garters, snap bottom—"

"It looks perfect." Caydon snapped the sexy piece of lingerie from the saleslady and quickly handed it to Jade.

"Go on in and put it on, honey buns."

Jade cleared her throat at the scorching look blazing his eyes.

Sweet sunshine! If looks could fuck, he'd be doing her right now.

She found herself nodding shakily and headed toward a secluded back door that said Fitting Rooms.

The area appeared to be empty and she headed to the far-end stall. Once inside she quickly stripped and put the sexy little outfit on.

Turning around she admired it in the mirror.

The saleslady was right. The man definitely had great taste. The see-through lace hugged her every curve, outlining her breasts and allowing her peaked nipples to poke seductively against the soft fabric.

And to her surprise the rest of it fit as if it were a second skin.

There was a quick knock at the door and to her horror Caydon stepped inside and closed the door behind him.

"Wow, you look hot enough to fuck right here and now," he whispered. "And you look downright horny."

"You're not supposed to be in here!" she whispered.

"Why not?" he chuckled. "I gave her a twenty to let me in."

"You didn't!"

"I did," he said proudly.

She resisted the overwhelming urge to throw her arms around his neck and start kissing him right then and there or better yet yanking his gorgeous cock out of his jeans and guiding it right into her hot and waiting pussy.

As if reading her thoughts he said softly, "That's the way I like my woman. Hot and horny for me. Those pleasure balls are working I take it?"

"You have to ask?"

He pushed her against the wall, and boxed her in with his large sinewy arms and brushed his lips against hers in a smooth feather light touch that made her senses riot.

"I have to feel you," he said huskily.

"What? Here? Now?"

"You sound properly shocked. How about I shock you some more?"

His large hand cupped under her soaked pussy.

Her body tightened with desire. Blood quickened in her veins.

God! She wanted to be fucked right now!

Reaching out she flattened her hands against the muscular expanse of his solid chest and arched her cunt really hard into his palm in a desperate attempt to grind herself into a climax. But his fingers quickly found the snaps and the material that had been the teddiette's panties fell away. Cool air brushed against her wet pussy but it did nothing to douse her fevered heat.

Two masculine fingers plunged inside her drenched vagina. They felt like two wonderful blades of lightning and she couldn't stop herself from gasping at the invasion.

"The pleasure balls have slipped down a bit, I'll adjust them."

"Caydon, I don't think…"

She wanted to say she didn't think this was a good place for him to be fingering her because she just might scream out her arousal but his mouth clamped over hers stopping her words dead in their tracks.

His lips were tantalizing, teasing and oh so yummy and she couldn't halt the tortured moan in her throat. Her eyes closed against the shivers of ecstasy as his fingers adjusted the pleasure balls pushing them higher into her vagina. Then he slid out.

Her body weakened against him when his thumb rubbed erotically against her swollen clit. Her cunt clenched in agonizing explosions and he kept his mouth sliding against hers capturing her moans.

When the orgasm faded away, he tore his mouth from hers and whispered huskily, "That's just a prelude of things to come."

Without warning, he unclasped the teddiette's underwire bra allowing her breasts to spill free.

He took her swollen globes into his hands, his thumbs harshly caressing her buds.

She closed her eyes, threw her head back and gasped at the erotic stirrings ripping through her breasts.

She could feel her nubs swell and harden as he drew them out and plumped them. He spent a good couple of minutes with each sensitized nipple until her pussy quivered once again.

"Keep your eyes closed, my sweetness," he whispered.

Before she could ask why she felt an unusual tug on her left nipple. The tug tightened a little and then a second later she felt a similar tug and tightening on her right one.

Jade's body quaked with desire.

"What are you up to?" she breathed wanting to open her eyes but not wanting to at the same time.

To her frustration, he moved away.

"Open your eyes, now."

Jade looked down.

Oh, my!

Her areolas, usually a hot pink had been turned to a pretty shade of knotted purple. And her nipples were a similar color. They were plump, stretched out and squeezed erotically between small nipple clamps.

Jade turned to look in the mirror.

Dangling from the nipple clamps were thin one-inch silver chains and at the end of each chain sparkled a tiny pink diamond, or at least what looked to be diamonds.

She highly doubted they were real.

Another tiny chain linked her two nipples by drooping between the valley of her exposed breasts down to her belly button.

"You like?" he asked softly as he pushed his male body against her naked back. She didn't miss the massive bulge pressed intimately against the crack in her butt and suddenly wanted him plunging into her from behind.

"Keep the teddiette and clamps on."

"Caydon…"

"Shh, you'll love it. I promise there's more to come."

Her head whirled. "More?"

He nodded. "Meet me in two hours at the restaurant around the corner. We're under the reservation of Minnelli."

Without waiting for an answer, he slipped out of the dressing room closing the door behind him.

Jade looked back at herself and exhaled a shaky aroused breath.

Her hair was a tangled mess.

Her cheeks were flushed a healthy pink as if she'd just been skiing all day in the mountains, her lips were swollen and red from his kisses and the tiny nipple clamps looked so erotic it just about drove her insane.

Now more than ever, she couldn't wait until they got back to her boat.

Jade grinned to herself.

It was her turn to pay Caydon back and she knew just how to do it.

* * * * *

The surprised look on Jade's face when she'd first looked down at her breasts and seen those clamps had turned Caydon's cock into a roaring serpent demanding immediate satisfaction.

By God, he'd wanted to take her right then and there in that dressing room. Wanted to ram his cock deep into her delicious cunt until everyone heard her mewl in pleasure.

He'd almost done it too if he hadn't already mapped out the things he wanted to do to her for the rest of the day.

"Will that be everything, sir?" The elderly salesman asked.

"Yes, that's great."

"Where would you like all this delivered?"

Caydon gave him the address of the marina where he'd docked Jade's yacht and the name of the boat.

"If you could just set it on the foredeck out of sight and I'll take care of the rest."

"This must be your first Christmas with the wife," the older man chuckled.

"Wife?"

The old man chuckled.

"I saw both of you earlier when you strolled by arm in arm. You were looking at Santa Claus. You're a very striking couple. I couldn't help but notice she was limping with a cane. She must have been in an accident. She looks familiar. Is she a model or something?"

"Or something," Caydon winked.

He didn't want to tell the salesman Jade had been a famous downhill skier or that she'd been on the front cover of every gossip rag in the United States a few days ago with her cute breasts blurred out making it quite obvious she'd been sunbathing topless.

"Mrs. Minnelli will be quite surprised, sir. Thank you very much for your business, sir." The elderly man handed Caydon back his credit card. "The delivery will be there within the hour."

"Thank you!"

A little beeping sound emitted from Caydon's watch startling him.

"I better get a move on. Meeting the wife for an early supper. Thanks again."

The salesman threw Caydon a wave as he slipped out of the store and back into the mall.

Suddenly he couldn't wait to get back to Jade and to the next surprise he had in store for her.

Chapter Seven

The restaurant Caydon had mentioned was beautifully decked out in seasonal garb. Green garland splashed with sprays of red rosehips intertwined with blinking gold lights were draped along the walls of the secluded booth the waitress had given her when Jade had told her she had reservations under the name Minnelli.

Romantic Christmas songs played softly in the background and the table had a traditional red and green theme giving the booth a cheerful and bright appearance.

The tablecloth was plain red cotton, the wineglasses were ruby-colored and the napkins were a charming forest green, the edges lined with red thread.

Jade couldn't help but laugh at the cute Santa Claus napkin rings or admire the gorgeous sphere-shaped Santa Claus ornaments set at the top of each place setting.

Stainless steel cutlery and silver plates sparkled in front of her and she realized not only was she starving for sex she was hungry for food as well.

As she allowed her gaze to wander out of the booth, she noted that there were no other tables visible from where she sat. But she was allowed a luxurious view of a tiny stone pond nestled in the nearby corner. It came complete with running water, floating lily pads and gold-sprayed wheat cone trees nestled in miniature French iron bathtubs that hugged wild foliage at the edges of the miniature pond.

Her heart scrambled into a mad pace, the instant she heard the distinct voice of Caydon speaking to someone nearby. She couldn't make out his words but when she peeked out of the secluded booth she spotted him conversing with a waitress.

The muscles in her cunt clenched tightly at the sight of him. Her breath backed up into her lungs and desire stabbed her body.

His jeans and white shirt were gone replaced by a pair of dark blue slacks and a gray shirt that stretched across his wide well muscled chest.

And he'd gotten a haircut and a shave.

Gosh, he seemed even more handsome now than two hours ago and hunkier than yesterday when she'd first met him.

Jade shook her head in puzzlement.

Yesterday morning her life had been so ho-hum. Today she was looking forward to spending the rest of her life getting fucked by this perfect male specimen with the nice juicy big cock.

The rest of her life!

And she didn't even know him!

Rein yourself in girl. You're getting ahead of yourself again.

She studied him as he laughed easily with the waitress.

Noted the confident way he stood. Loved the snug way his pants cupped his full ass. Most of all she loved the charming way he nodded his head in agreement with whatever the waitress was now saying to him.

His luscious lips were upturned into that sexy smile that made Jade's toes curl with excitement. But those cute dimples weren't playing along his cheeks like they did when he looked at her.

Oh pooh! She was reading too much into this guy again.

It seemed to be a very bad habit. One she hoped she could break once he decided it was time to leave her. Until that happened she was going to make the most of this man's company.

The breath stilled in her lungs when he turned and headed toward their booth.

Jade stuck her head back inside and waited for him.

"I missed you like crazy," he whispered as he slid onto the padded booth seat right beside her.

A delicious aroma of spicy aftershave washed over her senses making her dizzy with desire.

"I missed you too," she admitted truthfully. "A very nice haircut. Special occasion?"

His eyes roved to where her tight breasts were pushed up against the teddiette she wore beneath her T-shirt and shirt.

"A very special occasion. Those clamps still on?"

"Yes," Jade whispered as her blood boiled at his question.

She'd panicked in the fitting room as she'd redressed and seen the distinct outline of the clamps. Thankfully, when she'd put her loose shirt on top the outline had diminished to something she thought she could handle.

A hint of a smile teased his lips. "They comfortable enough?"

"They're driving me crazy if you want to know the truth. My nipples are on fire. My pussy is sopping wet and I want relief."

He grinned, obviously happy with her sexual torture.

"And the pleasure balls?"

"Waiting for you to replace them."

His eyes widened at her bold reply. "All in good time, Jade. All in good time. First though, I have another surprise for you."

"Dare I ask?"

Her heart cracked like a piston as he moved even closer to her, the entire side of his blistering body pressing intimately against hers. Hot masculine breath fanned her neck as he kissed her there and whispered, "Spread your legs."

Her eyes widened in surprise.

Quickly she glanced past him to make sure no one was watching and once again realized exactly how secluded this booth really was.

Her cunt creamed as she opened her legs wide beneath their dining table.

"I'm glad you wore a skirt today," he chuckled as his fingers burned against the inside of her knee.

So am I.

"Wider," he whispered.

She did as he said and she just about bolted out of the chair when his scorching touch trailed along the inside of her upper thigh toward her clit.

When he reached it, he immediately sought her plump labia.

"You kept the teddiette underwear off?"

"It's in my purse, soaked."

He beamed happily obviously pleased with the thought she was creaming for him even after he'd left the dressing room.

Jade bit back a gasp as he pulled and twisted tenderly on her flesh until they burned delightfully. Then he drew her labia apart making them sting with a pleasure-pain that brought tears to her eyes.

"Did you do anymore shopping while we were apart?" he whispered into her ear.

"Yes and I've got a surprise for you. Call it…" she inhaled a breath as he affixed something slightly heavy to one side of her labia.

A clamp?

Her pussy lip throbbed magnificently.

She spread her thighs wider allowing him easier access.

"Call it payback for what you're doing to me now," she whispered.

"I like the sound of that."

He attached another clamp to the same side, just a little further up. This one so close to her sensitized pleasure nub she had to hold onto the sides of the table to keep herself from reaching between her legs and rubbing herself into a climax.

He fondled her other labia until Jade felt it swell, then he attached two clamps to it too. They gripped her flesh firmly holding her cunt in a charming form of sexual bondage she found quite appealing.

His fingers slid ever so gently between her tortured labia and he began a slow seductive massage against her love button.

Moaning softly at the sensual sensations, she eagerly waited for him to lead her into another climax like he'd done in the dressing room.

His warm cheek brushed erotically against the arc of her neck as he buried his face there again, this time nibbling on her ear sending ripples of delight shimmering through her body.

"I would very much like to know what you have planned for me," his warm lips curved in a smile against her skin. "Perhaps I should masturbate you in order to get you to tell me."

She shivered. "You wouldn't dare."

Oh, please dare!

"I can tell by the glaze in your eyes, you'd love for me to do you right here."

His own eyes sparkled wonderfully.

"The waitress…"

"Don't worry about the waitress. She's busy getting our order."

Suddenly her clamped labia began to tingle.

"Caydon, what are you doing down there?"

He held up a small black remote box with a dial on it.

"Vibrating clamps. You like?"

"It's…different."

"Do they hurt?"

"They tingle."

"They've got little weights on them too."

"I feel them."

God! Did she feel them!

"With the same style of pink diamond drops like those on your nipple clamps."

"Not real diamonds, I hope," she joked.

"That's for me to know and you to find out. Aren't you glad you aren't wearing underwear? Might have been a little too much pressure. You can wear these clamps for hours without any trouble."

My god! Hours with these pleasing sensations rippling down there?

"I don't think I can wait that long, Caydon."

"Getting horny again?"

"More like still am."

"Sir? Ma'am? Your order is here."

Jade felt her face flame as she looked up to see the waitress Caydon had been talking to only moments ago standing right outside their booth with a cart overflowing with food.

"You work fast around here," Caydon chuckled.

Thankfully, he slipped the remote box out of sight and into his pocket. He leaned closer against Jade, presumably so the waitress couldn't see he had a hand beneath the table and between her legs.

To her shock, she felt his finger continue to slide erotically against her pleasure nub as if they hadn't just been interrupted.

Bastard!

Jade's hands tightened on the table.

"Newlyweds?" The waitress grinned.

"Not yet." Caydon replied as he increased the pressure on Jade's clit.

Son of a bitch! Lady, get out of here!

"Nice day outside, isn't it?" The waitress poured some water into their glasses. "They're calling for it to be beautiful all the way through the rest of the year. We'll have a very sunny and warm Christmas and Happy New Year."

It's always beautiful weather in Florida! Get out of here before I orgasm right in front of you!

Jade gritted her teeth as she quickly slid toward the pleasure awaiting her.

Obviously thinking they were very much in love, the waitress smiled sweetly at both of them and quickly placed the covered plates onto the table along with a pitcher of what Jade perceived as eggnog.

"Would you like me to pour?"

God! No! Get out of here!

The waitress' face blurred and Jade felt her body stiffening from the arousal.

"No, thank you, that'll be fine." Caydon's voice was so calm she felt like crashing her fists against his chest.

The waitress took her cue and quickly left.

"Caydon!" Jade whimpered a warning.

The pressure from his finger increased and Jade slid over the edge. The instant the wild explosion cascaded through her body his sweet lips swooped down over hers capturing her quiet moans.

Dinner was both torture and wonderful.

Her beaded nipples ached with arousal beneath the nipple clamps. The labial vibrating clamps kept her squirming in her chair. Several times, she tried to press her legs together to bring herself off but the clamps bit painfully into her flesh. Obviously, the manufacturer had taken that into consideration when they'd designed the naughty toys.

If she didn't already have her revenge mapped out in her head she would have insisted he take her to the bathroom and drive his gorgeous cock deep into her dripping cunt.

It seemed as if there was no end to the food.

Caydon had ordered maple-glazed turkey for them, complete with holiday mashed potatoes, peas and baby spinach.

During dinner they chatted about their likes and dislikes and when the waitress brought them their dessert, a scrumptious Berry Almond Trifle that arrived in a straight-sided clear glass trifle bowl that showed the irresistible palate pleasing layers of juicy red strawberries and plump blueberries, amaretto-soaked angel food cake and lip-smacking vanilla custard sprinkled with almonds, he prodded her about her childhood and how she got into skiing professionally.

"Well, my parents got us all into skiing. From as early as I can remember every winter we had skis strapped to our feet. Even after they died in an avalanche and we moved in with Gram and Gramps, I couldn't stay off the slopes. I loved the sharp sting of snowflakes on my face, the sound of wind shrieking past my ears and the adrenalin rush flowing through my veins as I raced at speeds over a hundred kilometers down the mountainside. I felt so alive. So in tune with nature. And then…"

"And then came the crash."

She nodded.

"You sound as if you'll never feel alive again. As if you'll never strap a pair of skis on."

"I will someday…but first I want to do something else."

"Such as?"

"Sail to Europe. It's always been a dream of mine. Now that I have the time I can do it."

She'd expected him to laugh at her dream. He didn't.

Instead, he frowned with concern. "All by yourself?"

Was he looking for an invitation? Did she want to ask him? Could she ask him? Her brain told her she didn't even know the guy. They were good in the sack but she really didn't know if she could have him around her for months.

Her heart told her they could get along wherever they went.

She decided to listen to her brain. The last time she'd listened to her heart she'd been betrayed by a man.

Sadness tugged at her heart.

No, she wouldn't ask him. He wasn't in her plans. Heck, she didn't even know what her plans were about the future, hence the idea for the ocean trip.

"That's the plan."

"Are you sure it's safe?" Concern etched his words. "I mean a woman alone in the ocean. Things could happen. Storms. Engine problems. You could get sick. You should hire a competent crew. At least then if you run into trouble…"

"I want to be alone. I need time to think about things." Like to think about what she really wanted to do with the rest of her life.

He nodded. "I understand. You're going on a quest. You are a brave woman and a very sexy woman and I want to take you back to the boat and have my way with you. Are you up to that?"

"God! I thought you'd never ask."

* * * * *

"Oh my gosh. Caydon what have you done?"

Jade said as she clasped a hand over her mouth in wonder.

Through the soft glow of evening dusk she spotted the row of champagne glasses, each filled with clear glass pebbles and each containing a flickering white votive candle, strewn along the mantel of what appeared to be a fireplace.

A fireplace, that sat smack in the middle of her yacht's deck.

"It's an electric fireplace. To set the mood," Caydon whispered as he helped her up the gangplank onto her boat.

"It looks so real. Even the flames look real."

She noted the two empty red Christmas stockings hanging near each end of the garland-dressed mantel.

Tears stung Jade's eyes as she stared at the flickering fireplace and then at the twinkling white miniature lights strung along the railings.

He'd made it look just like Christmas. All they needed now was a log cabin, fluffy snowflakes and a Christmas tree.

She shook her head in wonder. No guy had gone to so much trouble to do anything like this for her before. It seemed so…overwhelming.

She bit her bottom lip to keep herself from crying.

His warm hand touched her elbow.

"You okay?"

Jade forced herself to smile and nodded finding it hard to bite back the tears.

"Pop a couple of those chaise mattresses down in front of the fireplace and I'll be back in a few minutes."

When he disappeared into her yacht the rush of tears burned the back of her eyes again and she rubbed them away with her fists.

The pretty flicker of orange flames in the fireplace drew her attention. She found herself thinking about all those evenings she'd spent in front of a real fire with Beau in hotel rooms all over the world. The heat from the flames had blasted against them while he'd drilled into her the next day's ski moves. He'd always been business first, pleasure second…if pleasure is what she could have called it back then.

Gosh, she'd been so immature regarding sex and men but now she knew better.

Maybe her skiing accident in Cortina had been a blessing in disguise?

As she'd lain in the hospital bed, her pain numbed with morphine, her hip and leg plastered in a cast and the Italian doctor telling her in broken English she would never ski professionally again, Beau hadn't said a word. When she'd started to cry at the loss of her dream, he hadn't wrapped his arms around her in comfort. He'd simply shaken his head and walked out.

A few days later, she'd seen him on television announcing his new job coaching another professional downhill skier.

And that they were engaged, and she was pregnant with his child.

Son of a bitch!

Thank God, she'd met Caydon. He was a total opposite of Beau.

In bed and out. It was amazing how she'd responded to him and she'd loved all his surprises today and now this romantic fireplace...

Could Caydon Minnelli be *the* man in her future?

Jade shook the disturbing thoughts away. She needed to stay in reality. It meant this guy was just a fascinating fling who would get tired of her soon enough. In the meantime, she would enjoy all his attentions and the sizzling sex.

The clamps on her labia suddenly vibrated to life and Jade gasped at the sensual sensations it created.

Oh, the little bugger!

She'd give him his payback!

During the two hours they'd been separated she'd made a few purchases of her own and had them delivered to her boat asking them to specifically hide the goodies under the tarp in the bow.

Casting a quick glance over her shoulder to make sure Caydon wasn't around she quickly headed to the bow area. Peeking under the tarp she smiled at the shopping bags they'd delivered just as she'd asked. Caydon Minnelli was going to get his payback soon enough but first she needed sexual satisfaction.

Quickly she returned to the deck where she threw down some lounge cushions in front of the fireplace and gingerly sat down careful not to disturb the aching labia clamps or wonderful burning nipple clamps.

Caydon showed up a moment later.

"Here, I whipped you up some sparkling cranberry cocktail. You sip on it while I get the boat out of here."

"I don't think I can wait that long," she grinned as she accepted the martini glasses filled with the red liquid complete with dancing lime wedges on top.

"I doubt I can wait that long either," he whispered huskily. "But I'm thinking about the neighbors. They might call the police on us with all the noise that's going to be happening when I make love to you. I don't want us to be interrupted."

Jade swallowed at her excitement.

"Keep the cushions and yourself warm for me," he said and headed for the pilothouse.

Sipping on the cranberry cocktail she savored the delicate combination of vodka, orange liqueur and sweet cranberries. When she was almost finished with her drink she recognized the buzz of alcohol sifting through her brain and also realized, they were out of the marina, heading full speed for open waters.

No one was around but Caydon.

And he was watching her from the pilothouse with half-lidded lusty eyes.

Jade trembled.

Perhaps she should give the man a show?

She bit her lower lip thoughtfully. Did she have enough nerve to do what she wanted to do? Would she look like a fool dancing on the deck?

But why be shy?

She barely knew him. If she came off like an idiot, she'd probably never see him again anyway.

She grew painfully aware that she didn't want him to leave. She'd had such a lovely day shopping with him today, had exquisite sex with him last night and he'd even cooked for her.

Twice!

Maybe if she seduced him into staying at least for another day? Or maybe she could rig it so the engines wouldn't work and they couldn't return to shore, ever? Maybe she could make the keys disappear? Maybe she could make him fall in love with her?

Jade rolled her eyes and exhaled a frustrated breath.

He'd never fall in love with her.

He was just too sexy.

Too kind.

Too...poor?

That familiar niggle of doubt zipped through her. Was he trying to make her fall in love with him so he could go after her money like Beau had done?

Jade frowned as something else budged its way into her thoughts.

The other day when he'd first shown up to fix her engines, how had he started the boat while she'd slept? She always kept her key in her purse and the spare on a hook hidden deep inside one of the electrical consoles.

Had he gone through her purse? Maybe she'd left the key in the ignition? That would be the only explanation she could think of. She'd have to remember to ask him.

Later though.

Right now, the clamps were increasing in vibrations and really making her cream.

Looking over her shoulder she found him smiling down at her and holding that little black box in the air.

The tease!

She would show him she could tease just as good as she got.

Taking a last swallow of the cranberry cocktail, she set it down on the deck nearby.

Remaining seated on the cushions, Jade made sure he was watching as she seductively slid her shirt over her shoulders and let it slip off her body.

* * * * *

The sexy way she slid her shirt off fired Caydon's blood. He didn't understand why he was so attracted to her. Didn't understand why every time he saw her he wanted to mount her, pleasure her, romance her.

Quite frankly at this point, he really didn't care.

All he wanted to do was go down to her, help her out of those clothes and bring her the pleasure she must be craving by now with those clamps he'd placed on her. But if he did that then he'd miss the show she was putting on.

And he didn't want to miss this.

He watched anxiously as she slipped her blouse off to reveal the sexy jade-colored teddiette he'd purchased for her. Her breasts looked firm and high beneath the lace. He could see the way her large nipples poked at the material compliments of the clamps he'd attached to her buds in the dressing room.

His mouth watered as he remembered taking her juicy nipples between his lips and plundering them. His cock hardened as he remembered reaching under the dining table in the restaurant to pinch and prepare her velvety labia for the clamps.

He'd loved the rapturous tremors that had sifted through her body as he'd intimately touched her soaked pleasure nub and brought her to orgasm right before dinner.

And now as she slid the teddiette straps over her bare arms, he clutched at the wheel of the yacht and inhaled sharply at the sight of her silky globes spilling free.

Reaching for a nearby switch, he turned on the floodlights illuminating her.

She lifted her arms up and hands tunneled through her shoulder-length hair.

His fingers suddenly ached to sift through her silky mass.

Beneath the bite-sized clamps, her flesh looked a dark rosy color nestled in large pink areolas. The silver chains and pink diamonds sparkled brilliantly under the floodlights.

She looked up at him and gave him a magnificent smile as if she were encouraging him to come on down and get her out of the rest of her clothes.

Caydon swallowed.

His cock shivered.

His body tensed.

He dragged in a shuddering breath.

Man, he hungered for her body in a dangerous way. So much so, that he almost forgot to shut the engines off in his haste to get out of the pilothouse and down to her.

When he reached her, she was standing on the deck.

Her body moved in a slow seductive dance.

Succulent breasts swayed.

Beneath her skirt, generous hips sensually gyrated.

By golly, he couldn't wait to rip the rest of her clothing off and plunge his thick cock into her.

* * * * *

The warm Florida air caressed her bared, clamped nipples as Jade danced in carefree circles on the deck. She could sense him behind her now. Could feel the heat of his powerful desire washing all around her. Her heart thudded against her chest. Need coiled like liquid fire inside her cunt.

When she finally stopped twirling, their eyes met.

Every nerve ending in her body shivered when she spotted his dark heavy-lidded gaze.

The man wanted to fuck her.

And she wanted to get fucked.

Good and hard.

Her head spun with excitement as he reached out to her.

Long masculine fingers curled around the elastic waistband of her skirt, branding her belly where he touched her naked skin.

"I've been waiting all day to touch you like this," he whispered as he knelt on his knees in front of her.

She swallowed as he began to roll her skirt over her hips, her knees. It fell to the deck in a silent hush. His hot tongue dipped into her belly button and she gasped at the sultry sensations shimmering through her lower abdomen.

At the same time, his hand slid between her legs and she felt the pinch of the clamps as he loosened them one at a time. Fire burned into her labia as the blood rushed back into the plump folds while he removed the clamps.

Oh God! She ached for him.

Her labia pulsed.

Her puffy clit quivered with a fierce need to be massaged and soothed.

His breath blew hot against her belly. His tongue teased her button, poking and swirling in the tiny cave until she inhaled ragged breaths.

"Caydon!" she found herself whispering. Her voice sounded tortured and desperate in her ears.

Reaching out she slid her hands to either side of his head, her fingers sifting through his feathery hair as she guided his face down between her legs. Her mind reeled as his tongue licked a burning streak of flames against her fine curly haired mons. Fever raged through her cunt as he drove a long finger deep inside her boiling channel.

Jade couldn't stop herself from arching her hips at the quick invasion.

Without warning he inserted another finger and yet another.

She inhaled a sharp breath as he slowly pulled the pleasure balls out of her. Then he reinserted his fingers beginning a slow thrust, which threatened to destroy her.

Three fingers rammed into her, the sucking sounds shifted through the air.

Her soaked cunt dripped all around his plunging fingers. She was so wet for him, so eager to climax.

His head lifted and he looked at her. His face was flushed — his eyes a frantic bundle of need it just about made her have an orgasm on the spot.

"You're so tight, Jade. So unbelievably tight and so wet. I want to sink more of me into you," his voice sounded strangled. "I want to sink my whole fist into you."

The thought of having his fist buried inside her made Jade convulse in a frenzy of lust.

"Yes," she hissed. "Do me that way, Caydon. Do me. I need you inside me." She would do anything to have him in there.

Sweet sensations jumbled with pain as a fourth finger slipped inside. Her vaginal muscles ached with pleasure-pain.

She shivered at the large intrusion.

Her cunt burned.

Her mind fogged under the sexual torture.

His other hand slid between her legs. Masculine fingers pinched her aching labia, breathing more fire into her tormented flesh.

When he slid the calloused pad of his thumb over her sensitized pleasure nub, she climaxed.

Wailing under the harsh onslaught, she screamed out his name as the delicious storm of ecstasy took hold of her senses.

She bucked hard against his hand.

Moaned as his thumb seared against the spasming opening of her cunt.

Her pussy frantically clutched at this new intrusion as his thumb slipped inside.

My God!

His fingers and thumb filled her stretched her like she'd never been stretched before. Her entire body melted into acute sensual convulsions.

Her mind fragmented. Her legs went weak.

Jade's hands came off his head and landed on his broad shoulders, her arms felt like two trembling toothpicks ready to snap as she curled desperate fingers into his muscles in an effort to keep herself standing.

For a moment, she concentrated on the invasion. Concentrated on letting his entire fist inside.

But he didn't come in. His fist breeched her entrance.

"Too tight," he ground out. "This is as far as I can go."

Through heavy-lidded eyes, she watched the wondrous expression on his face as he stared between her legs. She could imagine him seeing his fingers and thumb disappearing into her. Could imagine how hot her juices must feel soaking his hand.

She sobbed hysterically as his knuckles rubbed and ground erotically against her sensitized clitoris.

Inside her cunt, a masculine finger massaged her G-spot.

Pleasure flowed through her whole body like a drug.

The sensations were unbelievable!

She threw her head back and let her hips gyrate on the massive penetration.

The orgasm made her cry. Made her laugh.

Made her scream out his name as she came all around his fingers and thumb.

The climax freed her like she'd never been freed before.

When it was over and he'd withdrawn from her, her legs gave out and Jade sagged against him like a limp rag doll.

He caught her in his strong arms.

With soothing whispers, he helped her onto the chaise mattresses she'd thrown earlier onto the deck.

Perspiration cooled her fevered flesh and his harsh breaths caressed her flushed cheeks.

She could smell her arousal as his wet masculine fingers sifted through her hair.

"Sleep, Jade. Sleep. When you wake up I have another surprise for you."

Did he say another surprise?

She wanted to ask him what he had in store for her next but when her eyes fluttered open, he wasn't there.

Jade sighed and snuggled into the mattresses.

Closing her eyes, she allowed her shuddering limbs to relax and listened to the gentle lapping of the ocean waves hitting the sides of her boat.

Did his surprise mean more sexual torture? Would he put more clamps on her nipples and labia? Or would he bring her more sex toys?

With a smile curving her lips, Jade fell into a slumberous sleep.

Chapter Eight

Christmas…

"Merry Christmas, sleepyhead."

A familiar masculine whisper into her ear made Jade's heart shoot into her throat.

She'd been fast asleep dreaming she'd been back on the slopes skiing at top speed, an ecstatic crowd encouraging her as she raced toward the finish line.

Crisp cold wind had slapped against her face, the sharp aroma of spruce gusting deep into her lungs. The scent of the forest had seemed so real. As if she were right there among the trees.

"Sleeping beauty, time for some more fun," he whispered again.

Opening her eyes she stared at the silhouette of a three-foot high spruce tree set in a huge white pot.

Pale blue miniature Christmas lights twinkled daintily along its branches.

Jade blinked and rubbed her eyes.

How odd, she thought sleepily, to have a fireplace and a Christmas tree beneath an open black sky filled with sparkling stars.

Under the blue glow of the lights on the tree, she noticed a scattering of presents.

She had to be dreaming.

"Wakey wakey, Jade. Time to decorate our tree."

Our tree?

"Caydon?" She turned her head to find him sitting on the deck beside her.

He wore a skimpy pair of bikini underwear laden with candy canes.

She couldn't stop her sharp inhalation at the quite impressive bulge pressing against the thin material.

His gorgeous smile slammed into her and she felt it as a wonderful punch to her gut.

In a flash, she remembered yesterday's events.

The pleasure balls. Shopping in the mall. Getting her nipples clamped in the dressing room, her labia clamped in the restaurant.

Coming back here to find the fireplace and then having wonderful sex.

And now a Christmas tree?

"Caydon? What are you doing?"

"Celebrating Christmas. It's midnight. Christmas is just starting. We have to get the tree decorated in her sexy garb."

Jade's mind whirled.

Decorate the tree? Celebrate Christmas?

Why would a man she barely knew want to celebrate Christmas with her? Why would he buy her Christmas presents and bring a real live Christmas tree onto her yacht?

She bit her tongue against the soaring questions just to make sure she wasn't dreaming.

Ouch!

She wasn't.

His grin widened. "Speechless?"

While she'd slept he'd turned off the spotlights but in the shadows she noted his dark hair was damp and tangled. A fresh scent of soap wafted through the air as he leaned over her.

Obviously, he'd showered, probably a cold shower, thanks to her slumbering off on him.

Guilt zipped a solid line into her. It didn't take hold though as he intertwined his fingers with hers.

"Come on. Get up. Time to decorate our tree."

He pulled her to her feet with ease.

Helping her into the snug terrycloth robe he must have found in her bedroom, he led her over to a bunch of boxes piled on the nearby deck table.

"Ornaments. Lights. Even silver icicles. Do you know how hard it is to find silver icicles in Florida?" he laughed.

"How long did I sleep?"

"I come bearing you all kinds of gifts and all you are interested in is your beauty sleep?"

Jade cheeks grew hot. "That's not all I'm interested in," she replied truthfully.

"Decorate first. Fuck later."

He handed her a small open box.

Her heart pattered at the little copper glass balls that gleamed up at her. Adorned with tiny seed-sized pearls and sprayed with lines of spun sugar they were the prettiest things she'd ever seen.

"I'm so sorry I fell asleep on you," she found herself saying as the guilt returned.

He threw her a rather serious look. "You can sleep on top of me later. I let you sleep for a reason. I wanted you nice and rested for this momentous occasion."

"You take your Christmas decorating seriously don't you?"

"Very. And you are my captive until this tree is decked."

"Your captive? Hmm, I love the sound of that."

"After that I'll be yours. You can do with me what you want until your heart is guilt-free. Feel better?"

"Whatever I want?"

His eyes flashed with heat. "Anything you want."

He drew a string of amethyst beads out of a box, and started a slow whistle of a romantic Christmas tune and began to decorate the tree.

Just looking at his long masculine fingers as they draped the beads onto the spruce branches made Jade's cunt juices flow.

She'd made love to that gorgeous hand. Had gyrated her hips, pumped her slippery pussy all over it while he'd tried to fist-fuck her. The fist fucking hadn't worked but part of his hand had been inside her.

She exhaled roughly as she remembered the fullness of him pushing into her.

His long thick fingers had explored her pussy, tenderly massaged her vagina and brought her to orgasm. Afterwards she'd simply collapsed and basked in her relief leaving him out in the cold.

Jade frowned.

His cock must be in one miserable hell as she continued to take pleasure from him and not give anything back.

It was time for her to give and for him to receive.

But first, they needed to decorate the tree.

* * * * *

Caydon didn't think he'd ever had so much fun decorating a tree. Or ever seen a prettier one even though it was only three feet tall.

Decked out in sprays of amethyst beads, gleaming copper balls, gold pinecones, miniature lights and silver icicles everything simply said Merry Christmas.

His whole life he'd enjoyed the Christmas season. Every year on Christmas Eve his grandfather Nonno, his pop and himself strolled into the hundred-acre woodlot his parents owned next to their grape farm in Tuscany, California and cut down a tree.

Laughter and cheers and play fights had abounded when they arrived home with their capture. After Nonno's careful trimming, everyone including his elderly grandmother participated in the decorating festivities at the stroke of midnight in order to hail in Christmas.

This year would be the first Christmas in his twenty-eight years that he wouldn't be celebrating with his family. Caydon smiled as he remembered telling his grandmother he might not be around this Christmas. He'd expected her to be disappointed, instead her watery blue eyes had sparkled happily, she'd clasped her hands together to her chest and cried out, "He's got a girl!"

Despite the fact he wouldn't make it home this Christmas, he wasn't the least bit sad. Gorgeous sexy Jade made up for his loss and she had turned out to be more than he'd ever dreamed. For the first time in his life, he felt totally at ease with a woman and had never felt so complete.

Hot feminine palms framed both sides of Caydon's naked waist and a beautiful velvety moist pressure slid along the back of his neck breaking him from his thoughts.

He grinned to himself.

His playful sex kitten was finally making her move. He'd seen the mischievous looks she'd thrown his way when she'd thought he was busily decorating the tree.

Every time he'd felt her hot gaze roving over his body his cock had hardened and tightened just as it was doing now.

He turned around and caught site of her devilish grin a moment before she planted a pair of sexy soft lips right onto his mouth. She tasted so delicious, so warm and so tender that he quickly became lost in a flurry of his arousal.

His balls swelled and tightened until they were two solid glass ornaments ready to shatter.

When he tried to kiss her back, she pulled away leaving him with an odd sense of loss.

"You're up to something," he said as she reached for his wrist.

"Actually, you're the one who is up," she giggled.

He followed her gaze down to between his legs just in time to see her fingers from her other hand curl around his waistband and tug his candy cane underwear down over his hips.

His cock sprang free standing straight up against his belly as if were Santa Claus' North Pole ready to be mounted by a warm spasming pussy.

"You've been growing harder and harder as we decorated the tree and I've been getting wetter and wetter," she teased.

Her grin widened. "The tree is finished. Now it's your turn to be my captive."

"What an irresistible idea."

Caydon tried to reach out to grab her but something soft and tight snapped around his wrist. Before he could blink, he felt the same thing snap around his other wrist.

He looked down to find both his wrists handcuffed in front of him.

"You're sneaky!"

She pouted prettily. "And so are you. Sneaking a Christmas tree on board with all these pretty looking presents."

"I can't help it if I like to surprise you."

"And I like to surprise you, too. I'll be right back." She disappeared from his view and the feeling of unease that had been haunting him on occasion since meeting her a couple of days ago quickly swept over him.

Cripes!

She looked so damned happy.

Happy and innocent.

Did she deserve him? A man who was far from innocent in the way of keeping why he was here a secret from her?

In fact, he was an asshole. A loser for not having guts and telling her the truth.

There was no absolutely no excuse not to tell her anymore. She would find out sooner or later from her sisters who he really was. When she did, it would be twice as bad as if he just spilled his guts now and took the fallout himself.

The handcuffs around his wrists suddenly made him feel more like a prisoner than a sexual captive. He yanked on them hard, suddenly wanting to be free, grimacing, as they stood strong.

"Why are you looking so worried?" she asked as she hobbled back onto the deck carrying a shopping bag.

Shit!

She'd ditched her terrycloth robe.

Totally naked she was bathed in pale moonlight, her beautiful breasts bouncing joyfully with her uneven gait.

His cock hardened as he spied the light bush of curly hair hiding her large labia and puffy clitoris from his view.

Her eyes sparkled with amusement. "Are you scared you might not hold up under my sexual torture? You're mine now, Caydon Minnelli. Totally mine. Want to see what I have for you here?"

He wanted to say no. Wanted to tell her to uncuff him so he could break her heart.

Instead, he forced himself to smile as she urged him down onto the mattresses dragging the big shopping bag with her.

"Hey, where'd you get that?" He nodded at the bag.

"When we split up in the mall you weren't the only one who was planning surprises. I did my own Christmas shopping for you."

She'd shopped for him?

Soothing warmth washed away his shame at not telling her his secret.

It was a good sign that she'd been thinking about him when they'd been separated. Maybe this could all work out in the end?

"Are you ready to be sexually tortured?" she grinned.

"Throw me your best shot."

Slipping her hands into the bag, she busied herself unwrapping whatever secrets the bag possessed.

When her hands came back out, his eyes widened with both shock and arousal.

He couldn't stop the soft curse from escaping his mouth.

"It's a pussy sleeve. You like?"

"I don't know. Is it better than the real thing?"

She giggled. "How about I let you be the judge of that?"

Caydon swallowed at the sudden dryness in his mouth. He'd heard the dangers of pussy sleeves. How they aroused a man to such heights that there was nothing else around quite like it…except for the real thing.

What an absolutely delicious idea and it was making him harder by the minute.

"Look what else I have for you."

From her fingertips dangled something unmistakable.

Shit!

Payback was a bitch.

"Nipple clamps?"

"Just returning the favor. The saleslady said they work wonders on a man."

"I've never had nipple clamps before," he admitted truthfully.

Jade's green eyes blazed. "Neither did I, until the dressing room. Trust me you'll love them and you'll love this too."

Her perky breasts jiggled as she drew out a small bottle. Pouring some of the clear contents onto her palms, he recognized the mouth-watering scent of cinnamon caress his nostrils.

"What's that?"

"Sensual lube. Cinnamon Christmas Kiss is the scent. It'll heighten your senses."

"My senses are already heightened every time I look at you."

"Hmm. Compliments and flattery will get you everywhere but not out of what I have planned for you."

She rubbed her hands together, smearing the lube into her palms.

As she placed her hot little palms over his nipples, he couldn't stop the sudden erotic shuddering of his chest muscles. Her lube-soaked fingers spent a few minutes on each of his buds, sensuously sliding over them, tenderly stroking, pleasantly plumping and tweaking his flesh until they were firm, big beads of quivering flesh and he felt as if he might go mad from the shimmering sensations.

First, she clamped one drawn-out nipple and then the other, tightening the teeth until he inhaled sharply as they bit hard into his sensitized flesh. When she was finished, his engorged nipples burned as if they were on fire.

"You're right. It feels good to have my nipples clamped. Damn good," he groaned.

And it looked erotic as all hell watching a woman clamping him.

She threw him an "I told you so" smile and wrapped her hot little palms around the thick base of his cock where she began to massage more of the warm gel into his stiff flesh.

Oh boy!

His cock quivered beneath her burning touch. Automatically he arched his hips against her hands wanting more. His hunger for Jade increased.

"We've got to lube you up nicely," she whispered.

She looked at him from beneath long lashes, her mouth set in determination, her warm hands slurping this way and that way making his engorged flesh tingle erotically.

From tip to base, her sweet palms massaged his massive erection.

Silky feminine fingers roamed over the swollen mushroom-shaped head of his thick length making his entire body tighten magnificently with anticipation.

Fevered blood coursed up his shaft.

He groaned at the wild sensations.

His heart raced. His cock literally felt as if it were on fire.

"How's that feel?"

"Like I want to be fucked."

"Perfect. You're nice and wet. Just the way I want you."

"Touché." He grinned as he remembered using similar words on her.

She grabbed the red and white-stripped candy cane decorated pussy sleeve and leaned over him, her hair tumbling in front of her face, hiding her flushed cheeks from his view.

Apparently, she was enjoying this just as much as he was.

Her seductive scent swept around him, drugging him. Her breasts looked swollen as they swayed, her nipples hard with apparent arousal.

Positioning the opening of the pussy sleeve over the pulsing head of his engorged cock, she pulled it down over his slick swollen shaft.

The sleeve stretched around his thick head like a tight glove.

"Shit!" he hissed as powerful sensations made his abdominal muscles clench.

"It's got ribbing inside," she whispered.

Inside the pussy sleeve, he heard a slurping sound as she eased it down over his thick throbbing flesh.

He grimaced as rich bursts of pleasure shimmered all around him.

Interlacing the fingers of both hands around the pussy sleeve, she moved it up and down his slick cock.

The ribbed insides of the stretched pussy sleeve massaged and scratched the entire length of his swollen flesh sending sensual shards of lightning racing down his shaft and slamming into his balls.

Caydon groaned at the fantastic impact.

His arousal throbbed.

He felt the need to spew.

Clenching his jaws tightly, he held himself back and allowed the wonderful sensations to wash all around him.

His scrotum tightened.

His breath stalled in his lungs as she twisted mightily.

He cried out at the pleasure-pain.

Watched in awe as the swollen head of his cock peeked out at the top of the sleeve. A dribble of pre-cum beaded at the slit.

Jade leaned over.

With the tip of her pink tongue, she licked the beads off his throbbing head and moaned her approval.

The power of that sexy sound made his whole body tense. He wanted to plunge his raw burning cock deep into her supple warm cunt. Wanted to feel her soft body bucking beneath him as he drove into her tight slit over and over again.

The need to fuck was reflected in her eyes.

"Jade?" His voice sounded strangled, desperate.

She laughed as she enjoyed his sexual torture and he caught his breath at the tiny crinkles that erupted at the edges of her eyes.

Shit! He'd never noticed that before. Never noticed how beautiful she looked when she laughed.

And when her mouth opened and she could barely slide her lips around the pussy sleeve, he jolted as her hot tongue laved the entire head of his cock.

Sweet mercy, she was going to kill him!

Suddenly her hands were on his shoulders and she was pushing him onto his back.

He lay on the mattress, watching in awe as part of his cock disappeared into her mouth. Soft hands clenched around his scrotum, squeezing ever so gently, encouraging him to climax.

He couldn't stop himself from thrusting his hips upward into her mouth, an animalistic groan ripping from deep in his chest.

"Jade!" he gasped as the entire thick length of his rock-hard rod quivered its need.

Shoving his hips harder at her face, he felt her hot mouth tighten around the top of the pussy sleeve, the ribbing inside clenched ever so erotically around his rigid rod.

He tried to reach out to her but remembered his hands were cuffed.

"Mount me!" he cried out.

She slid the pussy sleeve off him.

His cock had grown so tight and so hard, he didn't know how long he could hold out.

She came over him like a goddess, her brown hair flowing to her shoulders in wisps, the moon a halo around her head.

Her feet straddled both sides of his legs as she came down on him.

In the darkness he could imagine how her thighs were drenched with her arousal, could imagine how red and puffy her clitoris must look and how swollen her labia lips must feel.

Her eyes sparked heat as she straddled him.

He gritted his teeth as she teased his engorged cock-head with the tight opening of her hot cunt.

They both cried out as she dropped onto him, her wet cunt suctioning over his stiff flesh as if she were his very own hot pussy sleeve.

The current state of his impending release made him clench his eyes closed.

He cried out as he cut himself loose.

The explosion started in his balls, blades of white heat pounding into his shaft in a fierce blast that sent lights sparking behind his eyes.

He spewed his load right into her spasming cunt. He listened in awe to the suctioning sound of their juices mixing as her warm vagina sucked on his rigid cock eagerly draining him of his seed.

She rode him hard.

Her hips lifting.

Her hot cunt gripping him as she continued to slam down on his cock over and over again.

Her sexy moans mixed with his ragged groans as carnal sensations pierced his soul.

His mind swirled, his body spiraled beneath the waves of pleasure, leaving him dazed at the intensity.

When his orgasm died, he lay limp on the mattress, his harsh breaths tearing out of his lungs and shooting through the cool night air intermingling with her sensual whimpers of relief.

Tiny spasms from her vagina muscles continued to play with his softened cock as she kept him buried deep inside of her hot pussy and lay down on him, her soft feminine body curving over his rigid muscles.

Lifting his cuffed hands, he brought his arms around her head and down encircling her warm waist.

Her silky hair danced across his cheek and she nestled her head snugly into the curve between his shoulder and neck.

"I think I love you." Her softly spoken whisper sliced through the air slamming into his ears, clutching warmly at his heart and leaving him so stunned he could only blink in wonder.

I think I love you?

Had he heard right?

He waited for her to say it again but nothing came.

Should he say something? Should he tell her he knew he was in love with her? Should he tell her the truth about why he'd come here?

Seconds ticked away and he valiantly gathered his courage.

Yes, now was the time to tell her the truth. Now was the time to tell her he loved her.

"Jade?"

His answer was a soft snore.

Holy shit!

She'd fallen asleep on him.

Literally.

In the afterglow of sex people sometimes said things they meant or sometimes they said things they thought the other person wanted to hear.

But she had no idea that's what he wanted her to say to him.

She had no idea he'd fallen head over heels in love with her the instant he'd met with her two sisters and they'd told him things about her.

Like she was a kindhearted woman. Sensitive and loving.

Sexy as sin.

Well, the last part was his version.

Caydon smiled and cupped her curvy ass tightly with his handcuffed hands.

When she opened up her presents, he'd know if she loved him or not.

With that thought firmly in his mind, and Jade's juicy hot cunt wrapped tightly around his satisfied cock, Caydon drifted off to sleep.

* * * * *

Jade and Caydon made love again and again after they awoke at dawn.

They broke their lovemaking for breakfast and after that, they opened their Christmas presents.

Jade's heart had thumped wildly as his eyes lit up with both surprise and happiness as he eagerly ripped off the bows and shredded the cheerful Christmas wrappings she'd had professionally done while they'd been apart in the mall.

She'd gotten him a fishing rod, tackle box, a pair of cross-country skis, accompanying ski accessories and a generous gift certificate to a popular hardware store so he could purchase himself tools for his handyman trade.

In turn he'd given her things she'd need for a boat trip to Europe such as very detailed nautical maps of the ocean and Europe's waterways, an expensive compass-like object that he promised he would install on her yacht and some other nautical equipment her boat would need to get her to Europe.

There was a small fortune of equipment laying here on her deck. Stuff he couldn't afford on a handyman's salary. She wanted to tell him that he shouldn't have spent so much money on her. But she didn't want to offend him.

And he certainly wouldn't be getting her all these presents for her unless she meant something to him…or if he wanted to impress her…or he wanted something from her.

Uneasiness at the last idea made her frown.

Was Caydon another Beau? Did he want to buy his way into her graces in the hopes that he would have bigger fish to fry, so to speak, in the future?

Would she always look at every man as a potential Beau?

She had a couple of movie star friends who'd gotten taken in that way. Men who'd wined and dined them, made love to them, paid attention to them. Those attentive men had turned out to be gigolos or worse.

As the doubts rolled through her mind, Jade realized that her instincts were telling her to trust Caydon.

Caydon was not another Beau.

For years her instincts and Gram had told her not to trust Beau, she'd never listened.

Maybe it was about time she listened to herself.

"You're frowning. I don't think I like the looks of that."

"I thought you said it was too dangerous for me to go alone to Europe?"

"I did."

"So? What's with all this stuff?"

Her body tingled as he lifted her hands to his mouth and delicately kissed each sensitive fingertip one at a time.

"If you don't like these presents, I can take them back."

She caught the teasing glint in his eyes.

Trust him, Gram's voice echoed in her mind.

How could she trust a man she knew nothing about?

Sometime during last night when she'd made love to him she'd thought she might be in love with him. She might have even whispered it to him before she'd fallen asleep.

One thing she did know for sure though was she needed to trust a man sometime in her life and maybe the time to learn how to trust again was now.

"Well, I don't know if I want you to do that, Caydon. Maybe I'll need someone to show me how all this stuff works?"

Her pulse pounded and her body hummed as he stared at her.

She loved the intense way he looked at her. It was a look of caring, of joy, a look of confidence.

All those emotions couldn't be imitated.

Besides, her heart always burst with a warm fuzzy feeling at the sexy way his bangs blew over his forehead.

And she really enjoyed the way he fucked her.

Dear God, had she truly fallen in love with him?

"Thought you'd never take the hint, Jade."

"What are you are saying? That you want to come along to Europe with me?"

"What I'm asking is do you want me to come with you? You said you wanted to go alone so I don't want to interfere in your quest for whatever it is you're looking for. If you'd rather go alone I'll stand by your decision and I'll make your yacht as safe as I possibly can. I am a handyman, y'know."

"You would leave your job and go off with me?"

This was the question she'd been dying to ask.

"I'm self-employed. I earn a very comfortable living. I can do whatever I want."

Jade found herself relaxing. "I didn't know you were self-employed?"

A shiver of alarm zipped up her spine at the pained look that suddenly flooded into his eyes.

"Jade, there's a lot of things you don't know about me. Things I need to tell you…"

Desperation swooped over her and for some unknown reason she didn't want him to tell her anything right now. Things seemed just too good to be true. And she didn't want it to change.

"Caydon, I want you to make love to me. Right now."

And that's exactly what he did.

Over and over again.

He kissed her so deeply — it took the breath clean out of her lungs. He entered her quivering cunt with a devastating slowness that made her cry out in arousal.

And he made love to her so exquisitely that he removed any lingering doubts she had about him.

Afterwards they returned to the Tampa Bay marina chatting gaily as they made plans to head off to Europe first thing New Year's Day.

Jade's newfound happiness however was short-lived.

It was that same afternoon when all those plans exploded…

Caydon's cell phone was ringing up a storm when Jade stepped out of the shower and spotted it lying on the bathroom counter. Obviously, he'd forgotten it when he'd showered earlier.

A family member was probably calling him to wish him a Merry Christmas.

She smiled as she listened to him whistling away with those Christmas tunes while he prepared a late lunch for them out in the kitchen.

The cell phone continued to ring with insistence.

"Caydon! Do you want me to get that?" she called out.

No answer.

He kept whistling.

The phone kept ringing.

Surely, he wouldn't mind if she answered it for him.

"Merry Christmas!" Jade chuckled into the phone.

"Hello? Who's this? Where's Caydon?" A woman's voice echoed in Jade's ears.

"Jade."

"Jade?" The woman sounded puzzled.

"Who's this?" Jade asked politely. Perhaps it was his sister? Or his mother?

Oh God! Not his mother! Not yet. How would she explain a strange woman answering her son's cell phone?

"Sandy, over at Kidnap Fantasies. Can you please get him for me? There seems to be an emergency here and…"

A cold wave blistered through Jade.

Kidnap Fantasies? What the hell?

From behind her, she barely heard Caydon's bare feet slap against the floor as he entered the bedroom.

"He's um...busy," she heard herself saying.

Kidnap Fantasies? Had she heard right?

Her ears began to ring. Her head started to spin.

"Would you please ask him to call me back when he's...finished with what he's doing."

Finished? Her stomach clenched.

Did she mean when he was finished fucking her? When he was finished his job?

Oh God!

Jade jumped when the bathroom door burst open and Caydon stepped into the steamy room.

He was naked.

His cock was engorged, and thick and quite ready to start fucking her again.

Nausea stung her stomach.

He reached out and playfully caught her by the arms pulling her backwards into his embrace. She barely felt his large hot hands cup her breasts from behind. Ordinarily she'd be moaning against the erotic way his fingers tugged at her nipples but now she felt nothing but numbness.

"Hello? Jade?" The woman on the cell phone sounded impatient.

The cell phone trembled in her hand.

Kidnap Fantasies? Caydon worked for Kidnap Fantasies?

"Ma'am? Hello? Could you ask him to call me back? It's important."

"Um...sure."

"Fantastic. Merry Christmas!"

The line went dead.

Jade closed her eyes and tried to steady her frantic breathing. This couldn't be happening. It had to be some cruel joke.

Caydon worked for Kidnap Fantasies?

How could this be? She'd never mailed in that questionnaire.

"Who was it? A secret admirer I should be jealous of?" Caydon whispered against her ear.

"Kidnap Fantasies," she found herself whispering.

Caydon's hands stilled on her breasts.

Even with the mirror fogged by steam of her shower, she could see his face pale.

"Oh God, I didn't want you to find out this way. I can explain."

If that reaction didn't confirm what that woman on the phone had said, then Jade was an idiot.

Ice slid into her veins.

"Don't bother explaining."

"Please, just listen to me."

"Get your hands off me!"

"Sweetheart, it isn't what you think."

Hot anger burst inside her like an explosion and Jade tore herself from his embrace.

"You bastard!"

He reached out to take her into his arms again but she slapped his hands away from her. The thought of him touching her sickened her. She wanted him gone. Wanted him out of her life!

Grabbing a towel, she quickly wrapped it around herself.

Humiliation made her hobble past him and she rushed out of the bathroom.

God! She needed air. She was going to pass out!

Blackness hovered at the edges of her sight and she stumbled through the bedroom.

She made it outside just in time. The warm afternoon breeze blew against her skin.

It helped, but only a little.

"Jade, I wanted to tell you."

Shit! He'd followed her out here? The prick had nerve!

She whirled around to face him. The need to strike him was so brutal she almost did it, but held herself back.

"You fuck women for a living?"

"No, it's not what you think."

The bastard was denying it. He was a liar. Just like Beau.

"Get off my fucking boat!"

"Sweetheart…"

"Get out of here, Caydon!"

"Please don't let it end this way," Caydon whispered.

Oh God.

Her mind whirled. Caydon and Kidnap Fantasies?

He was still standing in front of her.

"Leave! I can't stand to see you. I don't want to ever see you again!"

His face whitened as if she'd struck him.

"Jade, I can't…I need to explain. I love you."

"Love? That's a joke! You're just like the rest of them. You're a loser. Just a gigolo."

"I can explain."

"Go away!" Hysteria edged into her mind. She felt like screaming. She'd do it too if he didn't leave.

She barely noticed a young couple on the nearby dock watching them.

He nodded. "Okay, take it easy. I'm going. Just take it easy. I'm going."

God! Why couldn't she cry? Why couldn't she slap him? Why couldn't she feel anything but this awful numbness? This horrible cold empty feeling?

She heard Caydon curse harshly as he jogged into the cabin.

A moment later, he erupted from the cabin wearing his jeans and pulling on his shirt.

"This doesn't change my feelings for you, Jade. I mean it when I say I love you."

"Go away. Please."

He didn't move. He stared at her long and hard.

She sensed he was expecting her to say something else but the numbness of shock was beginning to fade quickly being replaced by a pain so raw and ugly she didn't think she could survive it.

Regret, confusion and a dozen other emotions she couldn't put a name to flashed in his blue eyes.

"I love you, Jade Hart," he whispered.

Through suddenly welling tears, Jade watched as he turned and left.

Her legs trembled violently. Her stomach continued to clench with waves of nausea.

She closed her eyes and grabbed the steel railing for support.

What in the world was she going to do now?

His cell phone began to ring again.

Her eyes snapped open.

She couldn't bear to answer it. With shaky fingers, she dropped it over the edge of the yacht.

It hit the water with a splash.

The twinkling lights on their little Christmas tree caught her attention.

Fury, rich and violent slammed through her. Without thinking, she grabbed at a prickly branch. She barely felt the tingling pain of the spruce needles biting into her flesh.

Lifting the tree, she hoisted it overboard.

When she heard the giant splash, it seemed as if a dam suddenly tore lose inside her.

Anger, pain and other gut-wrenching emotions spun through her like a whirlwind. Jade slumped onto the deck amongst the strewn Christmas wrappings and presents they'd opened.

Frantically she wiped at the tears of hurt spilling down her face. Tears of pain that were breaking her heart. Suddenly she realized she was once again alone at Christmas. Just like she'd been last year when Beau had left her.

Chapter Nine

New Years Eve morning…

Jade had just paid and sent away the man who'd delivered all the boxes of dried goods and other things she'd need for her yacht trip to Europe when she heard the phone ring.

She debated whether she should answer it or not. Caydon had called many times over the past few days. Every time she'd seen his name appear on the caller ID screen of her phone she'd burst into another round of tears.

A quick glance at the ID screen showed it wasn't Caydon calling this time but her sister Lindsey along with Crista.

They were bearing down on her with a conference call.

Her anger burned even brighter.

Over the past few days she'd figured it all out. Lindsey and Crista's unexpected visit. Both of them getting her curiosity aroused so she'd fill out the Kidnap Fantasies questionnaire. Then the questionnaire had disappeared shortly afterwards.

Obviously, they'd somehow taken it and sent it to the organization.

And the organization had sent Caydon Minnelli, biggest cock in stock.

But why would Caydon buy her all that expensive nautical equipment for Christmas? Why invite himself to come along on her trip?

The only thing that made sense was her theory about him wanting to ingratiate his way into her life so he could get some sort of relationship going and get her money. Somehow, before he'd even met her he'd found out about her dream trip and used it to his advantage.

She should have figured that out easily enough simply by realizing he bought all those presents even before she'd told him about her dream of sailing to Europe.

And of course her sisters must have been the ones to tell him where she'd kept the keys to start her boat so he could "kidnap" her. But why would they tell him about her dream trip?

"You must have had a really good laugh reading my private fantasies." Jade hissed into her cell phone after flicking it on.

"Jade! I'm so sorry. We never read it." Lindsey sounded very upset. Served her right.

"It's all my fault what happened between you and Caydon," she continued. "If I'd just told you right up front and not taken that questionnaire to him everything would have worked out fine."

Jade's senses whirled.

"You met him?"

"We both met him," Crista chimed in. "We had to check out the merchandise to make sure he was suitable for you."

Oh my God! What was she hearing? Her two sisters had actually gone to meet the guy who would ultimately fuck her?

Insanity!

"Sis? You still there?" Lindsey asked softly.

"She's still there," Crista chuckled. "She can't stay mad at Caydon or us for long. Not after everything we had to go through to get them together. And boy you're going to want to hear what Lindsey had to do…"

"I don't want to know."

"Caydon Minnelli came to me in a vision through one of Gram's magical candles," Lindsey said softly.

A shiver of uneasiness zipped through Jade. Over the past two years, not including this one, Lindsey had sworn she'd seen visions in one of Gram's candles before it flickered and died.

Lindsey had pursued those visions and with the help of Gram's candles, Crista and Jeff had found each other.

"You saw him in the vision?"

"That's why we sent him to you," Crista said. "You know the first two visions led to love and this time Gram sent a message to Lindsey for you."

"Well, not this time," Jade snapped, the familiar anger churning up inside her chest again. "As far as I'm concerned Caydon Minnelli can go straight to hell."

"Would it help if I told you that I tried very hard to persuade him to meet you?" Lindsey said. "He told me he didn't believe in my visions and that he didn't want to meet you."

"He lied. He met me."

"Obviously he was intrigued by your questionnaire."

"Forget the questionnaire! I can't be with a man who fucks women for a living!"

"Jade!" Crista's stern voice hauled in her mounting anxiety. "That's uncalled for. Lindsey was following through for Gram."

"Well, I'm sorry but I didn't ask for Gram's help. And I didn't ask to fall in love with another gigolo."

"You're in love?" Crista said gently.

"A gigolo?" Lindsey asked.

Tears of frustration welled up and Jade couldn't stop the frustrated sob from breaking free of her chest.

"Oh great, now we made her cry." Crista sounded upset.

"Why do you think he's a gigolo? He's absolutely nothing like Beau," Lindsey said.

"For crying out loud! He works for Kidnap Fantasies. He makes love to other women for a living."

"Works for KF? He doesn't work for them," Crista blurted out.

"He owns it," Lindsey said.

"Owns it?" Jade hiccupped.

"He's a self-made millionaire," Lindsey explained. "He owns a string of hardware stores across the States and he invested in KF. Do you know how hard it was for me to even track him down and to get him to trust me enough to explain about Kidnap Fantasies?"

"How did you find him?" Curiosity was beginning to edge away Jade's anxiety, especially now that Lindsey had said Caydon didn't work for that…company.

"Gram found him. When I saw the name Kidnap Fantasies in the vision, I remembered seeing it written down somewhere. I went through Gram's old stuff we kept and found a paper with a letterhead that belonged to Gram's lawyer. On that paper was someone's scrawled handwriting, which said Kidnap Fantasies. So I took the paper to the lawyer, told him about Gram's candles, my visions and that I needed to find Kidnap Fantasies."

"And he told you he could help you?"

"No, he told me I was totally crazy. He told me to get lost before he called security."

"What did you do?" Jade asked.

"I informed him I wouldn't leave until he produced information about this Kidnap Fantasies. So I…handcuffed myself to his desk."

"You didn't!"

"She did!" Crista laughed.

"And you know what happened after that?" Lindsey asked.

"He told you Caydon's name."

"No. He left the office to go and get the security guard. I wasn't there two minutes when the man in my vision walked into the office. Caydon's face went so pale I thought he might pass out from shock," Lindsey giggled.

Jade could barely suppress her laughter at what Caydon must have thought seeing her sister cuffed to his grandfather's desk.

"What did he do?"

"He wasn't amused," Lindsey explained. "He thought his grandfather and I were doing something kinky behind his grandmother's back. When I explained everything about Gram, the magical candles and showed him the letterhead that said Kidnap Fantasies on it and your picture, remember the one on the cover of *People* magazine? That's when he told me what I was telling him was so unbelievable it just might be true. And you know what else?"

"What?"

"He couldn't take his eyes off your picture. His eyes just kind of lit up when he looked at you. Even when he was saying there was no way he was going to meet you based on my story he kept staring at your picture. In the end, he handed me that brochure of Kidnap Fantasies and a questionnaire for you. The rest is history."

"You told him about my dream trip to Europe?"

"Guilty," Lindsey replied. "I had to tell him what a wonderful person you are and that included your dreams."

"So? Are you going to make up with him?" Hope filled Crista's voice.

"I...I don't know where he is," Jade admitted.

Her Caller ID didn't display a person's number just their name.

Not to mention the way she'd kicked him off her boat on Christmas Day telling him she never wanted to see him again, he might not want to see her again.

"I have his phone numbers," Lindsey sang.

"Oh Jade, go for it," Crista urged. "You've already admitted you're in love with him."

Jade swallowed at her blooming excitement. "Okay, give me the numbers."

After getting his numbers and the promise she'd call Caydon, Jade broke the conference call with her sisters.

Slumping into a nearby deck chair, she gazed at the electric fireplace that had been too heavy to chuck overboard with the Christmas tree.

Caydon was the owner of Kidnap Fantasies? What kind of a man would create that type of a business? And why?

She frowned when she spotted something glinting off a string from one of the still filled Christmas stockings that hung off the mantle of the fireplace.

"What in the world?" Jade whispered as she stood.

Drawing closer to it, her mouth went dry with shock and she thought she just might start bawling right then and there.

Fluttering in the warm Florida breeze and tied to a pretty piece of gold tinsel was a big fat pink diamond ring.

Chapter Ten

Fifteen minutes before New Year's…

"Come on, Caydon, answer your damned phone," Jade grumbled anxiously into her cell phone as she lay in bed holding her hand up to the window admiring how the full moon's rays sparkled against the pink diamond ring she'd slipped on her finger.

She'd been calling Caydon off and on since Lindsey had given her the numbers. Earlier this morning she'd actually had him on the line but at the sound of his sexy voice she'd chickened out and hung up on him.

When she'd gathered up the nerve to try again she hadn't been able to get an answer anywhere. Not at his office, his pager or his home.

She'd wanted to apologize to him for her being such a bitch and not letting him explain. But she'd been hurt and humiliated by the telephone conversation with that Kidnap Fantasies woman.

Most of all she didn't like the fact he'd lied to her.

It had felt like Beau all over again. Lying to her. Hanging around her simply so he could manage her money and her career.

But Lindsey had said Caydon had his own money. So, he wasn't interested in hers. But what if he'd been dirt-poor? Would that have made her want to apologize to him? Want him back in her life?

Jade sighed.

She didn't know the answer to that question.

Poor or rich, all she knew was that over the last few days she'd missed her sexy man terribly and now she couldn't even find him.

As she watched the ring glisten in the moonlight, a fluttery happy feeling clenched the pit of her belly.

The pink diamond on this ring looked like the same type as the tiny diamonds that dangled off those nipple clamps and labia clamps he'd outfitted her with.

Had he been planning a proposal all along?

It sounded so insane and yet maybe, just maybe, Caydon Minnelli was interested in her. After all, he was interested enough in the questionnaire to come and meet her in the first place.

What about the ring though?

He wouldn't have tied this pretty ring to a piece of tinsel and hung it from her stocking if he wasn't serious about her. Right?

Jade frowned.

She'd ruined everything by not letting him explain. Ruined his plans to propose.

Swearing softly into the silence she flipped the cell phone closed and set it on the bed beside her.

It could be that he wasn't answering on purpose.

Maybe he'd changed his mind and didn't want anything more to do with her? Maybe she was being silly thinking that he wanted her after the way she'd freaked out and sent him packing.

Or she was just being dumb by keeping this pretty rock on her finger when she'd have to send it back to him anyway.

Oh but it was so pretty.

She shouldn't keep it, though. It wasn't right.

She tried to slide the ring off her finger but it didn't budge.

Great! Just what she needed.

She pulled harder.

Nothing.

She twisted it this way and that. Still nothing.

By golly, it felt as if it had been cemented onto her finger.

A slice of laughter slipped past her lips at the thought of having to have her finger cut off just so she could send him back the ring.

Suddenly she spotted a flash through the window high in the sky.

"A falling star!"

Quick make a wish! Gram's voice sailed softly through her mind.

"I want Caydon, Gram," Jade whispered longingly into the quiet of New Year's Eve. "I want Caydon back in my life."

The star disintegrated.

At that same instant, she heard the rumble of engines come to life. For a second she thought the owners to the yacht docked next to hers were heading out to celebrate New Year's. But she didn't see any lights on.

And then her yacht swayed just a little.

A gut-wrenching feeling clutched her gut as she felt her boat begin to move.

Oh my goodness someone was stealing her boat!

With her in it!

Fumbling in the moon glow she struggled to find the cell phone. The instant her hand touched the cool item she heard the soft sound of familiar whistling.

It was a New Year's tune.

It took Jade only moments to locate her robe and cane and hobble down the hallway, through the kitchen and out onto the main deck into the salt-scented ocean air. Maneuvering quickly and quietly up the stairs, she then entered the dimly lit glass-enclosed pilothouse.

Caydon Minnelli stood at the computer console. His legs slightly spread. His long fingers curled around the captain's wheel. His broad back was to her as he looked out the window and carefully steered the yacht out of the berth.

And he was totally naked!

His musky masculine scent drifted to her along the fresh ocean breeze teasing her nostrils. She couldn't stop the delicious lashes of lust from uncurling deep in the soul of her pussy as she savored the sight of his nice plump ass cheeks ready to be cupped into her eager hands.

However, she didn't dare touch him or press herself against his magnificent nude body.

At least not yet.

"I'd recognize that cute ass, anywhere," she whispered.

He stiffened in surprise, obviously unaware she'd come into the pilothouse. He stopped whistling and turned his face toward her.

His appearance shocked her.

Dark stubble stained his face, dark shadows haunted his eyes and there was an uncertainty in the way he held himself.

If she didn't know any better she'd swear the man had missed her. Maybe even pined over her?

She swallowed at the bright lust shining in his eyes and the sight of his nostrils flaring as he smelled the air.

"And I'd recognize the sweet scent of your arousal anywhere."

A shiver of anticipation raced up her back.

"You've got balls coming back here, Caydon Minnelli."

"Rock-hard balls, baby. Real solid and ready to spill deep into your sweet pussy."

Jade's cunt literally dripped with cream at his words.

God! She wanted him to fuck her. Wanted to feel his swollen shaft slide deep into her aching pussy. Wanted it more than her next breath.

"So?" he continued as he turned back around and maneuvered her yacht between the gently bobbing buoys that guided them out of the marina. "How come you've been calling me all day?"

Son of a bitch!

"Why didn't you answer?"

"And give you the chance to hang up again? No way."

"Why would I call and then hang up?"

"Because you did it once this morning when I answered. I wasn't going to let you get cold feet again."

"I didn't get cold feet."

"So what would you call it?"

"Changing my mind."

"I hear it's a woman's prerogative." There was a slight teasing chuckle in his voice. "So why'd you call me?"

"To apologize."

"I flew all the way out here for a simple apology?"

"That's all I'm prepared to give you at this point in time, Caydon."

Liar! Gram's voice whispered in her ear as plain as if she were in the pilothouse with them.

"So, I guess you've wasted a trip."

"Actually, Jade, I came all this way to kidnap you. And that's what I intend to do."

Jade's pulse picked up speed.

"And I came all this way to tell you that I should I have told you the truth right from the start."

"Why didn't you?"

He shook his head slowly. "I don't know. After your sister gave me your questionnaire, I realized I really wanted to meet you. But I wanted it to happen naturally between us, not because we were forced to meet. Lindsey explained about the magical candles and about your Gram and I thought maybe you'd think we belonged together because of her vision. I wanted to tell you why I had come. I tried...but I just couldn't. I had to believe it was natural between us."

"God! What we have together is very natural." Jade laughed as she walked up behind him and slid her arms around his lean waist. Muscles bulged against her fingers as she trailed downward and dove beneath his long hard cock to cup his swollen balls nestled in his tight sac.

He sucked in an aroused breath.

"What we have together can't be faked, Caydon. The minute I saw you standing there watching me, something inside my heart shifted into place. At the time, I wouldn't admit it. I couldn't admit that a guy might be interested in me...at least not the way I am with my leg and hip..."

"I think we covered all that, Jade." He pressed his warm ass backward against her belly.

Her cheeks grew warm at the thought that Caydon wanted her just the way she was.

"I know, I know. You suffer from the lady in distress syndrome."

"And by the way you're grabbing at my balls and the way your nipples are poking into my back, I'd say you're getting pretty distressed, Jade."

He grabbed her hands, pulled her fingers from his rock-hard balls and swung her in front of him, holding her against him as he now stood behind her. This time it was her turn to nestle her ass against him. His rock-hard cock pressed against the thin material barely clothing the crack in her ass cheeks.

"I do believe I have a remedy for your distress," he whispered.

His fingers intertwined with hers and he placed her hands on the steering wheel of her boat. "And you put it on your finger without giving me a chance to pop the question."

My goodness! She'd forgotten to take it off.

"I was just trying it on…and it got stuck."

"Stuck, huh?"

"Well, you try to take it off and see what I mean."

"Maybe it won't come off for a reason," he chuckled. "Maybe it's that falling star I saw a minute earlier. Maybe my wish of us being together is going to come true."

"That's the same wish I made when I saw it tonight," Jade whispered in awe.

"They always say if two people wish on the same star and for the same thing it'll come true for sure," Caydon said.

"No wish is going to come true until you tell me one thing."

He kissed the curve of her neck unleashing delicious little tingles through her body.

"What do you want to know?"

"This Kidnap Fantasies, what exactly is it?"

"Top secret."

"So I've heard."

Her eyes widened as she felt something clamp around one wrist and then the other.

Shit! He'd handcuffed her to the steering wheel!

"You steer. I have other business to attend to."

Pure desire ripped through her veins as she felt his fingers untie the sash on her robe. Warm air brushed her curves as he lifted the material over her hips and tied it into place with the sash so it wouldn't fall down.

"Tell me about it, Caydon. I want to know why you'd invent something like that?"

His hands settled on the curves of her hips. His hot breath embraced her ass.

"First of all, Sandy, the woman who you spoke with on my cell phone is relatively new at Kidnap Fantasies. She was given my private number over the holidays in case she couldn't reach the other partners. She shouldn't have revealed the organization to you. Only a select few know about it. She's been…reprimanded."

"Reprimanded? How?"

His hands smoothed tenderly over her ass cheeks. "Let's just say she's paid very well to follow orders…she won't forget this lesson. As to Kidnap Fantasies, I only invested in it. My partners invented it and they run it. They have personal reasons why they're doing what they're doing."

"So you really don't participate with…"

"With other women?" He gently bit into her ass cheek making Jade squirm from the sting of pain.

"Everything I told you was the truth. I'm not married and I've never wanted to be with a woman so badly as I want to be with you. When I saw your picture on the cover of that magazine your sister showed me I was hooked on you. When I read your Kidnap Fantasies questionnaire about you wanting a big cock and that you were open to new sexual experiences I just knew I had to meet you and make some of your fantasies come true."

"Now that you've kidnapped me and handcuffed me to my boat's steering wheel, where are you taking me? A secret island where you can fuck me 24/7?"

"If you call your yacht an island on the ocean."

"What are you saying, Caydon?"

Dare she hope? Dare she hope that he would say he wanted to come with her?

She held her breath as she awaited his answer

"I'm saying I'll be fucking you 24/7 all the way to Europe…if you want me to come?"

Her heart tripped wonderfully. "I want you to come all right. Inside me. Now."

"I can arrange that."

She couldn't stop the whimper of her excitement as she caught the reflection in the pilothouse window of him standing up behind her.

His hand slipped beneath her handcuffed arm and came around to settle over the swell of her belly. He pulled her back a couple of steps then instructed her to bend over.

She cried out as his hot fingers slipped between her legs and he pried her fat labia lips apart, his finger finding her swollen clitoris. With a firm pressure, he began a leisurely massage.

"Oh Caydon, yes. That feels so good," she whimpered.

"Just good?"

A finger slipped inside her hot wet cunt making her gasp her answer.

Heat scorched her skin. Her nerve endings flared to life. Her head spun.

The finger on her pleasure nub increased in pressure sending Jade's body spiraling toward her pleasure.

He continued to knead her clit until she literally felt the cream of her arousal dripping from her cunt.

She strained her hips backward pushing herself harder against his hand.

"There, that's the way I want you. Nice and wet and ready for me."

Delicious shivers rampaged through her body as his stiff swollen cock probed against the opening of her drenched pussy.

"Ready and willing to be fucked whenever I want it."

"How about when I want it?" she breathed.

"That won't be a problem. You want it all the time," he chuckled hoarsely. "Just like I want you all the time. Now brace yourself."

Before she had a chance to heed his warning and tighten her grip on the helm, he speared his long thick cock into her dripping cunt in one solid thrust burying himself right to the hilt, his hard balls slamming into her ass.

She cried out at the shocking impact. Her legs buckled and she fought to steady herself as he impaled her on his cock.

He stretched her open so wide her eyes teared up.

"Better than good?" he whispered in a tortured voice.

"Much," she gasped as her pussy walls clenched tightly around the long thick invasion.

"So what did you wish for that first night we saw our falling star?" he said between gritted teeth as he slid out and then sliced his solid erection into her tight wet slit burying himself right to the hilt again.

She wasn't the least bit embarrassed to tell him, especially now that his delicious cock was doing such wondrous things to her body.

"A trip to Europe…with you as my personal love slave on my yacht," she confessed.

"Your love slave? Really?"

"You sound surprised," Jade breathed against the pleasure threatening to swallow her whole.

"I had a similar wish." Caydon groaned as her vagina began to quiver around his intrusion. "I wished you would turn out to be *the* one."

Happiness washed over her. Through blurry tears, she looked at the pink diamond sparkling on her finger.

"I think I am *the* one…if Lindsey's vision and this ring is any indication. I can't seem to get it off my finger. So you won't be getting it back unless you want my finger too."

"I want your finger and all of you. Will you marry me when we get to Europe? Will you be my wife? Will you have my babies?"

"If you keep fucking me this hard we'll have one before we even get there," Jade laughed.

In the window, she saw his eyes flash with lust. His teeth clenched as he slammed his hips and penetrated her even deeper.

Jade hissed at the pleasure-pain as his cock slammed up against her cervix.

"You didn't answer my question. Will you marry me?"

She resisted the urge to close her eyes and sink into the pleasure. She wanted just one more moment with his reflection.

"Yes, I'll marry you."

A wonderful grin curled the edges of his lips.

"Happy New Year, Jade."

"Happy New Year, Caydon," she whispered back as her cunt clenched tighter around his enormous shaft and his finger continued to massage her love button.

Her last thought before she spiraled into her orgasm was she was really going to enjoy making babies with Caydon Minnelli.

She was going to enjoy it.

A lot.

About the author:

Jan Springer is the pseudonym for an award winning best selling author who writes erotic romance and romantic suspense at a secluded cabin nestled in the Haliburton Highlands, Ontario, Canada.

She has enjoyed careers in hairstyling and accounting, but her first love is always writing. Hobbies include kayaking, gardening, hiking, traveling, reading and writing.

Jan Springer welcomes mail from readers. You can write to her c/o Ellora's Cave Publishing at 1056 Home Ave. Akron, Oh. 44310-3502.

Also by Jan Springer:

The Last Candle

Katherine Kingston

Chapter One

Three years after the first vision, only one candle remained. Lindsey didn't like to acknowledge, even to herself, that she hoped the last message would be for her.

As usual Lindsey set up her tree the day after Thanksgiving and waited impatiently. Almost a month went by with nothing happening. By Thursday, two days before Christmas, she could barely stand to leave the room for fear she wouldn't see it happen. She fell asleep on the sofa that night.

The candle kept her waiting until almost two o'clock Christmas Eve before it flared to life.

Excitement and anticipation made her lightheaded as she looked into the vivid, golden glow of the blazing candle.

It showed her a man. Just his head, initially, but he was good-looking in a rough, unkempt way. Medium brown hair, with just a few threads of gray at the temples, was mussed and falling into his eyes in front. A couple of days' growth of beard gave him a sexy stubble, particularly since it surrounded a hard, but sensuous-looking mouth. The square jaw, long, straight nose and level dark eyebrows added up to a face that could belong to a model, with some improvement in grooming and a lighter expression. He seemed to be sitting, leaning back against a cinderblock wall, frowning at something she couldn't see.

Lindsey felt thrilling bubbles floating around in her stomach. Her pulse picked up speed.

Then she began seeing more of the scene, almost as though a camera showing the scene drew back to allow a wider-angle view.

Her excitement turned to dismay.

The man wore an orange jail jumpsuit and sat on a cot in a cell.

Well, crap.

He didn't look like a hardened criminal. In fact, clean him up a bit and he'd look like any other normal businessman. Well, maybe not exactly normal. He was too good-looking and too disturbingly, knowingly sensual for normal. But even more, a sense of barely leashed power, ambition and, right now, anger, radiated almost palpably from him. A hard man, a formidable man, under ordinary circumstances. Right then, he reminded her of a caged tiger. Dangerous.

Lindsey kept waiting for the rest of the story. But that was all she got. The view of the man in the jail cell.

It was all she needed, but she didn't want it to be that way. She knew what to do. She just didn't want to do it.

Act boldly.

But not stupidly, she argued back. Which was even more stupid. How could you argue with a ghost?

Anyway, the visions had asked her to do foolish, even stupid things before. They'd all worked out spectacularly well. She tried to see that as a guarantee this would, too, but another look at the man made her shiver. His eyes narrowed, and he seemed to gaze right at her as though he could see her. The raw fury hit her like a club in the gut.

She didn't dare. He was in jail for a reason.

Having delivered its message, the candle flared even brighter for a moment, almost blinding her, then it went out. For good.

And that was it.

The last thing she wanted to do on Christmas Eve was make a trip to the local jail and bail out an unknown and likely dangerous man. But…the visions hadn't let her down yet, even though each had seemed foolish, and sometimes even dangerous, at the time.

An hour later, Lindsey had managed to get lost trying to find the parking lot for the jail and then again once inside the government building that housed it somewhere within the maze of corridors and elevators. By dint of perseverance and questioning everyone she met, she finally found the right office.

It was only when a clerk asked her the name of the prisoner she was inquiring about that it occurred to her she had no idea, and that might complicate her mission. Once again, fate or otherworldly help came to her rescue, in the form of a man who had looked up from his desk nearby.

"I'll bet she's here for Greg MacIntyre. I figured he'd have some gorgeous woman come bail him out eventually. Guy that looks like that." He picked up a piece of paper from his desk and held it out to her. "You need a picture of him for your dresser, honey?"

Lindsey took it from him. It was a poor photocopy of a classic booking shot, showing full face and profile of the man from her vision, with a numeric label at the bottom. She nodded at the clerk, who asked, "You're posting bail for him?"

"How much?"

"Fifty thou," the clerk said.

"Oh, heck. I guess I better go find a bail bondsman."

"Do it quick," the clerk warned. "It's Christmas Eve. We're closing at four."

Lindsey looked at the clock. Two forty-five. "Can you recommend someone close?"

Fortunately there was one right across the street. The clerk gave her a piece of paper with the information she would need. Thirty minutes and five thousand dollars later, Lindsey took back the signed paper to the clerk.

"Have a seat," the clerk told her. "This will take a few minutes."

A few minutes turned into ten, then twenty, then thirty. Finally at five to four, the clerk returned, followed by the man she'd seen in the candle's glow. Her first reaction was an internal sigh of relief that she'd bailed out the right man. It didn't last long, chased away rapidly by the fear that followed.

She'd seen his smoldering sensuality and the anger that suffused him in the vision. It hadn't shown her how big he was and how aggressively male. She shivered under the impact of his riveting gray eyes looking at her with all his rage and fire on the verge of exploding.

He looked at her and frowned. "Who the hell are you?"

She opted for the safest response she could think of. "Lindsey Hart. I'm an attorney." She stuck out her hand.

Nothing could have prepared her for the impact when his palm wrapped around hers. Fire. Heat. Meltdown. Tingles crawled all over her skin, emanating from the hand he held. It stole her breath and flipped her heartbeat into overdrive. Oh, dear heaven. She was so not ready for this.

"Are you an associate of Tom Redmond?" he asked.

His voice was smooth, rich and deep with just an edge of bitterness, like the best dark chocolate. It sent shivers running up and down her spine.

She drew a deep breath to clear the obstruction in her throat. "Not exactly. Let's get out of here."

"Fine by me," he answered. "Have you got a car? Can you give me a lift?"

She nodded. They made an eerie trip out of the building, with lights going off in hallways behind them as offices closed up for the holiday. Greg wore the slacks of an expensive wool suit and a wrinkled dress shirt with the top two buttons undone. A red silk tie hung out of the pocket and the suit jacket was draped over his arm. He looked more like a businessman after a long hard day than someone just sprung from a jail cell.

The front of the car felt crowded with him in the passenger seat, and not just because his broad shoulders and long legs took up a lot of space.

She started the car, but before she pulled out of the parking place, she asked, "Where to?"

He stared out through the windshield, but she didn't think he was looking at the side of the city government building. "Who are you? Lawyers don't normally bail their clients out of jail."

"Lindsey Hart," she said. "And I am an attorney. But I'm not associated with Tom Redmond. He's your lawyer? He's a good one; probably the best."

"I know." He said it curtly, as though he wouldn't even consider anything but the best. "You haven't answered. What kind of lawyer are you, Lindsey Hart?"

"Actually I'm a tax attorney."

He turned to stare at her and rolled his eyes. "Oh, hell. Is someone investigating my tax returns, too? I'm clean. Squeaky clean. I don't cheat and I pay every dime I owe. Unlike some people I know." His tone turned from outrage to bitterness on the last sentence.

"I don't know anything about your taxes," she answered. "That's not why I'm here."

One dark, almost level eyebrow slid upward. "Then why are you here?"

"You aren't going to believe me when I tell you."

"Two weeks ago I wouldn't have believed it if someone told me I'd be in jail the week before Christmas. I'm learning to believe a lot of things I didn't believe before."

There were layers of meaning in his words. Below the reassurance that he would at least consider her explanation was something else. Suspicion—directed at her.

"This one is still pretty far out there," she said, wondering what he might suspect her of. Her instinct said it was more serious than just thinking she was a few crayons shy of a full box. It didn't make sense. What had that candle-vision gotten her into?

"Why don't you explain it as you drive me home," Greg suggested.

"All right. Tell me where to go."

Chapter Two

Greg watched the woman behind the steering wheel and wondered what she was up to. Lindsey Hart. The name rang no bells with him. She drove smoothly, competently, somewhat aggressively. She looked and sounded intelligent, except for that wild story she'd told him about seeing him in some kind of vision. In a flare from a candle lamp on her Christmas tree. She was also gorgeous, but that hardly mattered if she were the nutjob he suspected.

Was she one of those weirdos who followed news reports and hit on anyone who was featured? She didn't look the type, but then he'd never been in this position before and might not recognize the type. Worse, something about her tugged at him, made him too aware of her. The faint, appealing aroma of an expensive perfume, maybe, or the full curve of her bottom lip, made even pinker and riper because she chewed it gently, the only sign that she wasn't as cool and comfortable with this as she appeared. Or maybe it was the sparkle in her blue eyes, the glint of wry humor. She wasn't classically beautiful, but she had a warm prettiness that was more attractive.

They didn't talk much after she told him the wild story about the vision in the candle light and he gave her directions to his home.

When she pulled the car to the curb outside his apartment block, he wondered what he should say to her. What did she want? He was surprised she hadn't made any demands as yet. Before he could bring it up, though, she asked, "Have you got dinner plans? It's after five, and I haven't cooked a thing. Think we could find some place to eat on Christmas Eve?" And then, as though it just occurred to her, "Or maybe you have plans with family?"

He raised an eyebrow, and she blushed as it dawned on her how unlikely that was when he'd had to be bailed out of jail by a complete stranger. Maybe he'd humor her, have dinner with her and see if she'd tip her real reason for contacting him. "No plans. But I need to clean up a bit. If you don't mind waiting while I shower and shave, I'd enjoy having dinner with you."

She nodded. "I didn't have any other plans."

He couldn't help himself. "Why not?"

She looked surprised. "Why not?"

"Come on, lady. You're young, smart, well-off and attractive. You don't have to bail guys out of jail to get a date." He paused a moment. "I'm assuming you're not married or engaged." He looked at her hands. Her left ring finger was bare.

"I'm not," she answered. Her wavy, dark hair swung invitingly as she looked down at her own fingers. He wanted to bury his hands in the gleaming tresses. He wanted to taste her lips, especially the fuller lower one, to see if it tasted as good as it looked. *Whoa, doggie!* he implored himself. *We're going way too fast here.*

"You might as well come inside and wait," he offered. "I think I even had a bottle of a good Riesling, if you're interested."

"You're speaking my language," Lindsey said. She stepped out and joined him on the walkway. She moved with easy, lithe grace. Her hip-length coat fitted to her curves nicely and left her long, slender, jeans-clad legs free. The curve of calves and thighs under the denim was enough to set his pulse racing and his cock jumping. *Cool it down!*

He hoped he'd left the apartment in decent shape. He wasn't generally a slob, but when he got engrossed in a project, he sometimes let things like picking up the glasses and chip bags go. The surprise he got when he unlocked the door and entered, though, wasn't the kind of mess he was expecting.

It was freezing in the apartment, not more than a few degrees warmer than it was outside, which put it somewhere in the mid-twenties. "Oh, shit," Greg said, under his breath.

"How long were you in jail?" Lindsey asked. She pulled her coat tighter around her.

"A week."

Her eyebrows rose.

"I might have been a bit distracted before they arrested me," he admitted. *And forgotten to pay the electric bill.* So much for the hot, *private* shower, he'd been looking forward to for days. Geez, what else was left to go wrong?

He felt like kicking something—a lot of somethings, in truth. Things just kept going from bad to worse. No doubt the power company office was closed for the holiday, which meant he likely wouldn't be able to get it turned back on until Monday.

"I guess I'll have to see about a hotel room." And hope they'd accept his credit card. He couldn't remember if he'd paid that bill lately either.

Lindsey turned from surveying the apartment to look at him. "You can take a shower at my place. I'd like to change before we go to dinner anyway. Go pack your things."

Bossy lady, but he could handle that. Again he wondered about her real motivation. Could she have arranged for the power to be shut off? Possibly so she could offer him a place to stay? Why, though? And she hadn't offered him a place to stay yet, just the use of her shower. Something told him she was going to, though. Was she part of Marilyn's conspiracy? Good grief, she'd already gotten him disowned, fired and arrested. What else did she want?

He felt tired and disheartened, but Lindsey Hart didn't need to see that. More than anything else, he was furious, and she definitely didn't need to know that. "You might want to wait in your car," he suggested. "It'll be warmer there."

She nodded and turned to go back to the car. He could just make out the line of her hips as she walked out, but the way she moved…it set him on fire.

Dragging himself from contemplation of a complication he didn't need, he went back to his bedroom, gathered his razor, toothbrush, vitamins and hairbrush and tossed them into an overnight bag. As he grabbed underwear out of a drawer, though, it occurred to him he might as well pack for several days. He pulled a suitcase out of the closet and loaded the necessaries in. He traveled enough in his job—his former job— that packing was second nature. So much so, he caught himself as he was about to add extra dress shirts and another suit to the mix and replaced them instead with jeans and sweaters.

The cold seeped into his bones, even after he pulled on a wool sweater over his shirt, and his hands were just about frozen by the time he zipped up the suitcase and rolled it out. He stopped at the desk in the living room and pulled out his checkbook and a stack of bills from the drawer, stuffing them in the side pocket of his laptop case. Then he locked up and tossed the cases into the backseat of the car. They stopped briefly at the row of postboxes for the complex so he could pick up his mail, then they set off for her apartment.

Watching her drive was a pleasure. The hands that steered were long and graceful, with short, expensively manicured nails. The hands of a confident woman. He didn't understand her, but he'd go along with her, as far as she wanted to take this. As far as she wanted him to take her. What did he have to lose, at this point?

And if he was going down, why not grab what satisfaction he could find along the way? Especially when it came in such an inviting package and presented itself to him practically gift-wrapped and ready to wear.

"What were you charged with?"

"What? I'm sorry?" He had to drag himself out of unwise daydreams about what he'd like to do with Lindsey Hart.

"Why were you in jail?"

"Oh." The car suddenly felt too small. He felt too small. He didn't want to tell this elegant woman the whole sordid story. "Embezzlement. A damned neat frame-up. I didn't think she had it in her."

"Her?"

"My former fiancée. Also the boss's daughter. I was charmed by the package, shall we say? But it didn't wear well. I started trying to find the depths beneath the glitter, and unfortunately for both of us, I did. So I called it off. She called *me* every name in the book then called my uncle and cried so hard he was afraid she'd hurt herself, cried to Daddy and got me fired, and apparently cried to someone else who managed to set up a neat cheat that got me arrested for embezzlement."

"Wow. Busy lady."

"Yeah," he agreed. "Showed more ambition than I would have credited her with."

"Leaves you with kind of a problem, though."

"Indeed." He forced himself out of his maudlin misery. "Nothing I can do about it at the moment. And I've got a Christmas angel on my side. So maybe there's hope yet."

Lindsey didn't answer. He wondered if he'd offended her with the sarcastic edge he put on the words "Christmas angel". She pulled into the parking lot fronting a set of expensive townhouse apartments.

She parked, got out, and waited while he extracted his luggage before leading them to the door. Her place was impressive, neat and nicely decorated, but somehow comfortable. Right now it featured an amazing assortment of Christmas decorations. Beyond the extensively ornamented, eight-foot Christmas tree dominating one corner of the room, there were banners hung on the walls, star- and snowflake-decorated throws and pillows tossed on the couch and chairs, candles everywhere, an arrangement of red and gold ornaments on the mantel over the gas-log fireplace and swags of fir branches laced with strings of gold and silver bead trim over each doorway. The lady really got in the holiday spirit.

The one place in the room that didn't bear any Christmas decorations intrigued him enough to draw him closer for a better look. A glass-enclosed curio cabinet held several dozen figurines, in a variety of sizes and materials. But they all showed the same mythical creature—unicorns. Mostly white or pale colors, in various attitudes, with different sizes, shapes and colors of horns. He considered for a moment what it said about Lindsey Hart that she collected unicorns.

"They're symbolic of elemental male energy and sexual drive, you know," he commented to her.

"How do you figure?" She turned from the closet where she'd hung up her coat.

The lady had a very nice shape under the coat. Generally slim, but round where a woman ought to be round. Some very good places for a man to put his hands. His fingers tingled and his palms ached to explore some of them. He wasn't sure what was inside the package that was Lindsey Hart, but the wrappings were certainly appealing.

"The big, muscular horse body, with that very phallic horn right out in front. In fact, it's on top of his head. Leads with his...horn rather than his brains."

"I've known a few guys like that. But not all do."

He grinned. "Some of us hide it better than others."

"You include yourself in the 'hiding it better' category?"

"Up until a couple of weeks ago, I did."

"And you're letting it all hang out now?"

"Do you feel safe with me?" he asked.

She looked at him. Her blue eyes were sharp but bright with intelligence and amusement. "Not entirely."

"Then why am I here?"

Some of the amusement died. "I've learned that some risks are worth taking. I think I've learned how to know which ones."

"Trusting those 'vision' things?"

"And my instincts. The guestroom is the first door on the right." She pointed down the hallway. "It has its own bathroom, with shower."

He took the hint and dragged his stuff down the hall. He would have preferred his own apartment, but the hot water still felt wonderful, washing off the jail-grunge smell. The showerhead was high enough to accommodate all six feet and two inches of him. Normally he would have scoffed at the floral-scented shampoo, but the aroma pleased him and its suds made him finally feel clean again after too many days of confinement and unpleasant sanitary facilities.

By the time he'd toweled off, shaved and dressed in clean slacks and shirt, he felt life and confidence returning.

He wandered back into the living room and found Lindsey waiting there for him. She looked up and her eyes widened. "Wow. You cleaned up well."

"You say the nicest things."

"And you don't know how to deal with it."

He raised an eyebrow and looked her over. "You don't scrub up so badly yourself."

She gave him a wry grin. "You want the sharp, witty response, or the ego-soothing one?"

"Ego-soothing, of course. Always ego-soothing."

"I doubt it. But okay. Thank you and I don't know what to say."

"You've got to put more confusion and self-deprecation into that 'I don't know what to say' if you want it to be really ego-soothing."

She rolled her eyes. "And you've got to put less arrogance into 'always ego-soothing' if you want anyone to believe it."

He couldn't hold back a smile. He was starting to hope she would invite him to stay. This could be fun. In fact, he was going to be disappointed if she didn't. He'd manage to find some pitiful story about being alone at Christmas to get himself invited back, even if she didn't tell him not to bother with a hotel.

"By the way, what was the sharp and witty response?" he asked.

"Oh. I would have said, 'Actually I scrub up very badly. Especially dirty dishes and bathroom sinks.'"

He grinned. "Clever. Probably true, too. I'll bet you have a cleaning service."

She shrugged and stood up. "Yup. I believe in leaving things like that to the professionals."

"Of course," he agreed.

They went to a nearby restaurant that was open on Christmas Eve. Dinner conversation was pleasant and stimulating. He'd rarely met a woman who was so attractive, and yet felt no need to flaunt it or use it to entice him. Her sharp wit and incisive intelligence fascinated him as much as her well-shaped body and beautiful, sparkling eyes. They talked about their families, friends, jobs and travels during a steak dinner accompanied by a deeply fragrant, vividly fruity Merlot. He could have gone on all night, but when the waiters showed signs of wanting to close up, they got up and left.

They were in her car, driving back to her apartment, when she finally brought it up. "You don't have to go to a hotel, you know," she said. "I've got a perfectly good guestroom not in use right now."

"Are you sure that's a good idea?" he asked.

She shrugged. "No, but I'm pretty sure it's the right idea."

A few streetlights occasionally lit up her profile. He stared at her and knew she was aware of it.

"You're... It's going to be damned hard to keep my hands off you, you know."

She drew a sharp breath. After a slightly too-long moment, she answered. "You say the nicest things to me."

"It wasn't a compliment." He stopped. "Okay, it was. But it was also a warning. Take it seriously."

"I am. Are we talking rape or seduction?"

"Seduction. Geez, I'm out on bail for embezzlement. The last thing I need is…" The sudden recognition alarmed him.

"No, I'm not part of whatever conspiracy is being waged against you. Not that you'll believe me," she added. "No real reason why you should. Except I'm your 'Christmas angel'."

Greg sighed and said, more to himself than to her. "I wish I could believe in it."

She heard it though. "The whole magic and vision thing is a bit too much for you to swallow."

"When I was a kid, I believed all the stories. Santa Claus, the Easter Bunny, the Tooth Fairy. All of them. I was the last kid on the block to get the message, mostly because I didn't want to hear it."

"Life can be so disillusioning that way," she agreed. "Gram always said the real magic was in things too small to see."

She pulled into the apartment complex parking lot and stopped the car, but didn't turn off the engine. "It's after eleven and I want to go to midnight Mass. Shall I take you to a hotel or let you into the apartment?"

He weighed the pros and cons for a couple of silent minutes. The risks were considerable, the gains questionable. But he'd never met a woman quite like Lindsey. She fascinated him. Possibly she'd even cast a spell over him. She was completely different from selfish, vain Marilyn and most of the other women he'd known. What did it say about him, that those were the kind of women he was initially attracted to? That he was shallow, selfish and a bit vain himself? Probably.

There were risks. There were always risks. How much farther down could his life go?

He leaned across the center console, put a hand on her cheek and turned her to face him. Then he slanted his mouth across hers. It started light, just a salute and an initial tasting. But when their lips met, the kiss took on a life of its own and set off a firebomb in his gut. She was sweet and hot and deliciously inviting. His mouth belonged there and didn't want to be dragged away. Especially not when her lips twitched invitingly under his. She put a hand on his shoulder to steady herself and leaned toward him.

The fire poured through his body, making him lightheaded as the blood rushed to his groin and flooded into his cock. He swiped his tongue across her lips and exulted when she groaned softly and melted into his embrace. He nudged her lips apart and she opened for him, admitting his tongue into the hot, slick sanctuary of her mouth.

She held him firmly as he explored and the white heat surrounded him. It fired him, incinerated him until he no longer existed except as part of her. His cock ached to find similar entry as he strained to pull her ever closer, to join to her as fully as possible. But it wasn't possible. He'd known the woman less than twenty-four hours. How could his spirit feel like it had found home?

He tore himself away with an effort that left him shaking.

"Greg."

The sound of his name, coming from her in a shaky, ragged whisper, sent a surge of elation rushing through his veins. For a short while the only noises in the car were their ragged breathing as each tried to control their reaction and the hum of the car's engine.

"And I said earlier I didn't think I'd be able to keep my hands off you," he said when he could finally talk again. "Double that now. Are you sure you want to risk it?"

Her voice was still thin and shaky. "Double that now." She switched off the car and pulled out the keys. When she began to take one off the ring, he put a hand over hers to stop her.

"How about taking me with you to church?" he suggested.

Chapter Three

Lindsey had to take a moment to collect herself before she dared get on the road again. That kiss had shaken her down to her toes. It had to be one of the all-time great kisses. She'd certainly never experienced anything like it before.

The memory — and the implications — disturbed her enough to be a distraction during the service. Plus, every time Greg's shoulder or thigh rubbed against hers, tingles and tremors spread from the site. Since the church was crowded, that happened almost constantly.

She was in deep here, and it scared her half to death. She barely knew him and wasn't sure she understood him at all. Had she not seen his face in the candle's glow, she'd be running in the opposite direction for all she was worth. He was too sexy, too male, too overpowering for her comfort. Add to that intelligent, witty and good-looking, and the package was too good to be true. It was all just too much.

The vision seemed to indicate he was her destiny, but did he know that? Suppose he just wanted a quick fling and then goodbye? Would she ever get over it? He'd been arrested for embezzlement. Just because she'd seen him in the vision, she'd believed him when he said he'd been framed. But what if it wasn't true?

They drove back to her apartment after the service in silence. She was too tired to cope with anything more and expected he was as well. He followed her back into the apartment. Before he went into the guestroom he stopped and looked at her, with a gleam in his gray eyes that made her bones melt.

"I want to kiss you goodnight," he said. "But if I start I don't think I'll be able to stop, and we're both too exhausted to handle it. So I won't. But I didn't want you to think it was because I didn't want to."

She'd never been more sweetly *not* kissed. God, this guy was getting under her skin.

Greg MacIntyre filled her dreams that night and her dozing fantasies in the morning. They were hot dreams and naughty fantasies of him doing things with her she'd never allowed any man to do before. Things that she wasn't sure she'd ever really let a man do. In her dreams, and in her favorite fantasies, the man she loved dominated her, demanded she do his will and punished her when she didn't. In real life, she'd never met a man who'd dare make any such demand of her. Most of the men she'd met lacked the courage to stand up to her or the will to best her. They backed down from any debate or disagreement with her. She felt sure Greg wouldn't back down.

The smell of brewing coffee finally lured her out of bed around eight. Sleeping that late was a luxury she rarely had the opportunity to indulge.

She showered, dressed and put on makeup more quickly than normal. Greg sat in her kitchen, reading a magazine and sipping from a mug, when she got there. He looked comfortable, cheerful and altogether too handsome for her peace of mind.

"I love a woman who appreciates good coffee," he said, pointing to the gold bag he'd left sitting on the counter beside the coffeemaker. He stood up, filled the mug he had waiting and moved to the stove where a frying pan sizzled gently.

She looked around the kitchen. "You've been busy."

"Just trying to earn my keep," he said. "Have a seat. Pancakes in five minutes."

It was closer to ten, but with a cup of steaming coffee in her hands Lindsey didn't mind waiting. Besides she got to watch him work, a joy in itself. What that man's long, lean shape did for a pair of jeans was positively sinful.

"Merry Christmas," he said as he put a plate stacked with pancakes in front of her.

"Oh!" She couldn't believe she'd forgotten. "Merry Christmas to you, too."

He sat opposite her at the table with a serving of pancakes for himself. "What's on the schedule for today?" he asked her.

"As little as possible. It's Christmas. I don't have to do anything."

"Sounds like it doesn't happen often."

She shrugged. "About twice a year, maybe."

"So what do you do, when you don't have to do anything?"

"Read, watch movies, eat, listen to music."

"I noticed you have a pretty extensive collection of movies."

"Are you inviting yourself to the theater?"

"Is this a film festival? I'll even make the popcorn. If you have any."

"Couple of bags of microwave popcorn in the pantry cabinet. But not 'til later, please. I'm still drinking my coffee. Good coffee, too, by the way."

"Starts with good beans. Quality always comes through. How about you pick the first movie and I'll choose the next?"

Lindsey agreed and picked out her first choice while he turned on the DVD player. He took the disk she chose and inserted it into the machine while she turned on the Christmas tree lights.

"*Star Wars*?" he asked. "Are we going to do a marathon?"

"A movie marathon, maybe, but not a *Star Wars* one. Just the original one. One of my all-time favorite movies."

They sat on opposite ends of her couch. She took her usual spot on the recliner side. He settled into the other end and put his socked feet up on the coffee table. It quickly became evident that he'd seen the movie more than once, when he spoke a few lines right along with the characters. When they got to one of Han Solo's most famous lines, "Kid, I've been from one side of this galaxy to the other…" he did such a perfect imitation of it, she almost rolled off the chair laughing.

Lindsey did Leia's lines. Once they got to the battle scenes, however, they got so caught up they forgot about the mimicry. Lindsey thought it one of the movie's real strengths that, no matter how many times she'd seen it, she always thrilled and worried during the fights.

The phone rang just as the movie ended. "That'll be one of my sisters," she told Greg.

"Hey, Lindsey!" Jade said. "So did the last candle do something for you? Oh, yeah, and Merry Christmas."

"Merry Christmas to you, too. And to Caydon also. You two lovebirds still cooing at each other? You better be. I worked hard enough to get you together."

"Oh man, Lindsey, you are so sick. We've decided we'll stay together a while longer. Now quit avoiding it. Did the last candle show you anything?"

"Well, yes, but I'm not sure where it's leading."

"Is it a man?"

"Yes."

There was a heavy pause. "That's all? Yes? Details, girl, details. You can't just say yes. Is he good looking? What does he do? What's the story? Is he fulfilling all your wild fantasies?"

"Jade! What makes you think I have any?"

"Hey, I got that Kidnap Fantasies brochure from you, didn't I? Don't tell me you didn't read it over yourself. And get a bit excited about some of the scenarios?"

"Okay, you know I did. But you know why I got it."

"Yeah, your vision in the candle. Which brings us back to this year's edition."

"How is Crista? And Jeff and the baby? Have you heard from her yet?"

"Not today, but it's early for them. Now quit avoiding… Oh. He's there with you now, isn't he?"

"Yes."

"Are you doing wild and crazy things yet?"

"No!" It came out more sharply than she intended.

"Well, shoot. Don't wait too long."

"Is that how you plan to spend the day?" Lindsey asked.

"Oh, yeah!"

Lindsey smiled at the excited anticipation in Jade's tone. A year later, she and Caydon were still so hot for each other, it was risky for anyone to come too close when they were together. That candle-vision had terrified her, but it had worked out so well. If only…

"Lindsey! You still there?"

"Yeah. I've got a chicken I'm going to stuff for dinner, along with a couple of casseroles."

"And he's going to help you eat them, then he's going to stuff you and maybe nibble on a few other things?"

"Jade! Just because you're so lucky, it doesn't mean everyone is."

There was a pause. "Lindsey?" Jade's tone was less teasing and more concerned. "Is this really a problem?"

"I don't know yet. Okay?"

"Not okay, but I'll live with it for now. Call me when you get a chance and we'll talk. And have a Merry Christmas. Whatever that means for you right now."

"Thanks, hon. You, too. Tell Caydon I don't want to wait too long to be an aunt again."

"Um…Lindsey? You might not have to."

"You're kidding. Really?"

"I wasn't going to say anything yet, because I don't know for sure. But I think so."

"Oh, wow! That's fabulous."

They talked for a while longer, but Lindsey didn't let the conversation return to her own issues, knowing that Greg, in the next room, could hear her end of it so clearly. Finally she finished and went back to the living room.

Greg had left the TV on and found a station showing a football game, but he wasn't watching. He'd gotten up and moved across the room to her bookshelves. He'd pulled out a book and was thumbing through it.

She groaned mentally when she saw what he'd picked up. She'd forgotten her collection of erotica was still on the shelf — worse yet, if he looked at more than one or two he'd pick up the common theme. Or maybe that was a good thing. He might as well know about her secret fantasies. If they didn't match his, or if he was turned off by it, better to know about it now.

To her surprise, he made no comment, although he did raise an eyebrow when he noticed her watching him. He closed the book and replaced it on the shelf. "Ready to start another movie?" he asked. When she nodded, he picked up one he'd already pulled out. "My choice."

"*The Princess Bride*? I love that movie! 'My name is Inigo Montoya. You killed my father. Prepare to die!'"

He joined her on the last few words. His mimicry of Mandy Patinkin's repeated lines was better than hers.

They chuckled and joked their way through the movie. When they paused the movie for a lunch break, they even did an impromptu sword fight in her living room using rolled up magazines.

"Ah, you're using the Fribbleupagus maneuver," he said, when she swung and missed, nearly losing her balance. "Useful under some circumstances, but embarrassing when it fails."

She recovered and feinted toward him again. "I considered using the coffeetableus maneuver, but the terrain is a bit rough for that."

He backed her up with a barrage of short, quick lunges, until she was against the wall. He pushed forward and trapped her there, setting his hands on the wall on either side of her face, letting the magazine drop to the floor.

She looked up into his eyes. Deep in the gray depths a flame burned, and his mouth quirked in a wry smile. He was so close, the heat from his body warmed her, and the smell of soap and pine-scented aftershave lotion mingled with the essential male aroma of Greg. It went to her head like a double martini. She curled her hands around his biceps, exulting in the strength that held her pinned there.

"I'm going to kiss you," he warned, and then proceeded to make good on the threat.

She'd thought last night's kiss was the best kiss ever, but this one surpassed it. His lips explored lightly at first, then his tongue invaded her mouth, curled with hers and swiped the sides. Spurts of fire blazed through her, rippling along her veins and skin. A few men had tried, but no one had ever kissed her like this before. It blotted out all thought, stole her wits and replaced them with raw passion. Desire bloomed inside her like a flower opening to the sun. He was light, heat, rain, wind and soil, giving life to something new and glorious awakening.

She needed him closer. As if he read her thought, he pressed against her. The hard bulge of his cock nudged into her belly. His arms moved together and his hands closed against her cheeks, holding her fast as he drew off her lips, kissing a line across to her ear and down her neck.

She groaned when he licked hot circles on her throat. Need was a roaring wind in her ears, a storm thundering through her. His hands slid down from her shoulders to her breasts. They rested there a moment. No man had ever set her on fire this way. She looked into his eyes and saw her own wild longing and desire mirrored there. When she didn't object to his touch, he began to palm them gently, rubbing in small circles that set off a wild tingling in her nipples. Her breath grew harsher and faster. Her cunt swelled and moisture began to collect there.

He released her breasts but only long enough to dig his way under her loose sweater and up to her bra. He unhooked the front clasp and pushed the fabric aside. Her skin exploded in a fire of ecstasy when his fingers closed on the bare skin where the bra had been moments before. He looked down at her, and his smile was so joyfully delighted it reached into her heart.

She sobbed aloud when he stroked gentle fingertips across her nipples. The sensation knifed into her and through her like streaks of lightning. She was dissolving, melting against him as her legs went weak.

She moaned in protest when he drew back, rubbing a shaking hand across his face.

"I told you it would be hard to keep my hands off you," he said, his voice a bit ragged and his breathing harsh.

"So, why are you? I didn't notice I was objecting."

"Only because you weren't thinking either. Wait, that didn't come out exactly as I meant it. I mean, we barely know each other, and I want some things clearer between us before we take this all the way."

"You want. Does it matter what I want?"

He turned and smiled at her. "Of course it matters. I want to be sure I know exactly what you do want before we go there."

Lindsey deflated a bit and then felt a bubble of excitement well up deep inside as she considered the implications.

They made sandwiches in a somewhat tense silence and took them back to the living room to eat while they watched the rest of the movie. It soon had them laughing hard enough and reciting the Inigo Montoya monologue often enough to defuse the tension between them. But Lindsey couldn't help but remember the talk about "The Kiss" at the beginning of the movie. She already had two that she was sure surpassed the sweetest, most pure and loving kiss in the movie. Greg's kisses sent her reeling.

When the movie was over, they took a walk. The cold temperature outside meant they had to bundle up and walk quickly to keep from freezing, but the exercise felt good after several hours of sitting, and it put high color in their exposed cheeks. On their return to the apartment, Lindsey turned the gas logs on in the fireplace, made hot chocolate for each of them and chose her next movie.

While You Were Sleeping was one of her favorite romantic comedies. Greg admitted he'd never seen it, so there was no parroting dialogue during that one. They both laughed until they almost cried a couple of times. They paused it for a short break in the middle, and when he returned, Greg sat next to her on the couch rather than at the other end. Ostensibly it was so they could share the popcorn he'd popped in the microwave during the break, but he did put an arm around her shoulders. Lindsey didn't need any more nudging to get her to lean against him.

She'd always identified with Sandra Bullock's portrayal of the lonely token-seller. They'd each lost parents too early and had few other attachments. Lindsey understood why she had the fantasy about Peter Callaghan, the handsome young lawyer who stopped at her booth every morning. And Bill Pullman as his brother Jack made her want to hug him and go find one just like him.

If she had to choose, though, Greg likely had more in common with the handsome, sophisticated Peter than his down-to-earth brother.

When it was over, she had to take a break from the movie marathon to put together dinner. Since it was Christmas, and she had a guest, she wanted to do it right. Fortunately, she'd bought plenty of food and a good Chardonnay to go with the chicken. Greg volunteered to help and proved useful in preparing the vegetable casserole and the salad. He didn't balk at taking orders from her, and he didn't try to distract her. In fact, they worked quite smoothly together, like long-time friends.

He even helped her set the table and lit the candles she set out. He uncorked the wine and poured it while she put on soft Christmas music and turned out all the lights other than the Christmas tree, the gas logs and the candles. She would likely have done everything exactly the same had she been here alone, all by herself as she'd thought she'd be, and it would have been romantic, but empty. Greg's presence turned it into a sumptuous feast and a memory she'd treasure no matter what happened between them in the future.

He held her chair for her as she sat before he took the seat opposite. The candlelight cast flickering shadows across his face, but softened his features into beauty, emphasizing the strong line of his jaw, the hollows below his cheekbones and the sparkling lights in his gray eyes.

She was a good cook, though she hadn't actually done much of it lately, due to her crazy schedule. But her herb-basted roast chicken had never tasted so good, so deeply, richly satisfying. Just inhaling the aroma made her mouth water, and the taste lived up to that promise. The vegetable casserole had never come out so savory, the salad so lively, the bread so fragrantly crusty and delicious.

And the wine…it was a good Chardonnay, but not a Champagne. So why did it seem to fizz all through her system?

They talked all through dinner, though later she wouldn't remember a word of what they discussed. Their tastes in music must have come up, and recollections of how they'd spent previous Christmases. She loved watching the way his eyes crinkled when he grinned, the way his mouth quirked when he smiled. The sound of his voice was sweeter than music.

The wayward thought strayed through her head that she didn't know him well enough to be falling so far under his spell. It was dangerous. But it was also heady and exciting and it just seemed so…right. As though something hot and fierce connected them to each other in a unique way.

Would he make love to her that night? Her cunt oozed moisture at the thought of his hands roving her body, touching her in all the right spots, his cock filling her. Would he prove to be the lover of her dreams? She hoped for it.

He hadn't pushed it yet, other than the hot kisses he'd pressed on her. Those were so sweet and so full of promise. Part of her applauded him for wanting to take it slow, to get it right. Another part of her wanted to drag him into her bedroom right now, strip his clothes off and attack him.

"Lindsey?" He snapped his fingers, dragging her out of the reverie. "Judging by your expression, it was a pleasant daydream. I hope it involved me."

She hoped the candlelight would hide the flush she felt heating her face. "It did."

"Good." His face turned serious as he studied her across the table. He stood suddenly and moved around to take a chair closer to her and pull it nearer still. His fingers closed around her chin and turned her face toward him. "It's going to happen between us, Lindsey," he promised. "And it's going to be good. Very good. But it's not going to be fast."

His expression turned stern and commanding. His fingers tightened on her chin, not enough to hurt, just enough to tell her he was in charge. She could shake off his hold easily enough, but she didn't.

"You think you want it to be fast," he added. "You're impatient. And you like to have things your own way. You want it now. But that's not going to happen. Do you understand me, Lindsey?"

Her heartbeat sped up and something seemed to be blocking her throat. Excitement bubbled in her stomach, twisting it with a blend of fear and thrill. She hoped she understood. Had he sensed this about her, or was it just his natural inclination as well?

"Yes," she whispered. "I understand."

"Good."

He leaned forward and kissed her, lightly, sweetly, but with so much promise, her heart slammed against her chest.

"Greg…" She wasn't sure what she asked for.

He shook his head. "You've had lovers, haven't you?"

She nodded.

"Have any of them ever satisfied you completely? Made you feel like a complete and totally fulfilled woman?"

She sighed. "No."

"I thought not." He kissed her again, and this time he deepened it, pushing his tongue in. He tasted of her food and wine. He felt like heaven on earth when she put a hand on his shoulder to steady herself.

As the heat began to sing along her veins and her cunt swelled, he broke it off. "Let's clean up and do one more movie. My choice this time."

He cleared the table while she loaded the dishwasher. They put away the leftover food and made coffee. He left the wine bottle on the counter. Once the kitchen and dining area were clear, they took their coffee into the living room.

When she saw which movie he'd selected the shock and surprise jolted her all the way down to her toes.

Chapter Four

"*Secretary*?" It came out sounding both shocked and startled.

"You've seen it before?"

"Yes…" She gulped. "Have you?"

His knowing grin told her the answer before he said, "Oh, yes."

"Interesting choice." She hoped it came out sounding poised, sophisticated and nonchalant but suspected he saw right through the façade.

He inserted the disk and sat at the other end of the couch with the remote in his hand, but before he pressed play, he said, "Slide over here." He held out an arm.

She moved down the couch and sat next to him, stretching her legs out to rest on the coffee table beside his. One unexpected advantage of the position was that she had to slide down and was therefore unable to see his face without turning and craning her neck, nor could he see hers without an equal effort. There were parts of the movie where she was passionately grateful for that small bit of privacy.

He draped an arm over her shoulder and occasionally rubbed up and down her shoulder. Even through the light sweater, it sent delightfully warm tingles rushing through her. When he finished his coffee, he set the cup down on the side table and rested his now-free hand on her thigh. Throughout the rest of the movie, his fingers moved in circles, small and wide, on her thigh, venturing into the cleft between her legs occasionally. Even through the fabric of her jeans it was devastatingly sweet and amazingly aggravating.

With both hands on her, he had to feel when she occasionally squirmed while watching the movie. Lindsey had no desire to be a secretary, nor did she have Lee's scary psychological problems, but she could share the desire to be submissive to a strong, dominating man. When Edward Grey first spanked Lee, she almost jumped. No matter how many times she saw the movie, the first time always startled her nearly as much as it did Lee.

When it was over, she slid down a little more next to him and sighed. "I'm a sucker for a happy ending."

He was still for a moment. "Was it a happy ending? Some people think it's just a weird ending. How can they live like that?"

"I think it's perfect for them. They give each other what they need. They make each other happy. It may not be right for most people, but it was for them." She didn't turn to look at him.

"If you had to choose, which man would you want—Jack Callaghan, from *While You Were Sleeping*, or Mr. Grey?"

"Are you serious?"

"Entirely."

Lindsey thought about it for a few minutes. "I don't know. Neither, really. Or a combination of the two of them. I don't know if I could take either one full-time. But a tumble with either one would be exciting."

"Even Mr. Grey?"

"Yes! Even Mr. Grey. After all, variety and all that." Did he believe her, or did he hear the tiny quiver of combined fear and excitement in her voice?

To her relief he didn't push it. "How about some more wine?" he asked. When she nodded and started to stand, he gently pushed her back. "I'll get it."

He came back with the wine, sat down and pulled her onto his lap. Fortunately, he didn't question her about the movies anymore.

For a few minutes they both stared at the lights of the Christmas tree.

"One of the lights is burned out," he said. "It looks like it's the only candlelight on the tree."

"It's the one I saw the vision in. They always burn out after they flare up and show me their message. It was the last one."

"You believe in magic." She heard the note of doubt in his tone.

"Magic, miracles, call it what you like. Yes. 'More things in heaven and on earth.' Quantum physics. Frankly, when I read about that, it sounds a lot like magic to me."

"You saw a vision of me in the candlelight. You think I'm your destiny?"

"I think this is my destiny. Whether there's any more for us remains to be seen."

"You said other candles had shown you visions, and it worked out well when you acted on them. Tell me about them."

She did, starting with the dog for Joanna, and working through the Santa Claus incident for Crista, Kidnap Fantasies, Inc., and Jade's story.

"That was a pretty damn risky thing to do, wasn't it?" he asked. "A company that specializes in kidnapping people? They would surely attract some odd types."

She nodded and took a sip of wine. "Not as risky as it sounds. I knew some of the people enough to trust them. But there was definitely a risk that Jade might not really want it, or that she and Caydon wouldn't hit it off, or—plenty of things could have gone wrong."

"But you trusted and acted because your Gram had promised it would be all right." She heard something more than just the statement of fact in his words. A need or a yearning. She'd grown up with only Gram for a parent, but even so she suspected she'd gotten more loving care than he'd had from both of his cool, remote parents. From what he'd said of them, she had the impression they spent their time making money, entertaining friends or globe-hopping, and sometimes all three at once.

"And I did have a couple of previous experiences to bear it out."

He watched her for a moment with an odd expression on his face, then he turned to look at the tree. "Does the angel ever smile at you?" he asked. "She looks like she's been around a while."

"She was one of Gram's decorations. And...I'm not sure. Sometimes I've thought so. When I wasn't looking directly at her, I've thought I saw...something. In the corner of my eye."

"I'd like to see it. Maybe she'll smile on us, if it *is* right." Even he heard the wistfulness in his voice this time. He grinned wryly, and added in a very different tone, "Must be the wine, making me maudlin." He sat up a bit and shifted her. "It's getting late. I'm ready to hit the sack. But first...we never had dessert."

"Oh. I don't usually eat sweets."

"I guess I'll just have to get my sugar somewhere else." He turned her toward him, dipped his head, and kissed her again.

It was another spectacular, wonderful, memorable kiss. A kiss that made her cunt swell and moisten. He had clever fingers, too. His hands crept up under her sweater, unsnapped the bra again, and covered her breasts. Warmth surged through her, with little electrical tingles crawling along her nerves. She moaned deep in her throat as his palms rubbed over her nipples, making them bead up. His fingers closed over them, pinching them lightly, then harder, twisting them until they burned a bit. Fire zipped along her skin and veins and the pressure built in her womb. Whatever sweetness he took, he returned to her a hundredfold.

She grabbed at his shirt, pulled it free of his jeans and managed to work her hands up under it. His skin was warm and deliciously exciting. His belly was hard and muscular, with a light coating of hair that thickened as she brushed upward.

Heavy chest muscles twitched under her exploration. He jolted when she rubbed one of his nipples.

She wanted to see him. But when she pulled her hands out from under the shirt and began to unbutton it, he gathered both her wrists in one big hand.

"You have to earn this," he said.

"Earn it? How?"

"You'll see. Tomorrow."

"Tomorrow. How can you wait? I'm burning, on fire… I need you so badly, I'm about to scream with it. Why are you torturing me like this? How can you stand it?"

"It's not easy, but it's what you want, whether you know it now or not."

The glint in his eye made her squirm and her stomach tighten.

"What makes you so sure you know what I want?"

"Actually, I'm not entirely sure, which is why I'm not ready to take the chance just yet."

"You're driving me mad."

"A sweet madness, though." He kissed her again, but lightly this time. "To bed now. Separately. Oh, and I want a promise from you."

"What?"

"Don't touch yourself tonight. You'll be tempted, but don't do it. Save it for me."

"Why should I, you big, arrogant jerk? If you won't take what I'm offering now, why should I save it for you?"

"Because it will be all the sweeter if you do as I ask." His eyes narrowed when he added. "And you'll regret it if you don't."

A curling thread of excitement twisted her stomach into a painful knot. "I hope I don't end up hating you."

He didn't answer. By the time she finished checking the locks and turning out the lights, he'd disappeared into the guest bedroom and shut the door.

She woke next morning to the aroma of coffee again, but when she'd showered and dressed, and went down the hall, she found the apartment quiet and empty. The coffee was brewed, however, so she poured herself a cup, and found the note sitting on the counter beside the machine.

I hope you don't mind I borrowed your car keys. I need to get some things from my apartment. Back before lunch.

Beneath that he'd scrawled his name, Greg. His handwriting was bold but neat and easy to read. For a moment she couldn't help but wonder if she'd ever see her car again, and what else he might have taken.

Chapter Five

The doubts didn't last long. He had too much intelligence and too much pride to stoop so low and do anything so stupid. Besides, she'd seen him in the candle light. That had to mean something. And she just… She knew. He'd been shallow, selfish, vain, perhaps. But at heart he was an honorable man. Not a thief or an embezzler. She knew. She certainly *hoped* she knew.

She straightened up the apartment, checked her email, worked up a grocery list and wrote a few checks to cover bills. She wouldn't admit to herself that she missed him already and wondered what he was up to.

As the morning stretched on, she fretted more and more, then upbraided herself for her worries and the incipient loneliness. Why should she miss a man she barely knew? How had he insinuated himself so far under her skin in such a short period of time?

Still she breathed a sigh of relief and felt joy make her pulse leap when he buzzed her apartment to be admitted.

"You've got my keys," she reminded him. "They're on the same ring with the car keys."

"Oh. Right. Buzz me in anyway. I don't want to have to try each one to figure it out."

She had to resist the urge to throw herself on him when he came in the door. He had a duffel bag slung over his shoulder and dragged a large, wheeled suitcase behind him. A flare of suspicion roused again.

"Staying awhile?" she asked.

He shrugged. "Depends. But not all of this is clothes." He set the duffel down on the hall floor and pulled a bottle out of it, which he handed to her. "A thank-you gift. Actually, I plan to do better than that later, but there's not much open on Sunday morning, even the Sunday morning, the day after Christmas."

"Benedictine and Brandy?" The bottle was so cold it must have come from his unheated apartment.

"Ever tried it? It packs a punch, but I think you'll like it."

"No. Now?"

"Later. Did you miss me?"

"My tormentor? What do you think?"

He leaned over and kissed her in answer. He smelled of wool coat and fresh air from outside. His lips started cool but quickly heated as he clung to hers and made her mouth sizzle. She wrapped her arms around him and pushed herself against him. The man turned her insides upside down and twisted her nerves into a tight ball. His mouth moving over hers made her blood fizz and skin tingle.

After a minute he pulled back and stared at her with a bemused expression. "You missed me," he stated. "Almost as much as I missed you. What's for lunch?" He began to unbutton the overcoat.

"You assume I'm going to feed you?"

He turned and grinned. "I assume you're going to find it in your compassionate heart to offer sustenance to a man who's had nothing but a cup of coffee in the past fourteen hours. Seriously, I can heat soup with the best of them. Have you got any?" He hung his coat in the closet.

Twenty minutes later he ladled out steaming servings of New England clam chowder. Lindsey added toasted slices of bread. Watching him eat in daylight was as delightful as it had been by candlelight the previous evening. He was so handsome, and he had an innate grace, almost refinement, that made him incredibly appealing to her.

His gray eyes were bright with vitality and humor, except for occasional moments when he seemed to lapse into worry. Whenever he realized he'd done it, he yanked himself out of it and put the smile back into place. He had reason to worry; he was out on bail, but still facing trial for embezzlement. It appeared he was doing his best to forget it temporarily, at least.

"Do you mind it I turn on the football games? It's the playoffs."

"Giants versus the Redskins at one," she said.

"You're a football fan?"

"Not religious about it, but, yes, I like football. I like baseball and hockey, too."

"I can't believe some man hasn't snapped you up yet."

She fought down her surge of annoyance. "I do my own snapping, thank you."

He stared at her for a moment. "I imagine you do," he said, softly. "I brought a few games back with me. Want to play something while we watch and listen?"

"What kind of games?"

"Cards, Scrabble, that kind of thing."

"Oh. Anything but chess. Chess takes too much concentration."

"No chess. Of course, there's a twist on all the games."

"Oh?"

"You'll see."

"You're a tease."

"Yesterday I was a torturer. Now I'm just a tease? I'm not sure if I'm insulted."

"The day's young yet. You'll probably work up to more."

His smile was wicked and promising. "Count on it."

He helped her clean the kitchen and open cans of soft drinks.

"You're pretty handy around the kitchen," she told him. "And a fair kisser as well. I'm surprised some woman hasn't snapped you up yet."

His head jerked up and he stared at her, frowning, for a moment, before a wry smile broke through. "If that's payback, there's a bitch in here somewhere. I prefer to do the snapping, too."

Lindsey laughed. "Ever wondered how a pair of snapping turtles manages to mate?"

"Probably not face to face," Greg said. "Although maybe they enjoy the challenge of it. Or the…sting. Lots of possibilities. No apparent lack of snapping turtles in the world."

"True."

They took the drinks into the living room and turned on the TV to the game. Before they settled on the couch, Greg got a deck of cards. "You know Gin?" he asked.

"Haven't played in a while, but yes."

He nodded. "Here's the twist. No keeping score, just win or lose each hand. The winner gets to ask the loser a question—any question they want—and the loser has to answer as honestly as possible."

It surprised her, but sounded like an interesting way to get to know one another. "Okay."

He dealt the first hand while the Giants kicked off to the Redskins. She made her first interesting discovery about him even before they played more than a couple of cards. The Redskins made a successful pass on the first play and Greg cheered for it.

"You're a Redskins fan?" she asked in semi-serious horror.

"I grew up in northern Virginia."

"Oh, no." She rolled her eyes upward. "Gram, you blew it! He's a Redskins fan. How could you?"

"It's not a fatal disease," Greg said calmly. "It can be worked out. Your turn."

Lindsey sighed and picked a card. "I suppose."

She lost the first two hands quickly.

His first question wasn't at all what she expected. "How many lovers have you had?"

"What? Not your business."

"You agreed to the rules."

"You didn't tell me they would be intimate, personal questions."

"I didn't have to."

"Four! Okay? I've had four."

"Thank you," he answered. "Your turn to deal."

When she lost the next hand, too, he asked, "How many of them did you fall in love with?"

"I thought I was in love with two of them."

"You weren't?"

"That's another question. Win another hand."

"But you didn't answer the original question."

"Oh, all right! None. I wasn't in love with any of them."

Lindsey had already noted his strategy in the game and was both emulating it and working on ways to defeat it. She won the third hand, but it was more from luck than skill.

"How many lovers have *you* had?" she asked.

He had to think a moment. "Eight. But a couple may not count as lovers. They were more like one-night stands."

She wanted to follow up on that but would have to wait.

He won the next hand. "Have you ever done anything kinky? And if so, what?"

"Two questions. I'll answer the first. Yes."

Unfortunately he won the next hand as well.

"One of the guys liked to use a hairbrush. We brushed each other all over—including places we didn't have hair. And he put the handle into my…passage."

"You can call it a pussy," he said. "He didn't spank you with it?"

"No, he—hey, wait. No fair. That's another question."

"True," he admitted. "Okay. You get a freebie. Ask a question."

"Damn, I hate aping your questions, but I'm going to anyway. What kinky things have you done?"

"Oh, clever. Ask a broad sweeping question." He sighed. "Let's see. I'm not sure if you consider oral sex kinky. I've done it. Used silk scarves on one lady, and a vibrator on another. I've never had the nerve to ask anyone about the flogger or the nipple clamps."

Lindsey wasn't sure if he was rattling her chain, but it still sent a weird thrill into her stomach. She won the next hand as well, this time due to a combination of skill and luck. "What's your favorite, nonsexual thing to do when you have free time?"

His eyebrows rose. "Trying to change the subject? Play games."

"What kind?"

He shook his head. "That's another question."

But she lost the next hand, possibly distracted by the nice touchdown pass thrown by the Giants' quarterback.

"What are the three things a lover has done to you that you most enjoyed?" he asked.

"Talk about making the questions broader?" she said. "Now I have to start reciting lists?"

He just cocked his head to the side, gave her a wicked grin and waited.

"Okay. A moment. Yes!" The Giants made a two-point conversion. "Three things I've most enjoyed. The hairbrush thing. It was interesting feeling it on my skin. Otherwise, the standard making-love things. Touching my breasts and my pussy." Though she considered herself a sophisticated and experienced woman, Lindsey still blushed a bit talking about it so bluntly with him, when they both knew she wanted him to do those things to her.

He gave her an odd look. "You've had some pretty unimaginative lovers."

"Or maybe I just like it pretty straightforward."

He studied her face. "No. I don't think so. You're too clever yourself, too imaginative and intelligent."

"Maybe you'll just have to ask to find out."

"Deal."

She won the next hand. "What kinds of games to you like to play?"

"All kinds. I like tennis and racquetball, softball and hockey. I like card games, board games, word games and role-playing games. And I like bedroom games."

Her curiosity was boiling over so it was a relief to win the next hand. "What are your favorite bedroom games?"

"Actually there isn't much I don't like to play at in the bedroom. Favorites… Oh, the one where you're my captive and I have to tie you to the bed to keep you from escaping, but you're so beautiful I can't keep from ravishing you. Or the one where I'm the sheik introducing the newest member of the harem to a whole new world of sensual delights. Or the one where I'm training the new girl in the harem, but she refuses to cooperate and I have to punish her."

She drew a sharp breath and then hoped he hadn't heard even though she was sure he had.

The next game was longer and more tense. In the end, he won the hand, though, just as the Redskins scored to bring the game to a one-point difference. "Have you ever wanted to try something a few steps beyond 'pretty straightforward' sex?"

She felt the color flooding into her face and, for a moment, was tempted to lie. But that wouldn't be right or wise. If they were exploring their future, she owed him her honesty. "Yes."

He nodded. "Thought so."

The football game went to halftime and they took a break from the cards to fix drinks and snacks.

Over the course of the second half of the game, she learned that there had been only two women he'd gotten serious with. The first one finally broke up with him to marry a stockbroker with a house in Westchester and a summer home in the Hamptons. The second had been his fiancée, the boss's daughter. "I guess I don't have really great judgment about women," he admitted. "Maybe I have to be knocked over the head by a falling Christmas tree to get me to look beyond beauty and charm."

"Don't look at my tree," she answered. "It's not tipping. Even for you."

"It just blew out a candle light to bring me here."

"And that's the extent of the sacrifices it's making."

She also learned, even though she risked turning the conversation into something much more serious, that he was healthy and always used protection in his sexual encounters. "Even with Marilyn," he said. "Though there it was more because she didn't want to get pregnant."

She told him she insisted on the men she'd had relationships with using protection as well.

On the lighter side, she discovered that his favorite "toys" were a light flogger and a set of silk scarves. "You can do a lot of things with silk," he promised.

Lindsey admitted that aside from the hairbrush, she'd never used anything. She didn't tell him that the flogger sounded intimidating and she wasn't sure she wanted any part of it, and yet she was amazingly intrigued by it at the same time.

Toward the end of the third quarter, Greg won a hand and asked her, "How would you feel about being a man's slave?"

Her hands shook just a bit. "I'm not sure. The idea appeals to me as something I might want to try out for a short time. Maybe as a 'bedroom game'. But I don't think I could do something like that all the time. It's not me. I'm not that way. Just the opposite in fact. I can almost see myself as more of a dominatrix than a constant submissive."

The wicked grin slashed across his face again. "A dominatrix?" His eyebrows slid up. "Oh, yes, I can see that. We'll have to try that, too, though I'm not sure I can see myself as any kind of submissive."

"I'm not sure I see it either. But you like to play games."

She won the next hand and asked, "Do you see yourself ever settling down, having a family, a house, that kind of thing?"

For a moment his expression darkened. "I thought I was going to have all that with Marilyn. I'm ready for it. I've sown all the wild oats I want to sow. Right now, though, I'm not sure I have a future." He quickly dealt the next hand, as though he didn't want to dwell on those thoughts. He won it, too.

"Does the thought of being restrained while a man does things to your helpless body excite you or make you cringe?"

It took her a moment to control her fluttery breathing. "Both? I suppose it depends on what's being done to my helpless body. But then the point is I wouldn't have any say. I guess if I really trusted my partner, I'd find it pretty exciting."

The Giants scored again, but he won the next hand while she was distracted watching the drive down the field.

"How would you feel about being spanked, like Lee in the movie?" he asked.

Her pulse jumped and her voice wavered just a little, betrayingly, as she answered, "I'm not like Lee. I'm not into self-destructive behaviors. But, still… It kind of appeals to me, as long as it's not really brutal or anything."

He nodded. The game ended with a drive by the Redskins that would have won the game except that it fell short. The distraction helped her win that hand. "What would you most like from a woman during sex?"

"I—" She could tell from his expression that he started to say something glib but thought better of it. "Her trust," he answered instead. "And her complete submission."

They were both quiet a moment, staring at each other, beginning to measure the depth of their compatibility and perhaps their courage to take it farther.

Finally Greg turned away to stare at the screen, where the downcast Redskins trudged off the field. He didn't seem heartbroken over the loss, but he did set aside the deck of cards. "I think we've had enough of this. How about if we agree to one more question each?"

She nodded. "I'll ask first. What are the most important qualities you're looking for in the woman you marry?"

He was quiet for a minute or two and he frowned as he apparently looked inward. "It's changed in the last couple of months," he said. "Before all this, I was mostly about looks and charm. Now that's still important, but it has to come with intelligence, honesty, integrity, kindness and courage." He smiled in a self-deprecating way. "I don't ask for much, do I?"

"Not much," she agreed.

He shrugged. "My turn. What are you expecting from me, beyond wild, hot sex?"

Chapter Six

She couldn't speak for a moment, though she wasn't sure which hindered her more—astonishment at his phrasing or worry about the suspicion that prompted the question.

"I told you about the candles on the tree and the visions I've had in them. Each time I've acted on the vision, someone close to me was brought together with…with their destiny. A perfect mate…apparently, at least. They're all still married and all still gloriously happy and in love. This year…I was the only one left, so I hoped it would be my turn. I saw you in the candle. Are you my destiny? My perfect mate? I don't know. I guess that's what we're trying to find out. What I'm trying to find out. I'm not sure what your agenda is."

He watched her, his expression steady. Finally he shook his head and sighed. "Right now, the only long-term agenda I can wrap my mind around is figuring out how to get out of the mess I'm in professionally and legally. Until I do that I don't have a future to offer to any woman. If I can get it settled, though…" He stared at her, a deep, probing, serious look. But instead of pursuing that thought further, he shrugged, shook his head, and drew a breath before asking, "Okay, I know it's another question, but this one is too important not to ask. Why aren't you married and settled down already?"

Lindsey had asked herself that question more than once. She'd finally arrived at the answer, but it wasn't something easily admitted, especially not to a man who attracted her more than any she'd met before. She stood up and went to the window. What she saw surprised her.

"It's snowing!" A couple of inches had already accumulated on the ground while they were playing cards and not noticing. She sighed. "I'm not an easy person to live with," she admitted. "I have a strong personality and I don't suffer fools gladly."

"You're also attractive, intelligent and quick-witted. And I'm betting you intimidate most of the men you meet." She hadn't heard him get up and approach, hadn't realized he stood behind her until he spoke. His arms wound around her waist to pull her back against his body.

"I guess so."

"But you secretly want a man who won't be intimidated by you. Who, in fact, can dominate you at times, but not in a brutal, cruel or too-demanding way." His voice was behind and just above her ear.

Somehow the fact that they couldn't see each other's faces made it easier. She watched the snow coming down in a roiling maelstrom of large, puffy flakes falling thick and fast. "That's pretty much it. I've been looking for someone strong enough to take me on, but secure enough not to be stupid or brutal or cruel about it. Someone with enough wit and intelligence to keep things interesting." She sighed again. "I haven't met many men like that, and most of them get snapped up pretty quickly."

"There you go with that snapping thing again."

He moved a bit and then his lips were on her neck, nibbling at the tender, sensitive skin below her ear. It turned the blood in her veins to liquid silver, flowing hot and heavy. Tingles shot through her, running all over, down to her toes and out to the ends of her fingers.

His hands moved up from her waist to cup each breast in a palm. The heat of his hands penetrated through the angora wool sweater and her bra. She gasped as his fingers moved around, finding her nipples and brushing across them. It sent shards of excitement into her core, down into her womb, making it tighten. She hung onto his arms as her knees went rubbery.

He nudged the neckline of her sweater back with his lips so he could press hot, nipping kisses into her shoulder. He brushed his palms down the front of her sweater, along her stomach. When he got to the bottom edge, he pushed both hands up under the wool, found the clasp of her bra and dealt with it easily.

His warm palms closed over her breasts. Breath caught in her throat as his fingers brushed across her nipples. The rush of sensation forced a squeal of surprised delight from her. Lindsey sank back against him, reveling in the strength of his body that could support her. The tang of his pine-scented cologne tickled her nose. It mixed with a scent that was more basically male and uniquely Greg.

A harder nip on her neck right where it met her shoulder accompanied simultaneous light pinches of her nipples. She moaned loudly as sensation, mild pain heightening a brushfire of pleasure, tore through her. She gasped again and again as his lips, teeth, and fingers found ways to wring new delights. Heat and pressure swelled her pussy and moisture began to seep from it. Sobs tore from her as the continued assault on her senses had her head reeling, muscles straining, and blood roaring.

One of his hands moved down her body, slid over her stomach and her denim-covered abdomen, and continued down until it reached the cleft between her legs. Despite the layers of material between his fingers and her pussy, his first touch there sent an electric thrill, a bolt of pure, fiery energy, through her.

"You're so beautiful," he whispered in her ear. "And so responsive. We're going to make memories that will carry me through anything."

His touch worked an amazing magic on her body, transforming it from flesh into fire. Hunger became need and desperate longing. A single finger at her cleft turned desire into desperation.

When she thought she could bear no more, that she'd either have to jump him or run away, he released her. "Enough for now," he whispered. "More later."

She whirled to face him. "You're cruel. A tease and a tormentor."

"And you're loving it."

"You're driving me crazy."

"And you've been waiting for a man who could."

Without answering, she moved close to him again, wound her arms around his waist and pressed herself against him, head on his shoulder. As she absorbed the shock of being frustrated in her desire and the raging need slowly faded, it left behind something that terrified her.

"This is scary," she whispered.

"Scary, how?"

"I've known you such a short time and you're becoming too important to me. You don't know if you have a future, and I don't know if we're meant to share it even if you do. I don't know what it's going to do to me when you're gone. Would you let me help you fight for that future?"

He stiffened. Before she even looked up, she knew she'd see suspicion in his expression. To his credit, he tried to hide it, and his response was gentle and didn't cut her off completely. "I'm not sure. Let's wait and see what happens."

She considered several replies and rejected them all. No point in asking him whether he trusted her when the answer was so obvious. No point in berating him for it either. Why should he trust her? They barely knew each other, and he had no reason to believe her crazy story about a vision in a candle light.

He tipped his head down and kissed her gently. "Let's worry about it later." He looked past her at the window at the snow falling outside. "It doesn't look like any business is going to get done tomorrow if this keeps up for much longer, so you may be stuck with me a bit longer."

"I've taken vacation for the week anyway," she said, gathering her spirits and trying to steady her hands enough to get her bra fastened again.

"I'm on indefinite leave. Let's just rejoice then, that we have more time. I don't know about you, but I'm getting hungry. I brought a couple of lamb chops I found in the freezer. The freezer's not working since the electricity's out, but the apartment stayed so cold, they were still frozen anyway. I brought them with me."

She nodded. A second football game had started, though it involved teams neither of them cared about. They left it on in the background, turning to watch exciting plays, while they worked on dinner. Slowly the comfort between them returned as she chopped broccoli and he prepared a sauce for the chops.

After dinner, which included the candlelight and the good china again, he helped clean up and then proposed a game of Scrabble.

Lindsey agreed, but asked, "What's the twist on this one? There aren't any hands in Scrabble."

His grin set her heart on fire again. "No, but there are turns. We can create rounds. Say three turns each make a round?"

"Winner and loser based on total score for the three turns?"

He nodded.

"And…?"

He did a charming thing with a crooked eyebrow that almost made her throw herself on him again. "Winner of the round gets to ask the loser to do something."

"Is this related to Strip Poker?" she asked.

"Could be. If that's what the participants want."

Before they started, he opened the bottle of Benedictine and Brandy, and poured it into two small liqueur glasses he found in her china cabinet. The liquid sparkled in the candlelight.

"Small sips," he warned, as he handed her a glass. "This stuff packs a punch."

She appreciated the warning, because the burst of burning flavor that assaulted her mouth when she sipped startled her into nearly choking. Her eyes watered and her throat tingled as the liquid slid down. "Wow," she said when she could talk again. "Thanks for the warning. You weren't kidding. It's warm all the way down. But it has a nice flavor, too. It could grow on me."

They settled on the couch again, with the Scrabble board between them. The second football game ended as they were setting up, so he switched the channel to the weather station and let it be background noise.

Lindsey was pretty good at Scrabble, but because she wanted to see what he had in mind, she deliberately fudged the first couple of words, settling for a pair of meager six-pointers when in one case, she could have gotten eleven.

His wry, slanting look in her direction suggested he recognized her sandbagging. Nonetheless, he didn't hesitate to take advantage of it, and won the round of three turns easily enough.

"Strip Scrabble sounds good to me," he said. "Take your sweater off."

He already knew she wore only the bra beneath it. She peeled the sweater up and over her head slowly, watching his face as she did so. His eyes lit with pleasure as her upper body was revealed to him.

Lindsey desperately wanted to win the next round. She'd been dying to see him shirtless since the minute she'd laid eyes on him. Unfortunately the fulfillment of the desire had to be delayed. He won the next round and demanded she remove her shoes, socks, and jeans.

Again she moved deliberately, storing his reactions in memory for later pleasure. His eyes gleamed with interest. A hungry, predatory expression sometimes flashed across his face as she slowly peeled the jeans down her legs and stepped out of them. Even under her rattier clothes she loved wearing silky, high-cut, lace-edged underwear.

She felt a bit self-conscious sitting down to a play a game in nothing but her bra and panties. Maybe it helped distract him a bit, but he lost the next round, and obligingly removed his shirt at her demand. He aped her movements, undoing the buttons slowly, tantalizing her with glimpses of flesh. It was worth the wait. He had a magnificent chest with smooth, firm skin, well-shaped, toned muscles and a nice dusting of hair on his pectorals. Broad, solid shoulders narrowed down to a slim waist. Definitely yummy.

The next hand was delayed a few moments while the weather reporter finally got to the northeast. The snowstorm enveloping them looked ready to stay for a while, with predicted snowfall levels around eighteen inches.

"Doesn't look like I'm going to get the power turned on tomorrow." He didn't sound terribly disappointed about it. "Think you can put up with me for another day or two?"

"We'll manage," she said, making the words as dry as possible, a difficult task when she was actually feeling pretty delighted about it.

Greg won the next round. At his demand, she removed the bra. Lindsey wasn't embarrassed by her body. She was slender, and her breasts weren't large, but they were nicely shaped and didn't sag at all. He sucked in a hard breath as he saw them and let it out on a slow whistle. "You're beautiful." The words were thin and breathy, leaving no doubt about their sincerity.

Struggling not to be distracted by her state of undress and the way he kept staring at her, Lindsey concentrated on the game and won the next round.

"Shoes, socks, and jeans," she demanded of him.

He removed the requested items more quickly this time. She found herself sucking air while watching. Long, muscular legs bore a light coating of dark hair. He wore plain, white briefs on his slim hips, and the evidence of his enjoyment of their game bulged out the front of them. Greg MacIntyre was one glorious hunk of manhood.

Lindsey won the next round as well. He raised an eyebrow when she demanded he remove the briefs and asked, "You sure you're ready for this?"

"Do you have an ego or what?"

"That wasn't exactly what I meant, but no matter." He had to lift the briefs over the bulge to slide them down his legs. His freed cock sprang out, thick, hard and enthusiastically ready for action. It was a beautifully shaped penis, long and massive enough to fill her, threaded with a few veins standing out from the surface.

"You're certainly ready for this," she said, the words not quite as steady as she would have liked.

"It's the inspiration." His gaze roved up and down her body. "I have *got* to win the next round."

She suspected he'd been saving up some choice letters, and he won the next round easily. Her panties already bore the stain of her moisture, which seeped steadily from her pussy. The aroma of her sex filled the air as she slid them down her body, but after a moment she realized her own scent mingled with a heavier musk from Greg's desire. Again he stared at her body and his cock quivered with increased need.

"I want to explore every curve and fold of your body," he said. "I want to kiss every inch of you."

"Win the next round," she suggested. There were only enough letter chips for one more. A good thing, she decided. Seeing his gorgeous body, smelling the aroma, the memories of what his hands and mouth had done to her earlier all combined to rouse a surging tide of need that threatened to sweep her away on its torrent.

She couldn't concentrate on the game. She couldn't keep her attention on anything but him. His cock was so rampantly ready, so beautifully formed. It would fill her and… He won the final round, and the game as well, she suspected, though they didn't tally any final score. She waited for his final demand, wondering, hoping.

Greg swept the pieces back into the box in a pair of deft, impatient motions and set it aside. "Stretch out on the couch," he told her.

She did. He perched on the very edge of the sofa beside her hips. His expression turned serious.

"I'm not stopping this time," he said. "If you have any doubts at all about this, tell me now. I have protection, but I'm a demanding lover. You might find it more than you bargained for."

Her insides twisted in a frisson of excitement and fear. "I want this," she said. "I want you…and all your demands."

He still watched her, unmoving. "You have some doubts."

If he only knew. *Gram, you better be watching out for me here*, she prayed. She was about to commit her life, her health, and her future to this man. If she'd misinterpreted the visions, she was cooked. If he wouldn't learn to trust her, he'd steal her heart and her future and run away with them.

"Of course I have doubts," she admitted. "Don't you?"

His expression changed. A momentary flash of fear and sadness showed, chased away by a forced humor. "Right at the moment, no. Maybe later. But there is something very strong and very hot going on between us. I have no doubts about that."

"No, *that* I don't doubt either."

"Then let's stop thinking about it so much," he suggested.

Before she could answer, he dipped his head and ran his tongue over her left nipple. Lindsey did indeed stop thinking about anything after that but him and the things he could do to her. His fingers and lips moved over her breasts, stroking, bathing, nipping, sucking until she squirmed on the couch as the heat spread through her body. She became liquid fire. He drew a nipple into his mouth and sucked on it, then nipped down with his teeth, hard enough to bring a stinging pain that turned into fiery need. He soothed it with his tongue before he repeated it on the other nipple, then continued back and forth until both throbbed. Her pussy swelled and her womb clenched. She buried her fingers in his hair, grabbing handfuls of the silky strands and pulling.

Lindsey moaned and squealed as he fanned the spark of needed into a blaze with his clever tongue and fingers.

Greg kissed a line of damp, nipping kisses down her stomach and abdomen until he reached her cleft. After nudging her legs apart, he repositioned himself so that he could reach the folds of her pussy. He stroked with gentle fingers up and down the sensitive dips and hollows, sometimes trailing down the insides of her thighs with his palms, occasionally dipping a finger into her vagina. She moaned with each new delight he evoked from her, found spots she never even knew could be so sensitive.

"You're so ready for me," he commented, holding up a finger that glistened with her moisture.

"I've never been…so hot…for anyone in my…life," she said between pants. "Greg, you're—"

He found her clit and stroked it, drawing a scream from her as the shards of white-hot pleasure tore along every nerve and sinew.

The fingers of his other hand roamed up and down her thighs, and down along the cleft. The need was such an overwhelming hunger, she sobbed and begged. "Come into me. Please! I need you. Now!"

"Bossy, bossy!" he said. "For that, you'll wait another minute or two."

"Nooooo, please." Her clit throbbed. Her whole body throbbed with the building pressure. She needed him filling her to push her over and release it. "Now! Please!" She reached for his cock to tease him into doing as she wished.

He moved back, holding her down with a hand on her stomach, leaned over and pressed his mouth to her abdomen. He nipped again, hard enough to sting a little, then licked over it and moved down, down, until his lips were at her clit. His tongue explored her sensitive bud; he pulled it into his mouth and sucked on it until she screamed, on the verge of exploding. So close; she was so damn close. Her fingers dug into the fabric of the couch as pressure built far beyond what she thought she could contain.

She all but cried as he moved away for a second, but he grabbed a packet from his pants pocket, tore it open, and put on the condom.

Then he moved, stretching out on top of her. His cock probed and found its target. He pressed forward, gently at first, until he was sure she could accommodate his size. But she didn't want gentleness. The pressure within demanded power, speed, strength. Winding her arms around his shoulders she drew his chest against hers, his mouth to her face.

"Fuck me," she demanded.

The two words seemed to free him from all restraint. No more gentleness or caution, just flaming need and driving power. He pushed all the way into her. Her cunt spasmed around him, sparking even greater urgency. He drew out and rammed all the way in, fast and hard.

Lindsey lifted herself toward him, meeting his thrusts with her own violent desire and need. Each time he slammed home it wound a spring inside her tighter and tighter. She dug her fingers into the powerful muscles of his shoulders with the ever-increasing tension.

"Lindsey," he said, in a broken whisper. "Ah, God, you're so hot, so tight, so slick and smooth."

He pushed his fingers into her hair and kissed her hard between thrusts. "So beautiful. So right."

Their breath, forced out in hard pants, mingled.

Lindsey sobbed as the tension wound so tight, she couldn't bear it. His pistoning thrusts grew faster and harder yet, until she suddenly poised on the edge of exploding. He must have felt it. He pulled back out and waited a couple of endless, agonizing seconds.

"Greg!" She screamed his name as he dove into her again, filling her to the limit, jamming himself against her throbbing womb. She spiraled out of control then, exploding into a million pieces as the frenzied spasms of release rolled through her.

As though it were contagious, Greg pushed in one more time and jerked repeatedly as he climaxed as well. His face screwed up in agonized concentration, and he pumped into her until finally he halted and sagged onto her.

Lindsey welcomed the dear weight of his body on hers. She wrapped her arms around him and held him to her while the aftershocks rattled her and they each panted and gasped their way toward calm. His lips worked on her neck and shoulder, pressing grateful kisses into the tender skin at the junction.

When they were finally able to relax in the sublime peace of love fulfilled, he hoisted himself up so he could look her in the face. "I'm sorry it was so quick. Next time we'll do it slower."

Lindsey put her hands on his cheeks to frame his face. "I'm not sorry. It's been building between us ever since we met. We both needed it too badly to take it slow."

He nodded and pushed himself up and off her. "Let me clean up and get us a drink."

For a while Lindsey couldn't make herself move. She felt so wonderfully sated, replete with his loving. Greg had brought out a wildness in her she'd never suspected was there. Certainly no one before him had evoked that level of violent longing. Nor had any man ever worked her sensitive places so cleverly. Her system still hummed in the glorious aftermath of the best loving she'd ever known.

"It's still snowing," Greg said, from the kitchen. Lindsey got up and joined him. It felt odd to be walking around nude, but he was as well and seemed much more at ease with it. He stared out the kitchen window, watching the flakes swirling in the glow of a pole light in the parking lot. "It looks like there's a foot or more on the ground already. I've lived here five years, but I'm still not used to how much it snows. In Virginia, it snowed occasionally, but rarely more than a few inches. And that was enough to close schools, businesses, everything."

Lindsey shrugged. "We're more used to it. The plows are probably already out and the main streets will be cleared by morning. They're slow to get to the parking lot here, however. We won't be going anywhere tomorrow most likely. Good thing I've got plenty of food."

He handed her another glass of the liqueur. "And we've both got plenty of time right now. Let's retreat to your bed. How about a massage? And maybe that long, slow loving we talked about?"

Lindsey nodded. They took their drinks to her bedroom, where she pulled off the quilt.

"Satin sheets?" he asked. "My lady likes her decadent luxuries."

"A few well-chosen ones. Are you a decadent luxury?"

"Is that what you want?" He took a sip of his drink while watching her light several pillar candles. Their soft radiance filled the romance with a lambent, romantic glow.

Lindsey turned to him and studied his tall, straight, firm body. His brown hair flopped around his face, and a shadow of beard lent a rugged air to features that just escaped being too perfect. "Oh, yes, I want," she sighed, going to him.

She leaned against him, stomach to stomach, chest to chest, when he wrapped his arms around her. He tilted her head back and kissed, slowly, thoroughly, voraciously, learning every small hollow of her mouth, wrestling and wrapping her tongue. He rubbed up and down her spine as he kissed her, traveling down further each time. She started to melt into a pool of liquid heat as her pussy swelled again.

How she ended up on the bed, on her back, with his mouth still joined to hers and his hard, jutting cock probing into her belly would forever remain a mystery. But after a few minutes of drugging kisses that sapped her very will to move, he pulled away and rolled her onto her stomach.

"You're as beautiful from the back as you are from the front," he commented, while brushing his hand down from her shoulder along her spine over the mound of her left buttock and along her left thigh to the calf and finally her foot. "So gracefully rounded. Magnificent."

After massaging one foot and then the other, the hand traveled back up her body, along the right side, lingering for a moment at the line where her thigh met bottom, then proceeding upward. He rubbed her back, working on the muscles of her shoulders and around her neck until she was so relaxed she felt she could melt into the sheets.

The heat gathered more languidly, but just as surely, pooling in her belly and tightening her pussy when he turned his attention to her buttocks, stroking and rubbing them, even slapping lightly. The noise and the small sting startled her, but the moisture gathered at her cunt. Even she could smell its perfume when he nudged her thighs apart.

He rubbed the insides of her thighs, slowly, teasingly, always stopping just short of her pussy, until her blood boiled with mad need for him to touch her cleft. She squirmed and wiggled, trying to move herself against his hand, but he eluded her efforts. Just when she thought she'd scream with frustration, his fingers reached her cleft and stroked.

Pleasure hit, hard and explosive. His fingers brushed, rubbed and pinched the outer lips of her cunt, stroked the inner flesh, then found her clit and toyed with it until it was hard and her pussy wept for him.

Another ferocious climax approached, but before it could hit, he flipped her over and began to toy with her breasts again. He stroked her nipples, rubbed them until they fired at his touch, pinched and twisted until they burned a little. It all added to the fire growing low in her belly.

"Tomorrow we'll get out the toys," he promised. "Your breasts are going to love some of my things, and hate others."

She could only moan because his hand found her clit and began to work it again. He'd promised a long, slow loving and he delivered. He didn't hurry. More than once when he felt her beginning to tense, heading for a climax, he backed off and slowed down. She moaned and sobbed and begged him to complete it, but he cruelly refused. Then when the fire had started to wane, he used fingers and tongue and lips to stoke it even higher than before.

By the time he knelt between her legs she was desperate for him to fill her. He didn't though. Instead he dipped his head into her slit.

A thin, high scream broke from her when his tongue stroked the sensitive folds and found her clit. Pleasure was like a volcano, her blood and flesh, hot lava, with pressure building inside until she knew she couldn't contain it. He brought her higher and higher. When he drew the bud into his mouth and sucked, the volcano blew. She came apart. Sparks of light danced across her vision as she bucked and jerked with the repeated spasms of release.

He moved, stretching out beside her and winding his arms around her to hold while she recovered.

When she could talk again, she looked at him and said, "You get a gold star for keeping promises."

"Long, slow loving? It's good, isn't it?"

"It is good," she said on a happy sigh.

"And it isn't over yet." He shifted again, reaching for the packet he'd left on the side table.

Lindsey put a hand on his chest to hold him. "Oh, no, you don't. Not so fast. You got to torment me. My turn now."

He sighed and lay back. "I'm at your command."

She wanted to touch him all over, to explore his gorgeous lean body an inch at a time until she knew every bit of it. His chest hair tickled her palm, and his nipples beaded up into hard little knots when she stroked and tweaked them. The muscles that covered his strong bones twitched occasionally, and he moaned once when she pinched him.

His breathing grew ragged when she moved her hand down his hard stomach and abdomen. She skirted his engorged cock and rubbed along his thighs, exploring the hair-roughened hardness there. The different textures of his skin delighted her. His abdomen had smooth, silky skin that felt tight and firm, but the muscle on his hairy thighs rippled under her touch. After rubbing and exploring to her satisfaction, she nudged his legs apart so she could reach his balls.

No man had ever let her play with his body like this. With most of the others it had been a fairly quick coupling followed by sleep. Greg's openness was a revelation to her, one she took full advantage of.

His balls surprised her. Though coated with coarse hair, the skin below was soft, almost delicate. "Gently," he warned when she squeezed. She heeded his advice and handled the heavy sacs carefully. She ran her fingers back behind his balls, then forward to the long, harder length of his cock.

He groaned when she made a delicate exploration of its folds and bumps. The tip was some of the softest skin she'd ever felt, a satiny surface with the tiny hole at its center oozing a drop of fluid. For a moment she shut her eyes and reveled in the silky smooth feel of his secret flesh and the powerfully male aroma.

"I don't...think I can...hold it much longer," he warned, interrupting her reverie.

She felt the increasing throb of the blood pounding in his cock, the eager jump it took occasionally. When he reached for a packet again, she let him grab it, but then took it from him, opened it and rolled the rubber sheath onto him. She shifted, pushing herself up, and swung a leg across his stomach. His eyes widened in surprise when he realized what she intended, but the expression soon changed to delight.

Lindsey shifted backward until his cock rested against her pussy. A small push and its tip breached her opening, then she moved up and back again, sliding down until she impaled herself completely on him.

He gasped aloud as her heat and moisture swallowed him. She moved, cautiously at first, but with more enthusiasm and vigor as he surged upward to meet each downward push, and the fire built inside her again. With each thrust, his cock probed at a sensitive area within, making her jerk repeatedly. She leaned forward and held onto his shoulders, while he cupped her hips to help steady her.

A few more pushes and the tremors of release burst through her again. At the same time he jerked as well and moaned in ultimate pleasure. For several minutes they braced themselves against each other as repeated spasms of completion rocked them.

She collapsed against him, content to lay in a slightly awkward curve with her head resting on his chest, their bodies still joined. The peace was beyond anything she'd ever experienced, the intimacy of being quietly joined a revelation of what fulfillment really meant with the right person.

Finally he shifted her off him. He kissed her again before he left to go clean himself up.

Too sated to move, Lindsey dozed off but roused briefly when he returned. He lay beside her and drew her close. Her head rested on his chest. She fell asleep to the reassuring thump of his heartbeat beneath her ear.

Chapter Seven

The aroma of coffee floating down the hall warned Lindsey that Greg was already up even before she rolled over and realized he wasn't beside her anymore.

She found him sitting on the couch, bare feet propped on the coffee table, with a laptop computer open in front of him. He frowned at the screen while sipping from his coffee, and pushed a pair of glasses up his nose.

"Checking email?" she asked.

He started, then closed the laptop and took off the glasses. "Not exactly. Just getting some work done."

"Are you still employed?" she asked as she grabbed a mug from the cabinet.

He shrugged. "Honestly? I don't know. I doubt it. But my password still works to get into the company network."

Lindsey almost dropped the coffee pot. "What? They haven't disabled it? That's strange. Somebody's either very slow, very stupid, or…"

"Or what?"

"Or they're setting a trap for you."

His eyebrows rose. He stood and wandered toward the kitchen, twirling the glasses thoughtfully. "I'd considered slow and stupid, and counted myself lucky. I hadn't thought of the possibility of a trap. At least not that way. I should have. I can't believe I could still be that naïve. I should have thought of that."

"Maybe not. It's just we attorneys have devious minds."

"Why would they need to set a trap, though?"

Lindsey took a sip of the coffee. "Maybe the evidence against you isn't as strong as they'd like?"

"It was enough to get me arrested and arraigned."

"Doesn't mean they have enough to convince a jury beyond a reasonable doubt, though."

"How could they rig a trap to catch me online?"

"If your ID and password are still active, they could have something set up to trigger an alarm when you log in. If something else were to happen to the company's files or other information, it would be easy enough to make it appear you'd been responsible."

He stopped with the coffee cup halfway to his mouth and drew a deep breath. "I always thought of myself as pretty smart. I hate learning how wrong I was. I guess I've learned that lesson the hardest way possible." He rolled his eyes. "And dammit, the last thing I want to do now is start descending into self-pity."

"Even smart people can be fooled, especially if they're not expecting it from people they trust."

He laughed harshly. "You don't have to protect my ego. Despite my current self-recrimination, it's really pretty healthy."

"I'm not. I'm looking at facts and trying to work up the nerve to offer to help, knowing you don't trust me and you probably won't be willing to let me."

Surprise and an odd sort of pain mingled on his face, but he said nothing for several long moments. "Lindsey, I know you—"

"You don't have to apologize for it."

"Yes, I do. You've been extraordinarily generous—bailed me out of jail, given me a place to stay when my apartment wasn't livable, shared your bed, your body, and your joy. You have a right to expect more from me than suspicion and doubt."

"I do. But I don't expect it right away. Trust builds on experience. I just hope that now that you've recognized the dangers of trusting too much you won't go the other way and refuse to trust anyone at all."

"It's a point to consider."

That was all the concession she was likely to get from him right then, and it was enough. She had chores to catch up with, including checking her own email and some work correspondence that ended up taking most of the morning. He continued to work at his laptop, sometimes typing fiercely, other times just reading for long stretches. She could help him; Lindsey knew it without knowing exactly how she knew. Maybe the fact that Gram seemed somehow to have arranged this meeting, or possibly the sense that they had a destined future led her to believe she'd have a part in ensuring he did have a future. Of course, there was also her work experience. As a tax attorney, she'd had to deal with plenty of cooked books, unusual accounting systems and some straight-out fraud. She'd figured out how someone had perpetrated the deception in several cases, and in two had even worked out who had to be behind it.

Telling him that wouldn't make any difference just yet. She had to pray he would realize he could and should trust her before the snow melted, he got his electricity turned back on and he moved back home.

She made tuna salad wraps for lunch. While they ate, she asked, "Any more games this afternoon?"

His grin turned deliciously evil. "Oh, yes. Much more adventurous, too."

Her pussy swelled as she considered the possibilities, and she suddenly found it harder to sit still.

Once they'd cleaned up lunch, he brought out a large sheet of paper, some pencils, several colorful, multi-sided dice, and a pair of smaller pads. "Have you ever done any role-playing games?"

"Like Dungeons & Dragons?"

"Yes, but there's a near-infinite variety of them now. This is a sort of modified version of one. I'm the GameMaster. You're a kidnapped princess, trying to escape from a dungeon."

He went to the windows and closed the blinds, dimming the light in the room. "How's your supply of candles?"

"I love scented candles. I've got a drawer full."

"Good." He lit the three that sat out on the end tables. "More atmospheric lighting. You're escaping from a dungeon after all."

"I've no idea how I do that. In fact I have no idea how to play these kinds of games."

"Don't worry. It's not hard. I'll help you along. I'll be acting as the GameMaster, the person who runs the game and gives all the instructions for what happens and how to proceed."

Lindsey had no idea where this was going, but the idea of being a kidnapped princess in a dungeon suggested some dangerously thrilling possibilities.

"You wake up in a dungeon," he told her, getting into his GameMaster role. "You remember you've been kidnapped, and the kidnappers said you were going to be their Master's bride. You know their Master. You've been intrigued by him, but he's dark and dangerous. When he asked you to marry him, you refused. He wouldn't to take 'no' for an answer. So he's kidnapped you and brought you here. You're lying on a bed in a room lit only by a torch in a bracket on the wall. The door is on your left and it's closed."

The scenario reminded Lindsey of Kidnap Fantasies, Inc. She'd learned about them for Jade's sake, but the idea had excited her as well. "Okay. What am I supposed to do?"

"Tell me what you would do in the situation."

"Get up and try the door."

"Hmm. Can you believe it? The guards apparently forgot to lock it, so it opens when you lift the latch."

"Bad guards. So I open the door and go out in the hall."

"It's very dark in the hall. You trip over something on the floor."

"I go back and get the torch."

"Good idea. When you get back, you see the thing you tripped over is a small, ugly, gnome-like creature. It looks up at you and whimpers, then gets up and follows you as you pass it. The hall you're in ends suddenly, but dark passages go off to the left and right."

"I'll go to the left."

"You go a little farther and the hall ends at a doorway. An enormous troll blocks the passage."

"Can I go around him?"

"He moves to block your way."

"Oh." Lindsey looked up at Greg. "What do I do now?"

"You could try asking him to get out of the way."

"Please, Mr. Troll, would you mind letting me pass?"

Greg made his voice deeper and gruff. "If you'll take off your blouse and bra and leave them off, I'll let you pass."

"What? Lecherous troll," she grumbled. But she stood up and removed her shirt and bra.

"The troll gives you a long, hot look, then lets you pass." Greg gave her a long, hot look himself. "The gnome is still trailing along right behind you. The corridor you're in heads down a staircase. At the bottom you can go left, right or forward."

"I'll go right."

"You pass an odd place where the walls seem to glow. It doesn't do anything, except that when the gnome accompanying you passes by it, he seems to change shape for a moment, into the form of a man. You can't see his features, and it only lasts a few seconds. A little farther down the corridor, there's a cabinet."

"I'll open it and look inside the cabinet."

"Hmmm, seems to contain some spare armaments. A knife and a sword."

"I'll take them with me. Could come in handy."

"Indeed. Uh-oh. A spirit forms into a human shape right in front of you. He looks angry. 'You stole my weapons. If you wish to keep them, you must pay a forfeit.'"

"What's the forfeit?" Lindsey asked.

"You'll have to be punished for it. Not now but later. A spanking."

"Oh."

"Do you want to put the weapons back?"

Lindsey considered. He'd probably insist on carrying out the spanking at some point. "I'll keep them."

"So be it. You proceed along the corridor. Suddenly the gnome jumps out in front of you and blocks your way, making a bunch of noises that sound like a warning."

"I stop and look around."

"You don't see or hear anything, but the corridor is dark and you can't see very far ahead."

This was turning out to be a lot more fun than she'd anticipated. She could retreat into her mind and almost see the dark corridors and listen for strange movements. The sensual edge of danger and sexual experiment added an intriguing depth of excitement to it. "I take a couple of steps forward, cautiously."

"The creature with you continues to try to block your way and warn you off."

"I hold the torch up and out."

"Ah, you see a dense nest of spider webs ahead of you, with a bunch of black spiders running around on them. They block the corridor."

"Ick. I turn around and go back the other way."

"Good move. The spiders are not friendly. You pass the spot where there's that strange glow. Again the gnome seems to change shape into a man. You get a better look at it this time, though the view is brief. He looks very much like the mage that kidnapped you. You go on and get back to the stairs you came down. You can go straight ahead or turn left."

What did that bit about the gnome looking like the mage mean? Was the mage a shapeshifter and helping her out? Greg wouldn't tell her if she asked though. It was up to her to find out. "Straight ahead."

"The corridor continues for a while, then ends in a closed door."

"I open the door."

"You have a hard time with the latch. It seems to be jammed and doesn't want to open. The gnome growls at you."

Lindsey thought about it. "I keep trying until it gives."

"Okay. The door opens suddenly and bangs against the wall. Oops. Bad idea. You've woken a nest of sleeping satyrs. They're not happy about it."

"I run like hell in the other direction."

"Sorry, they're faster than you. They catch you quickly."

"Um, let's see. I use the sword to fight them?"

"No go. They're holding both of your arms."

"I'm in trouble," Lindsey admitted.

"The gnome creature suddenly growls at them. He seems to get bigger for a minute or two. The satyrs all turn to face him, and appear to be listening as he growls at them. Finally the one who appears to be the leaders says, 'The Master says we cannot have you. But he promises you'll be punished. So you go now. Leave us alone and don't come back.'"

"I'm outta there," Lindsey said. "Back to the staircase again. Sounds like I'm going to have a sore backside, too." She tried to make it light and sassy and wondered if she succeeded.

He raised his eyebrows. "That will be up to you. You still have three choices of direction now that you're back at the staircase."

"The one I haven't gone in yet."

"Okay, you enter a wide hall, beautifully decorated with tapestries and statuary all over. Comfortable, but rich furnishings fill the room, lit by a skylight well above that lets daylight filter down."

"Hmmm, nice, but how do I get out?"

"There are exits to your left and right."

"I think I'll go right."

"The corridor narrows and gets darker as you proceed. The gnome creature still accompanies you, and he begins to growl again."

"Now what?" Lindsey asked.

"Goblins! A group of four of them attack you."

Her pulse actually began to pound as though she really were in danger. "Yikes. Gulp. I swing my sword."

"This is where the dice come in. You roll the dice. If you get a five or more, you only kill one. Ten or more, two. Thirteen, three. Eighteen, all four."

Lindsey picked up the odd multi-sided dice and rolled them. Fourteen. "Got three of them. Does the fourth one demand I get spanked for killing his buddies?"

"The Master may demand you get spanked for having a smart mouth. While you're tackling three of them, the gnome takes on the fourth and defeats it. You now have clear passage down the hall. There are two doors at the far end. Before you get to them, however, there's a flash of light. The gnome disappears, and in his place stands the mage who kidnapped you."

"Oh. I turn and run in the other direction."

"He calls after you, asking you to wait, and promising that he won't harm you. He just wants to ask you a question. Once you answer, you'll be free to leave if you wish."

"His word of honor on that?"

"His word of honor."

"Okay. I'll stop and listen."

"Good. He tells you he brought you here because he wants you, and he wanted to show you all he could offer. The riches and the strange adventures. The way he…cares for you and wants to protect you and guide you. But it's entirely your choice whether to stay now. The door on the left will take you outside and you'll be able to go home. No one will chase after you. The door on the right leads into his personal quarters. The choice is entirely yours. One thing you should know, however. Should you choose the Master's quarters, he will insist you pay the forfeits you incurred on your journey."

Lindsey looked up at Greg, studying the expression on his face, the light in his gray eyes. It was a game, yes, but more than that, she realized. A test, of sorts.

"I'll take the door on the right. Do I win?"

"Depends on what you want. You win the Master's devotion. And his attentions."

"Sounds good to me. Are you the Master?"

"I'm playing him."

Lindsey gave him what she hoped was a come-hither look. She'd never tried it before so she wasn't quite sure how to do it. Apparently the effort was good enough.

He put the book down, stood up, came around the table to her side and drew her to her feet. After kissing her hard, but briefly, he whispered, "There are quite a few forfeits to pay. Perhaps we'd best get started."

Her couch divided the room in half. Flanked by two chairs, it faced the entertainment center on the far wall. Behind it was a set of shelves in one corner, and the dining area in the other. He guided her to the back of the couch and reached for the button of her jeans. "These have got to go. Kick off your shoes."

She did as he ordered. Slowly, almost maddeningly slowly, he unfastened her jeans, pulled the zipper down and slid them down her legs. Once she'd stepped out of them, he turned his attention to her only remaining bit of covering. He ran a hand lovingly over her silk-covered abdomen, enjoying the feel of the luxurious panties. "It's almost a shame to take these off," he said. "They look delicious on you. But they're in the way." He peeled them off her, rubbing the silk against her skin as he slid them down her legs. When they were off he bunched the fabric in his hand and brushed her with them, pushing the silk into her slit and rubbing them against her pussy. They came out again stained with her moisture. His eyes gleamed at that sign of her arousal.

"Now, turn around and bend over the back of the sofa."

A sudden stab of fear froze her for a moment. She couldn't deny that she wanted this, had wanted it for a long time, but still… What if he hurt her too much? What if he wouldn't stop, or it proved too much for her?

He brushed a gentle hand down the side of his face. "I won't hurt you," he promised. "Or not any more than you want. If you want it to stop, just tell me 'red light'. I'll stop whatever I'm doing, I promise. And I won't be angry or blame you. This is about things we do for pleasure. If it doesn't please you, then it doesn't please me, either. Trust me."

She stared into his eyes. Could she trust the honesty, the concern, the…love, she saw shining in them? *Gram, I hope you're right about this*, she prayed. She smiled at him and nodded, then turned around and bent over the back of the couch, putting her hands on the seat cushion.

It felt strange, scary and exciting to be in that position. Very vulnerable and open, especially when he nudged her legs slightly apart. He could see her cunt and her asshole. He could do whatever he wanted with them. Something about being at his mercy that way sent a thrill of excitement all through her.

Right then he wanted to touch. He brushed a hand along her spine, following the line down along the crack between her buttocks, fingers exploring that shallow tunnel and wandering across her asshole. Lindsey shivered with excitement and anticipation. He played with her for a few minutes before he took his hand off.

She couldn't bear to peek at him to see what he was doing. She waited, but wasn't kept in suspense long. After a few long seconds, he slapped her left bottom cheek. She jumped, but more in surprise than pain. It wasn't actually a hard slap at all, but it made a loud noise. It jarred and it stung, but not much. It was an interesting sting, though. It sent a small spiral of heat winding down into her cunt, making it feel tight and heavy.

The next few slaps, which alternated sides of her buttocks, had the same effect. A lot of noise, a bit of shock, a crisp bite that started as pain and turned to quickly to a buzzing excitement. It was bearable. It thrilled her right down to her toes. She wanted more.

As though sensing her reaction, he made the next few spanks harder. The bite got deeper, the sting a little stronger. Her excitement grew. They got a little harder still, enough to make her squirm and pant. After a few of those, he paused and waited for her to catch her breath, giving her a chance to protest or stop if it she wanted to.

She didn't want. She wanted more, in fact. They'd just scratched the surface of the wild and new sensations available this way.

He started spanking again after a minute. Her bottom had to be getting pink. A deep burn had begun sizzling there, stoked by each slap of his hand. It began to get uncomfortable, but she still had no desire to stop it. The heat continued to push into her womb and her cunt. She squirmed with each strike, and even moaned once or twice.

The blaze in her bottom began to feel like real pain, but perversely she still wanted more. It was a delicious pain that continued to spiral into ever-increasing pleasure. She wiggled more, squealing as harder strikes sent jolts of fire into her burning bottom.

Just when she thought she could bear no more and would have to ask him to stop it, he paused. His hand brushed over her flaming buttocks, soothing some of the ache, rousing even more desire. Her moisture was beginning to seep down her legs, she was so achingly ready and needy for him.

He hadn't quite finished spanking her, though. With one hand, he separated her bottom cheeks, while the other peppered the sensitive slit with light but sharp slaps. Those had her squealing, as much from the shocking sensations that blasted through her as from the burning sting that accompanied them. Then he brushed the hand down over her moist, swollen pussy that wept for his possession.

And he took possession of it. He claimed it for his own in a way so shocking and unexpected she almost melted with the surprise and delight.

With light, sharp flicks of his stiffened fingers, he spanked her pussy. Sparks exploded in her eyes every time his fingers landed. There might have been some pain mingled in the sensations it aroused, but if so, any discomfort got lost in the sizzling pleasure that made her arch and scream. Pressure built inside her until she knew she couldn't contain it.

Thrills rolled through every nerve and sinew each time he struck her pussy. Wanton sounds tore from her throat, moans and pleas and squeals of sheer delight. She arched her body even further and pushed back, eagerly meeting each flick.

Until finally, on one harder strike, she found herself exploding in a mushrooming climax that sent gigantic spasms tearing through her arched body. Her breath came in huge pants and she jerked repeatedly against the back of the couch, bouncing up and down with a release that outdid even the previous day's for magnificence and pleasure.

But it wasn't complete, and even as she heard the sound of his pants' zipper being dragged down, she knew what it lacked. He put on protection, nudged her legs farther apart and lifted her just enough to impale her with his cock. No gentleness, no careful entry, just the sharp insertion. Just what she needed. He lowered her again, letting her belly settle back against the couch. His arms wrapped around her. His hands found her breasts.

Two pairs of fingers closed over her nipples, pinching and twisting.

Lindsey didn't think she could still be so needy, but with him in her, the desire shot straight up through the stratosphere again. A more internal pressure built with his fucking. He banged away at her, hard and fast. She tried to wiggle herself up to meet each thrust and take it as deeply into herself as possible. Passion swelled to a rising tide that carried her far out of her experience.

Surging waves of orgasm broke over her again, swirling her with them. She screamed. Lindsey had never screamed with a climax before but this one was so huge, so overwhelming, the only way to bear it was to yell her joy out loud.

His cry of triumph as he came blended with hers. When it finally wore out, he rested over her, supporting his weight with his hands on the back of the couch, his breath whispering past her ear and his lips nuzzling the back of her neck.

Finally he recovered enough to move. He helped her to straighten up as well, then turned her into his arms, but held her out where he could see her face.

"Enjoy the adventure?"

"You have to ask?"

He shrugged, keeping his hands on her shoulders. "Hard to tell if I've gone too far."

She reached up to push back a few strands of brown hair that fell into his eyes. "Not even close."

The grin that broke through his serious expression worked its way into her heart. A surge of tenderness and possessive love filled her soul. This man was hers. She had no idea how long it would take him to understand that or learn to trust her, but it didn't matter. She had the patience to wait and the energy to ensnare him. If he didn't know it already, he'd learn.

"You just got a strange expression," he said. "Like a mountain lion sighting prey."

"Maybe. Or perhaps more like a princess who has just met her Master?"

"Ah, yes. That would be it."

She sighed. "At the risk of slipping into clichéd territory, I have to ask. Was it good for you, too?"

"Good? God, if it were any better, I'd be having a heart attack right now and dying a happy man."

"Oh, no. No dying here. You promised more games." She stopped and sighed happily. "Though, in truth, it's hard to imagine how anything could be much more fun than that."

"Failure of imagination," he accused. "Come on. You're much smarter than that."

"It's a failure of energy at the moment. Someone seems to have stolen all of mine."

"You want to rest while I fix us some dinner? In fact, I think I'm going to insist on it. I've had an idea."

"Care to share?"

His grin turned wicked and teasing. "I think not. You'll see."

Chapter Eight

Lindsey tried to get it out of him, but he refused to tell and finally chased her off to her bedroom, warning her to keep the door closed and stay inside until he came to get her.

She rested on her bed, reveling in the sated feel of completion. Though her bottom felt a bit rough, there was no residual pain at all. Her plain everyday sex encounters with her previous lovers had left her unprepared for and amazed by how thoroughly and eagerly her body responded to his rough treatment. It more than matched her secret fantasies.

His knock on the door woke her from the doze she'd slipped into. When she joined him in the living room, she discovered he'd moved chairs back and pushed the coffee table aside. A blanket was spread out over the rug. Plates and glasses rested nearby, including a bottle of wine in a cooler. A covered hamper sat beside them. Greg stood nearby, barefoot and shirtless. Lindsey had slipped into a tee shirt and a fresh pair of panties when she'd lain down. She admired his gorgeous, muscular chest for a moment

"An indoor picnic?" she asked.

"Not exactly. This is another role-play, only we're just going to play it, if you're willing. No paper or dice needed for this one. I'm an Eastern prince. You're the newest addition to my harem, but I'm so smitten with you, I've decided to train you myself."

"Train me in what?"

"Submission, obedience and how to please your Master. I'm aware that a spirited young woman like yourself will have difficulty bending your will to mine, but you'll learn. Some sweet lessons and some hard ones, but you'll learn."

She caught his drift, but had a few reservations about the scenario, especially when he produced a handful of long silk scarves and said, "Of course, since you insist on trying to escape from me, I'll have to tie you down."

He must have read the doubt in her expression because he added, "Same rules as earlier. If you don't like something or want to stop it just say 'red light'. I promise to stop whatever I'm doing."

When she didn't look convinced, he said, "You're worried about being tied down and helpless?"

"Wouldn't you be?"

She waited for him to take offense, but instead he took her concern seriously. "You have a point." He took a moment to think about it, but she saw when an idea occurred to him. He went and got her portable phone. "I'm going to leave this right next to you so you'll still be able to dial 911 if you're worried or think you're in danger."

"You're taking a bit of a risk yourself."

He shrugged. "I know."

Unless he was a truly master manipulator, it did seem likely she could trust him in this. But Lindsey truly hated and dreaded the thought of giving up all freedom of movement.

After watching her debate, Greg said, "Let's modify the game a bit. You've promised me you won't try to run away."

"No. Let's try it your way." *And, please, don't let me be making a terrible mistake.*

"A compromise. I'll fasten your ankles, but not your hands. Will that make you more comfortable?"

She wanted to kiss him, hug him, maybe even bow down before him. Instead, she just said, "Yes."

After asking her to remove the T-shirt and panties, he helped her lie down on the blanket, then he wound a silk scarf around each ankle and fastened the other end of each to the legs of a heavy chair. He put a pillow under her head so she'd be comfortable and then laid the phone down nearby, within easy reach.

"Reach out and take hold of the legs of the couch," he suggested. "Pretend your hands are tied to them." The couch was just above her head. Doing as he asked, stretched her arms out to their fullest.

"Now we'll begin your training," he said. "First I'm going to teach you some of what your body is capable of feeling." He had stowed some gear behind one of the chairs. He reached back there and brought out a feather. "Shut your eyes for this. Try to just feel."

Lindsey did.

The feather skimmed lightly down her shoulder and over her breast, paused to circle her nipples, then glided across them, and up and down. It teased with hundreds of tiny splinters of pleasure where it passed. She gasped and moaned as it prickled over the hard beads of her nipples. He ran it down her abdomen and up and down the insides of her thighs. It drew a squeal from her when it ran over her clit. Her cunt started to swell again and a twist of need spiraled down her belly.

She sighed when he set aside the feather. He rummaged around in the cooler and drew something out. Moments later she realized he had an ice cube, when the cold lump circled her breasts and sent shivers of hot excitement through her. She jumped when he touched it to her cunt, running it over her outer lips and then along the insides of her slit, where it breathed cold fire on sensitive tissue. "Greg," she gasped.

"Master," he corrected, slapping her cunt with stiffened fingers again, twice, in punishment.

A moan slipped from her throat before she said, "Master."

He crouched between her spread legs and ran the ice cube up and down her clit until she sobbed in pleasurable agony, then he pushed the melting remains into her cunt. Shards of icy heat exploded from it, spreading out along her nerves and sinews. His tongue made a maddening slow glide along her slit from just above her asshole to the peak of her clit. He probed into all her secret recesses, pushed a finger into her to explore the depths, and lashed her clit lightly with his tongue. She squealed and squirmed as the magic built a fire of need inside.

But then he backed away and moved to her side again. She moaned in disappointment.

"Slave," he said softly. "Now you know more of the pleasures awaiting you. You long for release, don't you?"

"Yes, Master." Lindsey didn't have to feign eagerness.

"Good. I'm going to untie you. If you want that release, though, you must not try to run away from me, and you must follow all my orders exactly. Will you?"

"Yes, Master."

He unwound the scarves from each of her ankles and touched her wrists. Then he stood.

"Now, come here and kneel in front of me," he said. "Shut your eyes for a moment."

The sounds of his movement preceded a metallic click. Then her right nipple was squeezed between his fingers. As he released it, something else closed over the tender tip, something bitingly tight. She drew a sharp breath. It hurt, but it hurt in an exciting way. He repeated the process with the other nipple.

"Open your eyes."

She did and looked down at her breasts. The clamps squished her nipples down almost flat, and the pain built to something ever sharper and more fearful. It was exciting but not comfortable. It throbbed with a fierce bite. He'd take them off if she asked, but she didn't want to ask. She'd rather suffer a bit for him.

Her head was even with his groin as she knelt at his feet. The bulge in the front of his jeans looked almost painful. He saw where she looked and grinned. "Undress me," he said.

She undid the button, opened his zipper, and slid jeans and briefs together down his legs. His cock stood out from his body, rampantly engorged. She reached for it, but he pushed her hands away. "Your tongue."

Lindsey leaned forward and licked him, from the base of his shaft right up to the tip. He tasted slightly, pleasantly salty. The aroma of his need teased her nose. The skin was fine and soft, almost delicate in places, though the shaft beneath was hard. Her tongue skimmed up and down, then around the knob at the top. Since it seemed to give him exquisite pleasure, she worked the ridge just below the tip extra each time she passed.

When he moaned or gasped under her attention, it sent a thrill rocketing through her. Knowing she could bring him to this, understanding how much power she actually had over him, even in this game of his Mastery, brought her delight. A surge of tenderness and love filled her heart.

Lindsey opened her mouth wider and took in the entire knob of his cock. She swirled her tongue around it and let it slide as deep as she could bear before she started to gag. He didn't press her to take any more, but let her set the pace and depth. She scraped her teeth over it carefully, then closed her mouth and sucked hard.

He groaned and buried his fingers in her hair as she worked him, making his cock harder yet and quivering with the need to come. His breath broke into loud, harsh pants.

Before they reach the explosion point, though, he pulled himself out of her mouth. "Your hands," he said, between pants. "Work me."

She did. His cock was slick with her saliva, so she found it easy to slide a hand up and down the rod. She wrapped the fingers of her other hand around his balls and kneaded them gently while she pumped. It didn't take more than a couple of minutes of that before he cried out sharply, jerked hard, and the cum spurted from his cock, landing on her chest and breasts. She continued to massage him until the spasms stopped and he was drained dry.

"Enough," he said, finally, sighing. He leaned down and kissed her hard on the mouth. "You've pleased me, slave. There's still much to learn, but you're making excellent progress. I think it's time for a reward. Are you hungry?"

Lindsey realized she was. It had been dark when she woke from her nap earlier, so it was probably dinnertime or even somewhat past. "Yes, Master."

"Good. But first…" He reached down and removed the nipple clamps with two quick flicks. She screamed in shock and pain. It hurt worse than when he'd put them on. He held her for a moment while she recovered, his clasp tender and gentle.

"Okay now?" he asked when her breathing had calmed.

She nodded.

He smiled and opened the cooler, then unloaded containers of finger foods. He must have added some things he'd brought back from his apartment to what he found in her refrigerator. Baby carrot strips, asparagus, olives, celery sticks with herbed cream cheese, cherry tomatoes, deviled eggs, chicken strips, cheese cubes, and an assortment of fruits and breads all came out of the cooler. There was enough food to feed several more people.

"Just one rule," he said. "Neither of us can feed ourselves."

"Oh. We feed each other?"

"Makes it more interesting, don't you think?"

"Definitely. Master."

He grinned at her, picked up a cheese cube and put it in her mouth. She licked his finger as she took it from him, and responded by holding out a piece of chicken and putting it on his tongue when he opened for it. He poured a sweet red wine into goblets for each of them, and they crossed arms holding the glasses to each others' lips.

It was a slow way to eat, but it was fun, interesting and different. They laughed when one or the other of them missed, pondered over choices of what to hand off next, and joked about phallic foods when he slipped a pair of slender carrot sticks into her mouth.

It probably took more than an hour before each was nearly full. He urged her to stop before she was replete and save room for dessert. Curiosity as much as a desire for something sweet kept her from eating too much.

Her reward for her restraint came when he took a can of ready-made whipped cream and sprayed a little on each of her nipples. She shivered as the sudden chill hit, but that quickly changed to heat in her system. He broke pieces off a pound cake, wiped them in the whipped cream and fed them to her and to himself. Her nipples were still a bit sore from the clamps earlier, but the cake brushing over her nipples aroused her as well, though not quite as much as seeing him eat the pieces he'd dipped in the cream.

When he asked her to spread her legs and sprayed the white foam onto her cunt, she squealed with the initial chill. But when the first piece reached her lips, replete with the aromas of cream and butter and her own juices, the heady taste made her moan and tighten. He fed her several more pieces before she protested that he wasn't getting any.

"I'll finish my dessert when you're done," he promised.

And he did. When she told him she'd had enough, he sprayed more whipped cream on her nipples and proceeded to lick it off quite thoroughly. The rasp of his tongue, slicked by the creamy smoothness drove her into a near frenzy. White-hot streaks of fire shot all through her body as he licked off every drop.

She almost jumped out of her skin, though, when he sprayed it on her cunt. The chill was a thrill of its own, but when his tongue rasped across the tender flesh, she jumped and squealed. Shards of raw pleasure, sharp as glass and almost as cutting, tore through her. Her womb tightened and her cunt wept into the cream.

His tongue worked on her clit even after all the cream was gone. She bucked and arched. Her whole being was fire and pressure, a volcano pushing upward. He licked up and down her slit, explored the opening and then moved upward slightly to draw the bud of her clit into his mouth. She screamed when he sucked on it and then nipped lightly with his teeth.

Lindsey dug her fingers into his shoulders, holding on tightly as the pressure built and built, until the volcano erupted with a cataclysmic burst. She bucked and jerked, racked with bone-jarring spasms of sublime release. She squealed like a madwoman and ended up nearly sobbing.

And then he completed it by thrusting into her again, filling her with his magnificent cock, pushing deep inside. She wrapped her arms around him to hold him to her and rode with him to a deeper, harder completion that left them both panting, breathless, and sweating.

They slept together on her bed that night, folded into each others' arms.

Chapter Nine

As usual, Greg woke before Lindsey. He lay quietly for a few minutes, watching her in the dim, early morning light. She wasn't the most beautiful woman he'd slept with, but her prettiness was more appealing than cold beauty anyway. Plus Lindsey had strength, courage, kindness and a wicked sense of humor that matched his perfectly. And she was such a sensuous creature, just beginning to plumb the depths of her own sexuality. He'd never truly expected to meet someone whose adventurous nature could match his own.

She could almost make him believe in magic.

He got up, showered, and went to the kitchen to brew coffee. A quick search of the fridge turned up the ingredients for omelets, so he grated cheese, crumbled and cooked the sausage, diced mushrooms and whipped the eggs. He fixed himself a slice of toast and left the rest of it on the counter, waiting for her to wake up.

He got out the laptop and booted it up. Conscious of Lindsey's advice, he didn't try to log into the company network. There were a bunch of records on his own hard drive, anyway, since he was supposed to write a year-end report on a product he'd managed and he'd started preparing for it right before the roof had caved in on him. Now he combed through the files he had, looking for clues to how someone had manipulated them to make it look as though he'd embezzled from the company.

He'd also turned on the Christmas tree lights. Something about their bright, festive colors and the glittering sparks they struck off the ornaments and icicles soothed him, relieved some of his tension.

Twice during the morning, he thought he caught a flash of light in his peripheral vision. Based on the angle, it could only be coming from the angel on the top of the tree. But that was absurd. It had no light of its own, though its golden wings and halo caught and reflected some. Each time it happened, though, it dragged him out of his preoccupation with the figures on the laptop, drawing his attention to the tree.

The second time, he looked up at the top of the tree, and he could have sworn the angel winked at him. But that was ridiculous, of course. He needed more coffee.

He hadn't made much progress by the time Lindsey wandered out. In truth, he was out of his depth on this. He'd never been a numbers guy. He generally only looked at the bottom-line sales figures and didn't worry too much about how those got there.

A quiet sigh slipped from him as he set aside the laptop and went to fix omelets for breakfast for them both.

After they'd finished eating and sat at the table with their coffee, Lindsey said, "You're a terrific cook."

Greg shrugged. "I enjoy it. I enjoy eating my cooking, too, so I try to exercise regularly."

"Don't want to lose that shapely figure."

He grinned at her. "Not until I'm old and gray and surrounded by grandchildren." If he didn't end up spending the next ten to twenty years in prison, he reminded himself.

She must have seen his expression change. Her own darkened as well. "Greg." She stopped and drew a breath. "Yesterday, on several occasions you asked me, either implicitly or explicitly, to trust you. And I did. Mostly, anyway. It wasn't always easy for me. I like being in control, being in charge. But I trusted you wouldn't hurt me and that what you were doing would ultimately benefit me. And it did." She grinned a heart-stoppingly lovely smile. "Lord, but it did."

"I aim to please."

"And you hit the target," she said. "But...Greg? Do you want our relationship to be anything more than sex?"

He wasn't expecting an assault on that front, so it took him by surprise. But he knew the answer and he owed her his honesty. "Yes, I do. We don't know each other all that well as yet, but there's undeniably something strong and compelling between us. And I think it's more than just sex, and I think it could be long-term. What about you?"

She nodded. "The same. But...there isn't going to be anything between us if we can't learn to trust each other. I made at least the first step yesterday. Can you do the same?"

"This is about letting you help me find out who framed me, isn't it?"

"It's about trusting that we are who we say we are. And that it's okay for each of us to be competent in different ways." She looked at him. "Greg, I'm a tax attorney. Do you have any idea how many balance sheets I've read? How many profit and loss statements I've dissected? How many general ledger reports I've pored over? I know this stuff. And I know how to spot when something's out of whack."

Her points were all valid. His only significant question in the matter related to whose side she was really on. And he knew the answer to that. His. Of course, it was his. Maybe partly because of the great sex, but more because there was a deeper connection between them, he believed she had to be in his court. They met and meshed on a level deeper even than sex.

"All right," he conceded.

"You'll let me help you?" She seemed shocked by his capitulation, as though she'd expected more of a fight.

"Yes. I can't say I was making any progress figuring it out on my own. I know Redmond, my lawyer, was going to subpoena some records and have someone go over them, but I'm betting they're not as adept at it as you."

She walked to him and kissed him. Over her shoulder, just in the corner of his eye, he saw another brief flash of light from the vicinity of the angel.

They spent the morning going through all the information he had. Lindsey didn't find any smoking guns in them, but she did find a couple of things that were strange. She finally asked if she could talk to his lawyer about the case. She wanted to see some of the things he would likely have subpoenaed.

Greg made the call to give his permission to release information to her, then handed the phone over to Lindsey. She and Tom Redmond discussed at length what each knew about the case and what the accountant had found. Judging from listening to Lindsey's side of the conversation, he thought the lawyer and accountant both agreed with her that Greg had surely been framed, but they hadn't yet located clear proof. Redmond agreed to fax over some of his information to her. There was some kind of a hitch, though. Lindsey agreed that getting it to her later that day would be fine.

"That's really all I can do for now," Lindsey told him after she hung up the phone. "I need those other files."

"Lunch, then?" he suggested. "And another game?"

"Another role-playing game? What is it this time?"

"We could do another role-playing. Or we could play Poker. With a set of specially modified chips. Call it Spanking Poker. Are you interested, or would you rather do something else?"

"I'm…interested." Though the words caught in her throat, a sparkle of anticipation lit her blue eyes. Eyes he could drown in. Eyes he could happily stare into for the rest of his life.

Over lunch, he asked her about her favorite treats, and began making a list as she rattled off suggestions.

"Gourmet coffee. I should have guessed that," he said as he noted down her responses. "Chocolate. Licorice whips. Licorice?"

"I like licorice."

He shrugged. "No accounting for some tastes. What else?"

"Doughnuts…ice cream sandwiches."

"Okay. I think it's safe to add DVDs and books to the list."

"Right. I like going to movies and the theater, too."

"Noted." He stood up. "Mind if I leave the clean-up to you this time? I've got to make some preparations."

"Go ahead."

He went back to the guest bedroom. It took over an hour to get everything ready. When he returned to the living area, he found Lindsey engrossed in a book. She set it aside.

"Ready? I like to set this up so there are no losers, only winners. We each have a different set of chips. These are yours." He handed her a box with a bunch of red chips. "Mine are blue. You'll notice each has a little tag I've pasted on. Each tag represents something you'll do for the other person." He picked up a few from his box. "Ice cream sandwich," he said reading the tag on one. "One cup of gourmet coffee. One movie of Lindsey's choice. These are like IOUs. You keep any you win, and you can demand I make good whenever you want."

"Sounds good," she said, "but what am I offering?"

"I did say it was Spanking Poker. You offer to take a licking with various implements."

"Implements?" The word came out on a squeak. "You mean like…a paddle?"

"Two different ones. And a pair of belts. A flogger. And a crop."

"You…have those things?" It came out as a kind of squeak.

"I brought them with me."

"Okay, I have to ask. How often to you get to use them?"

He shrugged. "Not very often. Call it a triumph of hope over experience. In fact…just once. But that relationship wasn't going anywhere."

"I don't want to know. So, if I play these chips and you win them, I give you the right to use whatever's on the chip on me?"

"That's the idea. There are numbers on the chips as well as a letter code."

"Number of hits?"

"Yup. Twos and threes for the paddle and flogger. Ones mostly for the belts and the crop."

She drew a deep breath. "I see." She stared down at the chips, swishing them around with a finger. "What does 'H' stand for?"

"Oh. I forgot. The hairbrush."

She suddenly blushed a nice, deep pink. He'd definitely hit on some of her fantasies here.

"So I bet spanks against the treats you bet?"

"That's the idea." He handed her a sheet of paper where he'd drawn a chart of equivalents. "You game?"

She studied the chips for a moment more before she looked up. "Why not?"

He leaned forward to kiss her. She tasted so sweet he couldn't stop himself from trying to take more and more of her rich heat. It flowed through him and collected in his groin, making his cock rise to attention, ready for action. He had to force himself to back away.

That was his Lindsey, playful and adventurous. He drew himself up short. *His Lindsey*? Where had that come from? If he had a future, maybe she would be, but he had his doubts. Not about where her heart lay. Not that anymore. But he couldn't bring himself to believe she could give him back a future. He'd have to start believing in magic again, if she did. But for now, he might as well enjoy what he'd been given.

"You know how to play poker?" he asked.

She nodded.

"Then shall we? I'll ante a chocolate. You ante a paddle stroke."

She put the chip in when he did. He shuffled and dealt five cards to each of them. He had nothing in his hand, but a king high. He bet three chocolates and she met it with three paddles. He discarded three cards and ended up with a pair of fours. She also discarded three.

In the ensuing betting she put up eight paddles and two belts to his DVD and coffee. His pair of fours beat her pair of deuces.

She won the next round with a pair of eights, taking his chips for two coffees and a handful of chocolates.

The next few hands went back and forth, though he won more than she did. After an hour or so, he had a nice pile of her chips, and she had some of his.

When it was his turn to deal again, he set the cards down instead and picked up a few of the chips. "I believe I'd like to redeem a few of these before we go on."

She drew a sharp breath and watched him. He stood up, took her hand, drew her to her feet and led her to the couch. He sat down right in the middle and pushed himself all the way back. "Unbutton your pants and come here," he said.

He'd moved far enough back that she could lay across his knees and keep the rest of her body on the couch. "I'm redeeming ten paddles—six light and four heavy—and two belts," he warned as he pushed her pants and panties down off her bottom. And a lovely, smooth, nicely rounded bottom it was. He brushed a hand over each mound, relishing the feel of her delicious, creamy white, soon-to-be-pink skin.

The bag he'd dropped beside the couch earlier was in reach when he stretched. He sorted through it and found the paddles and belt. He dropped the others next to him and raised the light paddle. He struck down sharply but not hard. The area turned white, then pink.

She let out a small squeal and wiggled delightfully. He snapped the paddle down on her other cheek. He delivered the next four with the light paddle at a slow, easy pace, enjoying her reaction to each slap. Though she moaned and squirmed, the sheen of moisture on her thighs revealed her excitement. His cock was hard as a rock and throbbing against her belly.

The heavier paddle left a bit more pink on her bottom, but he was careful not to swing it too hard. Four strikes left a nice sheen, but no bruising. Finally, he doubled-up the leather belt and swatted it down once on each cheek. She moaned after the second one and put her hands back to rub the slight welt that rose where the belt had landed.

"That stings," she complained.

He pushed her hand aside and took over the job of massaging away the burn. After a few minutes, she sighed and relaxed. He flipped her over and drew her up to sit on his lap. She all but attacked him, kissing him so hard it forced his head back. She wrestled his sweater up and shirt buttons open so she could fondle his chest. He allowed it for a while, but when she reached for his pants, he stopped her.

"We're not done with the game," he told her.

Her face almost melted in disappointment, but he knew making her wait would make her even hotter when the time came. When she went to pull her pants back up, he stopped her and asked her to take them off.

"I'll feel…" She stopped, grinned and shrugged. "Oh, why not?"

Why not, it turned out, was because it kept his cock painfully engorged to look over and see her bare pussy peeking at him. He felt sure she kept her legs open deliberately, teasing and torturing him.

She became more reckless over the next string of hands, betting bigger and more aggressively. Greg matched her and even maneuvered the betting higher.

Once he had a nice handful of her chips, he insisted on redeeming some of them again. He was surprised by her eagerness to get in position across his legs again. It relieved any worry about causing her too much pain. She wanted what he was giving her.

A faint pink blush still stained her bottom, but he didn't feel any heat there when he brushed a hand over the area. Using the back of the wooden hairbrush, he spanked a bit harder this time, but continued to be watchful for any indication she wasn't enjoying it. It didn't come. After ten swats with the brush and then four more with the heavier paddle, she squirmed a bit and once or twice had sucked in a hard breath, but she didn't protest or try to get away. Between strokes he caressed the reddening flesh with his palm, feeling the roughness and warmth. Twice he dipped his fingers lower down, into her cleft, and felt the moisture flowing there.

He finished this round with four smacks with the doubled-over belt. They made an impressive smacking sound as the leather hit flesh. Those had her jumping and moaning. When he was done, he massaged her bottom, enjoying the heat radiating from it.

Her breathing changed, and she spread her legs to allow him access to her cunt. He touched her lightly, then flipped her over again.

"Ten more hands," he said. "Then I'll redeem a few more and that will be the last time."

"It better be," she said. "Another round of that and you'll have to tie me up to keep me from ripping your clothes off and pouncing on you."

"I can hardly wait," he said, "Let's get to it."

"Why are you torturing me this way? Making me wait?"

"The better to eat you, my dear, when the time comes."

"The big, bad wolf wields a mean strap," she commented.

"Wait until you feel what the big, bad wolf can do with a crop," he said. "It will have you dancing."

"Oh!" She looked startled. "I don't know if…"

"I won't do anything you can't handle," he reassured her. "You believe me, don't you?"

She nodded and then grinned. "And I do love dancing."

The next ten hands took far too long. He wished he'd said five. But since he'd specified ten, they played ten. She won three hands, which added a nice batch of "treat" chips to her pile. He won the others and got more chips than he could safely redeem in two or three sessions, though he suspected she took a dive a couple of times just to make things move along faster.

When they finished the last hand, she jumped up, went over to the couch, and waited for him. But he didn't join her.

"Back around," he said. "Lean over the back of the couch again."

"I like it better over your lap."

"Not this time."

She pouted but did as he ordered.

It was a pretty pout, and he was tempted to kiss it away, but first he had other business to conduct.

Most of the redness of earlier had faded from her backside though he could still see where the last strokes of the belt had landed. He rubbed it a little and enjoyed watching her wiggle and tense in anticipation.

A sudden wave of pure exhilaration tore through him as he studied Lindsey's bent body. To have a woman like her—smart, classy, pretty, intelligent, and quick-witted—to have Lindsey willing to submit to him in this way made him feel like the king of the world. She was the only woman he'd ever met who could match him on every level—intellect, wit, humor, sensuality, and adventurous spirit. He could spend a lifetime exploring new worlds with her, and when they weren't doing that, just being comfortable with her.

If he had a future, he was going to spend it with her.

She wriggled in an enticing way, impatient to get started.

He picked up the light paddle first. The eight smacks weren't very hard, but they served to warm her up.

Next he picked up the flogger. It had a fall of ten or so strips of soft leather about eighteen inches long. It could pack a mean sting if used harshly, but when wielded lightly, it just produced an exciting burn. Or so he'd been told. He'd never actually used the thing himself.

"Flogger next," he warned her. "It has a different feel to it. Less jolting, but more sting. This isn't a heavy one, though, so ten strokes shouldn't be too hard to take."

She made no reply, though her bottom tensed a bit in anticipation.

Greg swung the flogger and brought the tails down across her rear end. It wasn't a hard strike and she didn't react visibly at all. Nor did it make any change in the pink coloration on her bottom left by the paddle.

He brought it down a little harder next time, but still not with any real force. She wiggled her bottom a bit but not in apparent pain. If anything, it appeared to be turning her on. With each further strike he increased the force he used slightly, until the tails started to leave pink streaks where they landed. The seventh and eighth strokes went across the backs of her thighs. Those made her jerk and her breath hiss, but she didn't complain. The last two were very soft, almost delicate strokes, aimed at the insides of her thighs, near her cunt. After the first of those two, she gasped and squirmed but spread her legs further apart, giving him an easier target for the last.

He was almost sure she sighed in disappointment when she heard him put the flogger down.

The crop worried him a bit. It felt heavy and he suspected it could easily deliver a blow harder than she could handle.

She started to rise, but he put a hand on her back and held her in place. "Not done yet. Ten with the crop and then it'll be over. This one's going to hurt more than the others. Tell me if you can't take it."

Lindsey nodded. He hoped she would stop it if it got unpleasant. She was a strong-willed woman.

His first stroke was little more than a tap. She didn't even flinch and it left no mark. The second time, he swatted a little harder, with the same result. Gradually he made each stroke a bit firmer, until on the fifth, she jumped and a red line stood out on her bottom where it bit. On the sixth, the crop snapped loudly as it kissed flesh. Lindsey squealed and wriggled. The seventh struck down low, just where her bottom joined her thighs. It drew a loud yelp. When she reached back to rub her bottom, he ordered her to keep her hands on the sofa. She hesitated, then complied.

The eight stroke was in almost the same place. She swore and jumped up, danced from foot to foot, and rubbed her bottom again.

"Yow," she said, "That stung!"

He gave her a moment to recover before he asked, "Can you take two more?"

She considered it a moment, a frown distorting her lovely features. "Yes."

"Get back in position, then. No jumping up or rubbing this time."

She nodded and leaned back over. Her bottom had several noticeable red welts spanning the cheeks. He struck across the fullest part of her buttocks. It hit with a crack that startled them both. She let out a sharp, gasping moan and started to rise, then caught herself and held herself in position, though her bottom swung from side to side in a way that made his cock nearly explode.

He made the last stroke the hardest yet. It cracked again, just below where the other one had stuck. Immediately, a wicked red line swelled. Lindsey let out a long wail, jumped up, and danced around the room.

"Ow, ow, ow," she moaned as she hopped and rubbed her backside.

He went to her, stood behind her, and put his arms around her. She shook a bit and her breath came on gasping pants. "Stand still a minute," he said to her. "Let me soothe it."

He dropped to his knees, put his lips to her buttocks, and kissed along the lines the crop had left. Her breath hissed out. With his hands on her hips, he traced each welt with his tongue. The rough skin rasped against his tongue, but the heat slammed into him and through him.

She moaned his name and went tense. He felt down along her hips, across her thighs and slipped a hand into her cleft. Moisture oozed down her legs. She sighed and then groaned when he slipped a finger into her cunt and sought her clit with his thumb.

"Greg," she said on a sob. "In me, please. I can't stand it anymore!"

He stood and picked her up. She yelped in surprise but didn't fight him. He carried her to her bed and put her down on it. While he ripped off his clothes and found another condom, she took off her sweater and bra.

She whimpered with need as he climbed onto the bed and lay over her. Her arms wound around his shoulders, drawing him close against her body so her breasts pressed into his chest. She clung to his mouth almost desperately when he kissed her, and sighed when his cock found her entrance and pushed in.

He moaned as her sweet, damp heat surrounded him. Any thoughts of trying to hold back, to make it last longer, died swiftly when she rose up to meet his thrusts, forcing him deep into her. He pumped and she tightened around him. Her fingers dug into his back while his hands tunneled into her hair, reveling in the silky feel. "Lindsey." Emotions surged to levels that matched the rampant plunging of his cock. "You're so beautiful. And so hot. The hottest I've ever known. The most wonderful I've ever known."

She dragged his face down and kissed him, but then her head fell back as the tension drew her body into a hard knot. He plunged deep into her, then pulled back, and each time the pressure in his cock grew. He felt her get tighter and tighter, hugging his cock, and he speared her more rapidly, until orgasm suddenly burst over her in series of rippling spasms that squeezed him unbearably.

He drew back, plunged in hard and shouted in triumph as the tremendous pleasure broke over him like a rapid thunderstorm, with lightning shooting across the sky and the rain of his seed flowing into her.

It took a while before the wild hammering of his heart slowed enough to let him think of anything but the aftermath of the pleasure of it. He let himself down a bit, so that he could rest against her, skin to skin, still joined in that most intimate way.

"Greg." She said his name on a shaky sigh. "God, you're good. This has been…the most memorable week of my life." Her words flowed more easily as her heaving breath calmed. "You've taken me places I only dreamed of going. Showed me things I didn't think were possible." She drew a sharp breath as an aftershock rolled through her. "Do you think…do you think you can be in love with someone you've only known for a few days?"

He bent down and kissed her, then drew back so he could see her face. "If you'd asked me that last week, I'd have said no. Today, the answer is yes. The memories we've made the last few days will be enough to keep me warm for a long time. For the next ten years or so, if necessary, and I'm convicted."

She reached up and touched his lips. "Oh, no. Those next ten years belong to me now. Along with the fifty or so coming after them. I'm not giving them up."

"I hope you have enough magic to pull this off," he said.

Chapter Ten

Lindsey woke from her doze, feeling deliciously sated and exhilarated at the same time. It surprised her how little pain she had in her bottom. Those last few lashes of the crop had packed quite a load of sting. The skin still felt rough and welted, but they didn't hurt at all. And earlier, the fiery sting had served to generate a bonfire of need in her.

Greg still dozed beside her. She was tempted to wake him, just to see again the love and pride in his gray eyes, but he looked so comfortable and peaceful, she couldn't do it.

Instead she got up, showered, dressed, and went to the fax machine in the guestroom that doubled as her office, to see if the papers Redmond had promised to fax her had come in. A stack of sheets sat in the output tray. She glanced through them enough to see they were what she wanted, and took them with her when she went to get a drink.

Greg came into the kitchen while she was wrestling with the pull-tab on the can of Diet Coke. Freshly showered and shaved, hair wet and slicked back from his face, he'd put on jeans, but no shirt or shoes. The sight of his bare chest roused the desire to throw herself on him that never seemed to be far away in his presence, but she was too worn out to act on the impulse.

He came to her, however and pulled her into his arms. "Let's go out for dinner to celebrate. It looks like the snow's melted enough to let us get out."

"What are we celebrating?"

He nuzzled her neck. "Us," he said in her ear. "Love. The beginning of something new for both of us."

"Yes," she agreed. "Greg? No matter what happens, I won't stop fighting for you."

He hugged her. "Right now, that's good enough for me. And because my future is yours, I won't stop fighting for it, either. No matter how long it takes."

She rested against him, feeling his heart beating against her, his breath raising the drying tendrils of hair at her neck. She loved the solid feel of his strong body, the pure male smell of him, the taste of his skin. She treasured the way he could take charge of her, making her submit to his will, and yet still respect her intelligence and strength. He made her body sing in new and different ways. A lifetime of sharing adventures, mock sword fights, new movies, and humorous slants on life, of exploring new places and ideas with him wouldn't be enough.

He took her to his favorite Japanese restaurant, where dinner was a show as well as a meal. The food was delicious and his company delightful. She thought it the most wonderful meal she'd ever had. They stayed there, talking about themselves, their families, backgrounds, travels, childhoods, likes and dislikes until the restaurant closed.

When they finally got back, they were so tired they went right to bed. At her request, Greg shared hers rather than using the guestroom.

As usual she woke to an empty bed and the aroma of coffee drifting from the kitchen. She found him standing at a window, staring out at the melting snow and the gray day that promised the possibility of more.

"We're just a few days away from a new year," he said to her without turning around. "One way or another, it's going to bring a whole new life."

"I was going to take my tree down tomorrow. Want to help with it?"

He nodded, then turned and came over to kiss her. "Sorry about my morose mood. It'll improve with some more coffee."

After breakfast, she settled down with the papers she'd gotten from Redmond, and the notes she'd made the previous day from the files on Greg's computer. Because it was so obvious, she almost overlooked the anomaly. It was only on the second time she worked through a particular column of figures that the odd total suddenly jumped out at her.

"Holy cow! Greg! Come and look at this."

He looked up from the book he was reading, came over to her, and studied where she pointed. "I have no idea."

"But it's one of your sales accounts."

He frowned and said, "I don't think so."

"According to the subpoenaed records Redmond faxed me, it is."

He stared at it a moment more before his expression changed. "Is this it?"

"I think it is. But…" Lindsey stood and went to pick up the phone. The lawyer was in the office. "Tom? I think we've got something for you. But to get the proof, I'm going to have to have Greg log into the company system. Yes, they apparently left his account active. I think there's a trap set in there, so I want lots of witnesses to exactly what he does while he's logged in. Can we meet in your office this afternoon?"

Redmond agreed and she hung up.

The conflict on Greg's face was almost painful. The dawning hope warred with his fear of disappointment.

"I don't promise anything," she said, "but I think this is the answer. We'll see this afternoon."

They arrived at Tom Redmond's office promptly at two. Two strangers were with him; Redmond introduced them as an accountant and an investigator he'd hired to go over the evidence. Lindsey showed him what she'd found and what she suspected.

"That's too simple," the accountant said, staring at her sets of figures.

"But it would be. Everyone knows Greg's a marketing guy, not a number-cruncher. The fact that it's crude would be part of their case. But even they know it's weak, so I suspect they've set a trap in there somewhere, which is why his login access hasn't been deactivated."

Redmond nodded slowly and looked Greg. "Have you been officially terminated?" he asked.

"Not that I know of."

"Okay. It's legit, then. Let's do it," Redmond said. Under the watchful eyes of the small gathered party, Greg booted up his laptop and logged onto his company network. Lindsey let out the breath she'd been holding when he was cleared for access. Her biggest fear was that she might have been wrong about them deliberately leaving his account open.

Greg did the actual typing, under the direction of Lindsey and the other two men, until they found what they were looking for.

"I'll bet that's it," the accountant said, pointing to a file on screen. "See if you can open it as a spreadsheet."

Greg did as directed, then opened up one or two other files when asked.

"Bingo!" the accountant shouted. "There it is."

Even Lindsey didn't see it at first.

"This code here," the accountant said. "Make a note of the number. Greg, go back to the account manager file. Now look what this code ties to."

The investigator whistled.

Redmond said, "I'll be damned. Looks like your ex-fiancée didn't think her allowance from Daddy was quite enough, so she killed two birds with one crime. Not only did she frame you for the embezzlement, she was channeling the funds back to herself. Not too bright, though. It was too easy to find once we started digging."

"But if Lindsey hadn't noticed that discrepancy in the sales figures, no one would ever have looked there," the accountant said. "Even we didn't because there was no reason to think there was anything strange there."

The accountant got a blank disk and had Greg copy the files onto it. He then shut the write-protect latch, put a paper seal over it and dated it. Greg logged out and shut down his computer. The other two men left, promising to get the information back to Redmond in a form he could take to court.

"Does this get me off the hook?" Greg asked when they were gone.

"Damned right it does." The lawyer clapped him on the back. "Congratulations. Looks like you've made a better choice of girlfriend this time."

"Far better," Greg said, staring at her. The emotion in his eyes made her pulse skip a beat.

"Treat her right," the lawyer warned. "Lindsey deserves the best and you'd better give it to her."

Greg grinned at him. "Count on it."

The lawyer wished them well, ascertained that Greg planned to stay at Lindsey's place for a few more days and told Greg not to do anything more about the situation until he called again.

Greg seemed almost dazed as they made their way back to the car and got in. He was quiet until they were back in her apartment. "You can't imagine what a relief it is to know I don't have to go back to jail or face spending a good chunk of my life in prison. I doubt I can ever repay you for that."

She thought about it a minute. "You can't imagine what a relief it is to finally meet a man who isn't intimidated by my intelligence or my law degree or my personality. A man who isn't afraid to be strong, to master me without being brutal or cruel. I'm thirty-one, and I was beginning to think it wouldn't happen. No matter where we go from here, I call it even. You've given me the best week of my life."

"Lindsey, now that I have a future, I want to give you many, many more weeks, and even years of great life. We've known each other a short time, but I think we both know this is different from anything we've had before. And I think we both know it can work. Let's have a long engagement to be sure we know it will, but not too long."

"Engagement? Are you asking me—"

"To marry me. Yes," Greg answered. "Will you?"

"Yes. Oh, heavens, yes." She threw herself into his arms.

Somehow they got to her bedroom, leaving bits and pieces of clothing behind as they went. The loving was long, slow, and sweet as they explored each other's bodies, found new ways to please each other and just spent time staring and whispering compliments.

Afterwards, they showered together and made love in there again with soap- and water-slicked bodies sliding against each other.

Lindsey was drying her hair when Greg called to her from the living room. "Come look at this!" The excitement and astonishment in his tone made her turn off the dryer and drop it on the counter.

She joined him and found him staring at her Christmas tree.

"The angel," he said, in a hushed, awed voice.

She looked up. The angel had no internal light, but it was glowing with a bright gold radiance that formed a vivid halo around it. Warmth seemed to radiate from it and imparted a peace and joy that filled her heart to the brim. "Gram?" she whispered.

The angel suddenly brightened even more, spreading a large pool of radiance around it. And in that liquid glow, Lindsey saw figures. Small at first, growing larger and clearer as she looked. Three women, three men and a small horde of children. "It's us," she whispered, recognizing the faces. "You and me. And my sisters, Crista and Jade, and their husbands, Jeff and Caydon. Those must be the children we're all going to have. Of course Crista's already started."

Lindsey felt the hot wash of tears dripping down her cheeks. "Gram, thank you!"

In a moment it was gone, and the plaster angel was just a Christmas ornament again. But the moment itself was embedded in her heart and soul.

Beside her Greg stirred and heaved a deep breath. "I guess I do believe in miracles now."

About the author:

Katherine Kingston welcomes mail from readers. You can write to her c/o Ellora's Cave Publishing at 1056 Home Ave. Akron, Ohio 44310-3502.

Also by Katherine Kingston:

Binding Passion

Crown Jewels (Anthology)

Daring Passion

Equinox (Anthology)

Healing Passion

Glimmer Quest 1: Silverquest

Glimmer Quest 2: Bronzequest

Ruling Passion

Enjoy this excerpt from
Happy Birthday Baby
© Copyright Lynn LaFleur 2003

The Birthday Gift

Jake watched Amanda leave the dining room. She was such a delight to be with, and not just sexually, although he had no complaints in that department. Simply being with her made him happy.

Patrick picked up the glasses and silverware from the table. "Need some help with this stuff?" he asked, following Jake into the kitchen.

"Nah. I'm just gonna rinse them off and stick them in the dishwasher." He set the plates on the counter next to the sink. "Is everything ready?"

"Everything you asked for. It's all in the closet under the stairs." Patrick placed the glasses next to the plates on the counter. "I'll bring the rest of the stuff from the dining room, then I'm gonna take a quick shower."

"Go ahead. I'll grab one after I finish here."

Patrick turned as if to leave the kitchen, then stopped and faced Jake again. "Do you think she suspects anything? I mean, I almost blew it today when I came in and caught you two." He grinned. "By the way, she has a great ass."

Jake chuckled. "Yes, she does."

Patrick quickly sobered again. "You're my best friend, Jake. I don't want anything to mess up you and me. Maybe you should find someone to do this who isn't related to you."

"It's you or no one, Pat. I won't let another man touch my wife, no matter how much I want to please her."

"So you're really okay with this? As long as *you're* sure, *I'm* certainly willing. Celibacy sucks."

"Yeah, I'm really okay with this." He motioned toward the door. "Go take your shower so I can take mine."

After Patrick left the room, Jake returned to his clean-up duty. As he rinsed the dishes and loaded the dishwasher, he went over the conversation he'd just had with his cousin. Yes, he was okay with this, more than he thought he would be. Ever since Patrick had walked in on them this afternoon, Jake had been fantasizing about this evening. He imagined all the things the two of them would do to Amanda…and he imagined the things he'd watch Patrick do to her.

It's In The Cards

A flash of purple caught her eye. A flash of purple always caught her eye for that was her favorite color. She could see just the top of a card on the bottom shelf of the display rack, hidden behind several other cards. Catherine frowned. She'd already looked at that row and she hadn't seen this card. There was no way she would've missed a purple card.

Unable to resist, she touched the part of the card that she could see. She felt…something. She didn't know how to describe it, but something electric, almost shocking, passed through her fingers.

Taking the card between her thumb and forefinger, Catherine slowly drew it out of the slot. The front was a deep, solid eggplant color with the words "Happy Birthday" in a flowing silver script scrawled across the front. There was nothing special about the card—no beautiful picture, no romantic saying, nothing that should draw her so intently to it, yet she felt compelled to look at it. Her fingers trembling, she opened the card, peered inside…and gasped.

It was him. Him. Her fantasy man. The man who filled her dreams at night, and her mind by day. The man she imagined in her life, in her bed, in her body.

She stared at the picture which took up the entire inside of the card. He reclined among rumpled white satin sheets, his torso propped up on several pillows. His handsome face was tan, with the beginning of a five-o'clock shadow covering his cheeks and chin. His deep brown eyes were half closed, a hint of a grin turned up the corners of his mouth. A corner of a sheet draped over his groin, but she could still see his bare hip. One arm was folded under his head, showing her his impressive bicep. Long, dark brown hair spread over the pillow. That same dark hair generously spread over his chest and tapered down his stomach until it disappeared beneath the sheet. Tanned legs, lightly sprinkled with dark hair, peeked out the other end of the sheet. His body was muscled in all the right places…not the muscles of a bodybuilder, but of a strong, healthy man.

The bulge in the sheet indicated that he didn't lack anything in that department…

One Thing To Give

Lindsay drew her bottom lip farther between her teeth when she saw Sam unlock the door to the storeroom. She glanced around the bar, searching for the other bartender. She didn't see him, but she could hear what sounded like dishes being shifted and stacked from the kitchen.

She had no idea how long Sam would be in that storeroom. If she was going to do something, she had to do it now.

Don't be a wimp, Lindsay. Go for it.

Lindsay sipped her Coke and took a deep breath. Grabbing her purse, she rose and strode to the storeroom.

It was a large room, larger than she'd expected. Long and wide, there were shelves along all the walls and down the middle, all holding boxes of liquor and glassware. She saw a door straight ahead of her that she assumed led to the kitchen, or perhaps was used for deliveries. She couldn't see Sam, but she could hear bottles rattling.

Laying her purse on top of a case of bourbon, she pushed the door shut and flipped the deadbolt.

The rattling stopped. "Monte?" Sam called out.

Lindsay leaned back against the door, her hands behind her for support. "No, it isn't Monte."

Unexpected

Linc took another step forward so he could see her better. At least, he thought it was a "her". The being inside the box was nude. She had pale purple skin, an oval, feminine face, dipped-in waist, and a small-boned frame. She had no hair anywhere on her body, nor any breasts, but Linc still suspected she was female.

She couldn't be more than fifteen inches tall.

Needing to sit before his legs gave out, Linc flopped down in a chair. He had no idea what to do now. Owning a fast-growing, successful computer and software company didn't prepare him for anything like this.

Linc had a basic knowledge of first aid, but that didn't include any medical help for an alien.

Alien. The term made him shiver.

Linc leaned forward and placed his forefinger against her neck. He could feel a faint pulse. Taking that as a good sign, he looked at her chest and detected the slight rise and fall as she breathed. Another good sign that she lived.

Now what?

Enjoy this excerpt from
A Hero Betrayed
Heroes at Heart
© Copyright Jan Springer, 2004

"Looks like we've caught ourselves a talking male."

"That's right honey. Now I'm ordering you to cut me down this minute or there will be hell to pay."

"There's a large bounty on the head of a talking male," another whispered, ignoring his command.

"Screw your bounty. I demand you to let me go."

"He must be one of those escaped educated sex slaves from last year's Slave Uprising."

Oh great! They thought he was a sex slave.

"Sex slaves are experts at pleasuring women," the cutest of the six said.

The women's blue gazes all brightened as they watched him curiously.

Uneasiness zipped up Buck's spine.

"Sorry ladies, but this guy ain't a sex slave. He's a free man, or at least I will be in a minute when you let me go."

"Quiet, slave, or it'll be the whip again!" the tall blonde snapped angrily.

Ookay, he could shut up. For a minute.

"We are not giving up this well-endowed male or the fun we've planned for ourselves just for a bounty!" The tall blonde addressed the others. Buck's hopes were dashed as all eagerly nodded in agreement.

The tall blonde spoke again, her harsh blue gaze clashed defiantly with Buck's. "And I, for one, do not want a male speaking while I fuck him. Perchance I should cut out his tongue?"

He didn't miss her hand slithering to the dagger strapped to her leg. Have mercy! These women were crazy!

"I have a better idea," another blonde chimed in. "We'll give him the passion poison now."

"The elders have warned 'tis dangerous to administer it without their guidance," one of them said quickly.

"But it will make him more obedient and quiet until they arrive," the tall blonde replied thoughtfully.

Oh man, he was screwed. Hopefully not literally.

"I'm up for a little danger." The woman who'd attacked his dick with an eager mouth grinned widely.

"I'm not interested!" Buck gasped as a whisper of panic threatened his sanity. "Cut me down. I've about had enough of this crap!"

The women's harsh intakes of breath made Buck tense. Obviously they didn't like being ordered around. The feminist movement was very much alive and well on this planet.

"The passion poison it is." The tall blonde smiled with smug satisfaction. From behind him he sensed movement. Before he could react, a sharp sting from a needle pierced the flesh of his right ass cheek.

He tried to swing himself away, but couldn't move more than a few inches.

He swore violently as the cool liquid flooded deep into his veins and spread an odd sensual heat throughout his tortured body.

The heat soothed the fiery whip welts, and languid weariness drifted through his limbs. He fought hard to keep his suddenly heavy eyelids from closing but knew he was quickly losing the battle.

"He's getting sleepy," the blonde who'd been sucking his cock giggled.

"It's too bad we'll have to kill him when we're through with him," someone else said. "His size would bring a fortune in the Brothel Town."

They were going to kill him? Oh boy, he'd really stepped into big-time trouble.

The whirring sound of the whip sliced through the air yet again and he gritted his teeth as savage pain snapped against his bare buttocks. This time however, the pain was brief, turning quickly into a savage erotic sensation that made Buck groan with want for more.

"It's working," a female uttered from somewhere nearby.

He shook his head to clear his fogging thoughts, but all that accomplished was giving one of the women free rein on his earlobe. She pressed a lusciously soft breast against his elbow as she nibbled on his flesh. Her warm silky hands slid wantonly over his sweaty chest until a hot ache throbbed throughout his body.

He found himself moaning at the wonderful sensations and to his horror he found himself craving more pleasure. His cock and balls grew painfully hard. He heard the women's sharp gasps and excited giggles.

"I've never seen a male so big!" one of them screamed.

"Take him down," another instructed in a rather hoarse voice. "Let's get him into the hide house. We'll get the Sacred Drink from him and then we'll let him rest. When he is fully adjusted to the passion poison, we're going to become women!"

Wild cheers pierced the warm evening air.

As they freed his limp legs, United States astronaut Buck Hero succumbed to the black tidal wave of sleep that swallowed him whole.

Why an electronic book?

We live in the Information Age—an exciting time in the history of human civilization in which technology rules supreme and continues to progress in leaps and bounds every minute of every hour of every day. For a multitude of reasons, more and more avid literary fans are opting to purchase e-books instead of paperbacks. The question to those not yet initiated to the world of electronic reading is simply: *why?*

1. *Price.* An electronic title at Ellora's Cave Publishing and Cerridwen Press runs anywhere from 40-75% less than the cover price of the <u>exact same title</u> in paperback format. Why? Cold mathematics. It is less expensive to publish an e-book than it is to publish a paperback, so the savings are passed along to the consumer.

2. *Space.* Running out of room to house your paperback books? That is one worry you will never have with electronic novels. For a low one-time cost, you can purchase a handheld computer designed specifically for e-reading purposes. Many e-readers are larger than the average handheld, giving you plenty of screen room. Better yet, hundreds of titles can be stored within your new library—a single microchip. (Please note that Ellora's Cave and Cerridwen Press does not endorse any specific brands. You can check our website at www.ellorascave.com or

www.cerridwenpress.com for customer recommendations we make available to new consumers.)

3. *Mobility.* Because your new library now consists of only a microchip, your entire cache of books can be taken with you wherever you go.

4. *Personal preferences are accounted for.* Are the words you are currently reading too small? Too large? Too...**ANNOYING**? Paperback books cannot be modified according to personal preferences, but e-books can.

5. *Instant gratification.* Is it the middle of the night and all the bookstores are closed? Are you tired of waiting days—sometimes weeks—for online and offline bookstores to ship the novels you bought? Ellora's Cave Publishing sells instantaneous downloads 24 hours a day, 7 days a week, 365 days a year. Our e-book delivery system is 100% automated, meaning your order is filled as soon as you pay for it.

Those are a few of the top reasons why electronic novels are displacing paperbacks for many an avid reader. As always, Ellora's Cave and Cerridwen Press welcomes your questions and comments. We invite you to email us at service@ellorascave.com, service@cerridwenpress.com or write to us directly at: 1056 Home Ave. Akron OH 44310-3502.

Discover for yourself why readers can't get enough of the multiple award-winning publisher Ellora's Cave. Whether you prefer e-books or paperbacks, be sure to visit EC on the web at www.ellorascave.com for an erotic reading experience that will leave you breathless.

www.ellorascave.com

NEED A MORE EXCITING WAY TO PLAN YOUR DAY?

ELLORA'S CAVEMEN

2006 CALENDAR

COMING THIS FALL